PRAISE FOR *THE DELUSION*

Impressive debut.
PUBLISHER'S WEEKLY

A complex and gripping tale that carries a powerful punch.
MIDWEST BOOK REVIEW

I encourage you to read *The Delusion*. It triggers your imagination about the realities of spiritual warfare.
JACE ROBERTSON, *Duck Dynasty*

Laura Gallier's book *The Delusion* is a very entertaining and thought-provoking read. It's full of relevant content no matter your faith perspective. I am excited to see its impact on bookshelves as well as on the big screen.
MAURICE EVANS, former NBA player

The Delusion is a great book that allows both teenagers and adults to dive in and get captivated by Owen's life. I couldn't put the book down as I found myself visualizing the details and looking forward to what happened next. The truths behind this fictional book are outstanding.
RODNEY BLAKE COLEMAN, M. ED., assistant principal, Anthony Middle School

The Delusion is a page turner that I couldn't put down, and neither could my husband and teenage son. Laura Gallier has a firm grasp on the challenges that our students face today, and her novel reveals challenging, eye-opening truths.
KELLY MARTENS, president and founder, Lighthouse for Students

As a film producer, I'm constantly looking for great stories. With *The Delusion*, Laura Gallier has delivered on all levels.
CHAD GUNDERSON, Out of Order Productions

I appreciate Laura Gallier taking the time to help us remember where the real battle is. *The Delusion* was a priceless reminder that we must be constantly exchanging the lies of the enemy, and our culture, with the truth of God's Word. The book is a fresh perspective on where our true power comes from: PRAYER. That's where the real victory is gained.

WADE HOPKINS, former NFL player and regional vice president, Fellowship of Christian Athletes

Laura effectively depicts the day-to-day battle between good and evil through powerful story and imagery. As a father, it is a wake-up call to the responsibility I have as the spiritual leader in the home, to recognize the battle that is raging and to stand firm for the sake of the next generation. *The Delusion* is a must-read for every father.

RICK WERTZ, founder and president, Faithful Fathering, faithfulfathering.org

---

Other books in the series:
The Delusion
The Deception

THE DELUSION SERIES

THE DEFIANCE

LAURA GALLIER

wander
An imprint of
Tyndale House
Publishers

Visit Tyndale online at tyndale.com.

Visit Laura Gallier online at lauragallier.com/delusion.

TYNDALE and Tyndale's quill logo are registered trademarks of Tyndale House Ministries. *Wander* and the Wander logo are trademarks of Tyndale House Ministries. Wander is an imprint of Tyndale House Publishers, Carol Stream, Illinois.

The Defiance

Designed by Dean H. Renninger

Edited by Sarah Rubio

Published in association with Jenni Burke of Illuminate Literary Agency: www.illuminateliterary.com.

All Scripture quotations are taken from the *Holy Bible*, New Living Translation, copyright © 1996, 2004, 2015 by Tyndale House Foundation. Used by permission of Tyndale House Publishers, Carol Stream, Illinois 60188. All rights reserved.

Mention of the King James Bible refers to the *Holy Bible*, King James Version.

The Defiance is a work of fiction. Where real people, events, establishments, organizations, or locales appear, they are used fictitiously. All other elements of the novel are drawn from the author's imagination.

For information about special discounts for bulk purchases, please contact Tyndale House Publishers at csresponse@tyndale.com, or call 1-800-323-9400.

ISBN 978-1-4964-3397-8 (hc); ISBN 978-1-4964-3398-5 (sc)

Printed in the United States of America

26	25	24	23	22	21	20
7	6	5	4	3	2	1

To Patrick—

I stand in awe of your ability to love.

You can't cast out a broken heart,

and you can't heal a demon.

DANA GRINDAL

ONE

NIGHTMARES WERE NOTHING NEW for me, but this one felt different, like more than just my subconscious randomly projecting terror. I was fully aware that I was dreaming, but every color was vivid; each dead leaf grazing my shoulders looked sharp and real. The lighting was strange though—neither day or night, but an unsettling charcoal gray.

I was standing alone, shivering, in a cornfield just beyond the Masonville city limits. There was nothing scary looming over me or chasing me down, yet fear had me by the throat, making it hard to swallow. I walked row after countless row of tall, withered stalks, searching for something.

But what?

The wind scraped sandy particles against my unshaven face. I held my hands open at my chest, and a sticky airborne substance began clinging to my palms and fingers. I recognized the ashen-gray death dust, but what was that black grit in the mix? The stuff started stinging—like needles were stabbing my face and hands, burrowing into my skin.

I turned and faced a small, dilapidated house in the distance, its white wood slats barely hanging on around shattered windows. The sound of running water compelled me to approach. The knob was missing, but I pushed the thin door open—what remained of it. A faucet was pouring over a small sink, allowing me to rinse the gritty death-dust off my hands. I still had no clue what I was supposed to find in this corn-field or why I was plagued by such crippling dread, but I couldn't shake the intuition that this nightmare held meaning.

The shimmering water—the same temperature as my hands—brought instant relief to my skin, but before I could enjoy the sensation a sudden movement above my head startled me. A horde of grungy brown bats that reeked like rotten meat swarmed in circles above the few rafters that were all that remained of the roof. There had to have been at least a hundred, each of their bodies the size of my fist. They spied down on me with beady red eyes. Bizarre as it was, I sensed they were mocking me. Their laughter sounded like a smoker's cough.

One by one, the devilish creatures began swooping down, collid-ing with my head and face. I swatted at them, but they didn't flinch. More came at me, mouths open, fangs bared. I ran out of the house and dropped to the ground, crossing my arms over my head. Tucking my chin, I saw the supernatural light around my feet, a welcome reminder that I was at the mercy of no evil, no matter its form.

For a fleeting second, a sense of reassurance displaced my fear.

But then I saw him.

The unmistakable purpose of the dream. The mystery I'd been searching for.

Inches from my aura, a pale face was jutting out from the dirt, frozen and dormant. A festering mouth, shriveled nose, and depraved eyes were all that breached the soil, along with a few long wisps of bone-white hair, swaying in the tainted breeze. Several inch-long black spikes poked up from the buried forehead—a blasphemous crown of thorns.

Molek.

The petrifying Creeper King lay motionless beneath the dirt, one eyelid drooping lower than the other while his jaw gaped open. His pointed tongue lay limp against a row of sharp teeth. His features were more human in proportion than those of the demons that formed his ragtag army, such a mix of feminine and masculine that his subjects could have just as easily hailed him as their queen.

Was Molek, the Lord of the Dead, dead himself?

Could a spirit-world principality actually die?

I took deep breaths, shielding my mouth with cupped hands, refusing to panic at the mere sight of him. The bats flew around me in every direction, faster now, a hurricane of hostility. I thought perhaps they were in turmoil over Molek's defeat.

Then, like a gallon of spoiled coffee being poured into a twelve-ounce cup, the bats dove headfirst into Molek's mouth, disappearing down his throat as if his lifeless chest, concealed underground, was somehow a vast cave. I thought I might barf.

I wanted to escape—to wake up—but the dream wasn't done.

As the last bat made its plunge, I heard something charging toward me, stomping with such ferocity that the ground shook. And it was coming from all directions, like I was surrounded—not just me, but all of Masonville. I could feel the intense hatred this force had toward me. Its determination to devour my town.

I braced myself, prepared to encounter a massive invasion of Creepers. Or some gruesome manifestation of evil I'd never laid eyes on before. But it was only a shadow, billowing toward me through the cornstalks like haunted smoke. It enveloped me and wrapped my face in icy darkness, whispering at me in high-pitched voices in a language I couldn't understand. But I didn't freak out—not until the whispering shadows started choking me. Freezing, invisible claws constricted my airway.

I hit my knees. I tried to yell but couldn't make a sound.

That's when everything went completely black, and I feared I'd gone blind. I flailed my arms, swinging fists in the dark.

My lungs became so desperate for air, I was sure they were about to explode. Then an electric-red bolt of lightning pierced the darkness above my head and struck my right forearm with an explosive boom.

Before the pain had time to register, I sat straight up in bed, my mouth open even wider than Molek's had been in the dream, gasping for breath. My dog, Daisy, whined at the foot of the stiff mattress.

I reached for my phone but still didn't know my way around the musty room well enough to find the bedside table right away. I'd moved out of my upscale apartment and into this hole-in-the-wall two weeks ago, and even though I'd save thousands on rent over the next few months, I was already second-guessing my decision.

I'd nobly agreed to live in this free makeshift room in the back of Ray Anne's church—upstairs, behind the sanctuary—because of some recent acts of vandalism against the church. Also, it was helpful to lie low here instead of at my apartment after my identity had been outed at the occult's auction block.

Pastor Gordon was working to raise money to renovate the late-80s building, which would include a new high-tech surveillance system. In the meantime, I'd volunteered to keep an eye on things at night. If anyone tried to break in again, it was my job to call 911. But there was no helpline to dial when a nightmare invaded my sleep.

I'd been having them every night since I'd moved in here, but tonight's was the most heart pounding by far.

I breathed a little easier when glimmering light radiated through the sheer curtains covering the only window in the room—a set of paned-glass double doors leading to an outdoor balcony overlooking a grassy field and pond. Custos was out there, keeping watch. Still, I was way too on edge to lie back down. For one, this cluttered room didn't feel right. It had given me the creeps since the moment I'd moved in, even though it was in a church and I had yet to see a Creeper or their hateful graffiti on the property. And now that dream . . .

I replayed the whole thing in my mind—Molek buried and lifeless while another form of terror closed in. Something just as vicious and powerful. Maybe more so. And that dramatic blast of lightning.

For months—four, to be exact—I'd nearly driven myself crazy wondering what had become of Molek since the night I'd seen Watchmen drag him and his spirit-realm throne off my forested acreage. Had Ray Anne and I managed to succeed the next day at following the instructions in Arthur Washington's prophetic letter, Molek and his Creeper army would be banished from Masonville, Texas, for good—in which case, it wouldn't have mattered to me where they were now. Well, except that it sickened me to think some other town might have Molek lording over their spiritual atmosphere in furious retribution over having lost ours. But since I'd seriously fumbled the mission that day back in April, I wasn't surprised that my acreage, along with Masonville High, remained crawling with Creepers.

Unfortunately, I was now faced with Arthur's disturbing warning outlining the consequence for failing our mission. "Unthinkable darkness and sorrow" would come to Masonville—hence my obsession with finding out where Molek was and what his next move would be. He'd already done such devastating damage; I couldn't imagine what *unthinkable darkness and sorrow* could possibly look like.

I leaned and flipped on the nearest lamp, then opened the squeaky drawer on the nightstand where I'd tucked Arthur's decades-old envelope with my name on it. No, it didn't literally say *Owen Edmonds*—or *Ray Anne Greiner*. But both she and I remained convinced the letter inside had been written specifically for us, decades before we were born.

I reread the final statement for the millionth time, the sobering prediction that still seemed absurd to me: *What happens in Masonville will affect the spiritual condition of the rest of the nation and the world.*

The whole planet of people. No pressure.

My thoughts dragged back to my nightmare. The longer I mulled over it, the more unlikely it seemed. Bats mocking me? Molek dead and buried? Far-fetched, for sure—even for the paranormal realm. And yet the location of the dream carried a hint of hope. Molek was outside Masonville city limits. I considered the possibility that the Watchmen had banished and beat him so badly, he was no longer a threat to our town. Even if another wave of horror was rolling in, it would be satisfying to know Molek was deported and disarmed.

With my knees bent at my chest, I tapped my foot against the mattress, eyeing the cluttered bookshelf across from me. What had made me think this dream was any different from all the other nerve-racking ones I'd had? The only answer: a gut feeling. The problem was, my gut had led me in the wrong direction before—*way* wrong. But sitting here alone in this cramped space, my bedsheets in a wad around me, it nagged me still.

I'd been asking God to reveal where Molek was, to give me an unmistakable sign of some kind. Had he answered me in a dream?

I wanted to jump out of bed, drive past the town's *Welcome* sign, and start searching cornfields, but if I went now, at four o'clock, I couldn't bring Ray Anne—and I wanted her with me. It's not like I was afraid to go alone or before sunup. It's that Ray and I were a team, inseparable partners in the mission to defend Masonville and protect the world.

I wanted to be more—as in, life partners—and last spring I'd gone so far as to get down on one knee, bare my soul, and practically beg her to marry me. She'd just stared at me a minute, while her family and friends stood by, mouths open, but she finally gave a tearful reply. "I want to say yes, Owen, I really do. It's just . . . this feels rushed." She hugged me, then drove the dagger the rest of the way through me: "I'm so sorry. I can't."

It crushed me, but it's not like I could really blame her. We were only nineteen, and plus, I'd done some idiotic things and had a lot to prove. So we committed to doing the boyfriend-girlfriend thing and giving our relationship more time.

I switched off the retro-looking lamp, but hard as I tried, couldn't go back to sleep. Finally, as much as I wanted to wait for Ray before venturing into the cornfields, I gave up on that, too.

I threw on jeans and a T-shirt I grabbed out of a dresser that had to have come from Goodwill, then shut and locked the door to my room and traveled the narrow second-story hallway. I turned a corner, then walked to the center of the old cherrywood choir loft—unused for at least a decade—overlooking the sanctuary from the back. I stared down at the empty pews, the long benches as comfortable as back braces and old-fashioned as phone booths. They were barely visible in the dim floor lighting. Four sections, some two dozen rows each. *Surely if vandals were coming tonight,* I told myself, *they'd have made their move before now.* The previous break-ins had all happened before 2:00 a.m.

The longer I stood there, the only person in the entire building, the more I battled the disturbing sense that I wasn't alone—a familiar feeling I'd endured off and on since I'd become a spirit-world sensor. But it was getting stronger lately. And right now, it was like I could feel someone staring up at me from among the pews. Something threatening. It was so tangible, I could have pointed to the exact spot where the unwelcome gaze was coming from: the center aisle down below, three or four rows from the stage.

The experience played on one of my worst fears—that I might

somehow lose my spiritual sight. Or just as dreaded, that a certain species of Creeper could somehow elude it. But I had to consider that the sensation could have been nothing but a paranoid superstition, symptoms of post-traumatic stress brought on by all the repeat exposure to spirit-world terror I'd suffered.

Be with me, Lord.

I'd been going out of my way lately to react to situations with faith, not doubt. A new outlook for me.

A text hit the burner phone my father had given me, and yeah, I jumped. It was from an unlisted number—aka, him: **I hope you are well and you're seeing things improve in your town. Have you been able to team up with other Lights, as you call them? It's the strategy we've employed here, and it's proving fruitful. I think of you often.**

I'd only met my dad for the first time a few months ago, but I already knew this was so like him. Texting me in the middle of the night from Uganda, offering advice to help me turn the tables on the spiritual war raging in Masonville. His advice was usually easier said than done, but at least he cared enough to give it.

Turning my back on the feeling of being watched, I slipped out a side door and got on my Ducati. Other than the rumble of my motorcycle's engine, there was no sound or traffic this time of night. I kept checking my rearview mirrors. I swear, a black Suburban had been tracking me lately. But right now, it was just me and the town of Masonville, alone together. Her, a captive to painful secrets and tormentors, and me, dead set on freeing her and exposing decades of corruption.

The string of local abductions had come to a sudden, suspicious stop after the night I'd become an eyewitness to the selling of human beings—the horrific exploitation of teenagers and children. The elaborate ceremony had ended in chaos, scattering the buyers, members of Masonville's secret occult society, but there was now an increase in kidnappings in surrounding counties—they hadn't stopped poaching children, only switched up their hunting grounds. And since they'd all seen my face that fateful night, I knew I'd better watch my back.

I turned onto the main stretch of highway that led to the outskirts of town and gassed it. My former tutoring student Riley came to mind.

I wondered if she'd been taken down this very road against her will on a night as dark as this one, only to be auctioned off states away, purchased through some encrypted wire transfer by a shell of a human being who'd already sold his own soul to the kingdom of darkness. She was only seventeen.

What kind of person *buys* another person?

There were multiple situations I couldn't think about for long without getting nauseated, and Riley was one of them. I still saw her face around town now and then, on tattered *Missing Person* flyers. Like the other victims, she deserved justice, even if all that was left of her was her discarded body. I winced at the thought.

The stoplight next to Masonville High changed to red, and I succumbed to the pointless delay, eyeing the school and surrounding moonlit acreage. As usual, there were Creepers scurrying up the building like roaches and clinging to the suicide memorial fence, still covered in pictures and stuffed animals and faded fake flowers that dated back to my senior year. But the Creepers had a new area to roam now—the freshly-bulldozed field behind the high school. Soon, foundations would be poured for a new middle school and elementary. About the worst place in America to construct buildings to house more students.

My mother's parents had donated more than enough land to the school district to allow for additional campuses, a highly deliberate move on my grandparents' part, for sure. They knew an extreme infestation of unseen forces of destruction covered the land, lying in wait to devour souls—the younger, the better. Sick as it was, my grandparents had gone out of their way to ensure that evil's appetite for human suffering would remain fed, even after they were dead.

I still owned the 1,253 acres they'd willed to me that bordered the school district's property, but of course I had no say-so whatsoever about what the city chose to build on their side of the boundary line. Now that the oil and gas industry was more profitable than ever in Masonville and the teen suicides seemed to be a thing of the past, people were breathing easier and talking expansion. On top of that, an increase in local law enforcement was credited with stopping the abductions, conveniently blamed on organized crime, and just like that, the bond passed practically overnight to build two more state-of-the-art, shark-infested schools (spiritually speaking, of course).

I was sure I wasn't the only one in Masonville who had concerns over putting new campuses right next to one that had suffered a mass shooting, coupled with the highest suicide rate in the country, just two school years ago. But by now, I understood: the secret society ran this town, not the everyday people. It was the same underground occult group my grandparents had raised my mom in before she ran away at sixteen years old.

I pulled off the road just past the *Welcome to Masonville* sign. It seemed like a lifetime ago since I'd first seen that sign, when my mom and I moved here from Boston. Not long after that, my eyes were opened to the invisible realm. In those early days, I'd have given anything to get my ignorant, blind life back, but now, my supernatural awareness was as vital to me as my physical senses. More so at times.

The first cornfield outside town stood some fifteen feet back from the road, not shriveled and dead like it had been in my dream but growing ripe for harvest. I concealed my bike among the stalks, then walked one identical row after another. The air was clear and crisp in the sparse moonlight, not an ominous, gritty gray.

I wished I'd have thought to grab my big flashlight. The constant aura on the ground around me was glorious, but not far-reaching enough to show me much. I put my cell in flashlight mode and swept it around. I was used to seeing huge shadow-like streaks darting in the night, but that was on my forested land, defiled by centuries of violence, overrun with Creepers. Out here, beyond the city limits, all was still, as vacant as the streets on my drive over.

I so desperately wanted the same atmosphere for my property and the schools built on its soil.

Someday.

There was no path to follow, and I contemplated whether to change directions or keep forging straight ahead. I took a random right, second-guessing my decision now to come here at all—to take a dream so seriously that I was out of bed at five in the morning, searching a vast cornfield for a spirit being's revolting face in the dirt.

Am I really doing this?

I ignored logic for the moment and traveled deeper into the maze of crops, stopping at times and using my foot to slide fallen leaves back, exposing the bare ground. Nothing but soil, every time. Had I expected to simply stumble on Molek?

Time marched on, and as the first hues of sunlight colored the sky, I spun on my heel, content to give up and get back to the church and get some sleep while I still could. But then, to my left, I spotted an old weathered structure among the rows of corn. A little dilapidated house with white wood slats barely hanging on around shattered windows.

TWO

IT WAS SURREAL, staring at the exact thing I'd just seen in my dream. Dilapidated wooden slats. Old busted windows. Two beams where the roof used to hang. I approached the house and shone my phone light through a broken window. There was no running water, like in my dream, but I was still intrigued.

It would be a short walk around to the front of the square-shaped house, and I was anxious to get there and inspect the ground a few steps from the door—the spot where Molek had been laid to rest in my dream, pounded into the earth by mighty Watchmen. Who else could do that kind of damage to him?

I was mid-stride when a threatening howl echoed through the field—not the cry of some four-legged animal scavenging for rodents, but the groan of an unearthly creature. A Creeper on the prowl. I pressed my back against the side of the house and waited. There it was again— several at once. A pack of them.

A gentle breeze swept over me in the sunrise, a stark contrast to the threatening wails drawing closer. I pressed harder against the rotting wood, careful not to exhale too loudly.

When all became quiet, I made my move, inching forward and spying from behind the corner of the house.

I'd never seen anything like this. Not even close.

There were six squatty creatures, about three feet tall and muddy brown. They formed a tight cluster with their backs to me, their heads lowered. One of them extended a pair of bony, bald wings—shaped like a crooked umbrella—into the unmistakable silhouette of a bat. That's when I connected them with the horde I'd seen in my distressing dream, but these were way bigger.

My pulse kicked into high gear. *I know what they're staring at.*

I had to see for myself.

Instinct said to remain hidden from hate-filled demonic forces like these, but courage demanded I take action. I gazed down at the divine aura around my Adidas—the light that had never stopped shining since the moment my shackle had busted off my neck, liberating my soul. And I reminded myself that light triumphs over darkness.

Always.

Well . . .

Unless we welcome evil into our lives and become its naive friend. A lesson I'd learned the hardheaded way, but at least I knew better now.

I squared my shoulders and strode toward the giant bats—a hybrid species of Creeper with a specialized spirit-world function, no doubt. The wind wafted their overpowering stench my way, as rotten as it had been in my nightmare.

Any second, they'd see me, but I was determined not to care. I belonged to a superior kingdom.

Still, it startled me when, all at once, they twisted their thick necks and looked back at me. They didn't have cute bat faces with puppy-like features but flat, gnarly snouts and beady red eyes.

I froze.

But not for long. I willed myself to take one step at a time, praying, defying fear.

When I came close enough that my light nearly grazed the bats, they took flight. Their wingspan was about as wide as my outstretched arms. They swarmed in speedy circles above my head, but they didn't swoop down on me. Instead, all six of them hurled insults at me, their voices a chilling, raspy whisper. They called me names like *coward* and *weakling* and *orphan* and threatened to spy on me and attack at night while I slept, smothering me to death.

I knew I was awake, but the experience was so freakishly disturbing, it felt like I was dreaming all over again.

Stay focused, Owen. I'd come here for a reason. A crucial one.

Sure enough, standing out like a patch of snow on dark desert sand, Molek's face was a foot away from where I stood. Just like I'd dreamed, his right eyelid hung lower than his left. Was there anything on earth or beyond so petrifying as his hollow pupils?

The pit of hell came to mind.

I stepped closer, determined to make sure there was no sign of life. If he didn't react to my aura contacting his skin, he was dead for sure.

It was surreal to see the Lord of the Dead's face illuminated in heavenly light. It exposed tiny fissures in his milky-white skin—a web of cracks, like he was made of porcelain and had suffered repeat blows. He didn't gasp when my light hit him, but then again, Creepers don't breathe. But he didn't twist or flinch or cry out in anguish either.

That settled it for me. "He's dead."

I would have liked to have seen exactly when and how he'd met his fatal ending, but all that really mattered was that he was finished—that it was possible for a seemingly immortal being to die.

This was worth celebrating.

I gave him a last look, ready to walk away; the badgering bats were growing unbearable. But something caught my eye—my spiritual vision. A substance coated the inside of Molek's gaping mouth, blanketing his tongue. Death dust mixed with tiny black specks. The mystery substance that had stung my skin in the dream.

Despite the chaos and cruelty swarming overhead, I lowered onto my hands and knees, squinting into Molek's mouth.

What *was* that stuff?

I bent my elbows, putting my face as close to the Creeper corpse as I could bear. He'd always reeked of burnt flesh and sulfur, but there was only a faint trace of it now. I never thought I'd see the day my breath would graze Molek's unresponsive cheeks.

But then I stopped breathing, because . . .

He looked straight at me.

And blinked.

THREE

I LEAPT BACK IN ONE KNEE-JERK MOVE. Molek groaned—not the predatorial kind, but a suffering wail. The Lord of the Dead was alive but hurting. Not quite dead but dying.

Or so it appeared.

What if this was an act? An elaborate plot to deceive me all over again?

The bats still traveled in every frenzied direction, spitting their curses. I stepped back but kept my gaze fixed on my archenemy. The nightmare that had led me here now seemed more like a demon-induced trap than a divine revelation.

I knew what to do—what name to call on for protection—but something heavy clamped down on my right shoulder. I spun around, ready to fight with the only weapon that had ever proven to work in spiritual combat—faith-filled words. But thankfully, there was no need to defend myself.

The familiar old man gazed at my face. No smile today, but calming assurance poured from his golden-brown eyes, peering from beneath the brim of his straw cowboy hat.

"Hush." That's all he said, just barely above a whisper, yet it sent the bats flapping away.

"Please." I grabbed his plaid shirt sleeve, layered under the same overalls he always wore. "Stay awhile."

He had a way of disappearing as quickly and unpredictably as he showed up, gracing me with a few vital answers to mysteries no ordinary person could possibly solve, then leaving me hanging, desperate to know more.

I would have liked an explanation of where he'd been the past few months and how he'd found me out here, in the middle of nowhere, but I had an even more important question. I pointed to Molek's dirt-framed face. "Is he really dying or just faking?"

The old man narrowed his eyes at the assassin. "Principalities can't be killed the way you understand death, but they can be banished to outer darkness, as good as dead."

"Where's that? Tell me how."

He kept his gaze fixed on Molek. "When wicked reigning powers lose a major territory to the Kingdom of Light—a town as coveted by evil as this one—they're banished to the furthest, darkest, most torment-ing chambers of hell. You've already been told how to send Molek there."

Arthur's prophetic letter. The call to gather the people of Masonville onto my land for an unheard-of time of spiritual devotion, purging the land of the sins of the past. The way I understood it, in the spirit world, my acreage remained stained with innocent blood, and the only way to wipe it clean was to express remorse to God on behalf of the unrepentant guilty people, long dead now.

Even though I'd never had the chance to tell the old man about Arthur's instructions, he somehow had a way of knowing pretty much everything, so I wasn't completely surprised he'd just referenced the prophecy. "So, it's not too late?" I asked.

He shook his head. "Trust me, if it was too late, you'd know it. You'd see that the tables had turned."

"But even if I find a way to get people onto my property, how will I make them believe me enough to cooperate and pray?"

I'd known from the moment I'd been handed Arthur's call to action that it was unrealistic. A town of mostly shackled people doesn't care about the spiritual history of a piece of land, much less want to gather on it to do something as seemingly absurd as ask God's forgiveness for atrocities committed a long time ago. And after months of reaching out repeatedly to all seventeen student pastors around here—a ton of churches for a community our size—only six had finally agreed to meet with Ray Anne and me on the front steps of Masonville High this Sunday.

We hoped they'd want to join forces with us and persuade more people to join the mission to purge the school and my land of evil, but judging by how difficult it had been just to schedule an initial gathering, Ray and I had our doubts.

What's more, Masonville was home to occult worshipers who were working against us around the clock, evoking and empowering the very evil we were trying to expel. Deranged as it was, I'd seen it with my own eyes: they wanted Molek to reclaim his position of lethal authority over our town.

The old man folded his arms and tilted his head to the side. "You believe the mission is to pressure a crowd of people to meet up on your land so you can try to convince them to go through the motions of some prayer exercise they think is useless?"

He'd basically nailed it. "Well . . . yeah."

"That wouldn't fix a thing. It's a process, young man—guiding people to the truth so that they actually understand and *want* to join the cause." He glared at Molek again. "Your faith and action up to this point have kept him off your land, separating him from his army and the students. That's no small thing, but it'll only last so long. He's relentless. Until he's banished for good, he'll keep trying to find a way to rise up and reestablish his throne. If that happens, you're looking at generations of suffering and warfare."

"Yeah, I realize that." It was weird how this extremely nice man had a way of frustrating me. I always felt like a jerk afterwards for having been impatient with him. I forced a polite tone. "I want Molek gone, cast into outer darkness, like you said. But I don't get how to convince people to do their part."

He patted my shoulder, completely patient with me, as always. "Again, it's a *process*, Owen." It was strange, but I didn't recall ever having heard him say my name before. "Molek has to be starved out of town as one captive soul after another comes to the Light and learns to defy him—his lies and temptations. Only then will gathering on your land make a difference. While you work to that end, pay attention to what circumstances come your way. Who's put in your path and why."

I took another satisfying glance at Molek's restrained body, buried alive. "He can't tempt or lie to anyone in that condition."

The old man lowered to one knee, hovering over the regional Creeper King as if studying his otherworldly features. Molek's eyeballs rolled back behind his eyelids and shook within their sunken sockets, like he was having a seizure. "Even in his absence," the old man explained, "his demonic subjects carry out his mission, shooting his deceptions like flaming arrows at people's minds. Provoking crippling thoughts and painful, disheartening emotions."

I stared at the mysterious cowboy, now more intrigued with him than the Lord of the Dead. "Who *are* you? How do you know all this?"

"Focus on what matters." He scooped up dirt and tossed it on Molek's exposed face, and it stayed there, the physical realm colliding with the unseen. "You have to find your people."

"Meaning . . .?"

"Seek out and band together with those chosen by God and destined to believe your account and join you in the mission. Together, the handful of you can turn this town around and overturn evil."

It was like déjà vu, only I knew why the scenario felt familiar. "My father basically just told me that."

The old man nodded, like he was one up on me again.

"I'm meeting with some church people this Sunday," I said. "Is it them?"

Still kneeling, he looked up at me with a small yet reassuring smile. "I have no doubt it will become clear to you when you find the ones called to serve alongside you."

What a relief. People were being divinely stirred to believe and assist Ray and me. How else would we ever convince them?

Molek groaned, drawing our attention. "We need a battalion of armored Watchmen to stand guard here," I said. "Look what a beatdown they put on Molek. They need to strike him again if he starts to move."

The old man stood and rubbed the dirt off his palms, the soil only a slightly darker shade of brown than his skin. "Heaven's army dragged him and his throne off your land, outside city limits, but the beating that left him this impaired came at the hands of his own kind."

"Are you serious?" I'm sure my eyes were wide.

"In desperation, Molek summoned wicked cosmic powers that outrank him to descend on Masonville and help him reestablish his throne here—to combine their heightened destructive powers with his and devastate the town. They came, but they punished him severely for fumbling his assignment to begin with."

I rubbed anxious circles on my chin, staring up at the morning sky, processing things out loud. "So even though these cosmic beings hate Molek, they're willing to team up with him to try to destroy us?"

"All wicked forces hate one another," the man said. "It's the nature of their kingdom. But this town is a vital territory to their global plan. Their mission demands that they work together to see Masonville fall."

There it was again. The idea that the world's fate was directly tied to ours.

"Who are these superior rulers?" I thought maybe he was referring to the bats.

"Rulers of satanic darkness that preside high in the atmosphere over America. Seven of them have descended on Masonville, severely increasing the intensity of their influence on the people here. They're larger in stature than Molek and far more wicked."

So, it wasn't the short, squatty bats. And *far more* wicked? How was that even possible? Yet it fit. This had to be the greater evil Arthur's letter had warned about. The meaning behind the shadow that had brought me to my knees and tried to suffocate me in my nightmare.

The old man nodded solemnly at the broken-down house. "More than a century ago, that sat among others just like it on your land, during Caldwell's plantation era. Unthinkable evils were committed within those walls, but it was eventually abandoned and hauled off. Dumped out here." He shifted his weight toward me. "Think about it: if that house was restored and occupied now by a wholesome tenant, wicked men couldn't enter it again, but since it's vacant, they could walk in anytime and make themselves at home—men even crueler than the ones who lived there before."

"Okay?" He seemed to be making some kind of analogy, but I struggled to follow it.

"And so it is with Masonville." He faced me. "It's not enough to have driven Molek off your land and out of town. The people here are empty without the Light. So evil has come in greater strength and number to fill the vacancy. It's how wicked forces operate, generation after generation."

I raked my fingers through my hair, already feeling the heightened stress. "Please stay and help me."

The old man made no commitment—or reply. Instead he led me away by the arm, turning our backs on Molek and the house. Thankfully I had enough sense to get my phone out and pin the GPS location before we got very far.

"It's not your job to pick a fight with the seven Rulers," he explained. "Stay focused on finding those assigned with you to the mission, and together, gather the townspeople on your land to fulfill the sacred, scriptural promise you've been given."

He let go of me, and we walked side by side between rows of ripening corn. "Know this," he warned. "If Molek regains his strength, rises from the earth, and joins the seven Rulers, they will triumph, and the decades of heightened darkness will begin—here and in regions far beyond."

"And countless people my age and younger will pay the price," I added. I'd already learned from my father that hell's end goal was to wipe out my generation and the next from the face of the earth, since no generation before us was so called to expose and defy evil's agenda. Through every twisted means possible, demonic overlords and underlings were frantically working to kill us off. And based on the ancient historic account, Molek was among the most notorious assassins of young souls.

"How can Molek regain his strength?" I asked.

"You'll know soon enough." He reached toward my eyes, and of course, I squeezed them shut. He cupped his hands over my eyelids. Totally weird. "Be caring, young man, and you'll see what you need to, when you need to. You both will."

I knew he was talking about Ray Anne.

He removed his hands. I blinked a few times and nodded,

remembering a strange but proven paranormal principle: when I looked at people through eyes of compassion, so to speak, I saw hidden burdens and bondages on them that I couldn't detect otherwise. It was totally bizarre, but then again, lots of supernatural things are—from a human perspective, anyway.

He resumed walking, a brisk stride for a man his age. I kept up, eager to learn more. Everything I could. "Where are the seven Rulers right now?"

"All over town, working to spread their own influence and outdo one another, even while on a joint mission. But more days than not, at dusk, they commune on your land. At least a few, if not all seven of them."

"Where on my land?"

"The place most associated with death."

No surprise. I was confident I knew the spot.

The wise old man looked up and around, a cue I recognized by now. "Don't leave," I said. "Please, stay and help for once."

He shoved his hands in his deep denim pockets and grinned. "Haven't I always been there when you needed me?"

He'd definitely saved me on more than one occasion. Most recently, he'd come to my rescue after I'd been gagged and hog-tied in the woods, freeing me just in time to rescue little Jackson from his sadistic captors. But he'd said he'd meet back up with me at the scene of the crime that night and never did. "How come you bailed on the occult ritual, when I broke up the ceremony and stole Jackson back?"

He smiled wider, showing his gleaming white teeth. "I was there."

"Oh." In all the chaos, I must have overlooked him.

He glanced over his shoulder. "I have to go, but I'll see you again." He instructed me not to follow, then turned and walked away in the middle of me asking, "What's your name?"

I stood there all of two seconds, then dove between cornstalks, determined to follow in spite of his warning. But he was gone.

It figured. He was a marvel all his own.

I left the cornfield and drove toward Ray Anne's house, squinting into the rising sun. She loved when I had updates, and man, I did today.

I'd just passed Masonville High and was driving alongside my wooded property when a pale-faced teenage boy came stumbling out from the tree line, holding hands with a dark-haired, olive-skinned girl, both dressed in jeans and hoodies. In late August, in Texas.

They were both shackled. At first I thought something dark and freakish blanketed their faces, but when I looked a second time, there was nothing on them.

I circled back and pulled off the road, curious about the scary face thing and also wondering what they'd been doing in my woods. It was six-thirty on Wednesday morning, the first week of a new school year—a weird time to go walking the trails. When I parked and turned my engine off, they angled away from me, marching through knee-high grass back toward the woods, lurching forward at times like their equilibrium was way off. His blond hair pointed in every wild direction. She latched onto his skinny waist to keep her balance. They had to be freshmen. Maybe eighth graders. And both naive enough to think if they ignored me, I'd just go away.

"Hey," I called out.

The boy looked back and mumbled something. I ran and caught up to them, planting myself in their path. "What are you guys doing out here?"

She looked up at me, but he pulled his hood down, covering half his face while tugging on her hand. "Come on, Zella." When she didn't move, he let go of her and strode toward the trees without her.

She was a petite girl, only as tall as my chest, with dimples that made her seem innocent, but her brown eyes were glassy and bloodshot. And roaming all over the place. "Please don't call the cops on us." Her eyes pooled.

I wasn't sure why she thought I'd call the police, but before I could say anything, she turned and tried to catch up with the guy—her boyfriend, I assumed. But she tripped over her own Nikes and slammed onto the grass.

"Are you okay?" I went to her and reached to help her up, but she dodged my hand.

"We got it." The boy sighed, turning back and working to get her onto her feet, obviously as high as she was.

"What are you guys on?" There was no sense playing dumb. I'd been around enough of my mom's druggie boyfriends to spot users without any second-guessing.

He finally got the girl up, then faced me. "Nothing." After that, his syllables slurred together, but it seemed like he said, "Just leave us alone."

That's when it hit me.

"Gentry?"

I recognized him. Gentry Wilson, Lance's little brother—a lot taller and thinner than he used to be. I hadn't seen Gentry in a while, not since Lance went from being the best friend I had in this town to one of my worst critics.

Gentry stared at me with an open-mouthed, blank expression, his brain clearly not firing on all cylinders. I placed a brotherly hand on his shoulder and asked again, "What are you on?"

He shrugged my hand away and stared off into the distance. "Why would you care?"

I leaned down so I could look him in the eye. "Gentry, it's me. Owen Edmonds. Remember?"

He hardly glanced at me, but then again, his mind was frying. This wasn't the same giggly kid who used to follow Lance and me around and try to shoot hoops with us in their driveway and beg me to drive him around on my motorcycle. The memories must have triggered compassion in me, because the next thing I knew, I had an up-close look at the most grotesque bondage I'd ever seen.

FOUR

GENTRY'S FACE WAS COVERED IN METAL—a thick mask, dark copper-brown as an old penny. Horizontal, cylindrical bars formed small slits over his eyes and mouth. At the bottom of the contraption, just above his shackle, intertwined strands of barbed wire stretched all the way down his chest to his gut, where they were attached to a dagger that plunged beneath his ribs. Into his soul.

I swallowed hard.

I guess I didn't have the same compassion for the girl next to him—Zella, he'd called her. Her identical mask and barbed wire were faint and see-through, hardly visible to me. Just enough to know they were there.

"You guys . . ." I was at a loss.

Zella leaned and looked past me, then gasped and ran toward the woods as fast as a drug-impaired person could. Gentry was on her heels. I sighed. It occurred to me to move on. Forget about them and drive off and go see the love of my life. But since the old man had just instructed me to pay attention to the people I happened to cross paths with, I stayed put and looked around for what could have spooked them.

I spotted a white Ford Taurus that had pulled off the road behind my motorcycle. When I saw the driver, a sense of dread came over me, like a big barbell was suddenly strapped to my chest.

Detective Benny.

Good cop by day. Bad all hours of the night.

He bolted out of this car, leaving the door open, hollering Zella's name. He glanced my way but kept moving. In spite of his protruding gut, he chased after the kids, dragging six shackle-tethered chains behind him, four cords swinging from the back of his head. He'd gained a chain since I'd first met him, and I was sure he'd keep adding more. There were no Creepers attached to him, but I was convinced it was only because his oppression went deeper. His demons were hunkered down inside, influencing him from within.

He emerged from the trees a minute later, out of breath, pulling Gentry and Zella by their long sleeves. "This deviant behavior will not be tolerated." Detective Benny, playing the part of a model citizen. An upholder of justice and order.

He acknowledged me with a courteous nod while leading the masked kids to his vehicle, as if there was no twisted history between us and he hadn't threatened—however subtly—to harm me if I ever came forward with what I knew.

"Where are you taking them?" This man had the connections to have me killed, but I couldn't stay silent while he took off with two minors. For all I knew, they'd end up missing. Sold in a human auction like the one I'd spied him at, on my very own property.

The detective opened the car door to the back seat. "I'm going to see that they get home safe, where they belong."

Safe was the last word I associated with him. That and *honest*.

Zella lowered herself into the car but kept her feet planted in the grass, blocking him from shutting her in. "I was on my way home, Dad. I swear."

It was like the barbell on my chest fell and rammed my stomach. This corrupt man was raising a daughter? No wonder she was on drugs. And didn't want me calling the cops.

Detective Benny made a sharp sweeping gesture with his head, warning the girl to move her legs. She did, and he closed the door on her and Gentry. He looked at me before sliding into the driver's seat. "You stay out of trouble, you hear me?"

Aka, I'd better continue to keep my mouth shut. I nodded as if I hadn't been working behind the scenes for months, gathering information so I could eventually expose every camouflaged criminal and occult member in this town. But if I wanted to live long enough to see justice served and protect my mom and the other people I cared about from retribution, I had to go about it the right way and at the right time. The local news reporter lady—my unlikely ally, Elle Adelle—was discovering and confiding in Ray and me that Masonville's satanic society was every bit as cutthroat as the Mafia, only with a paranormal twist. They summoned powers of darkness to do most of the dirty work of harming people for them.

I knocked lightly on the door of Ray Anne's garage-turned-apartment, hoping she was awake, knowing Jackson was probably still snoozing in his crib, nestled within arm's reach of Ray Anne's bed. She'd taken on an enormous responsibility when she agreed to take temporary custody of someone else's baby—my ex-girlfriend's son. Adding to the strangeness of the situation, Jackson's father was Dan Bradford, the school shooter who had gunned Ray Anne down, but she never seemed to connect any dots of resentment back to Jackson.

Ray Anne opened the door with Jackson on her hip, still dressed in her pant-style pj's, her blonde hair thrown into a sloppy ponytail that struck me as gorgeous. Even after all this time, I found myself starting to lean in, as if she'd welcome me with a kiss. Ray Anne still clung to her overachieving goal to save her first kiss for her wedding day. Hard as it was, I didn't pressure her and had even managed to hold the line the *one* time she'd let her guard down and made herself vulnerable to me. I was holding onto hope that if I just stayed the course and didn't blow it, I'd be the one she'd marry. Then nothing with her would be off limits.

Jackson reached out with his tiny arms, straining so hard to get to me that his pacifier popped out of his mouth. He was eight months now, old enough to grin from ear to tiny ear every time he saw me. He'd also started calling me *dada*. What was I supposed to do? Letting him believe I was his dad seemed almost as cruel as scolding him for saying it.

I snatched him out of Ray Anne's arms and tapped my finger on his miniscule nose. As usual, he giggled and kicked his little legs. It was weird taking care of a baby at our age, but at least Ray's mom liked to watch him a lot and kept some playpen sleeper thing in her bedroom so my girlfriend and I could stay out late pretty much whenever we wanted. Honestly, I never thought I'd get so attached to a baby, especially one that wasn't mine. Jackson made me want to devote every ounce of energy I had to making the world a better place for him.

Way better.

Ray Anne walked over to her laptop and typed something, already at work on her online classes, determined to earn her nursing degree. She paused to rinse a sippy cup in the sink. I lowered myself into a chair at her two-seater breakfast table and bounced Jackson on my knee, looking at the tiny, concentrated glow emanating from his heart. It's not like he could understand my conversations with Ray Anne, but it still felt wrong to talk about invading forces of evil in front of him. But I had to get Ray Anne up to speed.

I started at the beginning, describing the details of last night's nightmare. She abandoned her chores and sat across from me, nodding every five seconds like she always did when I told an important story. I'd gotten to the part about the swarming bats when she held a flexed hand in my face, silencing me, staring at the backside of my forearm, of all things.

"What *is* that?" She pointed just below my elbow.

I examined my arm, and . . . *wow*.

There was a symbol on me. More like under my skin. It looked like small red glowsticks had been implanted in a strange pattern. Or like I'd been tattooed with luminescent ink.

Ray Anne ran her finger over it. "It feels warm. What in the world is it?"

I didn't know, but the fact that I could see it on myself was a good sign it was most likely from the Kingdom of Light. Bondages born of darkness weren't visible to the bound person's own sight. Plus, the symbol bore light—but I didn't put as much stock in that, since I knew by now that dark forces could fake divine illumination.

I studied the odd mark, mulling over whether it was ancient

hieroglyphics or a futuristic code or maybe symbols with no earthly source at all. One thing was certain: it was supernatural. Then I remembered . . .

"It's right where the lightning struck me."

Ray Anne gasped. "What!"

"In my dream," I told her. "I haven't gotten to that part yet."

"Oh."

As I resumed my story, her gaze drifted above my head to the wall behind me.

"What?" I asked her.

She ran her fingertips along the cuff of her long-sleeved sleep shirt on her right arm. "It's just, I had a weird dream too last night. Ramus knelt in front of me and touched my arm below my elbow."

Ramus was the Latin name we gave the Watchman who frequently watched over Ray Anne.

Still holding Jackson, I reached with my free hand and pushed her sleeve up, holding my breath. "Are you kidding me!" Sure enough, Ray had the exact same symbol as me, in the same place.

She was speechless, but only for a second. "I can't believe this!"

This was new and cool and definitely worth exploring, but just then an explosive boom startled us to our feet. It was like speeding Mack trucks had slammed in a head-on collision right outside Ray Anne's house. Jackson kept slobbering on the leather bracelet my father had given me without the slightest flinch, so we knew this was no traffic accident—no earthly commotion at all.

I followed Ray Anne out the door, holding Jackson as I scanned her driveway and the front yard and the airspace above us, then all around. The only unusual thing was a wad of black fabric lying in the street like someone had balled up and tossed tattered sheets on the pavement. No big deal, except that when a pickup truck drove past and ran it over, the vehicle and the heap never made contact.

"That thing's paranormal," Ray Anne said.

We headed down her driveway, illuminating the cement with her aura and mine, picking up on the faint sound of whimpering. It reminded me of the way Daisy would whine when I'd set her on the vet's table.

Ray Anne peered down her street, then froze with her arm out stiff, shielding Jackson.

"What?" But as soon as I asked, I saw it.

They had to have been traveling toward us at like eighty miles an hour—a caravan of Creepers, advancing as thunderously as a herd of wild horses, only these were carnivores, frothing at the mouth. They encircled the fabric heap in the street, ignoring us completely while taking turns striking the balled-up mass with clenched fists and kicks. A voice like a small child's cried out, so agonizing Ray Anne instinctively covered Jackson's ears, momentarily forgetting he couldn't see or hear any of this.

The assault continued, eliciting more high-pitched, unbearable wailing. Ray Anne lost sight of common sense and set out to intervene, as if she could shield whatever was wrapped in the fabric. I grabbed her arm just below her glowing symbol. "Wait!" We had no idea what was shrouded in there, but I was sure it wasn't a human child.

Don't get me wrong; Creepers didn't spare children the torment of whispering in their tender ears or stalking them at night. In fact, a few nights ago, Ray Anne had seen a hooded one looming over Jackson's crib while he slept. She woke up and commanded it to go, but I was confident that even if she hadn't woken, Jackson's robed, shield-bearing Watchman would have appeared and protected him. Surely Heaven's army would never allow a child to suffer the kind of merciless Creeper beating unfolding in front of us now.

All at once, the Creepers stopped their attack on the heap in the street and turned their battered heads in the same direction. Then they took off, taking their insatiable hunger for violence elsewhere. Ray Anne and I stared at the pummeled bundle, now jostling from within. She inched forward and reached toward it, as if she could peel back the layers and peek inside. Despite how easily spirit realm beings penetrated the material world, we'd found no way to physically maneuver spirit-realm matter.

Ray Anne came to her senses and stepped back, then gripped my hand. Jackson twisted in my other arm like he was bored and wanted down, but I wasn't about to let him crawl near that thing. I squeezed

Ray's fingers. "Let's move back." I wasn't afraid, just cautious. There was no telling what manifestation might emerge. But Ray Anne insisted on standing right where she was, in her purple-striped fuzzy socks, waiting.

It was like watching a creature pry its way out of an egg, hatching little by little as strips of fabric parted to the sides. At last, a trembling hand emerged—clawed and bony like those of all Creepers, but only about the size of Ray Anne's. And how do I explain the color? Imagine a raw turkey breast—pasty-white with a hint of pink.

Ray Anne searched my face. "What is it?"

I shrugged. I had zero sense of where this was going—what kind of Creeper this was.

A pair of wide, circular eyes peeked out from the cluster of cloth. They had big, dark pupils, more like a dog's than a devil's.

The thing whimpered again, like it was scared and suffering excruciating pain.

Finally, its entire bald head emerged. Ray Anne gasped. I probably did too. It had a Creeper's face—a bare skull with no tissue, covered only by an ultrathin layer of skin. But somehow this one wasn't scary, maybe because it had such huge, unthreatening eyes and smelled like a skunk—gross but not nearly as nauseating as other demons.

All base-level Creepers have war wounds and gashes, but this thing was marred with bruises. But how? From what I'd observed, Creepers didn't have blood—the essence of life and very substance of bruising.

It was hunched over, its skin-and-bone legs tucked against its body while still nestled in the black material. I recognized the fabric now as the stuff Creepers draped over themselves, but this evil spawn was bare-chested, like its robe had been ripped off its body and was now falling away in shreds.

It locked eyes with Ray Anne. It's not like she was teary eyed with compassion or smiling at the thing, but her brow wasn't exactly furrowed in revulsion either.

"Ray Anne, don't you dare feel sorry for it."

She huffed. "Like I ever would."

That's when a Creeper that stank like rotting fish came barreling through the air from behind us. It used its pointy elbow to deliver a crushing blow to the side of the pathetic Creeper's head, evoking a pained wail, then continued to pound the weakling.

I thought maybe Ramus would appear, but apparently the Kingdom of Light saw no need to shelter us or intervene.

Man, what I would have given to have been there to witness Molek suffer his violent ambush, outnumbered and outmatched by his own merciless kind. I couldn't harbor that kind of vengeance toward a human being without inviting chain-link bondage onto my neck—my soul—but there was no spiritual law that forbid me to hate evil. The way I saw it, I'd better hate it. Anything less meant naive vulnerability.

This second-round assault ended after the defenseless pale-pink Creeper was rammed in its side so hard, it went rolling down the pavement, dragging shreds of fabric with it. Its body appeared no more than four feet tall. Ray and I noticed a big pothole where the small Creeper had been. That crater hadn't been there when I'd pulled up to Ray Anne's a few minutes ago.

Another full-size Creeper seething with anger barged onto the scene, getting its furious licks in.

"I wonder why they're torturing him." Ray Anne winced with every blow.

"The same thing happened to Molek, but his attackers were Cosmic Rulers."

She turned and faced me. "Tell me!"

We went back inside, leaving the puny Creeper to its excruciating fate, and I told her the rest of my story. I kept pausing, both of us compelled to eye the sensational, glowing mark on our arms.

Typical Ray Anne: once I explained everything, she insisted we needed an even more detailed communication plan for Sunday afternoon's meeting outside Masonville High with the student pastors. I agreed we needed to explain Arthur's call to action to them as clearly as possible, but I reminded her, "The old man said there's people destined to help us. If they're the ones, they'll join us; if they're not, nothing we say will convince them."

In the meantime, Ray suggested we go to my land at dusk to spy on the Rulers. "Shouldn't we try to figure out their specific assignments?"

I told her it was worth a try, but only if we could stay hidden and undetected—no getting caught and provoking a conflict. I wasn't one to go picking fights with demons, but Ray Anne? Her bold bravery was unmatched.

"Did the old man describe what they look like?" she asked.

I sniffed the air, then handed Jackson to her so she could change his diaper. My affection for the guy had its limits. "Only that they're bigger and somehow way more wicked than Molek."

The truth was, nothing could have prepared us for the night's encounter.

FIVE

THE SUN SANK BEHIND OUR BACKS. Thankfully this time I'd remembered to bring my five-watt LED flashlight. I was careful to slow my pace through my wooded acreage so Ray Anne could keep up. She'd miraculously survived the Masonville High shooting, but still felt the aftermath in her weakened stamina and achy abdomen. Her diagnosis of infertility was yet another life-altering effect, but neither of us had brought that up in a while. Too depressing.

I led the way toward the Caldwell family cemetery, where a dozen of my ancestors had been buried some hundred and fifty years ago. As Ray and I dodged tangled shrubbery, I envisioned the two ornate, black-streaked tombs that stood side by side in the center of the graveyard like silent soldiers on a never-ending night watch. The remaining graves were crowned with decrepit headstones covered in peeling whitewash, all tilted in random directions. As crooked as my ancestors had been.

The small cemetery was encircled by a rusted iron fence that conjured the morbid image of a cracked rib cage framing disintegrating organs. There'd been bloodshed all over these woods, but the cemetery was the most obvious spot I associated with death. My best attempt at locating the Rulers.

Ray Anne and I took the same path I'd traveled the night I'd discovered the heinous cage out here on the old auction block, imprisoning abducted children. Sadistic history repeating itself on the very same soil.

We continued to weave our way through the oaks and cedars, ignoring the occasional Creeper whisper. I had goose bumps—not the exhilarating kind, but uneasy jitters. Every so often, bright streaks of dazzling light zipped by us, as fast as a falling star but moving horizontally, among the trees. I was sure it was Custos, and yeah, it was comforting to know that he was making the journey with us—and maybe Ramus as well. But it was also sobering: Heaven felt the need to dispatch reinforcements for tonight's stakeout. That had to mean we were about to face some degree of danger.

By the time we approached the cemetery, Ray Anne was out of breath but so eager, she took the flashlight from me. As the sunshine faded with every passing minute, she aimed the light around, then kept the beam fixed between the two arch-shaped tombs, illuminating a relic I'd forgotten about. A statue of Mary, carved in white stone, seven feet tall if I had to guess. The robed figure held a naked baby Jesus against her chest with one hand. The other one extended palm up, as if beckoning all to draw near. But trust me, there was nothing inviting about her stoic expression or stone-cold child.

Ray Anne studied the art piece. "She's so serious. And sad."

I eyed the pouty infant. "So's the baby."

Ray Anne walked to the iron fence, chest-high on her. She attempted to lean in and read the nearest headstone, but weeds and decades of discoloration made it impossible. I checked the time on my cell, hopeful I'd led us to the right place.

"We should back up and take cover," I told Ray Anne. But before we had a chance to move, she latched onto my arm so hard, her nails dug into my skin.

Like floodwater swirling into a manhole, the cluster of graves and the fence and the surrounding trees began to spin in the first hues of moonlight. Fighting dizziness, Ray and I ran back, distancing ourselves from the phenomenon. An entire football field's worth of physical matter rotated faster and faster until the earth, towering trees and all, caved in the center, sinking into some kind of paranormal vortex.

Like a black hole consuming an entire galaxy in seconds, the Caldwell cemetery and surrounding forest were sucked away and replaced by absolute darkness.

We were used to feeling the unsettling, icy presence of evil, but this was something else entirely. An overwhelming sense of exhaustion came over me, like I'd been shot with a high-dose tranquilizer gun. The weariness was mental and emotional too, tempting me to collapse and succumb to sleep right then and there. Ray Anne slouched over, bending under the weight of oppression while struggling to switch off the flashlight, trying to hide from whatever was coming.

I fought the severe fatigue enough to pull her close and take refuge with her behind the thickest tree trunk I could find. A level of evil we'd never endured before was headed our way.

There was a deep, dissatisfied moan, much louder than any human could make. Birds and small earthly creatures began to scurry overhead and around our feet, sensing the urgent need to scatter. Droves of Creepers flocked to the scene, perching in trees and hovering midair. Several noticed us and even charged at us, hissing and growling, but our light was impenetrable.

Ray Anne leaned into my side, both of us shivering. Our combined body heat was no match for the freezing spiritual air. I tried to grip the tree trunk in front of me but lacked the strength.

"*Open the gate!*"

We couldn't see who had spoken, but his voice was as loud and assertive as lightning striking a powerline. At his command—spoken in English—the dark void lit up, revealing a massive crater, as if a fiery furnace was being stoked below. I understood now what we were seeing.

The pit of hell was open before us, right there on my property. The sudden heat was beyond intense, but I had no doubt that it was the anguished humans' cursing and wailing that made Ray Anne cover her mouth and wince. Untold multitudes wept in eternal suffering. There's no sound like it in all the universe. No way to accurately reenact it on earth. And I still couldn't reconcile how a merciful God could possibly allow such a place to exist—much less create it.

Ray Anne started to cry, and it hit me; she'd never glimpsed into hell before, like I had. Never come face-to-face with the irreversible doom that awaits shackled humanity.

The horde of onlooking Creepers stayed uncharacteristically still as a huge, horrid object rose up from the pit. It was a sloppy, cone-shaped conglomeration of human skulls and bones strung together so that they came to a point some thirty feet beneath a flat, circular platform that, from where I stood, looked like it was paved with white pebbles. Or God forbid, teeth. The thing came to a stop, hovering above the fiery crater.

At last, a huge being emerged from the forest and stood at the edge of the pit, gazing at the bone-filled oddity. Ray Anne hushed. The creature was as tall as a two-story building, with the skin-and-bones frame of a Creeper, but his face resembled a wolf's, only without fur. He was draped in a green, kingly robe and wore a gaudy gold crown with an upside-down cross on his forehead. His bloodshot eyes had deep creases under them and blinked slowly and heavily. His head would drop into his chest like he was nodding off, then snap upright again.

Most troubling were the waves of extreme exhaustion that kept sweeping over me, so intense I could hardly keep my knees from buckling and my mind from wandering into meaningless dreams. Sure, Molek had had a dizzying, disorienting effect on me my senior year, when I'd been shackled, but this was even more severe. I knew I should be on guard and alert, paying close attention, yet all I wanted to do was curl up and abandon the mission for sleep.

Ray Anne couldn't keep her grip on my arm, and I knew she was suffering under the spell too.

My head was too heavy for my neck. I hunched, and my cheek pressed against hers. "You okay?" It was like my tongue had been injected with Novocain and could barely move.

Nothing about this was right. Two Lights, under the control of wickedness without either of us having done one thing to evoke it? And yet we needed to experience this—to understand first-hand what had descended on our town, seeking the destruction of all who lived there.

Custos emerged seemingly out of nowhere, facing us and placing his giant hands on top of our heads. "The Spirit of Slumber has no authority over you," he commanded, without any need to raise his voice.

I'd never heard him speak English before, but right now, he needed us to understand.

And just like that, my energy returned, surging from my gelled hair to my illuminated feet. Ray Anne wrapped her arms around my waist, holding on to me again. Custos had not only provided a heavenly intervention but a much-needed lesson. Now I understood: Cosmic Rulers projected oppressive power into the atmosphere like a frequency, so that all within its reach felt the effects, even unprovoked. While reigning high over the United States, Slumber's signal transmitted to every city and state—to every person in the country—but having descended on Masonville, the intensity of his signal was off the charts, bringing the immense oppression—some kind of spiritual slumber—to the people here.

That said, Cosmic Rulers' domination can be refused with God's authority.

With a single step through the air, the Spirit of Slumber stood on top of the massive floating platform, which began rotating slowly above the pit, as if floating in a whirlpool. And I know this sounds as outlandish as it gets, but the bones began to speak and praise him in numerous earthly languages—English included—lavishing him with words of affection like, "I adore you," and, "You are mighty and strong." Yet the voices were wailing, like they were being forced to worship against their will.

Another platform just like the first rose from the fiery chasm, and a Ruler of equal height emerged from the forested shadows. This one was bulky and draped in vibrant blue. His entire face was masked in dark brown metal with narrow slits over his eyes and mouth, identical to the revolting veils on Gentry and Zella. Twisted strands of barbed wire oozed out of the being's chin like metal drool, creeping down his chest and encircling his arms, then coiling like cobras around numerous daggers he held in each hand.

I'd had bouts with loneliness before, but this . . .

This was a misery all its own, like no one knew me or wanted to or cared if I lived or died or went missing without any explanation. Even with Ray Anne pressing against me, the sense of isolation was soul-crushing.

"I'm here," I told her, looking to somehow ease the pain she was bound to be feeling too.

Custos was there again. Ray and I shielded our eyes from his blinding brilliance as nearby Creepers dispersed like roaches fleeing a floodlight. He pressed his huge palms against our stomachs this time, his fingers extending all the way to our necks. "The Spirit of Addiction has no authority over you."

Instant relief, followed by a sinking realization. *Is that the feeling that drives my mom to drink?*

Now was not the time to ponder the distressing thought.

As the Spirit of Addiction stepped onto his own grisly platform, a third Ruler arrived. This one was arrayed in solid gray and hunched over like an elderly man, even though he was built like a ten-ton monster. Instantly, it was like a fist pressed into my chest, knuckles digging through my muscles and into my heart, infusing me with such crippling depression, I wanted to run away but lacked the motivation to bother.

Ray Anne let go of my hand, and we both groaned as all sense of contentment was swallowed by emptiness and longing and an overbearing desire to be left alone.

"The Spirit of Depression has no authority over us." I was suffering so badly, I asserted spiritual authority myself. But Ramus appeared beside us and pointed to the peace-sucking principality.

"Despair," he corrected me, so radiant I could hardly look at his epic armor for the brief moment he was there.

I cleared my throat, acting in spite of the debilitating stress on my soul. "The Spirit of Despair has no authority over us."

It worked.

The hunchbacked Spirit of Despair let out a barbaric grunt, and two Creepers stepped out of him—one after the other, exiting like a swinging door was hinged to his torso. They rushed away as another Creeper slipped out of the Spirit of Slumber's back and ran into the woods.

Ray Anne tugged on my arm to get me to bend down. "The Rulers house and release lower-level Creepers to carry out their assignment."

I nodded in agreement.

Soon, all three Cosmic Rulers stood atop floating platforms, orbiting above the simmering pit like uninhabitable planets, heads swaying as if reveling in the echoes of insincere praise from the bones.

Then a fourth giant entered the scene, this one bat-faced with ruby-red eyes, like the bats that had badgered me in my nightmare and in real life, but with gums flared, like a pit bull in a dog fight. He wore an obnoxiously-bright red robe, and Ray and I watched in silence as multiple Creepers fled his body too.

No fatigue came over me this time. No despair. Instead I was overtaken by such furious rage, my entire body tensed, from my clenched jaw to my locked knees. I didn't trust myself to be near Ray Anne. Although aggression toward women was among my most hated human violations, I felt like I was fully capable of yanking her by the arm and shoving her. More than capable—I *wanted* to.

Ray Anne pushed me away, obviously battling the same hostility. I was popping my knuckles when Custos spoke into my ear. "Strife."

I wanted to punch someone or wrestle something to the ground. But I knew the insanely intense urge wasn't mine, and I'd better confront it. I popped another knuckle, even as I spoke. "The Spirit of Strife has no authority over us."

Ray Anne sighed, then raised herself to her tiptoes and threw her arms around my shoulders in a tight embrace. "Thank God that one's over."

But the weird thing was, for me, it wasn't. The fury had lifted somewhat, but not completely. I managed to hug her back, keeping my predicament to myself.

The Spirit of Strife stepped onto his own suspended podium of bones. The heat raged hotter on my cheeks as the simmering fire flashed brighter, and all four Rulers gazed down into hell's open chamber. That's when those atrocious fat bats I'd seen in the cornfield—all six of them—came charging out of the pit, flying in ungraceful circles around the Rulers.

"We've marked all thirteen." The raspy-voiced bats spoke in unison—and in English, a huge advantage for Ray and me. "Every one of them must die."

I was sure they were delivering intel on behalf of their detained master, Molek.

Three Cosmic super-Creepers nodded in uncontested submission, but Slumber dared to pose a request—in English again. "Give us until the new moon."

I could hardly believe my eyes when one of the bats opened its mouth and extended a tongue as black and thick as a whip and lashed the Spirit of Slumber's head, sending him careening off his platform into the blazing chasm. "That's too late! Kill them at once!" Then came a slew of profanity mixed with such vile threats, Ray Anne covered her ears.

One thing was certain: as effectively as the kingdom of darkness collaborates to destroy humanity, its agents have nothing but spiteful contempt for one another.

The bats flew up and disappeared into the night sky—on their way back to Molek, I imagined. Meanwhile, Slumber climbed out of the pit as if an invisible net stretched up and onto the ground. He stood and faced the crater, still heavy-eyed and nodding off. The three remaining Rulers dismounted from their hovering platforms, stepping back onto land, and the bright inferno began to dim. The spirit world shifted and swirled back to the wood's natural setting.

As the Caldwell cemetery spun into place, my stomach churned. I wrapped my arm around a tree to keep from staggering and held Ray Anne with my other. By the time everything came to a standstill and I regained some sense of balance, the Rulers were gone, yet the spectating Creepers remained.

And there were voices coming from the old Caldwell graveyard.

SIX

You wouldn't think staring at something fiery bright in the spirit realm would create a need for physical eyes to adjust to the darkness of earth's night, but that's exactly what happened to Ray and me. We stood a short distance from the Caldwell cemetery, blinking and blinking. We'd had no time to process all we'd just witnessed, and already we were being confronted with another mystifying scenario.

Little by little, as my eyes adjusted to the moonlight, I spied what looked like people climbing and hopping over the rundown fence into the graveyard. They spoke in hushed tones as their spirit-realm chains clanged against the iron bars—an audio overlap of dual realms that I always found disorienting. The silhouettes clustered in front of the two arched tombs, by the Mary statue.

"What are we supposed to say?" A giddy young voice. A girl, from the sound of it.

"I'm scared!" someone else said, provoking satisfied cackles from the onlooking Creepers.

"You should be." A boy, for sure.

I could see five people now: two ponytails, one head of long hair, and two ball caps. No Light aura around any of them. They were all wearing dark pants and long sleeves.

"Say it, Gentry!"

Ah. Gentry—and Zella too, I figured—plus three of their friends. They stared up at the stone-carved Mary and used their phones' lights to illuminate her face and one another.

A kid wearing a hoodie and a backpack—Gentry, I was pretty sure—stepped close to the sculpture, tilting his head back like he wanted to make eye contact with her. The gawking Creepers looming overhead all leaned in.

"Mary, Mary, there's a secret only a few do know. If we ask you kindly, you'll let your real tears flow."

"Now, watch this!" one of them announced. Zella, I think.

There was a silent pause, followed by gasping and muffled screams as they took pictures with their phones.

"You see anything?" Ray Anne whispered to me.

We were too far back. I took her hand, and we marched toward the spectacle, refusing to slow our pace as Creepers swooped down and lurched at us. I found myself stomping unnecessarily hard, still simmering with aggression left over from that Cosmic Spirit of Strife.

A girl spun around and faced us. "Who's there?"

"It's okay." I tried to act normal and collected, even though I didn't feel like myself. "We just want to know what you guys are doing."

I hopped the fence without Ray Anne. She couldn't risk agitating her injuries.

They all had their flashlights aimed at me now. "Are we in trouble?" a trembling girl with glasses asked.

"No." I glanced up at the Mary statue. Thick cobwebs draped down her veiled head like feeble strands of hair, though I couldn't tell if they were physically there or a spiritual reality. "What's the deal?" I asked.

Zella stepped beside me and pointed up, sober tonight, it seemed. "See her tears?"

A dark streak lined the statue's left cheek. I reached toward it.

"Don't!" Zella swatted my arm. "You'll make her mad, and she'll haunt you."

"Enough, Zella." Gentry spoke up. "It's none of his business."

I crossed my arms. "Uh, this is my property. Everything that happens out here is my business."

There was a collective *oooh*—the overly dramatic, immature kind.

I sighed. "What grade are you guys in?"

Zella pointed to herself, then Gentry. "Ninth." The other two girls and the remaining boy were sophomores. "We're in a group together at school," Zella said. Whatever that meant.

I refocused on the stone-carved Mary. I swiped her cheek, unafraid of any supposed retribution for touching her.

"You shouldn't have done that." Zella shone her light on my finger, damp and dark red now. "It's blood."

"Well?" Ray Anne called from the other side of the fence.

I made a closer examination of my fingertip. There was no denying it. "It does look like blood."

"Isn't it the coolest thing *ev-ver*?" a smiling girl with braces said. The surrounding Creepers stirred.

"No, it's not cool. It's evil."

They all rolled their eyes like I was old and lame.

I turned to Gentry. "Where'd you learn that chant?"

He took a big gulp and hesitated. "Just some girl . . . my brother dated a few months ago."

I didn't know Lance had had a girlfriend after Meagan, but then again, how would I? Our friendship hadn't survived past high school. It was hard for me to picture him with anyone except Meagan, but she'd been dead for over a year. Even so, I still suffered from agonizing memories of her . . .

My hand unable to make contact with hers as her petrified soul reached for me in anguish.

Don't think about it.

"Who's Lance's ex-girlfriend?" I wanted to know.

Gentry gave me a lopsided grin. "A hot blonde that drove a red BMW."

It was like I could feel the synapses firing in my brain, connecting seemingly random bits of information to form a clear picture. There was only one young blonde I knew of who'd driven a red BMW around Masonville. "Veronica?"

"That's what they called her on the news, but her real name is Eva," Gentry said.

There was no telling how many names she'd gone by. She was a fraud, like the rest of her occult colleagues. And now I realized my suspicion about Lance was spot on. He *had* been one of the masked security guards at the human auction, no doubt inducted into the secret society by his then-girlfriend.

"She brought you out here and showed you this?" Ray Anne asked Gentry. He nodded. "When?"

He shrugged. "Before she got locked up."

"Wait a minute." The girl with glasses pushed her friends aside to get to Gentry. "Your brother dated that gangster girl that got arrested for kidnapping a baby?"

After Veronica had been hauled to jail for abducting Jackson, Detective Benny had released a cleverly spun web of lies to the public, saying that the abductions were gang related. But Elle had determined to report the truth, supported by evidence—until a man in a ski mask rose from the backseat of her Audi one night and held a knife to her throat, vowing he'd come after her husband and their little boy if she dared challenge the detective's statements.

But this sophomore girl with glasses and a shackle had no clue about any of that, and naturally, she'd believed what she'd seen on the news. Like most people do.

Gentry looked past her, at me. "We'll leave, Owen." He tugged anxiously on the straps of his backpack looped around his shoulders. "Please don't call the cops."

This time I understood why they dreaded involving the police. I didn't want Detective Benny coming around anymore than they did. "I won't," I said, "but you guys can't come back here. Understand?"

All five of them nodded.

I had no clue how the statue was crying bloody tears, but it was obviously a paranormal trick intended to captivate, then somehow trap and torment young, ignorant souls. I'd never once seen or heard of God performing a meaningless miracle just to draw a crowd.

The students climbed back over the fence and began the trek toward the main street beyond the woods. I followed, walking next to Ray Anne and behind Gentry, shining my flashlight and working to ignore the commotion of Creepers moving through the trees in all directions. "What's in the backpack?" I asked Gentry.

He sped up his already-hurried pace, and so did his friends. I caught up to him and asked again. This time, he stopped and faced me, his eyes plastered wide. "Um, just matches and outdoor stuff." He took another big gulp as the others rushed ahead—except Zella, who stopped to wait for him.

"Tell me the truth, Gentry." I stepped close, realizing now how much his facial features resembled Lance's. There was no sign of the horrible mask—the Spirit of Addiction's influence. I assumed it was because Gentry wasn't high tonight. At least not yet. That or I lacked compassion for the guy at the moment.

I nodded toward his backpack. "Whatever you're doing or dealing, just say it."

He rubbed his tongue in circles against the inside of his cheek and averted his eyes—the same thing my mother always did whenever I ventured to bring up her issues with alcohol.

"You don't know what things are like for me." He spoke so softly now, I barely heard him.

"So tell me." I leaned in, already aware of some things about his life. His overly demanding mother. His quick-tempered stepdad. "You and me, we go way back, Gentry. You know you can trust me."

He sighed. "I gotta go, okay?"

It dawned on me that he'd probably heard Lance talk all kinds of trash about me. No wonder he didn't trust me.

I thought about reaching and unzipping his backpack—what could he do to me? But once his dope or JUUL or whatever was in there was out in the open, all I could do was lecture him about it like some overbearing parent, and I knew that was useless. So, I stood there, shining my flashlight at him, hoping the weight of my gaze would at least make him think about things.

That's when I spotted a black horizontal streak in the crease between his chin and his neck, above his shackle. It was like a thin, sloppy tattoo that ran the length of his throat.

Ray Anne obviously noticed it too. "Do you have a mark on your neck?" she asked him.

She and I both knew it was there. The issue was, did he?

He shook his head with a crinkled nose, rubbing back and forth on his neck—over his shackle, but it's not like he could feel the freezing metal. "Can I go now?"

He caught up with Zella, and Ray and I trailed them out of the woods. They all refused a ride home. Ray Anne and I knew the risk they were taking walking the streets of Masonville, especially at night, but it's not like we could force transportation on them.

I hurried to the church on my motorcycle, hoping no one had broken in while I was supposed to be on night duty. Most nights, I stayed up until at least 1:00 a.m., listening, just in case. All the while enduring that unnerving sense I was getting in my room lately.

I took a shower in the tiny bathroom attached to my claustrophobic space, the cinder block walls painted a warm vanilla color that still didn't make the room cozy. I collapsed onto the uncomfortable bed—the only place to sit other than the floor—bored and restless and seriously homesick for my apartment. My 55-inch TV and king-size mattress were in storage, along with nearly everything else I owned. But this church-guard gig was the closest thing I had to a witness protection program.

I glanced obsessively at the awesome red-glowing symbol on my arm while researching the phases of the moon. I quickly discovered that the next new moon was just ten days away, which meant that, unless evil's plan was interrupted, the thirteen people marked to die—whoever they were—would surely be dead before then. Maybe even in the next day or two.

Don't get me wrong—I cared. But ten days or less? That was hardly enough time to figure out who the targets were, not to mention coming up with a game plan to protect them from the Cosmic Rulers' death plot.

Facing impossible situations was getting old fast.

I found a pen in the nightstand and used the blank space on the back of a Chinese take-out menu to make my best sketched replica of the supernatural imprint on my skin: מגן. I snapped a pic of the drawing and texted it to my father. **Any idea what this could mean?**

For reasons I still didn't understand—and that still irked me—he'd warned me not to risk texting or saying anything personal, even on the burner phone he'd given me, for fear it could be intercepted. Of course I'd asked, "By who?" He'd said it was safer for me that I didn't know. So, I didn't mention the symbol being on Ray Anne and me.

I strummed my guitar a little while, my go-to diversion when I needed to chill out, then lay down and stared at the tacky speckled ceiling, rehearsing the assignments of the four overlords—Slumber, Addiction, Despair, and Strife. And I speculated about the assignments of the remaining three, contemplating dysfunctions common across America. I also replayed the bats' instructions—Molek's malicious plot . . .

"We've marked all thirteen. Every one of them must die."

"Kill them at once!"

I tried to piece together who the thirteen might be, and also why the kingdom of darkness wanted them dead so badly and so quickly. And I imagined ways the Rulers might go about it.

Another school shooting by a demon-possessed gunman?

My stomach churned. I hoped not.

"Lord . . ." I worked to keep it a humble request instead of an impatient complaint. "Help me understand."

It took a minute, but I paused breathing in the middle of an exhale when a connection registered: Gentry had a paranormal mark on his neck. Was that it? Was he one of the thirteen people on Molek's hit list, marked to die? Yeah, I had a new supernatural mark too, but mine was born of Light. Not at all like Gentry's jagged black streak.

Thinking to the monotone soundtrack of the spinning box fan in the corner of my room, I tried to come up with another explanation for the mark on Gentry, but I only became more convinced he had to be a target. I still had no clue why, though.

I shoved my pillow over my head, like I could actually smother the disturbing mental image of Gentry's black line, as if his throat was scheduled to be slit. I remembered the way he used to be, when he was younger. He'd looked up to me and trusted me enough to tell me what Lance never dared: that behind closed doors, his stepdad drank all the time and was brutal toward all three boys in the house. And his mom did nothing about it.

Of all people, I could relate to having an alcoholic parent. Also one who refused to confront reality.

Right now, I needed a break from harsh realities. I flipped on the 1990s television set and tried to get interested in some lame Western, but I was still plagued by intruding cosmic feelings of strife-filled hostility. I decided to mute the TV and focus on God, desperate to know what he wanted from me, especially concerning Gentry. So I asked him out loud. Then I lay there, honestly not expecting any response. Yet an internal whisper came. More like an inner *knowing*.

FIGHT FOR HIM.

It was so subtle, I could have dismissed it as a coincidence—my mind merely recalling the old man's advice that I help people. But I knew better. Although I didn't hear it often, I was starting to recognize that inner voice. All peace. Zero hostility.

"How, Lord?"

I waited and waited but heard nothing but the box fan. I sat up and clutched a pillow against my chest. This wasn't the first time I'd felt the overwhelming responsibility to save someone's life, to protect a person from diabolical forces that he—or she—never suspected existed. But when it came to rescuing lives, I'd lost more times than I'd won—an undeniable fact I couldn't escape, even after I unmuted the TV.

God, help me.

I wondered what other forms of witchcraft Eva (aka, Veronica) had introduced Gentry to and how they related to his mark for assassination. There are no coincidences in spirit-realm operations on either side of the kingdom equation, light or dark.

It was late, so instead of calling Ray Anne, I texted her, explaining what I believed about Gentry's mark.

I got out of bed and was brushing my teeth, hoping I'd be able to fall asleep soon, when there was the loud sound of glass shattering somewhere beyond my room. I slammed my hand down on the faucet and turned the water off, standing at attention. Then came another noise . . .

A baby crying?

Daisy's nails tapped the dilapidated wood floor as she paced in front of the locked door of my room, her gaze fixed toward the hallway on the other side, ears raised like she heard the crying infant too. Or some intruder.

I grabbed my flashlight and my Louisville Slugger, then stood poised by my door. It occurred to me to call 911. The problem was, I didn't know which realm the crashing sound or whimpering had come from. A squalling baby made no sense in either dimension.

I clung tightly to my trusty baseball bat and opened the door ever-so-softly, flipping on the hall light before beginning my cautious descent down the hallway. I made it to what was becoming my familiar stakeout—the second-story choir loft. I leaned forward against the waist-high balcony and shined my flashlight down, scanning the sanctuary. None of the stained-glass windows were broken, but the infant's cries were so loud now, I was convinced someone had abandoned a baby in one of the pews.

I charged down the stairwell and flipped light switches on the panel at the back of the sanctuary, illuminating the whole sanctuary and stage. It was clear the cries were coming from my left. I hurried over there, my heart racing, convinced that any second now, I'd find a newborn. The distinct sound led me down the aisle of the second-to-last pew, where I stood looking down at the precise spot where, based on everything my ears were telling me, a baby should have been.

But there was nothing there.

I lowered to one knee and searched the floor. Just gray tiles.

Surely this blindness had nothing to do with me lacking compassion.

I rose to my feet and scanned the surrounding pews but was quickly drawn back to the original spot—the unmistakable source of the crying. It was so real, I reached down, as if I could touch the child. But my hand only brushed the tan pew cushion.

I felt the uneasy sense all over again that someone was looking at me, spying on me from behind my back. I spun around and eyed the center aisle near the stage—the exact location where I'd sworn an invisible stalker had loomed the night before.

I was already questioning my sanity when the freakiness escalated to a whole new level. As if some sort of frequency was vibrating against my chest, I could physically feel the presence across the sanctuary now—so tangible I knew it was moving up the aisle, headed in my direction.

I wanted to sprint out of there and speed away on my motorcycle, confident my dog could fend for herself for the night. But no. That's not how faith responds.

"God hasn't given me a spirit of fear but of power and love and a sound mind."

It didn't take long before I felt the unseen threat looming at the end of my row, undeterred by my use of Scripture. I stood facing it, sideways between two pews, the mystery baby still crying hard. When I sensed the presence advancing, coming directly toward me, I gripped the back of the bench on my left and balled my right hand into a fist.

Lord, help me!

I stood my ground with every shred of courage I had. Every ounce of bravery God provided.

For a single, agonizing second, I felt something horrific pass by me—more like through me. It was like my old stalker, that Creeper named Murder, was back, invading unseen and breaching my aura.

Believe it or not, the situation actually got worse. From the sound of things, the invisible baby fell off the pew onto the cold tile, then its cries moved away from me along the floor until they grew faint—seemingly outside the building, fading into the night.

I didn't move for a while. Just stood there wondering if, God forbid, I was losing my spiritual senses, then second-guessing what I had or hadn't just experienced. I wished this was just another vivid nightmare.

Needless to say, I didn't sleep well. At 8:00 a.m., Ray Anne called, out of breath and begging me to come over. It wasn't until I turned onto her street that I spotted a black Suburban in my rearview mirror. I pulled over in front of a random house, unwilling to lead them to Ray Anne's. The vehicle, with its dark-tinted windows, passed me and kept driving, but I still found it suspicious.

The SUV didn't circle back, so I went ahead to my girlfriend's.

Mrs. Greiner had taken Jackson for a walk in his stroller, so Ray Anne and I sat alone in her garage apartment, side by side on her futon.

It was awesome to have her all to myself, but she was anxious and fidgety. I put my arm around her shoulders, but she stayed tense.

"Something happened this morning," she said, "while Jackson was sleeping."

"Okay?"

She pulled her knees into her chest and rocked back and forth. "I was watching a YouTube video—some man talking about spiritual symbols—and I felt a blast of cold air, then saw something out of the corner of my eye. I looked up, and just like the other day, a hooded Creeper was hovering over Jackson's crib, peering down at him. Its back was to me, but I could tell this time, it wasn't built like a normal Creeper. And there was no odor.

"I commanded it to go, and it groaned—not in pain, but like it was really furious—and balled its fists, but get this: the hands looked normal, like a human's. Then it turned and glared at me. I got a clear view of its face before it vanished, and Owen, I'm telling you . . ."

She was trembling now. I pulled her close, into my side. "Go ahead."

"It was Veronica."

SEVEN

"RAY, YOU KNOW CREEPERS CAN APPEAR AS PEOPLE."

"I understand, but the way she stared me down—it looked *just* like her."

"Trust me, I know." I still carried humiliation over having fallen for Molek's manipulation—his cruel disguise as my father, the one man I'd been desperate to meet my whole life. Then there were the spirits that looked like Walt and Marshall, and Lucas too, all exact replicas of departed people, sent to torment and trick me. The charade finally ended the night I beheld each of them in their true form: Creepers, not human spirits. No shred of humanity at all.

I'd never be so gullible again.

"Ray, we have to focus on resisting the Rulers and purging my land of evil—there's no time to waste. This is just a distraction to scare you and derail your focus." Maybe the same was true for last night's crying baby ordeal, but I was still too confused by it to even bring it up.

She stood and faced me, her arms crossed. "I get what you're saying, and I know Veronica's in jail, but still, I'd feel better if I had concrete proof."

I stood and pulled her to me. "You mean more proof than the fact that she's behind bars three hours away at the Hilltop Correctional Unit? Ray Anne, she wasn't here. It's physically impossible."

She looked away and twisted a strand of her beautiful long hair. "I know you're right. I mean, of course there's no way. But . . ."

She paced the room, still talking about it. I meant to listen, but my gaze drifted to her legs. Off topic as it was, they looked really good in her denim shorts. She'd lost muscle tone after being injured, but her thighs and calves were built back up now, as attractive as they'd been in high school.

"Owen, my gut tells me Veronica's up to something, even though she's in jail."

Gut feelings. The new normal in my faith-based world—a total antithesis to how I'd lived my life as an atheist. It had its risks and its rewards.

"Ray, take it from me—gut feelings can be way off." I gazed into her captivating blue eyes. "Jackson is completely safe from Veronica. It was an imposter Creeper, but you ran it off. Mission accomplished. Now, don't go taking matters into your own hands. You do *not* want to go see Veronica in jail."

I was sure that was exactly what Ray Anne wanted to do, and I had to talk her out of it. According to Elle, and based on what I'd witnessed myself, Veronica was a witch. I'm talking a full-blown, spell-casting, devil-conjuring witch. I didn't want Ray Anne anywhere near her.

I finally made an offer I thought might calm her. "If it makes you feel better, Ray, I'll go question Veronica myself. Just please, don't go near her."

It took some convincing, but Ray Anne finally agreed to keep her distance and let me handle it.

I switched to a new subject before she could change her mind. "You hear from Jess lately?" A dismal topic, but it was the first thing that came to me. Ray Anne sighed while walking to her small desk on the far side of the room. I was already aware Jess hardly ever bothered to call and check on her son, which I found inexcusable, probably because I knew what it was like to grow up not knowing one of my parents. Jackson was worlds away from both of his. But he'd hit the jackpot when he got Ray Anne. No one loved as deeply as her.

Ray Anne powered on her laptop. "I haven't heard from Jess in three weeks. I hope she's okay."

Although Ray Anne never admitted it, I got the idea she was relieved that Jess took little interest in Jackson. Jess had a legal right to show up and take him back any time, and by now, Ray Anne was intensely, irrevocably attached. I'd warned her like a million times to guard her heart, but she couldn't help herself.

Neither could Mrs. Greiner. She entered in typical fashion—no knock—and rolled Jackson's stroller into the center of the room, then gave me a warm shoulder pat. While unstrapping Jackson and hoisting him into her arms, she accidentally called him Lucas, her deceased son's name. Ray Anne and I looked away, pretending not to notice. Mrs. Greiner set Jackson on the floor with some toys, kissed his head, then hurried out of the apartment, teary-eyed.

"I feel so bad when she does that." Ray Anne stood motionless, wrestling with her own unhealed emotions, I think. The two-year anniversary of her brother's suicide was just a month away.

Mrs. Greiner opened the door again and poked her head in, clearing her throat like nothing sad had just happened, suppressing all trace of grief. "Ray Anne, while I was on my walk with Jackson just now, Dr. Bradford was driving in our neighborhood, and he pulled over to say hello. He asked who the baby was."

Ray Anne slammed her laptop shut. "Mom! What did you say?"

Mrs. Greiner winced. "Calm down, sweetheart. I just told him his name. It was obvious to me Dr. Bradford has no idea Jackson is his grandson. I can't believe Dan didn't tell his dad he's a grandfather." She teared up again. "Kids need their grandparents."

Ray Anne picked Jackson up and held him close. "It's not our place to tell Dr. Bradford anything, Mom. Please don't ever discuss Jackson with him."

Mrs. Greiner huffed. "I don't see why not."

Of course. She didn't know what Ray and I did—that Dr. Bradford was fully aware Jackson was his grandson. I'd seen Dr. Bradford in the woods the night of the auction, shouting curses from behind an animal mask, consenting that Jackson be fatally harmed—the little guy would have died if I hadn't rescued him. I was sure at the time the masked man was Dr. Bradford, and I hadn't questioned it since.

"Mom, Dr. Bradford abused his own son. Dan would show up to school with black eyes."

"You can't honestly believe his father did that, Ray Anne," Mrs. Greiner scolded. "Dr. Bradford single-handedly supports Masonville's food pantry, and he's underwritten and participated in medical mission trips to Mexico for over a decade. Such a warmhearted, generous man deserves to know he's a grandfather."

Ray Anne had been convinced her mom was too fragile to handle the truth about Masonville's occult society and had warned me more than once to never disclose anything about it to either of her parents. But I felt the need to at least clarify, "Making some hefty tax-deductible donations and a few trips to Mexico don't mean Dr. Bradford is a warm-hearted man."

Mrs. Greiner pursed her lips, visibly annoyed with me, and inten-tionally kept the conversation between her daughter and her. "All I'm saying, Ray Anne, is the man has a right to know about his grandson and see him. Spend quality time with him."

"No!" Ray Anne clung tighter to Jackson, like someone was trying to rip him from her arms. "*No one* has my permission to take Jackson out of this house, away from me, understand, Mom?"

Mrs. Greiner furrowed her brow. "That's hardly fair, Ray Anne. Now may not be the time, but you and I need to discuss this."

Ray Anne glared, unrelenting. Mrs. Greiner studied her daughter as if she knew something was off. Finally, she shut the door. I was surprised it didn't open again. Mrs. Greiner was the most obsessive woman I'd ever known, especially when it came to her daughter.

Ray Anne sighed. "Can you imagine if Dr. Bradford got his hands on Jackson?"

I shook my head. "No, I can't. I'll never let that imposter get any-where near him."

Ray Anne put Jackson in his playpen, then went to her computer, printed off a document, and handed it to me—a spreadsheet listing the four Rulers, including their assignments, features, even garment colors. So Ray Anne.

"Why do they speak English?" she asked me. We'd nearly always heard demons talk amongst themselves in their own otherworld language—choppy syllables, not at all like the Watchmen's flowing dialect.

I gave her my best theory. "The old man said the Cosmic Rulers reign high in the atmosphere over America. Maybe they're so entrenched in our culture, so familiar with us, they use our language."

"Makes sense, I guess." She clutched my hands. "You're up for going back tonight, right? Maybe the other three will show up."

"For sure."

She reached out and gave me a hug. I held her tightly, overcome with gratitude to have her in my life. We finally let go, and though I hated to ruin the mood, I felt the need to warn her, "Ray, please pay attention to your surroundings and be on the lookout, especially for a black Suburban. I think Detective Benny has people tracking me, and they may be keeping tabs on you, too."

Ray Anne turned and watched Jackson roll onto his back, obviously more concerned for him than her own safety. She gave me her word she'd be aware.

We discussed our plan, and by the time I left, we'd clarified next steps in order of the most urgent, encouraging each other that we had nothing to fear. Our most pressing priority remained the student pastors—hopefully they were destined to join us, and starting this Sunday, would get busy helping recruit people to gather on my land and follow through on Arthur's mandate as soon as possible. In the meantime, Ray and I agreed that we had to try to solve the urgent mystery of Molek's thirteen targets and find a way to protect them, starting with Gentry.

I was walking my bike backwards down Ray Anne's driveway when the sound of whining stopped me. There was that pale-pink Creeper, huddled in fetal position in the dirt behind the hedge of bushes that lined the brick of Ray Anne's garage apartment, its scared-skunk scent wafting in the midday breeze.

I commanded it to leave, and it whimpered, then hobbled on all fours into the middle of Ray's front yard, not a shred of fabric covering its naked, detestable skin-and-bones body anymore. It collapsed, pretending it could go no further, but I asserted heavenly authority again: "Get off this property." The sorry excuse for a Creeper didn't budge, as if it couldn't comprehend my command. But I knew from experience that Creepers understand every word people say, and they're also well aware of property lines. They're just relentless trespassers. But Lights have a right to evict them. A responsibility to make them leave.

Dealing with one or even a few usually wasn't much of a challenge—at least now that I understood the heavenly authority I carried. But evicting the vast army that had staked claim to my acreage and this town over a century ago, along with seven Cosmic Rulers? That took more than one or two Lights saying, "Get out."

I commanded the pale-pink Creeper to flee a third time, and the thing finally started moving again, using its elbows to drag itself inches at a time, crying as if scooching over the grass was torture. It was the first time I'd ever witnessed a Creeper shed actual tears.

Ray Anne stepped outside. "What's going on?"

She looked on as the pathetic Creeper finally toppled over the curb into the street, where a gang of full-size Creepers emerged from a nearby gutter and took turns beating the weakling. Ray Anne lowered her head and went inside.

Not me. I stayed awhile and watched the thing suffer.

That afternoon, I parked my bike between students' vehicles in the Masonville High lot, just like old times. I had an idea to run by Principal Harding. If she agreed to it, it would serve a couple of purposes, including allowing me to be on campus another school year without the hassle of tutoring students.

It didn't matter how many times I'd seen Creepers crawl up the three-story school building and peer down from the edge of the roof, it still made me cringe. And clench my fists in fury.

The front cement steps were littered with nearly-see-through Creeper notes inscribed with all kinds of dates and initials—evil missions—no two alike, from what I could tell. The lowercase word **death** was scribbled on the front brick of the school in wide, spirit-world letters that stretched above and all the way across the four main entrance doors. A not-so-subtle reminder that I was entering a war zone, one that still bore signs of Molek's influence.

I whispered, "Lord, give me mercy and compassion." I wanted to see *everything*.

Same as last year, stepping into the freezing foyer triggered a flood of unwanted memories. I could practically hear the blast of Dan's rifle.

Students made their way to class, hurrying before the bell rang, and I dodged them on my way to the administration offices, enduring the familiar yet still disturbing symphony of chains colliding and dragging on the tile floors. Creepers thronged the halls, attached to people, hovering midair, gathered around trash cans—you name it.

Even though I felt no sudden rise in compassion, and it was so faint I almost missed it, I saw a mask of addiction on a student who walked past me, followed by another. Months ago, my entanglement with evil had weakened my senses; were they getting stronger now? Unfortunately, that possibility conflicted with the invisible-crying-baby incident, so I gave up on analyzing it for now.

As I neared the office, I started really missing Ray Anne. She'd captured my heart in these halls.

It was still hers.

I ducked into the foyer of the admin offices and introduced myself to the shackle-free lady seated at the front desk, then asked if I could please speak with Principal Harding. The soccer-mom-looking woman glanced up at me from her computer, sitting up straight in her chair, but my breath caught as I saw a shadowy form of her—her soul—slumped over, a chain layered around her neck and dragging onto the floor. Her soul's forehead nearly grazed her keyboard, bent by the burden of oppression. The lady's physical form smiled politely at me while she used a handheld radio to page Harding. Meanwhile, the slouched, shadowy version of her groaned.

Without causing a scene, I uttered under my breath, "Spirit of Despair, you have no authority over her." I couldn't stop myself from wincing when her hunched soul strained to turn its neck, gazing up at me with despairing eyes, yet remained bowed with suffering.

So much for my attempt at liberating her. I figured that the lady—no doubt depressed and suffering within—had to take authority herself, on her own behalf. Or at least agree with my declaration for her. But she probably had no clue the miserable sense she was living with was the effect of a Cosmic Being permeating our atmosphere. And just like some deficit in my soul had obviously allowed Strife's influence to stick, keeping me agitated, something in her invited Despair's power.

"Mrs. Harding welcomes you to go to her office." The nice lady's face smiled while her soul wept. And she was a Light.

I stared as long as I could without making a scene, then walked the familiar path to Harding's office, attempting yet again to win my own internal battle. "Spirit of Strife," I uttered under my breath, "you have no authority over me." But that abiding sense of aggression still brewed in me, like an app running nonstop in the background on my cell phone.

I stepped into Harding's office and . . .

What. Is. Going. On?

She was seated behind her same ol' desk, bound in the same ol' shackle, but now there were thick cobwebs all over the place, from floor to ceiling—the same kind I'd seen binding critically ill and dying people to their hospital beds in the ICU. And come to think of it, clinging to the Mother Mary statue.

To make matters worse, Principal Harding was shrouded in webs too. A paranormal manifestation, no doubt.

She stood and extended her arms, inviting me into a kind embrace. The white fibers stretched from her head all the way down to her high heels and were also layered around her chair and desk, like she was tethered to her office.

I only managed to give her a hug because I closed my eyes and made it quick. When I stepped back, I saw that the light around my feet had incinerated the webs around hers. That was cool.

I lowered into the chair across the desk from her. Thankfully, by now I was pretty good at acting normal when nothing around me was. She asked how my education was going, and when I told her I was still enrolled in online community college classes and still undecided on a particular degree, she removed her glasses and demanded to know what kind of student passes up the chance to go premed at Boston U.

"I wanted to stay and make a difference here in Masonville."

She slid her glasses back on and shook her head.

"There's a freshman student I'd like to help," I told her. "Gentry Wilson. He's going through a hard time. Have you assigned a mentor to him?"

She pursed her lips and leaned back in her web-covered chair. What kind of Creeper was spawning that stuff?

"We're in the process of matching certain freshmen with mentors," she said, "and Gentry's at the top of our list. But Owen, you're so young. We're looking for wise people with extensive life experience. Accomplished adults."

She'd basically just insinuated I was a juvenile nobody going nowhere, but this wasn't the time to get defensive. We sat in silence a moment, long enough for me to observe the webs subtly moving and shifting, like poisonous vines growing at an accelerated rate. Strands started stretching over Harding's glasses. I would have asked how long this had been going on, but it's not like she had a clue.

I stood, not only because I wanted to be taken more seriously but because I couldn't stomach sitting there any longer, watching her be overtaken by webs. "I know I'm young, Principal Harding, but Gentry has looked up to me for a while now, and he respects me." Hopefully on some level, anyway. "Please, give me a chance. I know I can help him."

It took some more back-and-forth, but she finally agreed to give it a try, providing his parents approved. I could only hope Lance hadn't run me down to them. He was away at the police academy for now, so thankfully, not likely to interfere.

As I turned to leave, I spotted an easel with a large foam board—a digital rendering of the soon-to-be-built middle and elementary schools. I sighed and faced her again. "You know better than anyone, Principal Harding, that this school has seen more than its share of tragedies. And student suicides and violence tend to happen in clusters, stopping for a while, then starting up again. What happens if it gets bad around here once more, and there's two more campuses full of students close by—even little kids?"

She stood and rearranged an already neat stack of papers on her desk. "Let's not be superstitious, Owen. It's not like the soil is cursed." She grinned, oblivious. At least I hoped she was. I couldn't imagine Principal

Harding being part of the secret society, but then again, I'd never suspected Detective Benny until I straight up busted him.

"Our strategies here are proving effective," Harding said. "Masonville High's mentoring program has gained national recognition, and we've taken the utmost measures to increase security and protect against any future acts of violence. I've also instituted specialized, need-based support groups for students this year and hired a new meditation instructor—a proven, upstanding member of the community, highly experienced in the art of promoting mental and emotional well-being."

"Who?" I wondered who had replaced Veronica.

"Melanie Benny."

My jaw dropped. "As in, Detective Benny's wife?"

"That's the one."

My gut churned. His wife was bound to be as corrupt as him. Another occult member instructing students. Man, those people were intentional.

"Mrs. Harding, are you sure about her?" I knew it wasn't my place, but given the circumstances . . .

She folded her arms. "Excuse me?"

I covered my tracks with a polite goodbye, hoping I hadn't offended her and ruined my chance to be Gentry's mentor.

I drove back to the church in the late-afternoon drizzle. While I was waiting on leftover pizza to finish heating in the microwave in my room, my dad responded to my text about the symbol: **Check the Hebrew alphabet.**

I sat on the floor with my Mac and did an online search. Sure enough, between quick bites, I learned my dad was spot on. The mysterious mark on my arm and Ray's was a combination of Hebrew letters—the primary original language of the Bible's Old Testament.

I pasted the letters into Google Translate, selected the English translation, then dropped what was left of my slice of pizza and stared at my computer screen . . .

Defender.

Wow.

The way I saw it, Heaven had given Ray and me an official title and seal for our mission. We were commissioned to defend our town and rid it of evil's long-standing infestation, ultimately helping protect our nation and others around the world. In the immediate future, we were to identify and defend the thirteen people targeted to die. Surely both missions were related somehow.

I called Ray Anne, and she was as amazed as me.

I'd started researching if there was any biblical significance to the number thirteen, when the church secretary slid two pieces of mail under my door. I crumpled an ad flyer and tossed it across the tiny room, scoring a basket in the trash can, then eyed a white envelope, hand-addressed to me from the Texas Department of Corrections Hilltop Unit.

My stomach sank. I only knew one inmate there.

I tore open the envelope and unfolded the enclosed piece of paper. A single statement was written in pencil in childlike handwriting, in the center of the blue-lined sheet: *I SEE YOU.*

Was Veronica trying to scare me?

"Give me a break." I huffed and balled the letter and envelope into a wad so I could score another trash can basket. But an unnerving squeal, like damp fingers dragging on glass, stopped me. And I heard whispers. Female, it sounded like.

Surely no vandals would try to break in here during the day, with the church staff at work in their offices at the other end of the building.

I stood and faced the glass-paned double doors, wishing the sheer curtain panels and rain weren't obstructing my view of the balcony. I heard the slippery sound again and spotted movement.

I was sure now: something was definitely out there, pressing against the soaked window.

EIGHT

I PULLED THE WHITE SHEERS BACK, then slapped a hand over my mouth. A pair of muddy bare feet were pressed against the glass, climbing the windowed door. They looked human—female—Caucasian and petite. But how could any human, man or woman, climb the side of a building?

They couldn't. This had to be demonic.

I ran downstairs and outside into the afternoon drizzle, then stood in the damp grass, facing the balcony and scanning the brick exterior of my room, including the space above—a storage room, I'd been told. I didn't see anything, and as best as I could tell from ground level, there was nothing looming on the roof. But there were whispers that sounded like they were coming from up there—whispers just like the ones in my nightmare, come to think of it.

I looked behind and above me, searching the air, but all was clear.

"Lord, what is this?"

The voices got louder, but I still couldn't make out what they were saying.

I stayed outside until my clothes were soaked and I was chilled—a response to the frigid presence of evil, not the summer rain. I ventured back inside, content to dismiss the unnerving whispers for now.

Why would the church building suddenly draw this kind of

paranormal disturbance? The only reasonable answer was *me*. It's not like the satanic kingdom was going to ignore a person marked by Heaven as a *defender*.

I traveled the narrow hallway toward my room, wishing I could go see my friend Betty, the closest thing I'd ever had to a grandparent. I needed her advice and, I admit it, one of her reassuring hugs. Unfortunately, her grandmother Dorothy's health was in a steady decline, and some weeks ago, Betty had driven her to Louisiana, where they were spending time with family—for as long as Dorothy had left, I imagined. So, this wasn't exactly the best time to bother Betty, even when, for example, a whispering Creeper disguised as a woman had climbed up my balcony door.

Then again, she of all people might have some advice for me.

I called her, and the sound of her hello instantly eased the tension in my shoulders. I asked her how she was doing, and Dorothy too, resisting the habit of making our whole conversation about me and my always-urgent dilemmas. But after she explained that Dorothy was living out her final days pain-free and at peace, Betty invited me to confide in her.

I told her everything that had gone down in the last two days. All of it, including the weirdness outside my window minutes ago. "What do you think is happening?" I asked her.

She reminded me of the significance of my life calling and that I was bound to meet fierce resistance. Then she encouraged me, "Stay focused on Scripture, especially the red-letter text."

Jesus' words were printed in red in some Bible translations, I knew.

Maybe it was juvenile of me, but I didn't want to hang up. Betty and her little old lady friends had majorly come to my rescue when I'd entangled myself with demonic deceivers. They'd supernaturally barricaded my apartment against intrusions from the Lord of the Dead himself—and even came back and redid it after I messed it up.

But maybe I needed to learn to stand on my own now. Wage war without a mother figure holding my hand, doing the work for me.

I thanked Betty for her time and reluctantly told her goodbye.

I changed into dry clothes and sat on the hard floor, leaning against my bed. I felt lonely in this room, somehow more so than when I lived alone in my apartment. And my spiritual ears were still picking up on those grating whispers. It sounded like they were drifting into my room from the storage room overhead, but instead of charging upstairs and inspecting things, I took Betty's advice.

I opened my Bible to where I'd left off in the book of Mark, working to tune out the unnerving audio interference. As Betty suggested, I focused on the red-letter text.

As I read, it occurred to me that Jesus was kind and merciful and all, but what I liked the most was how he didn't put up with religious elitists' hypocrisy and garbage. And he cast devils out of people on a daily basis and told the guys who followed him to do it too.

I used to agonize over how to free people from Creepers, whether they were just bound to them or completely possessed, but I was fairly confident I understood now, based on how Jesus dealt with *demoniacs*—possessed people.

I finished the chapter, then closed my Bible and straight up asked, "God, give me a chance to try casting a Creeper out of someone."

That got me thinking . . .

Why didn't Ray Anne's pastor, Gordon, ever do a sermon that exposed the tactics of our evil opponent? He only spoke of demons metaphorically, like, "Don't let the demons of your past steal your joy today." How about, "Don't give demons open doors to infiltrate your mind and chain themselves to your soul so that your thoughts and words and impulses are dominated by evil and ruin your life, wounding the people closest to you in the process"?

While I had a decent amount of appreciation and respect for Gordon, I had yet to claim him as *my* pastor. Sure, I went to church here every Sunday now with Ray Anne, but it still felt like her church, not mine. The kind of church I envisioned didn't seem to exist. I was hard-pressed to describe it, except to say, it would have been less regimented and formal—no stiff pews, for sure—and the pastor would teach about prayer and spiritual warfare and helping hurting people instead of spending half the sermon reminding us how badly we needed to pool our money together to pay for a bigger, more modern building—with a 3.5-million-dollar price tag. And if it were up to me, anyone battling demons could get them cast out if they wanted, on the spot.

Just thinking about it stirred the unwelcomed hostility that had been quickening my pulse off and on since the night before. The intermittent, high-pitched whispers weren't helping.

But it wasn't up to me how Pastor Gordon ran the church, and it's not like I was going to start my own.

Pastor Owen Edmonds.

Ridiculous.

I may not have been the pastor type—and yeah, I'd also passed up the opportunity to go to med school and become a doctor—but I was as committed as ever to helping heal people. Treating invisible wounds of the soul. At least I wanted to. I had a lot more to learn.

I tried to take a nap before it was time to meet Ray in the woods at dusk, but it's kind of impossible when devilish whispers are seeping through the walls. The more I prayed for them to shut up and go away, the more voices I heard. I didn't like that at all.

Ray Anne and I hid behind the same wide cedar we had yesterday, spying on the Caldwell Cemetery in the setting sun, waiting to see if any Rulers showed up. The air became overpowered by every kind of rancid smell as a host of base-level Creepers converged on the scene. Ray and I braced ourselves, holding tight to one another.

I could have stayed that way forever.

Too bad she wasn't ready to hold on to *me* forever. It still pained me that she'd turned down my marriage proposal, even if her reasons were fair.

I hadn't seen him yet, but I knew which Ruler was coming by the weight of exhaustion that bore down on my body and soul.

"Spirit of Slumber," Ray Anne uttered, "you have no authority over us."

Done.

And here he came, stomping through the woods—*my* woods—as if he owned every square acre. The spectating Creepers stirred like MMA fans watching a prizefighter take the ring. There was no swirling earth or spirit-world portal this time. Instead Slumber loomed in front of the cemetery, ranting to the surrounding Creepers in a spirit-world language—scolding them, it seemed.

Either he didn't realize Ray and I were there, or he was powerless to do anything about it. Still, she and I stayed hidden, content to steal quick glances.

I'd just squeezed her hand, assuring her I was by her side and all was okay, when a certain mental picture barged into my mind, vivid and detailed. I recognized it as the first pornographic image I'd ever come across as a kid while searching something random online—a picture that woke something in me that day. I'd vowed to Ray Anne never to look at that stuff. She had zero tolerance for porn, and, duh, I knew it was wrong—a pathetic portrayal of manhood and totally disrespectful to women. That's someone's daughter or wife or mom. But all of a sudden, right now, it was like I had to have it. Even a peek.

Here came a giant being—another Ruler—clawing its way out of the earth, then standing next to Slumber. Never, in my most outlandish imaginings, did I *ever* think something like this could exist.

It was too dark at night to see his facial features or garment color, but all that mattered were his eyes. They radiated dim light and were twice as big and elongated as any Creeper's I'd seen. There was no pupil or misshapen iris or anything remotely typical about them. Instead, both eyeballs were, like, display screens, streaming pornographic images.

Ray Anne pressed her eyes shut and bent over like she might barf. As for me, I intended to look away but only wanted to stare. Desperately. And I felt drawn to the monster, like an overpowering suction was tugging on my arms and legs, coaxing me to walk to him and stand as close as I could. Get as close of a look as possible.

I wasn't sure how long I could stand there, leaning away.

Ray Anne stood upright again and gazed at the tempter. She stayed that way, and I knew, innocent as she was, she was enduring her own battle.

I didn't see Custos, but I sensed he was near, his peaceful presence clashing with the filth trying to invade my soul. I heard him whisper the Ruler's name, his all-consuming assignment. I wish I could say I acted immediately, but it was an all-out fight. A vicious war between good and gross throwing punches inside me.

God must have given me strength, because finally, the words came tumbling out: "Spirit of Lust, you have no authority over us."

The crushing temptation lifted, and there was instant relief, like soaking in a bathtub after having climbed out of a dumpster. At the same time, I was super agitated, enduring the misery that arose when something I really, really wanted was withheld. I'd seen base-level Creepers named Lust before, and even messed up and drawn them to me, but this Ruler had evoked something far stronger—an utterly depraved hunger that had snagged me in an instant, like fishhooks plunged into my soul.

Ray Anne faced away from me, hunching over again like she still might barf. I focused on breathing slow and steady.

The two Rulers—Slumber and Lust—spoke back and forth in English again. Their tone grew harsher and more aggressive as they accused each other of breaching one another's territories, staking claim to various neighborhoods around Masonville. They mentioned certain streets, including the last names of specific households they both insisted they owned.

Slumber named a family, the Carters, and Lust raged, "*I* built the dwelling there!"

I had no idea what that meant.

It took Ray and me both off guard when Lust reared back and shoved Slumber, sending him sailing backwards, passing through trees like they were mere shadows. Slumber roared from somewhere in the distance, and Lust fled the scene, clawing down into the same patch of earth from where he'd emerged, as best as I could tell. The spectating Creepers began drifting away, and we knew then the ordeal was over—for now, anyway.

Seated behind me on my motorcycle, Ray Anne clung to my waist as I started the drive to her place, both of us fighting drowsiness—the natural kind, from needing sleep. While traveling the road that ran alongside Masonville High, mostly vacant at night, we spotted a remarkable radiance a short distance away. Ray tapped fast on my shoulder, signaling for me to gas it—both of us fully energized now.

I pulled off the road in front of Masonville High, and we could hardly jump off my bike fast enough.

We were just in time.

My girlfriend and I stood hand in hand at the curb, smiling as wide as we could. One armored Watchman after another came exploding out of a shimmering oval in the sky, sprinting to the ground at an astounding speed, then filing shoulder to shoulder across the empty Masonville High parking lot, facing the school building. They were as tall as the lot's streetlamps, and the circular platinum-looking shields they held at their chests formed a perfectly straight row.

There wasn't a Creeper in sight. They'd all hunkered down inside the school and underground, fleeing like defeated cowards.

There was a pause, then another armored platoon came charging down from the night sky, forming a second line in front of the first, only this group lowered to one knee. It was an archery battalion with bows and arrows strapped to each warrior's back. I held my breath, knowing that any second they'd launch arrows into the school, aiming for Creepers' unprotected heads and chests.

There had to be fifty Watchmen present by now—more than I'd ever seen gather at once.

As the supernatural soldiers held their positions, a beaming-white horse as big as an African elephant charged onto the scene, galloping over Masonville High toward the warriors. A mighty rider sat tall on its back—a robed Watchman with a hooded cloak over his head and back, as bright as a meteor storming the atmosphere. Without any use of reins, the Watchman stopped his warhorse and dismounted in front of the militia, then strode up and down the line, rallying his troops in their poetic, heavenly language. I could see now that under his shining silver cloak he wore armor, with an ornate helmet beneath his hood.

I could hardly wait to watch the warriors storm the school, pulling Creepers out of hiding by their long, scrawny limbs, then flinging them miles away. Or better yet, maybe they'd march right past the school and confront the Rulers in the woods, engaging them in a heated battle.

I wasn't sure what had triggered the Watchmen's arrival, but all that mattered was that they were here. And from the look of things, ready to charge.

Ray Anne was as speechless as I was.

The commanding Watchman faced his men—colossal Watchmen,

perfect in stature—and slid his hood back so that it piled around his armor-clad shoulders. I breathed a disappointed sigh when he removed his platinum helmet and rested it against his hip. Hadn't they come here to do battle?

But as I continued watching the one in charge, I let go of Ray Anne's hand and stepped forward, my mind reeling.

The commanding Watchman—the one leading the radiant troops . . . I knew him.

Knew him well, I liked to think.

Who would have thought my God-assigned keeper, Custos, was a general in the most sophisticated, dominant military in all of creation?

NINE

I WANTED TO RUN TO CUSTOS, waving my hands and shouting, "Hey, it's me! I'm here!" But the presence of Watchmen inspires an intuitive respect that doesn't allow for spastic outbursts or casual hellos. Besides, Custos was on duty. Who was I to disrupt him?

I was sure he already knew I was there, anyway. I believed he knew exactly where I was at all times. That's how aware and protective God is—of his Lights, yes, but I'd seen him dispatch Watchmen to rescue shackled people too. I'd been there when a Watchman showed up to save Jess's life—not once, but twice—and she never claimed to even believe in God.

And the scent . . .

If I could have bottled the Watchmen smell, people would have paid a fortune for it, even without knowing where it came from. And the way it feels in their presence—if only *that* could have been compressed into a pill. No one would bother with drugs or get drunk or have so much as a depressed thought.

All eyes were on Custos, still facing the line of kneeling archers who were backed by a row of standing soldiers with shields. As for Ray Anne's and my eyes, they were watering, physically reacting to the blazing-bright spirit-world. But I was so enthralled, I didn't want to shut them.

Custos gazed up toward the dazzling heavenly portal, and a third stream of Watchmen flooded Masonville's airspace. These wore robes instead of armor, with golden circular headbands resting like crowns on their flawless heads. And these new arrivals clutched long, electric-blue wand-shaped objects in each hand, sizzling with some kind of current, like mini lightning bolts.

In precise unison, the Watchmen holding shields did an about-face, standing face-to-face and toe-to-toe with the electricity-carrying ones. They exchanged warm smiles like they'd been a brotherhood since the dawn of time. Ray and I couldn't help but smile too.

All motion ceased, and intensity hung in the air like a nuke was about to drop. Custos lowered to one knee, his helmet still in hand while his face angled toward the heavens. He belted out a command in the heavenly tongue.

That instant, like some kind of rehearsed dance, the Watchmen with shields turned them faceup like tabletops, holding them at their waists. Then in unison, using those electrified rods, the robed Watchmen pounded their sticks on the shields in a steady, single-beat rhythm that struck a kind of terror in me—not tormenting fear, but an undeniable awareness that this army had annihilation power. The epic drum corps's tempo reverberated against my chest, and I thanked God out loud that I was not their enemy.

At a precise moment in the cadence, the kneeling Watchmen with bows and arrows strapped to their broad backs bent down and began pounding the parking lot to the beat with clenched fists, while the ones with electric wands raised their hands above their crowned heads and hit their sticks together in the air. A sound went out like nothing I'd ever heard—or felt. It was like jet engines blasting with every beat. Ray and I both felt the power in the cement beneath our feet. The divine frequency traveled through our shoes, all the way up our legs and through our bodies.

The archers on bended knee didn't shoot a single arrow. Instead they got all the way down, facedown on the parking lot, prostrate on their stomachs. And they started weeping loudly, pleading in their native language—to their Creator, no doubt.

That really threw me. These were astonishing beings built for battle—why come here and sob?

The other Watchmen took turns chanting, several together at once, shouting what sounded like a war cry.

Hissing, wailing, and anguished howls began seeping from the school—petrified Creepers whimpering from their hiding spots. I held out hope this was a preattack ritual, and any second, the Watchmen would rise and advance. But they just kept up their passionate cries.

Custos remained on bended knee, hands raised, worshiping. I think they all were; it just didn't look like anything I'd ever envisioned or witnessed. It was a loud, fervent mix of pleading and chanting. Even the horse had its head down, like it was paying homage.

I turned to Ray Anne. "This is incredible, but I thought they came here to fight."

She looked at me, teary eyed but grinning. "Owen, they *are* fighting. Their worship is drawing God's presence here—that's bound to be evil's worst nightmare."

Oh . . .

Hand-to-hand combat had its place between Watchmen and Creepers, but apparently there were other ways to inflict damage on the kingdom of darkness. The way I now saw it, hell had recently unleashed heightened, cosmic evil on Masonville, but Heaven wasn't just sitting idly by, tolerating it. God's forces were ramping up the fight too.

The Watchmen carried on for nearly an hour, changing formations at times with military precision, marching to the beat.

"Owen, that's it!" Ray Anne searched my face. "We should follow their lead and worship here with the student pastors this Sunday."

Maybe she was on to something, but I couldn't wrap my mind around what that would look like. Don't get me wrong—it was the coolest thing *ever* to witness the Watchmen's synchronized worship. Truly profound. But a handful of humans gathered on the front steps of Masonville High, beating a drum and marching around, crying and singing with our hands in the air?

Besides Ray Anne, the only person I could envision actually doing something like that was Pastor Gordon's son, Ethan—the med school grad who'd crushed on my girlfriend but failed to win her away from me.

All at once, the Watchmen ceased moving and bowed their heads, holding their positions like exquisite statues until they broke rank in line order, swarming the sky. They charged up through the air and disappeared into the beaming oval.

Custos stood and slid his helmet on—even more impressive than the other fighters. Like a noble general, he held his post until he was the last one remaining. Then he mounted his majestic horse and raced toward the heavenly portal, pausing midair to look back—at me, I like to think.

"Owen!" Ray Anne didn't care that an occasional vehicle was passing. She spun around like she was back on drill team. "How amazing was that!"

I might have danced too, if I could have ignored my pride. And been more coordinated.

Ray and I got back on my motorcycle, and as I started the engine, she pointed ahead. "What's that car doing?"

The familiar Suburban was parked on the shoulder, headlights facing us, windows too dark to see inside.

I drove fast toward the vehicle, invigorated by the Watchmen's boldness. As we passed it, I slowed exaggeratedly, so whoever was in there would know I was on to them.

They didn't follow us.

Around ten o'clock, after I'd dropped Ray Anne off, I stopped by Gentry's house—an ordinary one-story. I used to love hanging here with Lance. It was weird walking up the driveway after all this time.

It was a little late on a weeknight to go knocking on the door, but I had to check on Gentry. If I was right about the meaning of that black line across his neck, his life was on the line. And if I'd really heard from God like I thought I had, I'd been told to fight for him.

I was questioning things now, mainly because I still had no sense of direction about how to intervene, and I couldn't stomach the thought that yet another life might be lost because I wasn't wise enough or spiritual enough to piece together how to protect him.

And there were twelve more unnamed souls on the Cosmic Rulers' hit list. If any or all of their lives came to ruin, I'd feel responsible for them, too.

Gentry's stepdad answered the door and shrugged when I asked for Gentry. "He ain't here. I never know where that boy is. His mama and I gave up months ago on trying to get that kid to do right. He's hopeless."

Hopeless? Kind of harsh.

He seemed eager to shut the door.

I was headed back to my bike when I spotted Gentry struggling to pry into his house through a window. I hurried over just in time to watch him drop to his bedroom floor like dead weight, mumbling to himself.

"Are you okay?" I tried a couple of times to get his attention, but it was no use. He was out of it. I shut his window and walked away, hoping that the next day I'd find him sober. And alive.

When I pulled up at the church, the infamous black Suburban was idling across the street, on stalking duty. I didn't have the luxury of calling the cops and reporting it—not in this town. But I did shoot my father a text: **Being followed.**

For once, he texted back immediately: **No need to fear.**

Not afraid, just annoyed, I replied.

I was exhausted and fell into bed, mindful of how grateful I was for the financial inheritance from my father's parents. Yes, I seriously resented the spiteful motive behind it—a bribe to persuade my mother, pregnant with me, to abandon my father and annul their marriage—but the money kept me from having to worry about employment right now. The way I saw it, I had a job; it just didn't pay. Transforming Masonville's spiritual atmosphere deserved my full-time attention. My online college classes got the leftover scraps.

I turned onto my side and fluffed my pillow, wondering if Custos would show up outside, or maybe even inside my room tonight, and how it would feel to be near him now that I knew who he was. A superior among superiors. I never would have imagined I could have admired him even more.

As usual, I had a restless night. I slept past noon the next day, and I might have slept later had an annoying racket not woken me. I didn't have to open my eyes to know something was traipsing around on the balcony outside my room. Then came the distinct sound of my half-dead potted plant—a housewarming gift from Ray Anne's mom the day I moved in here—toppling over, the clay pot shattering.

As I lay there in my sunlit room—groggy, working to pry my eyes open—I sat up and spotted Daisy next to the bed, her gaze fixed on the locked double doors that open to the balcony. Was some injured bird flapping around out there, or . . . ?

My good-natured Labrador retriever lowered her head and growled, flaring her gums. So, maybe the demon woman was back, lurking on the balcony, trying to scare me in broad daylight. Whatever the commotion was, I had to get up and face it.

By the time I slid on a pair of jeans and peeked out the sheers, the noise had stopped. Sure enough, my potted plant was in a broken heap. But there was no person or animal out there, earthly or otherwise.

I opened both doors, invigorated by the feel of the warm summer breeze against my bare chest.

I took a deep, energizing inhale, walking out onto the balcony, three times the size of the one at my old apartment. I reached to grip the wood railing in front of me, but something in my peripheral vision stopped me mid-stride. I turned to my left, and there she was. Veronica, in a flimsy white tattered dress that draped below her knees, her back pressed against the handrail. My stomach dropped like I'd been pushed off the balcony. Her feet were bare and muddy, just like the pair that had climbed my window the night before.

She smiled, but her green-eyed glare was narrowed and hostile. "I see you, Owen."

My knee-jerk reaction was to dive back into my room and slam and lock the doors. But after a few panting exhales, I threw the doors open again, ready to confront the demonic imposter and drive it away with the Name above all names. But it was already gone.

I didn't waste time pacing around and coming unglued. Instead I took Daisy outside for a potty break and scanned the property. I looked over my shoulder a lot, but I refused to be scared or let my focus be derailed.

Daisy sniffed the wide-open lawn, and I shook my head, annoyed by my latest realization: dark forces insist on playing mind tricks, even when their charade is a tired act.

That *wasn't* Veronica—not today and not at Ray Anne's yesterday, brooding over Jackson's crib.

I went back inside the building with my dog, and the pastor's administrative assistant—a plump, friendly lady—spotted me. She stopped me, handing me an envelope she said had arrived in the mail for me today. From the Hilltop Unit penitentiary.

Another one? Seriously?

Back in my room, I trashed the letter without opening it and got busy cleaning up the broken clay pot and mound of soil on my balcony. But curiosity got the best of me. I dug the letter out of the trash can and ripped into the envelope, unfolding a piece of notebook paper identical to the first, a childish handwritten statement in the center, in pencil again: *You're as easy to break as your pitiful little plant.*

Then a signature: *Eva.*

TEN

Anger welled up in me like a tsunami barging past the shoreline, gaining momentum with every passing second. I didn't have to put up with this—Veronica's threats and bullying. And using a fake name, Eva, was as childish as her handwriting.

I wasn't surprised she was tag-teaming with enemy forces to conspire against me—against Ray Anne and Jackson, too. But I wanted her to know I was onto her. I wasn't the same naive guy she'd met months ago.

I decided I'd make the three-hour trip to Gatesville, Texas, tomorrow. Just show up unannounced at the Hilltop Correctional Unit on Saturday, when they were open for visitors, and tell the witch to her face that if she didn't stop playing evil mind tricks on Ray Anne and me, I'd . . .

Okay, I couldn't come up with any leverage at that moment, but I still felt the need to confront her.

I stopped by Gentry's house again, but he wasn't there. How was I supposed to warn and protect someone who was always physically or mentally not home? And as willing as Ray and I were to try to intervene somehow on behalf of the thirteen targets, we had yet to figure out who all but one of them were. But I already knew that just because an assignment is from God doesn't mean it's easy.

Ray Anne had plans with her mom that day, so I sat alone at a table in a coffee shop with my Mac and forced myself to do schoolwork, even though a statistics course had *nothing* to do with *anything* that mattered in my life.

A snooty-looking lady in a floral dress was seated at the table next to mine. She kept taking lingering glances at me, looking me up and down and mumbling under her breath. The man sitting across from her did the same. But that was nothing new. Ever since I'd intruded on the occult ceremony and rescued Jackson, certain people around town—occult members, obviously—would recognize me and spew curses at me. I knew that's what they were doing because it never took long before one or two of those hideous black serpents would come out of their mouths, squirming down their bodies and snaking their way over to me—identical to the one I'd watched crawl out of Hector's mouth and slither undetected through Riley's lips last school year. But every time a serpent was loosed at me, the Kingdom of Light aura glistening around my feet prevented it from climbing on me.

So I didn't flinch. Just sat there sipping my frap, ignoring the couple's abuse.

I happened to glance at the date before I closed my laptop—August 30. Yikes. The sun was setting on my mom's birthday, and I hadn't stopped by or even called her. I hurried to H-E-B to buy a box of her favorite Godiva chocolates and a card. A funny one. Sentimental never fit her.

I picked out some flowers, too. While the shackled florist, who looked about my age, tied ribbon around the bouquet, she kept nodding off. Not physically; her shadowy soul bore the burden of Slumber's presence. But I only witnessed her condition after eyeing a gruesome skull tattoo on her hand and wrist that made me feel sorry for her. Trying to be cool, I guess, she'd permanently memorialized Murder's face on her skin. It looked just like the Creeper that used to stalk me.

I made the short drive to Mom's. Even after her life-saving surgery, she rarely reached out to me—only when she needed something—but I'd been making a point to call and say hello a couple of times a week. My way of being caring without having to endure going to see her. The last time I'd sucked it up and stopped by the house about a month ago, it was beyond filthy, but more than that, she was still drinking. Never mind that alcohol had nearly killed her. I didn't trust myself to see the wine glasses scattered around without going off about it. But today, I had to put up with it.

I parked outside my old house, my mom's childhood home, and stood in the driveway a few moments, marveling at the manicured flower beds and new outdoor lighting, plus the fresh paint job on the two-story farmhouse. Major improvements I'd never dreamed my mom would actually get done. But not everything was pretty. A Creeper had tagged the word **doomed** across my old second-story bedroom window—the black, scribbled letters so fresh, they were dripping.

I rolled my eyes.

I used my key to let myself in. My mom entered the living room from the kitchen, dragging her numerous chains. She reached out like she couldn't wait to squeeze me. Weird.

And that wasn't the only thing that was different. She had on trendy jeans and a blouse with no wrinkles, her brunette hair was curled and long enough now to sway past her shoulders—and shackle. She hadn't looked this pretty and healthy since . . . well, ever, that I could remember. And yeah, she was wearing makeup and had also gained a little weight, thank God, but it was more than that. She was smiling from ear to ear, beaming despite having no internal light to speak of.

I handed her my gifts, and she held me in another tight embrace, like she was an affectionate person. "Thank you, Son. I'm so glad you're here."

Most people would probably celebrate their mother's apparent life improvements, but it was so out of character for *my* mom that my stomach sloshed with apprehension. "Um . . . who are you?"

She laughed—a fun-loving, easy laugh. Again, so *not* her, especially considering she and Wayne had recently called it quits. My mom couldn't handle breakups.

I smiled back at her but was still leery. For some reason this whole experience was intensifying Strife's hostility in me.

I took a wide-eyed glance around the living room. It was spotless.

Like, impeccable. And instead of the stink of fermenting alcohol, the room smelled like roses. There were a dozen light pink ones in a crystal vase on the coffee table. And as if things weren't already over-the-top, she had jazz music playing. "What's going on?"

Mom escorted me by the hand to the sofa, practically dancing, her chains scraping the hardwood like old times. "Have a seat, sweetie."

She'd never once called me *sweetie*.

I moved a throw pillow, meticulously tilted the same angle as the rest. She sat facing me, scooting until her knee touched mine. She reached for my hands. "I've made a decision, Owen, and I'm not going back." She squeezed my fingers and smiled. "I've quit drinking. For good this time."

My stomach grumbled, but not with hunger. Right or wrong, I was agitated. How many times had she promised before? Gotten my hopes up, only to relent and relapse? All her failed attempts had ever done was cause me to resent her even more.

But sitting across from her now, face-to-face, I wanted to forget the past and be kind. Find a way to genuinely believe her and tell her congratulations or something. But I couldn't shape my mouth around any words at the moment.

I was used to her mostly pulling away, but today, she leaned toward me—close enough that I could tell there was no alcohol on her breath. And come to think of it, no metal mask on her face. If *anyone* would bear the mark of Addiction's presence in Masonville, it was her. And surely I had enough compassion for her that I'd have seen it if it were there.

Right?

"I know I've committed to sobriety before, Son, but this time is different. I give you my word."

Her *word*? I resisted an eye roll. "How's it different?"

She tucked her chin and blushed, grinning while nibbling her bottom lip. An all-too-familiar gesture.

"Mom, tell me you're not doing this because you've met some guy and convinced yourself if you clean up your life and pretend everything's good, he'll actually stick around."

I'd seen that one play out more than once. It always ended in shouting matches and slammed doors, my mom begging some two-timer to stop packing his suitcase and realize how much she'd changed for him. *All* for him. Then would come the screeching of tires down the driveway, at which point my sobbing mother would lock herself in her bedroom and binge drink while I figured out how to fix dinner for myself and do the laundry when I was too little to pour the heavy bottle of detergent.

I wiped my clammy palms on my jeans and took a deep breath, working to tame the scalding lava of old resentment—a brewing volcano of unforgiveness that, if allowed to erupt, would earn me chain links around my neck. Cumbersome soul-baggage I'd already shed—twice.

"I'm doing this for myself, Owen. For you, too."

"That's your only motivation?" I searched her face. "There's no man involved?"

"Sometimes fate sends people into our lives to help us," she said. "What's wrong with that?"

As an atheist, I'd never believed in fate, but it sounded more ridiculous than ever now, knowing how strategic God and forces of evil are. But my mom didn't believe in God.

No, it was worse than that. I think she was terrified of him.

She clutched my hand in both of hers. "Owen, do you remember when you were four years old, and you fell into that sewer pipe in the field behind our apartment and got stuck?"

"Kind of." Most of my childhood memories were cloudy.

"It was the middle of December, and by the time I found you, you were freezing and struggling to breathe. There was no time to call for help. But right then, that kind man showed up, and his arm was just long enough to reach down and pull you out—surely you recall that."

"I remember you carrying me home, but I don't remember any man rescuing me."

"Well, Son, my point is, sometimes it takes another person to help us out when we're stuck in life, but that's a good thing—nothing for you to be upset about." She reached and hugged me again. "You mean the world to me, Owen, and I want to change for you."

Her tender words were as unexpected as the mopped floors. And was she saying *I* was her motivation to change?

She held both my hands now, her eyes pooling. "What do you say?"

I had seconds to choose a response. To interrogate her about her motive or express faith in her. I cleared my throat. "I'm proud of you." It wasn't easy, but I'd pulled it off. And sincerely wanted to mean it.

"Thank you, honey." A third icy-metal hug. More than she'd given me over the course of the last year, I think. "Oh, I have something for you. Wait here."

She went bouncing up the stairs, all peppy, while I stayed on the sofa, still admiring the place. I wasn't surprised to find a cleaning service's business card on the coffee table. I already knew this had to have been a professional job. But the next card I spotted took me off guard—handwritten, tucked among the pink roses: *You deserve this, Susan, and much more. Love, Brody.*

I leaned back into the sofa cushions, way back, and popped my knuckles. I didn't know if Dr. Brody Bradford had arranged for the lawn and house to be overhauled, and maybe even paid for it, or if my mom had done it all herself to impress him, but either way, their doctor-patient relationship was obviously more than that now. And her supposed commitment to sobriety was one-hundred percent about another man—a conniving manipulator steeped in the occult, depraved beyond comprehension.

While at death's door, my mom had committed to put me before her boyfriend for once—Wayne, at the time. But her pledge obviously hadn't lasted any longer than their unstable relationship. There was a lot she didn't know about Dr. Bradford, but she knew that he was the *last* man I'd want coming around our fragile two-person family.

How dare she say she wanted to change for me? I had nothing to do with this.

My mom returned with a plastic bin the size of a shoebox and held it out to me. "I gathered your childhood keepsakes."

Was I supposed to be grateful that she didn't want them anymore? Or that everything she'd kept of mine from birth until my high school graduation fit into one small container?

"Thanks." I took it without looking at her, aware I was in serious danger of giving in to bitterness toward her and compromising the condition of my soul. I also knew if I didn't get up and leave, I'd probably say something that would draw Creepers to the scene.

She followed me to the door, her brow furrowed. "You're leaving already? Why?"

I stood with my back to her, my hand on the doorknob, working my hardest to tame my tongue. But that had never been a strength of mine. "For a second there, Mom, I thought maybe I could believe you." Resentment took over. "But I should've known better."

I could have said a lot worse, but I'd still crossed a line. I hadn't even made it to my motorcycle when a Creeper, Accusation, rose out of the cement, hovering in the driveway, looking between my mother and me. I recognized it as a longtime stalker of hers, even though I was the one to blame for its arrival this time. Mostly.

She took steps toward me, her brow furrowed even deeper now. "Why are you being so discouraging, Owen?"

I sat on my bike, eyeing her distraught face. *Because we both know you'll always be a miserable drunk.*

I saw it for what it was—a thought Accusation had hurled at my mind, hoping I'd stab her with it.

"I'm sorry, Mom. I really do wish you the best."

I shot the demon down.

My thoughts went in the right direction after that—toward the right kingdom—even while my emotions kicked like a pent-up bull.

Lord, help me. I prayed it under my breath all the time lately.

And I prayed it the whole time I backed out of my mom's driveway. And the entire drive to my shabby room at the church. By the time I was seated in my spot on the floor, I'd found the strength to ask God to help my mom, too. That felt like a victory, along with the fact that no Creeper had detected unforgiveness and pursued me and pinned me down, coiling chain links around my neck. Still, I'd be more at ease once Ray Anne looked me over and confirmed there was nothing on me.

I called her, and neither of us felt like spying on any Rulers in the woods tonight. We weren't easing up on our mission—not at all. We were just sick of staring at evil. We agreed to do something normal, like take Jackson out for ice cream.

It should have been a relaxing, easygoing evening, especially after I got to Ray's house and she assured me there was no metal on me. But this is *my* life we're talking about, remember?

ELEVEN

RAY ANNE AND I STOOD HOLDING our Marble Slab ice-cream cones, waiting for the pregnant cashier to ring up our order. It was awkward, standing next to Ray Anne with a close-up view of the baby's tiny shimmering light emanating through the woman's tight T-shirt, from inside her belly. A crushing reminder of Ray Anne's infertility.

For me, the issue was settled. I was prepared to give up having biological children in order to marry Ray Anne. But the way Ray was fidgeting and angling away from me right now, I got the impression she was still really struggling with it.

We sat at a small square table, and Ray Anne gave Jackson bites of her Dutch chocolate ice cream. She kept eyeing the cashier and frowning. "You were right. Those metal masks are awful."

"Hmm?"

"You don't see it on her?"

The woman looked normal to me. Distracted and maybe a little sad, but that's all.

"Addiction's got her," Ray Anne said. "I feel so sorry for her baby."

I glanced back again and still couldn't see it, but then again, Ray Anne had always been a much more compassionate person than me.

I looked toward the door just in time to catch Ethan walking in with a young brown-haired woman I'd never seen before, both wearing medical scrubs. And both Lights.

The only time I'd talked to Ethan in recent months was to confirm he was coming to the student pastors' meeting this Sunday. He was filling the role at the church for now, until they found a permanent hire. Pastor Gordon had never mentioned the open position to me, but it's not like I'd expected him to.

And at church on Sunday mornings, Ethan was onstage singing in the choir—one of the featured ones out front, with his own microphone. So our paths hardly crossed.

I held my breath, hoping Ray Anne's face wouldn't light up like a firecracker when her eyes met his. She swore she didn't feel *that* way about him, but there was no reason to assume he'd stopped liking her. How could he? Ray Anne was the whole package.

He spotted us and approached our table, wrapping an arm around the dark-haired girl's shoulders like maybe they were more than friends. "Hey, guys."

Ray paused wiping chocolate off Jackson's chin and tilted her head back. She didn't light up. It was worse than that. She nearly gasped, like the sight of Ethan with a girl stung like a slap to the face.

I gnawed the inside of my cheek, working to convince myself I'd just read way too much into Ray Anne's reaction.

Ethan introduced his doctor friend, but I didn't catch her name. I was too preoccupied watching every nuance of his interaction with my girlfriend. He stood close to Ray Anne, and the two of them chitchatted while the brunette and I exchanged sympathetic smiles. *You feeling left out too?*

Ethan said something about meeting up here tonight with his coworkers. Meanwhile, my supernatural eyes picked up on cobwebs all over the girl. I still had no clue what force of evil was doing that to people, Lights and Shackles alike, or what it indicated.

I stood and threw away my napkins, working to give off a cool vibe, like I couldn't have cared less that, only months ago, Ethan—a pretty-boy ER doctor in his midtwenties—had professed to having feelings for Ray Anne. And she'd admittedly wrestled with the thought that maybe he was more her type than I was. For the sake of her own happiness, I'd released her to be with him.

But she'd chosen to come right back and commit to me. To *me*, I reminded myself.

I sat back down, and finally, Ethan and his girlfriend—or girl friend—left us to place their order. Ray Anne flashed me a smile like she had nothing to hide. And for the record, I trusted her. She wasn't, and never had been, the cheating type. Unfortunately, the thought of her having even the slightest hint of a crush on Ethan was maddening. And the extra strife brewing in me wasn't helping.

Ray Anne and I cleaned off our table, and before leaving, to be polite, I turned to give Ethan a farewell handshake. But when he reached out, I stood there staring. More like glaring.

How's that possible?

The defender seal. On his right forearm.

It glowed just like Ray's and mine. The exact same Hebrew letters. But it was *our* special assignment—hers and mine. Our connection with Arthur's prophecy. Exclusive to us.

I finally shook Ethan's hand, hoping Ray Anne hadn't noticed the mark on him, nor the uneasiness on my face.

Did this mean he was one of the people chosen to help us carry out our mission?

It was bound to, but I stood there racking my brain, trying my hardest to formulate an alternative—anything except him being called to team up with Ray and me. Yeah, he was one of the student pastors I planned on asking help from on Sunday, but surely God cared enough about me to exclude Ethan. That was a distraction I didn't need right now. And certainly Ray Anne didn't either.

Hard as it was to admit, even just to myself, I couldn't get rid of the fear that Ethan would win my girl's heart away from me eventually. And that perhaps God actually wanted the two of them to be together, given Ethan's lifelong commitment to holiness—a stark contrast to my own blemished record. The truth was, Ethan was a more spiritual man than I'd ever be, even with my supernatural senses.

I'd taken comfort recently in Ray's and my matching seals, our identical heavenly callings as defenders, but now that he had one too . . .

I wanted to crush his fingers. Instead I released our handshake and forced a smile.

Ray Anne stood by the exit, waving goodbye, oblivious, it seemed.

I walked over and opened the door for her, grateful we were leaving. As she rolled Jackson's stroller out of the ice-cream shop, more people in scrubs approached from the parking lot—five or six of them, laughing like they were blowing off steam after a long shift at the hospital. And leading the way was none other than Dr. Brody Bradford, his charming smile masking a darkened heart.

Ray and I knew this could happen—that we could run into Dr. Bradford somewhere, and he'd spot Jackson. But she still wasn't prepared to face him, as evidenced by her loud gulp and trembling hands.

I gently grabbed the stroller from her, trying to head straight to the car and avoid coming face-to-face with the malicious doctor, but he called our names and strode to us like a man on a mission. Because he was. "Hello, Owen. Good to see you, Ray Anne." He stepped close, then lowered to the ground, eye-level with Jackson. "I saw this little guy with your mom. Remind me of his name?"

Even if I was wrong and the man sporting the revolting ram's mask at the sick ritual hadn't been Dr. Bradford, everyone in this gossipy town knew by now that Jess had left her child with Ray Anne. And surely Dr. Bradford would have connected the dots that his own son was the boy's father. But this man operated in deceit, not honesty.

Jackson wailed like he'd just been pinched, like he knew this man was dangerous.

"This is Jackson, Jess Thompson's son." I told the straight up truth. I'd been doing that a lot lately.

Dr. Bradford could have won an Academy Award for the performance that followed. Shock overtook his expression, the grin fading from his suntanned face, erasing the dimples in his cheeks. "Jess? You mean . . ."

He stood, searching our faces like he was just now making the connection. Ray Anne teared up. I angled the stroller away from the doctor, feeling a fierce instinct to protect Jackson.

Dr. Bradford motioned for his coworkers to go inside without him, then put his hand on my shoulder. It was chilled, as usual. "Owen, you and Jess had a son?"

What an act—a mind game, really—and yet he was so good at it, I almost wondered if he was actually sincere. But of course, he wasn't. Not only had I been an eyewitness to his deadly motives toward Jackson, but the boy looked just like Dan. Like Dr. Bradford, too, from certain angles, even though I'd always tried to suppress the thought. It was obvious whose lineage he came from.

I'd had enough. "You know good and well I'm not his father."

Dr. Bradford stepped even closer, encroaching on my personal space. "Are you saying this boy could be my son's?" When I said nothing, he raised his voice. "Please tell me!"

I couldn't believe Ray and I had set out on an easy trip for dessert, and now it looked like I might have no choice but to get physical with Dr. Bradford. How dare he get in my face and shout like that?

I took a big step back, fuming, but kept my voice down. "You know exactly who Jackson's father is, and you were there, at the occult ritual in April, when we rescued him from you and the others." It was a huge risk to be so outspoken—deadly, even, in this town—but silence and secrecy had to be challenged at times. Times like this.

Dr. Bradford grabbed the sides of his head like he was trying to control his thoughts with his fingers. "No. I got out years ago. That's in the past."

My jaw dropped at the same time as Ray's, both of us shocked by his open admission that he'd been in the occult—not that I believed he'd ever quit.

He rubbed hard up and down on his face like he was losing his mind. Then he lurched at me, grabbing both my shoulders so that I bowed up, ready to defend myself. But all he did was plead. "I wasn't at any ritual last April—I swear. And if they're out to hurt my grandson, so help me . . ."

He dropped to one knee and stroked Jackson's head. The baby was crying even harder now. "I'll never let them harm you," Bradford said.

He stood again, and by now, Ray Anne was in tears too, freaked out and confused. He patted her back like he really cared. "Ray Anne, I'm here to help. I was aware Jess left town some months ago, but my son never once mentioned a child. You shouldn't bear this burden alone."

"She's not alone," I said.

"He's not a burden," Ray Anne added.

Dr. Bradford's eyes were glossy. "How can I help?"

I didn't hesitate. "By staying away from Jackson. And my mother, too." I was sure he had ulterior motives toward my mom, not that I'd nailed them down yet. I'd seen Dan's bruises in high school, inflicted by his own father—this man. He had no business spending time with *any* woman or child.

Dr. Bradford's bottom lip quivered. The performance of a lifetime. And as he and I stood there, locked in an intense mutual gaze, I saw something dark flicker in his eyes. The sickening sign of possession.

As if he knew what I'd seen, he worked to cover his tracks. "I still battle demons from my past—I admit that. But I am not the monster you think I am." He stared longingly at Jackson. "And I want to be in my grandson's life."

Ray Anne sighed and lowered her chin. Those were the very words she feared.

"Dan terminated his parental rights," I said. "And for now, Jess has made Ray Anne Jackson's guardian, and she isn't letting him out of her sight."

Bradford gave a defeated, single nod. "I don't want to interfere. I just want to do what's right by the child." He looked at Ray Anne. "Do you need financial help?"

I stepped between my girlfriend and him, recalling the vile words I'd heard him bellow out from behind his gruesome mask. "She doesn't need anything from you." I put one arm around Ray Anne and steered the stroller with the other. "We're leaving."

Bradford stood there, watching us the whole time we strapped Jackson into his car seat, until I drove Ray Anne's Hyundai off the parking lot.

Ray Anne was still distraught when I parked in her driveway and turned the ignition and lights off. I sat still in the driver's seat, focused on being a good listener while she talked hysterically fast, making up one doomed scenario after another, each ending with Jackson in Dr.

Bradford's lethal hands. "I mean, what if that man arranges to have me killed, Owen?"

As much as I wanted to assure her it would never come to that, could I, given what I'd already seen Bradford attempt?

I couldn't stomach the thought of more harm coming to Ray Anne, or God forbid, her death. But since fear was not an option for either of us, I redirected my attention. "Don't talk like that, Ray Anne. We can't think that way."

She was shaking all over and gasping, crying thick tears. It wasn't like her to come unglued, but when it came to that little boy in the back seat . . .

It didn't surprise me when a fanged Creeper, *fear* carved in its forehead, began circling outside our vehicle, peering into the moonlit car at Ray Anne through her passenger-side window.

To be clear: every single Creeper inflicts fear, no matter its rank or assignment; some just bear the actual name and targeted mission.

"Ray, sweetheart, we can't panic."

She saw the mongrel pressed against the glass and released her head back onto her headrest. "I can't believe I just drew that thing here. I don't want to be afraid. It's just . . ." She turned and eyed Jackson as he slept. "He means everything to me."

I saw it as my responsibility to calm her, to say something reassuring that would drive fear from her heart—and off her driveway. But she flipped on the vehicle's interior light and spoke first. "Why are you making those fists?"

"Huh?"

Sure enough, my hands were clenched so tight, my knuckles were white. "Um . . ." I hesitated, not wanting to appear unspiritual. Unattractive to her. But I couldn't lie to her. Not anymore. "I've been battling this annoying, like, hostility ever since we encountered Strife."

She put a comforting hand on my bicep. "He has no right to put that on you."

"I know, and I—"

All of a sudden, my issue wasn't so important anymore. Not compared to what I was seeing on her.

Slowly, I reached and placed my finger under her chin, gently tilting her head back, examining her throat. I lifted her hair so I could look at the back of her neck. I didn't mean to flinch.

"What's the matter?" She searched my face. "Do you see something?"

When I didn't answer, she flipped the passenger sun visor down and scanned her reflection in the small mirror.

I didn't blame her for wanting to know, but I'd have to be the one to tell her. Experience had already taught us that we rarely had the ability to behold our own bondages, even with our visionary gift, and it definitely wouldn't show up in a mirrored reflection. But she was already wringing her hands, battling fear. Now seemed like the worst possible time to deliver the news.

There was something thin and black coiled around the top of Ray Anne's spine, at the base of her shackle-free neck, wrapping all the way around her throat, just beneath the surface of her skin. It was stretched across the same spot as Gentry's jagged mark of assassination, only this thing had girth, like it was a creature, not just a mark.

I recognized a serpentine curse when I saw one.

How had it gotten inside Ray Anne—a Light—and when? Her neck had been fine a few minutes before.

"Is there something on me?" She demanded to know.

It was another one of life's defining moments—a crossroad of internal conflict. I could tell her the horrifying truth and risk her anxiety skyrocketing, or I could fib and act like everything was normal. But there was no way to spare *myself* the unsettling reality. A snake twisted around her spine was bad enough, but its tail tucked beneath her chin like that . . .

Was she marked for assassination too?

The thought of Ray Anne dying was among my most paralyzing fears—the horrific notion that I'd try with all my might but again fail to protect her, and this time, all would be lost.

I knew the kingdom of darkness was no match for ours—the mighty Kingdom of Light—yet hard as I tried to resist it, fear was staring me down too now. Literally. The stalking Creeper leapt over the roof of Ray Anne's car and glared through my driver's side window. Our light kept it outside the vehicle, but our fretting must have been giving off some kind of spirit-world pheromone, keeping it enticed.

She gripped my hand. "Owen, whatever's going on, be honest with me." Her gaze bored into the side of my face. "Please."

Months ago, I'd committed to stop protecting her from harsh realities, trusting that she could handle the truth, however dire, and we could get through anything together. But *this*?

I took a deep breath, placing my palms on either side of her petite neck, my eyes locked on hers—those beautiful blue eyes that always melted my heart. And I defied evil's plot. "This curse of death has no authority over her, no right to claim her. In Christ's name."

Ray Anne's lips narrowed tight while her eyes pooled again, feeling a mix of anger and sadness, it seemed. I released my hands and watched, astounded, as the black streak faded from her neck like evaporating smog. "Ray Anne, it's gone!"

But just as quickly as it had dissolved, it came back, as dark and defined as before.

I threw my hands up, exasperated. "I don't understand."

She ran her fingers across her throat and winced. "I have that line, don't I? It went away, then reappeared?"

"Not just a line," I reluctantly admitted. "A curse, Ray Anne." I swallowed hard. "A snake."

I thought she'd freak out, but instead, she got completely quiet. Neither of us said anything for several minutes. Just sat motionless, our eyes forward, listening to the innocent rhythm of Jackson inhaling and exhaling. Until Ray Anne voiced a confession. "I never used to be afraid of what might happen to me or even of dying, if it came to that. But now that I have this child to care for—"

I knew where she was going with this, and I couldn't sit back and allow her to make such a hopeless statement. "Dr. Bradford's not going to get his hands on Jackson, and you're not going to die, Ray Anne." I turned in the driver's seat and faced her. "Think about it. This scenario—it's evil's way of playing on our deepest, darkest fears to try to stop us in our assignment. It's anxiety based on what's happened in the past and dread about the future, as if the worst thing that could ever happen to us is going to. But it's not, Ray. We can and we *will* overcome this. You believe that, right?"

I'd never seen her like this, so filled with doubt. She wrapped both arms around her gut as if she was bleeding out, like she'd been shot all over again. It was lonely, trying to have enough faith for the both of us. Such an odd reversal of roles.

She peered into the darkness through the windshield. "I know it's wrong and faithless, and I feel guilty for that." She had an unfamiliar blank stare. "But I'm seriously afraid this time. *Really* afraid."

I leaned over the middle console and pulled her toward me, guiding her head to my shoulder, intent on holding her for as long as she'd let me. I wanted to comfort her with a bold promise—a solemn vow that absolutely nothing bad would happen to Jackson or her because I'd never allow it.

But . . .

What if I can't stop it?

I didn't know if the thought had come from me or was shot at my brain from Fear, still circling the vehicle, but it was enough to stop me from making any promises. And to make my heart pound.

Eventually, Ray Anne got out of the car, and I unstrapped Jackson from his car seat. Our light sent Fear into the neighbor's yard, now ironically afraid of us. I walked Ray to her garage apartment door, carrying Jackson's limp body in my arms. I didn't want to leave either of them, but it wasn't like I could stay the night. That was way off limits.

She took Jackson from me and hugged me, squeezing him between us while pleading for me to keep my cell with me at all times and make sure the ringer was on. I swore I would.

I lowered onto my motorcycle, wondering which was worse: seeing that black serpent in Ray Anne's neck or witnessing the most faith-filled person I knew completely cower to dread.

I started my bike, and from the edge of Ray Anne's driveway, Fear growled at me like demons do.

"I command you to go, in Christ's name."

It didn't. Because it didn't have to. It had a spirit-world right to torment fearful people, and Ray Anne was eaten up with fear tonight. I sat idling in the driveway as Fear charged into the air and landed on her roof, pacing back and forth over her room. Above Ray Anne's bed, as best as I could tell. I prayed out loud for God to send Ramus, her divine protector, and thank God, he came immediately. Fear leapt off the roof and ran through the air, far and fast.

My night-watch duty demanded I get back to the church, but I hated to leave. I finally backed out of Ray Anne's driveway and spotted that scrawny pale-pink Creeper in the moonlight, crawling through the lawn on all fours toward Ray's apartment—as if I hadn't run it off already. But before Ramus reacted, it got pulverized by a pack of Creepers that appeared to show up for the sole purpose of smiting the weakling and hauling it away.

Nice.

My sleep schedule was way off, but it's not like I would have slept peacefully anyway. I thrashed on top of my mattress, knowing I should trust God, and Ramus, to watch over Ray Anne, yet I was restless with worry. It didn't help the situation when, at 2:00 a.m., there was a loud thud, like something had slammed the floor in the storage space above my room.

Maybe it was overreacting, but I called the cops. Thankfully the operator patched me through to an officer who'd proven trustworthy in times past. Officer McFarland agreed to come check things out. I followed behind him as he inspected the dusty third-floor storage room, dragging three chains behind him—a nice man who worked hard to put bad guys in jail, yet wasn't liberated himself. At least he *seemed* nice. You never could tell around here.

I wanted to talk to him about getting free—shedding his metal for the Light—but I still didn't know how to bring it up in a way that would make sense to a shackled person. And I did *not* want to see those freaky black scales overtake his eyes like had happened before when I'd broached the topic of faith with bound people.

Beat-up tables were leaned against the walls throughout the large storage space, and there were stacks of chairs and a few old-school chalkboards—but no robbers or vandals. "There are lots of rat droppings," McFarland pointed out. "They scurry at night. I'm guessing that's what you heard, but you were right to call me. Would be good to put some traps out."

I picked up the pole of an American flag that was lying on the floor. "Maybe the rats knocked this over." Not everything was paranormal.

I followed McFarland out of the room, down two flights of stairs and to the church exit doors, wondering the whole time how much he did or didn't know about his colleague Detective Benny.

"Officer McFarland?" He faced me, and there was no going back. "If I had some concerns about someone on the Masonville Police force, how would you suggest I go about reporting it?"

He nodded slowly, a concerned look on his face. "Well, I'd say you best go talk to Detective Benny."

I cut my eyes away, gnawing my bottom lip.

He cleared his throat. "I see. Well, if you have evidence, you should take it to the state police."

"Okay. Thank you."

It's not like that had never occurred to me. Unfortunately, Elle and I still didn't know who we could and couldn't trust, even on a state level, and telling the wrong person could cost our loved ones and us our lives.

He started to leave, then turned back. "Son, I've been Detective Benny's right hand for fifteen years, long enough to know he shoots straight."

I was careful but clear. "Well, you know what they say. Sometimes the right hand doesn't know what the left hand is doing."

He stared at me long and hard. I thanked him again, then closed and locked the doors, praying I'd at least piqued his suspicions. And hoping he really was one of the good guys.

Upstairs in my room, I scooted Daisy out of my spot in bed, then lay down, ready to try to finally get some sleep. I didn't react to another thud overhead. *Rats*, I assured myself.

But then I sat up straight in bed. Those high-pitched whispers were back.

TWELVE

HUSHED VOICES POURED INTO MY ROOM like a sewer pipe leak in the ceiling. Unintelligible words. And there were more thuds, like pounding and stomping.

This wasn't rodents.

I prayed, but like before, the foreboding voices only got louder. That didn't exactly build my faith. But it did help me to hear what they were saying. I picked up on words like *attack. Fear. Death.* Then the most unsettling: *Ray Anne.*

My heart sank, but not my adrenaline. I threw my sheets back, prepared to beat these evil trespassers at their own game—whoever or whatever they were. I determined I'd pray even louder and longer than they were carrying on, until Custos and his soldiers hopefully arrived and ripped the tormentors from limb to limb. Or wing to wing. Molek's ghoulish brown messenger bats had vowed to come after me at night. Maybe it was them, mumbling in high-pitched voices and flapping around the storage room, knocking stuff around.

My feet hit the floor, and there was an instant commotion on my balcony again, loud enough to make Daisy jump down off the bed and whine. I didn't hesitate—just threw the double doors open, more irritated than scared. But I still flinched.

Veronica stood facing me in the moonlight, balancing barefoot on the narrow balcony handrailing.

"I see you." She smiled, but it wasn't kind. A strong gust swept across the balcony, but it didn't even ruffle her thin dress or long hair.

"I know you're not her." I stepped boldly to the center of the balcony. "You're a demonic pretender."

She shook her head with a belittling hum. "Poor orphaned Owen. Always a step behind."

It was a cruel thing to say, but evil is always vicious—to everyone. And dishonest. "This won't work on me. Not again."

She crossed her arms against her chest. "Silly boy. It's already working." She smiled wider. "You're in my intentions. Always." And with that odd remark, she fell backward off the balcony. I charged forward and leaned over the railing, searching for her—for her imposter—but it was gone.

There were no more whispers after that. Just the sound of my box fan and my noisy thoughts as I tried to come to grips with what in the world could be happening in the spirit realm.

The next morning, Saturday, I was laser-focused on what I needed to do. On my way out of the church, I called Elle and told her where I was headed. I hadn't expected her to drop everything and meet me at a prison three hours from Masonville, but she said she had her own list of questions for Veronica. Fine by me. Elle was an expert at extracting information from people. Plus, she said she was able to call and use her media status to set up a face-to-face interview with Veronica versus having to talk to her through a glass barrier using one of those germy prison phones.

As I drove off the church lot, I spotted the black Suburban parked on the side of the road, but I made it past the outskirts of town without being followed. The open hill country roads were always where I did my best thinking. I let myself daydream awhile about what it might be like to move far away from Masonville. Just pack up and start a new life, with Ray Anne, of course. Settle some place where the spiritual atmosphere wasn't off-the-charts toxic. But what kind of soldier defects at the height of a heated war?

By the time I pulled up to the penitentiary, I'd organized my thoughts and felt prepared to face Veronica. Mostly, anyway. I hadn't seen the woman since the night she'd rammed a knife into my left bicep, completely demon possessed. So I wasn't sure what it would be like to be around her now.

I secured my helmet to my bike, eyeing the security watchtower. There were Creepers perched on top and also roaming around the jail yard inside the tall barbed wire–lined fence, but what surprised me was the situation on the roof of the whitewashed Hilltop building.

I'd always assumed a prison would be covered top to bottom with Creepers—at least as many as crept up and down the exterior of Masonville High. But I'd never imagined a platoon of armored Watchmen would be patrolling the roof, moving at crazy-fast speeds and grabbing hold of any Creeper that dared try to slip into the building. I stood there watching as a Creeper slithered on the ground on its belly, hands draped at its sides, working its way toward the building. A Watchman leapt off the roof and drove his armored heel into the demon's back, stuffing it down into the earth like garbage compacted in a landfill.

So apparently God didn't just hand criminals over to the satanic kingdom. And who knew? Maybe there were family members, and people on the inside even, who knew how to wage spiritual war. The mere possibility energized me.

Elle parked next to me, and together, we entered the building and requested to see Veronica Snow, then went through the security process. We were instructed to take a seat at a certain rectangular table in a stark-white room, where we stared at the empty brown chair across from us.

It gave Elle and me a chance to discuss her ongoing effort to track down Masonville's abduction victims, including Betty's niece Tasha Watt and my friend Riley Jenson. "I don't know if either is still alive," she said quietly, "but I believe I know the city where they were both taken, at least initially. Washington, DC."

"Who took them?" All these months later, I was still desperate to know—to hold someone accountable.

"I don't know who abducted them and transported them, but I've narrowed the order down to a certain coven in DC."

"They placed an *order*? For people?" I cringed. "What's a coven?"

"An underground group of witches and warlocks. A branch of the occult."

It was the sort of idea that, a few years ago, I would have scoffed at, dismissing it as conspiracy theory nonsense. I knew now it was anything but.

Elle covered a yawn. "Sorry, I'm so exhausted lately." I wondered if it had anything to do with Slumber's presence in Masonville, but she explained, "I'm up all night. There's all these noises in my home, like the pots and pans are being tossed around in the kitchen cabinets and someone's stomping up and down my stairs. But when I look, nothing's there."

I leaned toward her, trying to avoid the guard overhearing. He kept a close eye on us from the corner of the room. "You know it's the presence of evil, right? They've been haunting my place at the church too. Stomping around the room above me and breaking things on my balcony." And whispering, but Elle couldn't hear spirit-world voices.

"I know it's supernatural." She tapped her pen on her pad of paper. "I have a theory about what's going on. Pay attention to my dialogue with Veronica."

Now and then, a female inmate passed by us, escorted by guards down the hallway. There were some Creepers inside the jail, but they were all attached to guards and convicts—evils these people had personally ushered in and probably swapped with one another, I concluded, since the Watchmen outside weren't letting unattached Creepers in the building. What I didn't understand were the shadowy figures darting around the room, passing through walls the way spiritual bodies do. They looked like Creepers posing as teenage boys.

Elle's quick mention of the facility's history solved the mystery: this place was believed to be haunted by the young men housed here in the 1800s. A superstitious lie, but it was enough to motivate Creepers to play the part.

Veronica entered, led by a guard, and I barely recognized her. She'd been stripped of all her makeup, but it was more than that—it was like all trace of her natural beauty had been wiped away as well. She was average-looking at best. Oddly so.

Her hair was flat against her head and gathered into a ponytail at the base of her neck, at her shackle. She wore a white jumpsuit, and her hands were cuffed in front of her. But it was her expression that was most unfamiliar. Sad, bloodshot eyes, like she was broken and fragile—hardly the lioness I'd known before. And nothing like the replica of her that had been frequenting my balcony.

I didn't know what to expect she'd do when she saw me, but I'd have never guessed she'd walk over and put her head on my shoulder and cry. "Owen. Thank you for coming."

Did she think I was here as a friend?

She finally backed away and sat. I waited for the guard to remove her cuffs before introducing her to Elle. They shook hands, then Elle got straight to business, starting with questions about the missing students' involvement in Veronica's mediation program in the days leading up to their disappearances. Veronica kept pressing her right hand to her heart, like she was filled with compassion for the abducted girls, but when Elle asked if she had any knowledge about what had happened to them and where they might be, she swore she didn't.

I think Elle found that as hard to believe as I did. She turned up the heat. "Did you kidnap Jackson of your own volition, or did someone put you up to it?"

Veronica tucked her chin into her chest and rocked forward and back like a toddler wishing someone would hold her. "I can't talk about that."

"Without a lawyer present?" Elle asked.

"Without putting you in danger," she whispered. There were two guards watching our every move now.

Elle leaned across the table and assured Veronica she was willing to take the risk in order to get answers. That's when Veronica shifted her pitiful gaze to me, her formerly-striking green eyes a dull gray. There was no hint of the seduction she'd always come at me with before. "I didn't want to hurt Jess's baby—I swear. I—I didn't have a choice. I wasn't thinking clearly." She winced. "I didn't mean to harm you either that night, Owen."

It was a charade as dramatic as Bradford's. I wondered if it was to support a plea of insanity at her upcoming trial.

"He's been brainwashing me ever since he brought me to the United States." A tear spilled down Veronica's cheek.

"Who?" I asked her. "Where are you from?"

Veronica clammed up until Elle asked, "Who's your handler?"

I had no clue what a *handler* was, but Veronica got wide-eyed, then glanced over her shoulder at the guards before staring down at the table. "I was born in Russia, but my parents were very poor and sold me to an American man who promised to take care of me and provide me with a much better life. I was eight years old. But I didn't go live with his family like he'd promised. He put me in a boarding school with other children whose parents had given them up too, and he . . . would come see me every few weeks." She slumped so low, her chin nearly rested on the table.

It was obvious the visits hadn't been good.

"Is this man from Masonville?" I asked.

She nodded. "People think he's a noble man who cares for people and wants justice in Masonville, but . . ."

She stopped there, but I was already confident I'd put two-and-two together.

"Tell us who he is so we can stop him and help you." It sounded like Elle was sincere about helping Veronica.

Veronica shook her head no over and over.

"Your handler instructed you to take Jackson." Elle didn't ask but gently asserted.

Veronica finally gave a subtle nod, crying loudly enough that the guards stared even harder at us. Those shadowy boys flocked to her, glaring at her with stern, vengeful eyes as she poured her heart out. Or pretended to. "All these years, I did everything he told me—*everything*. And look where it got me. The pain and destruction I've suffered and caused."

Elle reached into her purse and pulled out a bookmark, of all things, then slid it across the table.

"Sorry," Veronica said, "I can't take anything."

"I know." Elle placed it in her hand. "I just thought you'd like to read it."

Veronica read just loud enough for Elle and me to hear. "Even if my father and mother abandon me, the LORD will hold me close." She set the butterfly-adorned bookmark facedown, and more tears streamed her pale cheeks.

I took over the conversation, determined not to be swayed by theatrics. "Listen, Veronica—or Eva—whatever you call yourself. I'm not opening your letters anymore, and there's no use in sending a Creeper— some demon masquerading as you—to taunt me or Ray Anne. She and I both know what's going on, and we're not afraid."

At least I wasn't.

"Please help us understand, Veronica." Elle was a pro at keeping her tone firm, yet compassionate. "Have you been casting spells on us?" Elle gestured to herself, then me. "Loosing witchcraft on our homes? You've been ordered to, am I right?"

"It's not me!" Two shadowy boys on either side of Veronica gripped her head, pressing their spirit-world fingers into her scalp, then pushed her down so that she banged her forehead on the table over and over, sobbing and babbling. Elle's eyes went wide, but she reached for Veronica's shoulder, hoping to make her stop, but she wouldn't. Or couldn't.

I sat tall in my chair. "In Christ's name, give up your deception and go."

Yeah, we'd now officially caused a scene—a weird one—but get this: the teen boys morphed into towering Creepers, the word haunting marred on every single one of their vile faces. They went rushing out of the room, slipping out through the walls.

One of the guards spoke into his two-way radio, about us, I assumed. Elle raised her eyebrows at me, but Veronica didn't acknowledge anything. She sat still now, her arms crossed tightly at her chest like she was bound in a straitjacket. "Okay, I'm choosing to trust you, Owen." She spoke just above a whisper. She glanced at Elle. "Both of you."

We assured her she could and moved our chairs closer. She spoke quietly, yet frantically. "There are certain chosen cities around the country that have already fallen to Cosmic Ruler control. Masonville is the final atmosphere that must fall in order for Molek to rise up and destroy America."

Of course the insatiable Lord of the Dead wanted to exalt dominion over the whole nation—why hadn't I come to that conclusion already?

I voiced my next question out loud. "Why Masonville?"

She didn't bother answering me. "There are locals and also covens across the country, assigned by Molek and collaborating with my handler to release curses around the clock on Masonville, especially those working against his plan." She eyed Elle and me. "You two are prime targets." Then her gaze locked on me. "And Ray Anne is . . ."

"Ray Anne's what?" I asked.

Veronica withheld a response to that question too.

"My handler has ordered me to do my part, to loose curses on you guys like he's taught me since I was a child." Veronica's voice quaked. "But I refuse to do anything he says anymore. So I probably won't survive much longer."

One of the guards—the taller of the two—approached Veronica, motioning for her to insert her wrists back into a pair of cuffs. I glanced at the clock. There was over a half hour of our visitation time left.

"Excuse me?" Elle glanced at the clock too. "We're not done—why are you taking her back?"

"Time's up," he mumbled.

Veronica locked eyes with us, silently begging us not to protest. "I'm coming," she politely told the guard, then whispered a final time. "Those letters you're getting aren't coming from me, Owen. I'm done with that life."

The guard studied all three of us, more inquisitive than he should have been. When a pointy-hooded witchcraft Creeper emerged from the floor with one of the guard's chains fastened to its wrist, I became convinced the man was there on assignment—another operative in the occult.

Elle stood. "Thank you, Veronica."

As we watched her being escorted away, I asked Elle, "Do you believe a word she just said?"

She exhaled, retrieving the flimsy bookmark off the table. "Most of it. But not the part about being done with that life. Even if they're sincere, SRA victims almost always get manipulated into going back."

"SRA?"

"Satanic ritual abuse," Elle clarified.

My gut sank. Veronica wasn't the only victim I knew.

On our way out of the building, I felt the need to caution Elle. "Don't get sucked into feeling sorry for Veronica or believing anything she says."

Elle handed me the girly bookmark, then fished her keys out of her purse, speed walking, as usual. "I feel for anyone who's been raised in the occult," she said. "Such unfathomable mind tricks and cruelty. That said, you don't have to tell me to be objective and on guard."

I walked beside her through the parking lot, comfortable enough with her by now to tell her, "My mom was raised in the occult—an SRA victim—and she made it out and never went back." It was about as personal as anything I could have shared, although Elle's lack of reaction made me think she already knew.

I stopped as a thought hit me. Maybe *that* was why Bradford was pursuing a relationship with my mom. So he could try to coax her back in. I'd never considered the possibility before. But surely she'd *never* go back to that life.

I kept the troubling thought to myself, but Elle planted more concern in me. "Honestly, Owen, I'm not sure about your mother's current involvement or lack thereof."

I huffed, offended at the notion, even if her suspicion was fair.

Elle opened the driver's side door of her Audi. "I'm aware of your mother's history and defection from the occult, and also how your father, Stephen, fought to protect her from their retribution when he and your mother were married."

I clutched her arm before she could duck into her car. "Wait a minute. How do you know all that?" And why hadn't my own father told me?

"Your ancestors played a key role in Masonville's history; I've made it my business to uncover your family's business." She actually paused to put a stick of gum in her mouth. "Look, if you want the whole story, you could always ask your parents." She said it with that know-it-all attitude that had grated on me from the first time I'd seen her reporting on TV. "I only have some of the facts—seems to me you'd want to take the lead on that one."

Naturally, I wanted all the facts and truth I could gather about my parents' history, but Elle didn't understand. My mom refused to speak of her past, especially about my father, and him . . . he was so secretive, he and I could hardly communicate about *anything*. I'd been restricted to a few vague texts here and there on a burner phone.

Elle shut herself in her car, then lowered her black-tinted window. "I'll be in touch soon, but in the meantime, do you know how to stop the evil that a nation full of witches is loosing on our homes? That's more your area of expertise than mine."

"Not really, no. But I'll figure it out as fast as I can." Add that to the other pressing dilemmas that already needed my attention and solutions.

"I sure hope so," Elle said, "'cause it's terrorizing my family."

She put her car in reverse, but I didn't want to let her go without asking, "What's a handler?"

"A person in the occult who uses mind-control techniques and manipulation to dominate a vulnerable person—you know, get them entrenched in the secret society so they're too afraid and brainwashed to get out. They mostly target children and teenagers."

I bent down, eye-level with her. "I think I know the phony peace-keeping Masonville man Veronica described as her handler."

She checked her rearview mirrors and lowered her voice. "I have my suspicions too. And wisdom demands that we stay as far away from him as we can for now—you hear me?"

I nodded, then extended the bookmark to her. "Here."

"Keep it."

I tried handing it to her a second time but there was no use. She drove off. I stuffed it in my back pocket, thinking maybe a bookmark would somehow come in handy soon. Elle had a way of giving me random objects I didn't know I needed until suddenly, they were exactly what I had to have.

I was tense the whole drive back to Masonville, wondering if Veronica would send word to Detective Benny that Elle and I had come asking forbidden questions, hardly minding my own business like he'd threatened me to do.

The more I mulled it over, the surer I was: Detective Benny was Veronica's handler.

THIRTEEN

THAT AFTERNOON, RAY TEXTED and said her mom was babysitting Jackson. That meant she and I could spend time together. Music to my ears.

Around 4:00 p.m., I stopped by Gentry's house *again*, but he was gone. I got the idea he'd rather be anywhere but home. The new moon was only six days away, and the Cosmic Rulers had been warned not to wait that long to carry out their assassinations. Meanwhile, I'd made no progress intervening in Gentry's life and had only thought up one way to try to identify who else made up the thirteen marked for elimination, but I couldn't execute the plan without being allowed to roam among the students at Masonville High.

I told myself that black snake tail wrapped around Ray's neck coincidentally resembled the mark of death, and she definitely was not one of the targets. The thought that she might be gave me anxious shakes, so I suppressed it at all costs.

I may have had *defender* supernaturally sealed on my arm, but I felt like *disqualified* was more accurate at this point.

On my way to Ray Anne's, strong gusts of wind blasted against my motorcycle, as if even the weather was determined to work against me. I confided in God. "Lord, you see that I'm trying. Please don't let me fail."

What else was I supposed to do?

Don't give up came to mind.

I knocked on Ray Anne's garage-apartment door, and from the timid way she asked who was there, I could tell she was still crippled with fear—though I didn't see the Creeper version anywhere at the moment. But that pale pink one was back, curled up in a ball beneath the bushes outside her room like a drunken squatter, pretending to sleep.

Surely Creepers don't rest.

I'd confront the thing in a minute. My first priority was to check on Ray Anne.

She opened the door an inch and peeked out, as if it might not be me, even though I'd just said it was. And despite the summer temperatures, she was wearing a sweater that bunched up around her neck, all the way to her chin.

She invited me in, and I told her, "I know you're grossed out or embarrassed or whatever about that thing around your neck . . ." *In* your neck, but there was no need to phrase it that way. "But please, Ray, don't feel like you have to hide it from me. You've seen horrible things on me before, and you didn't back away or hold it against me."

I hugged her, but her arms hung limp at her sides. "I'm a monster, Owen."

"No." I let go and looked into her terrified eyes. "You're being attacked."

She huffed, then started gathering Jackson's toys off the floor and chucking them into a plastic bin like she was pitching fastballs. "Why would God let this happen to me?"

Ah. The real issue.

I followed her around the small room. "Ray Anne, we'll figure everything out. He'll show us."

"I'm not so sure about that."

Really?

I'd only seen this serious of a scowl on her face once, back in high school, when she'd thought she'd caught me kissing Jess. She'd gone into a furious rant about how she couldn't trust anyone, shouting up at the starry sky. At God. But she'd been quick to come to her senses that night and trust him all over again. And also me.

"Babe, you know you can't talk like this." I followed her into the makeshift kitchen area—a minifridge with a microwave stacked on top. "You'll draw dark forces, and they'll—"

She spun around and faced me, her cheeks flushed red. "Stop trying to solve everything, Owen, as if I need you to fix me!"

Wow. This attitude from her was as unexpected as my mom's sobriety and spotless house. I was tempted to get offended, but I knew better than to make this about me. Ray Anne was hurting, and I needed to be there for her. But I had to pause and at least allow the thought to register . . .

It's scary when you know someone so well and they act way out of character.

There'd been a lot of that lately in my world, mostly corrupt people swearing they'd changed for good. But here was Ray Anne, the most faith-filled person I knew, second-guessing if God could even be trusted and yelling at me just for suggesting he could.

Sure, I wanted to yell back at her, especially since that annoying inner hostility was all over me. But I still had a choice, and I chose to be calm—yes, to try to get through to Ray Anne, but also to hopefully stop evil from closing in on the scene if I could.

I stepped back and gave her some space, trying my best to be empathetic, even though it didn't always come naturally to me. "Ray, remember how, not that long ago, I was lugging around chains and cords and had no clue how I'd ever get them off me? It all worked out, didn't it?"

"That's you. I'm not supposed to have . . ." She didn't finish her cruel remark, but she and I both knew what she'd been about to say.

So much for my good intentions. Like a volume switch cranked all the way to max, anger surged in me.

I stepped back again, putting even more space between us, then spoke my mind. "Ray Anne, are you saying *I'm* the kind of person who deserves to have baggage, but not you—cause you're too good for that?"

She stood there with her arms crossed and her lips pressed tight, as if her new shade of lip gloss was *Resentment*. But finally she broke, shedding a tear. "I just never thought I'd have some snake in me and feel like I'm looking over my shoulder all the time. It's like I'm completely defeated."

Sure enough, there was scampering overhead. Creepers flocking to Ray Anne's roof. The very thing I'd tried to prevent.

I approached her and held her tight, coming to some important conclusions. "Ray Anne, think about what's really happening." I moved my hands to her shoulders, guiding her to look up at me as I made my own confession. "That Spirit of Strife has some kind of hold on me—I've been feeling it since the day we encountered him. And it's obvious the Spirit of Despair is getting to you. I mean, you know you're not normally a discouraged person.

"As for that snake," I told her, "it's bound to be some kind of curse. But just like there's freedom from chains and cords, we know there has to be a remedy for curses. We just have to figure out what it is."

She sniffled a few times and her voice quaked. "I know we can fight this."

Thank God, my brave Ray Anne was sounding more like herself. The stomping on the roof came to a sudden standstill.

We both eyed our defender seals, still glorious and glowing on our arms, and I prayed right then and there for both of us—that we'd quickly come to understand how to combat the attacks being hurled at us. Our worst fears, intentionally being thrown in our faces.

I got Ray Anne caught up on everything that had gone down with Veronica, and she eventually suggested we head to the Caldwell Cemetery this evening for another stakeout. There were two more Rulers we had yet to uncover. I wondered whether she could handle it right now, but I didn't ask. If she said she was up for it, the only respectful response was to believe her.

On our way out the door, I pointed to the pale-pink trespasser. "That thing is relentless, but it's got to go."

"They'll just hurt him again." Ray Anne pulled me by the hand toward her car. "Just leave him."

"*Him?* Don't you mean *it?* And Creepers deserve to get hurt." Anger began to cluster in my sternum again. The idea that this devil was actually getting her sympathy . . .

"Ray Anne, you can *never* feel sorry for evil or allow it to stay close."

She opened her driver's side door. "He's outside. It's not like he's in my house."

I clutched her arm, stopping her from getting in the car. "Listen to me. This is no different than when I was interacting with a spirit and you warned me to stop. I didn't listen, and you remember what that cost me."

"I get that, but I'm not interacting with this one. I would never do that."

I couldn't believe what I was hearing. "You think it just *happens* to be hanging out here, outside your door, with no agenda whatsoever?"

"Owen, all I'm saying is he's not doing anything scary or harmful."

"That you're aware of."

She sighed. "Don't you think we have much more serious battles to fight?"

I knew no matter how gently I tried to say it, if I accused her of being deceived, it would start an argument, which would evoke a flurry of evil and not only hinder my relationship with Ray but ultimately sabotage our joint mission. So instead I turned around, marched right up to the unholy weakling, and commanded it to leave all over again. I was so loud, Mrs. Greiner came running out of the house, Ray Anne's dad behind her.

"Everything's fine." It was basically true. There was a problem, but I was handling it.

Her parents went back inside. Meanwhile, that Creeper stopped pretending to be asleep and started limping down Ray Anne's lawn, hobbling toward the curb. But before it could get there, a pair of big greenish-gray hands reached up from beneath the ground, up through the grass, and drove pointed claws into the mongrel's back. It howled in agony, of course, still masquerading as a victim.

Ray Anne grimaced. "What was the point of that, Owen? He was only sleeping."

I huffed. "Did you really just criticize me for sending a Creeper away?" My anger spiked higher, my neck instantly tense and hot. "Evil forces are never neutral, much less innocent, Ray Anne. You know that."

The pale-pink Creeper was dragged underground, thrashing and screaming, leaving a bloody mess in the grass. I pointed to the nasty maroon spot. "Creepers don't have blood, Ray Anne. This is all a trick."

She gazed at the stain from where she stood in the driveway. "The Bible doesn't say if they have blood or not." She faced her car again. "Can we go now?"

I'd been living with the nagging worry that Ethan might come between Ray and me at some point, but never in a million years would I have imagined a Creeper would. It seemed to me that's where this was headed—her pity for the "poor thing" creating resentment toward me for hating it.

I got in the car but sat silently in the passenger seat while Ray drove us to my wooded property. I mulled over whether I should tell her how her instability was making everything feel odd and unsafe to me. Ray Anne had always been a rock, keeping me anchored to truth and reality. Well, at least she'd always tried to keep me on the right path. But it was like that determined girl had gone missing, replaced by someone gullible and fragile I didn't recognize.

I hadn't felt this lonely in a while. Or this concerned about Ray Anne. But would it do any good to tell her that?

The sun had nearly set as she and I stood a distance away from the Caldwell Cemetery, both quiet, anticipating that the final two Rulers might show themselves. That Bloody Mary statue—as I'd started thinking of it—and the "miracle tears" it had cried remained a mystery, but it wasn't important compared to the other unsolved situations weighing on me.

Standing in the woods, sensing nothing but an occasional Creeper-tainted breeze, my racing thoughts were in serious need of sorting. I got my phone out and typed in my notes app:

1. Find how to get serpent/curse out of Ray Anne.
2. Identify all 13 people marked to die plus how to protect them—ASAP.
3. Come up with plan to fight back against witches and warlocks haunting Elle's place and mine.
4. Will the student pastors be willing to help us tomorrow?

And finally, the one I'd been keeping to myself.

5. Am I losing my mind, or has some invisible form of evil been spying on me, toting around a crying baby?

Even now, standing next to Ray Anne, I felt the invisible presence.

I read back through my list and shook my head. They didn't exactly have how-to videos for stuff like this.

I put my phone in my pocket and assured Ray Anne we were okay. She was gasping at every sound, even leaves rustling. I could tell she was trying to be her adventurous self but failing.

We waited for over an hour, but nothing happened. Honestly, I was relieved no Rulers showed up. My instincts had been right—Ray Anne couldn't have handled it.

I held Ray's trembling hand the entire walk through the woods back to her car. This wasn't the Ray Anne I'd fallen in love with, but I was already committed to her without any official vow—for better or worse.

On the drive to her place, I contemplated what I needed to do that night, back at the church—more specifically, what I needed to confront. I would've liked to have had Ray Anne there at my side, standing strong with me, but in her condition, she had no business attempting any kind of spirit-world standoff. Especially one like this.

FOURTEEN

I SAT ON THE CORNER OF MY BED with my Mac in my lap, willing myself to ignore the unsettling vibe I always got in this room. And the miserable suspicion I was being watched.

I searched up the definition of *curse*: "An invocation for harm or injury to come upon a person; to will one's misfortune as an act of retribution or revenge."

I stared blankly at the bookshelf in front of me, connecting the dots. "Evil people are loosing curses on us."

I couldn't vouch for the sincerity of Veronica's supposed withdrawal from the occult, but I had to admit, her explanation of certain things made sense—mainly her account of Molek rallying the satanic world's human servants to work against those of us called to free Masonville of his tyranny.

I wondered how it worked. His minion bats delivered their master's marching orders to Veronica's handler, and he communicated with covens around the country? Or did the demonic bats descend on secret gatherings of witches and warlocks to deliver instructions directly?

However it worked, the concept also aligned with Arthur's prophetic warning that the outcome of Masonville's spiritual battle would be felt far beyond our city limits. Demon-devoted people around the country had their eyes on our town, plotting against us, willing Masonville to cave to dark powers as part of some spirit-world takeover strategy for America. And if Veronica was right, Masonville was the *last* targeted city still standing—the outcome here would be felt around the nation.

The realization added to the immense pressure to achieve our mission, but at the same time, I remained confident these evil peoples' dark powers were no match for the power of God. The way I saw it, we Lights had only one disadvantage, but unfortunately, it was a big one: *ignorance*. Satan's vessels were trained to tap into supernatural powers. Meanwhile, Ray and I were still trying to figure out how to skillfully wield our spiritual weapons, and Elle didn't seem to have a clue. I'd learned a lot since the day I'd shed my shackle, but circumstances demanded I learn more. And fast.

There I was, my mind consumed with the reality of spiritual attacks, when the sudden sound of footsteps began closing in, advancing down the hallway toward my door. I slammed my laptop shut and jumped off the bed. My heart banged in my chest like it wanted out.

I knew I shouldn't be afraid, but my jumpy, adrenaline-charged body wasn't convinced.

I grabbed my Bible off the bed and held it in the air, as if throwing the Scriptures at a spirit-world enemy might somehow accomplish the same thing as quoting them.

Then came a knock. "Owen? You there?"

I let out a massive sigh. Pastor Gordon, working late, apparently. Ethan's father, but I tried not to hold that against him.

I opened the door and invited him in. There was no place to sit, so we stood in the center of my room, our auras overlapping. He stuffed his hands into the pockets of his tan slacks, calm and easygoing, as usual. I tried not to fidget.

"How have you been?" His familiar smile was wide and kind. I welcomed the comfort.

"I'm, uh . . . yeah, doing good." It was easier to just say that.

He thanked me for my willingness to keep an eye on the church property and told me he was proud of the spiritual growth he'd seen in me lately, I guess because he'd observed me sitting in church every

Sunday for a while. And I supposed Ray Anne had told him I'd stopped talking to evil spirits.

I wanted to confide in him about Molek, to find a way without sounding insane to tell him that a high-ranking demon mentioned in Scripture was plotting with seven Cosmic Rulers to decimate our town. Our whole nation and world, ultimately. But before I could find the words to even begin, he started pacing a small lap around my cluttered room and talking.

"I'm sorry the accommodations here are so lacking. Wait until you see the facilities after the renovations are complete. As soon as I raise the funds, this entire campus is getting the face-lift of a lifetime."

"That's cool." I tried to sound interested.

"Owen." He faced me. "How well do you know Dr. Brody Bradford?"

"Um . . ." I wondered where this was going.

"I was told he used to mentor you in high school."

Never ended up happening, but okay.

"I know he and his family have been through a lot in recent years," Gordon said. "My heart goes out to him." He patted Daisy on the head, then made his point. "We're looking to gain support from benevolent folks in the community to underwrite the cost of building renovations and also enable us to purchase this land. The property was originally leased to us at no cost, but the owner is now demanding that we purchase all twenty acres. We don't have the funds for that, Owen. Which is why I'm asking if you'd mind making an introduction between Dr. Bradford and me."

Oh. A fundraising connection.

I was torn, partly because Gordon had building improvements and real estate on the brain while hell's best fighters were out to annihilate our town—the people, not the buildings. His ignorance was annoying. But I also knew I needed to cut the man some slack. He'd been mostly caring toward me, and I'd seen him care for others; he didn't *mean* to be blind and totally oblivious to the big picture. I guess my thoughts counted as compassion, because that's when I saw it . . .

Like a semi-transparent shadow living inside of him, Gordon's soul nodded off. His physical head stayed upright, facing me, but his soul's head dropped down to his chest, eyes closed, then popped up again, retreating into his skull, beyond my sight.

"You're under Slumber's influence." It just came out.

"Excuse me?"

I pressed my eyes closed and rubbed my eyelids. How was I supposed to handle this?

I finally asked if he and I could go sit somewhere and talk. I followed him down the hall and downstairs. He flipped on the lights, and I sat next to him on a back-row pew. On the other side of the sanctuary from the freaky-baby-crying incident.

I warned Pastor Gordon I was going to sound crazy, and there were certain things I couldn't elaborate on. Then I just flat-out told him Masonville was on a spirit-world hit list of sorts—though I still didn't know why our town—and seven Cosmic Rulers were here to wreak havoc. I didn't go so far as to mention Molek's history on my land, but I did name the assignments of the five Rulers I knew of and even admitted I was dealing with the unwanted effects of Strife's presence. "And I mean this with no disrespect," I said, "but your soul has been nodding off the whole time I've been talking to you. Slumber has a hold on you."

He sat stiff as a robot, his mouth gaping while he searched my face like he'd just met me for the first time. "That's some story."

"No, it's more than that." I grabbed a Bible from the shelf attached to the pew in front of us. "This stuff's in here." I thought about turning to the chapters in Leviticus and telling him about Molek after all, but I flipped to 2 Chronicles instead, the seventh chapter. "Look." I pointed to the exact verse quoted in Arthur's prophecy, then gave my best summary. "It says if God's Lights—I mean, his people—will humble themselves and pray and stop doing the things he says not to, he'll respond and heal our land. Cosmic forces will lose their grip on Masonville, their power to oppress us. And I bet people's spiritual blindness would be healed too, so they could finally see the truth and come to God, then get free from their own demons." I spared him the description of the slimy scales that overtake the eyeballs of the spiritually blind—as they had mine at one time, I'm sure.

"It's a beautiful promise," Pastor Gordon said, eyeing the text I'd just paraphrased.

"We have to *do* this, Pastor. Like, literally gather whoever's willing and begin praying—and keep praying, until there's enough people in Masonville to pray on my land—where tons of evil has happened. Then we'll fill plenty of Watchmen bowls and saturate the property, so no demons are left standing."

Okay, I'd accidentally gotten too descriptive at the end, but it was true. I'd witnessed colossal Watchmen immobilize a horde of Creepers by dumping supernatural bowls of liquid prayers on the demons' helpless heads. It was epic.

Gordon smiled at me while his soul nodded off yet again. "Owen, I love this new zeal you have. Have you ever considered pursuing a seminary degree? It would serve you well to gain a solid understanding of Scripture."

I cleared my throat, my body tense with impatience. "Did you hear what I said? We have to act—work together with others to reach our whole town with the truth before things get much, much worse around here. Lives are at stake. Souls."

Gordon looked toward the stage, lost in thought, it seemed. "I tell you what. I've got some excellent books on prayer in my office. How about we go get them now, and I'll lend them to you?"

Correction. He wasn't lost in thought. He was asleep at the wheel, too spiritually drowsy to even comprehend what I was saying, much less react.

At least I now understood how the Cosmic Spirit of Slumber operated. His influence put people's spiritual drive to sleep. All sense of fight and urgency pacified, like how Jackson would doze off while Ray Anne sung him lullabies. Something in Pastor Gordon—the condition of his soul—made him susceptible to Slumber's oppression.

I could only hope the student pastors would be awake at our meeting tomorrow.

Gordon walked me to his office and gave me a stack of books, then left for home.

Back in my room, I decided I'd read the books soon, but right now, duty called. It was late, but I had no intention of sleeping. Honestly, after what I'd just witnessed, I loathed the thought of curling up in bed. It was time for combat.

The best defense is a strong offense, right?

I grabbed a dusty stack of blank note cards I spied wedged between two books on the bookshelf and prepared for war. I googled Scriptures about God's power over Satan and started writing them out, one per card.

The spirit world must have known what I was up to, because I'd hardly finished writing on the first card when there was a commotion outside, on the balcony. I kept writing, fast and fired up, my handwriting messier than usual. I sat leaning against the bed on the hardwood floor, asking God the whole time to please commission his Watchmen to be with me—and to go with me when I set out in a minute.

There was an instant glare outside, shining through the sheers on the windowed doors. I peeked out.

The disturbance on the balcony had stopped, but Custos stood mid-air in the distance, facing the building with six more armored Watchmen at his side. Their sculpted arms were bowed out, poised, it seemed, to twist the neck of any Creeper that dared to come near.

That's what I'm talking about.

With my face pressed against the windowpane, I scanned the grassy property. Daisy started barking her head off right before I heard the sound of women wailing. Then I saw them. Several mounted lights shone down from trees, giving just enough illumination for me to observe them, huddled shoulder to shoulder in front of the pond. Young and old, light skinned and dark—all draped in tattered dresses that appeared soaking wet, hanging loosely to their shins. There were several males in the mix as well, their slender bodies draped in the same thin white dresses. All at once, the pack of them charged through the grass on bare feet toward the building. Toward me.

I refused fear, choosing fight over flight.

I watched through the windowed doors, ready to face whatever form of intimidation tactic they came at me with—whatever manifestation of witchcraft was being loosed on me. That had to be what this was.

I watched in astonishment when the pond people—some forty Creepers masquerading as humans—left the ground and began crawling swiftly up the brick building like human spiders. I braced myself for their arrival, but they passed up my room. I took a courageous step outside, onto the balcony, and witnessed them disappear one by one into the storage space above my room, passing effortlessly through the brick exterior.

There was stomping overhead, as loud as before, and once again, whispers seeped through my ceiling and walls.

Custos and his platoon remained poised in the air, hovering, even though their armor had to have weighed a ton. When the last crawler pried her way into the building, the Watchmen rose higher and fanned out, surrounding the third-story storage room.

I took that as my cue.

I grabbed my stack of note cards, ran down the hall, then charged up the rickety flight of wooden steps to the plain brown storage room door at the top. I didn't pause to weigh the seriousness of the situation, and I didn't let their intimidating whispers derail me. I turned the knob and flung the door open, flipping on the light and barging inside in one swift move.

Then I froze.

FIFTEEN

THEY WERE EVERYWHERE. Women and girls and several men and boys, all in thin tattered dresses. They walked sideways on the walls, upside down across the ceiling, and at random slanted angles midair. But no matter their direction, their soaking-wet hair stayed pasted to their cheeks and shoulders and backs. They uttered angry chants, passing through material objects as if the room were empty.

They left footprints everywhere—dark-red stains. The same sickening color dripped from the hem of their soaked gowns, puddling all over the floor.

Out the windows, I saw Custos and his soldiers. Their heavenly light poured in, clashing with the infestation of evil, yet not driving it away. Custos peered in through a window straight at me and gave a subtle nod, as if signaling me to take action. All at once, the prowlers faced me, then rushed at me without having to take actual steps. Their glaring eyes appeared human, yet their pupils were small as pinpoints.

The door slammed behind me as they pressed in just beyond my aura. All of them. They cursed me, commanding me to suffer and go insane and give up and die. Sure enough, black snakes came slithering from mouths and out from under dresses, as thick as water hoses. As long as broomsticks. But the serpents couldn't breach my light or crawl on me, thank God.

I knew what to do. I'd just done it this morning at the jail and seen it work. I pointed at the witchy Creepers. "In Christ's name, I command you to give up your deception and go!"

That shut them up—but there was no metamorphosis into Creeper form.

A petite girl directly in front of me chuckled. She looked about thirteen. "He doesn't know."

They all laughed at me hysterically. Like the bats had in my nightmare.

"I don't know what?"

I realized I'd just made a wrong move. Asking Creepers questions gives them an unnatural advantage, like a lion rolling over and exposing his belly to a pack of hyenas. So, I immediately repeated the command for them to stop their deception and go.

"Say it over and over, Owen. It won't work."

I knew that voice.

"We're as human as you. We just have superior power."

Here she came, gliding through the paranormal crowd until she stood in front of me. Veronica, dressed and drenched like the rest.

"You're an imposter," I said, declaring the truth.

She pressed her index finger into my chest, and I felt it, like her hand had substance. "You're the imposter, charging in here like some man of faith."

They all snickered.

"You have no faith, Owen. No spiritual knowledge. No depth or understanding of the Source. No real conviction." She inched forward, as close as she could get to my aura. "Poor baby," she said. "You don't even have parents."

That young girl mocked me with a sarcastic pout.

"All lies," I said.

Veronica's face was a breath away from mine, though she wasn't breathing. "Your mother never loved you or bothered being there for you. And your father . . ." She shook her head. "He never wanted you."

I knew it was useless to defend myself against her false accusations, and yet I gave in. "My father didn't know he had a son. He would have wanted me."

"Oh, but he did know. Full well." She tilted her head to the side and whispered in my ear. "You're unwanted, Owen. An orphan. Totally alone in this world. You always have been, and you always will be. It's what you deserve."

Her words sliced through me like a samurai sword. That's what evil does—pinpoints our soul's deepest wound, then brutalizes it with lies.

I didn't have to take this. The kingdom of darkness is aggressive—I had to be also.

I read the first card in my hand. "Christ disarmed the spiritual rulers and authorities. He shamed them publicly by his victory over them on the cross."

The whole nest of them launched into a rage, yelling and releasing more snakes and flailing their arms like they were falling.

I read another card, turning the verse into a personal declaration this time, shouting it. "No weapon turned against me will succeed. God will silence every voice raised up to accuse me."

Veronica growled in my face, flaring her gums like a wild beast as the cluster disbanded, covering their ears and rushing to the far end of the room.

One by one, I read through the Scriptures. By the time I'd finished, every dripping figure was on the floor, convulsing like the Word of God was attacking their nervous system.

At last, I watched out the windows as the Watchmen rose above the building. The blinding radiance lifted, and the anguished mob went rushing out, flinging themselves out the same west-side wall through which they'd entered. With my face pressed against a window, I watched them race to the pond, then run into the water and sink out of sight.

"Yes!" I threw my fists in the air, reveling in having done something right this time. Something that totally worked.

Every last one of them was gone from the room, along with the slithering snakes. The red puddles and footprints were gone too—every trace of them. Custos and his battalion moved on as well, their work done here.

I marched downstairs to my room and collapsed on my bed, smiling, feeling like I'd just downed an extra-large double-shot of espresso. I could hardly wait until sunup. I'd call Elle and tell her exactly how to purge her home of the nighttime hauntings—demons impersonating people, likely appearing identical to the witches loosing them on us.

I sat up in bed, with no intention of sleeping. "That phony form of Veronica said some mean things, Daisy." Yeah, I talked to my dog sometimes. "But none of it was true."

I spotted the plastic box my mom had given me and figured now was as good a time as any to dig through it. She'd saved a few of my honor roll certificates, some report cards from random school years, a plastic baggie with two of my baby teeth. Gross.

There was also a small stack of photos. A few of Mom and me at the lakeside carnival where she used to take me when I was little. Me blowing out candles at the kitchen table when I turned thirteen. No, fourteen—the year we moved three times.

There was one of me at bat at a Little League game. I played one season of baseball in the fifth grade since the boy next door played, and his mom offered to let me ride with them. My mom hardly showed up at my games, so I knew the neighbor lady had likely taken the picture.

I stared at my munchkin face in the photo, recalling how my coach would crush his paper cup and hurl it at the ground every time I struck out—which was a lot, because I'd never swung a bat before joining the team.

Then I saw something strange, in the right-hand corner of the picture.

Wait . . .

I rushed to my lamp and held the photo next to the bulb. I rubbed my eyes and blinked. "That can't be right."

Even wearing a baseball cap and sunglasses, there was no denying who was in the stands, watching me play ball nearly ten years ago.

What was my father doing there?

SIXTEEN

MY HANDS WERE SHAKING. Not from fear, but with seething anger. The kind that makes you want to drive too fast and keep going until you're somewhere far and secluded.

I'd learned to accept that my mom had lied to me my whole life. Most alcoholics lie, especially to themselves. But my father?

Furious as I was, something in me—in my damaged psychology, I guessed—wanted to make excuses for him. I stood in the center of my room, trying to convince myself there had to be a good reason that, although he'd known he had a son, he chose to hide from me.

He must have cared, or he wouldn't have bothered coming to my game. Right?

But I couldn't suppress the obvious: there's never an acceptable excuse for a father to intentionally let his kid grow up without him. And to think that all this time I'd been feeling sorry for Jackson because his mother had failed him and his father had given up parental rights. I was basically in the same sinking boat.

My father hadn't been unaware of my existence, like he'd led me to believe. He'd *abandoned* me.

And that Creeper posing as Veronica knew it and had used it against me, aware it would torment me to the core.

Forget the burner phone. I snapped a picture of the photo with my own cell and sent it to the number I had for my dad, along with a text: **Never knew you had a son?**

That wasn't satisfying enough. I sent another: **Please don't contact me ever again.**

That still didn't quench the anger, but what more could I do? I hurled my phone at my mattress.

I couldn't remember the last time I'd been this irate, if ever. I stomped back and forth in the tiny room—it felt like a maddening jail cell now. And here came the Creeper Rage, thrusting its mangled head through the painted cinder block. Then my old enemy Demise. But neither had the guts to set foot in my room. As unspiritual as I felt, the aura around my feet still shone bright, keeping demons out.

Both Creepers backed away.

I dropped to the hard floor and leaned back against the metal bedframe, considering packing my bags and leaving Masonville once and for all, as if I could run away from my dad's betrayal. I was exhaling into my cupped hands when a brood of spirit-world serpents came spewing out from under my bed, then spread out and slithered all over the floor and walls and ceiling. Forked-tongued curses. Another manifestation of witchcraft, aimed at me by people I didn't even know.

"Leave, in Jesus' name!"

The serpents sank into the walls and floor, but kept slinking around, refusing to go.

And how's this for bad timing? That horrible baby started crying again—right outside my door, from the sound of it. But there was no sense in looking. Even if it was there, it wasn't *there.*

I faced the door and commanded the tormenting presence to go, along with the snakes again. I ordered them to leave the church building and surrounding property. They didn't, so I read the cards out loud again—the exact same verses that had just cleared out a storage room packed with demons parading as humans. But the baby kept bawling and the snakes kept slithering.

I couldn't believe how quickly the spirit-world tables had turned on me. The thrill of my victory snatched away by serpents and a sobbing infant that increased the foreboding sense I was under spiteful surveillance.

"Custos!" I stood in the corner of my room, waiting, stomping my foot, but he didn't come.

I finally sank hopelessly into my bed and pulled the sheets over my head, reminding myself that the snakes couldn't get past my light to crawl on me. But then again, one had managed to breach Ray Anne's skin. I piled all three of my pillows on my head and tucked them over my ears, not because I thought it would protect against the snakes but in a useless attempt to block out the aggravating sobbing.

For the first time in a while, I seriously questioned my sanity.

Lying there suffering, I sifted quickly in my mind through the life events that had led to this moment. As committed as I'd been to my life calling and mission to help heal this town—and as impressed as I was with my defender seal—I was beginning to come to grips with a sobering realization: *The bigger the assignment from God, the bigger the satanic attack to try to block it.*

It's not like I'd had some fluffy idea about what it would be like to walk out my destiny and reclaim Masonville from the powers of darkness. But I'd somehow mistakenly assumed that overall, it would be exciting and fulfilling and . . . okay, heroic.

But *this*?

For the first time since I'd read Arthur's prophecy and accepted the supernatural call, I second-guessed if it was remotely worth it.

Sunday morning came, and I hadn't slept. The baby had squalled on my doorstep until sunrise. That was one reason I didn't feel like going downstairs and sitting in a pew—passing the offering plate, listening to Pastor Gordon preach like everything in Masonville was on the up-and-up, then passing the plate again, in case his sermon had inspired people to give more to the building fund. But I was starting to like the worship part a lot—the glistening, reassuring light it ushered into the atmosphere, even though it meant having to watch Ethan sing center stage.

I chose getting out of bed over staying closed off in my reptile-infested room and missing a chance to see Ray Anne.

In the foyer, I downed a couple of donuts, eyeing the entrance doors the whole time, waiting on Ray to arrive. She walked in and gave me that heartwarming grin of hers. But she ducked her head as she approached, fiddling with the collar of her blouse, trying to cover the scaly curse.

She didn't tell me hello or ask how I was—just blurted out, "Veronica was back at four o'clock this morning, spying into Jackson's crib again. It's her, Owen, I swear."

I spun her around and rubbed her tense shoulders. "It's not her," I insisted all over again. "And you know how to make Creepers leave—you're the one who first showed me."

I hoped to encourage her by explaining how things had gone down at the church last night with "Veronica" and the horde, ending my story at the victorious part, where the Scriptures on note cards drove every dripping-wet oppressor away. I spared her an account of the rest of my defeated night. Uncovering my dad's abandonment. Tormented by snakes and a wailing infant that refused to leave me alone no matter what I commanded or quoted.

"I know what I'm supposed to do," Ray said, "But I got so scared, I couldn't speak. She only left 'cause Jackson's Watchman showed up, the dark-headed robed one with the shield on his back."

"*You*? Too scared to speak?" I rubbed the sides of her chilled arms. "You're fearless, Ray Anne. This isn't you."

"I know." She pressed her lips together, straining to hold back tears. "But I can't shake it. I'm terrified."

"Of what?" I was no shrink, but common sense said if we could figure out what she was afraid of, we could start combatting it. But I wasn't prepared for the onslaught.

"I'm afraid Veronica is gonna hurt Jackson—take him at night while I'm sleeping, and I'll never find him again. Or Dr. Bradford is going to demand visitation rights, bribe some judge to approve and expedite it, then steal Jackson away from me and finish what he started in the woods. Maybe he'll have me killed first so I'll have no chance of protecting Jackson or trying to find him when he goes missing. Can't you imagine it, Owen!" Tears flowed, right there in public. "I don't understand why God is allowing this—haven't I been through enough?"

I couldn't get a word in.

"You're bound to want to break up with me, Owen, seeing me like this." She stared at the grayish tile floor and rubbed the back of her neck—the black coiled clump she knew was there but couldn't touch. "It's not like I blame you. You don't have to pretend you still want to be with me." She cupped her mouth with a trembling hand and took deep breaths, like she was on the brink of a nervous breakdown.

I wanted to hold her and try to embrace away her fears, but this was no time to coddle her. Not *her*, the fiercest girl I'd ever known. She needed to be reminded of who she was, the unshakable courage she'd always possessed.

I took her by the hand and led her outside the church, to the grassy side of the building where we could be alone. "Look at me, Ray Anne." She wiped her cheeks, then tilted her chin up, squinting in the sunlight. "I'm suffering through some hard things too right now, and yeah, it gets scary sometimes. But we can't assume or expect the worst, and we *cannot* cave to fear."

"I don't want to be afraid," she said. "I just feel so alone."

I lowered to one knee, not to propose again but, like, as a sign of humility. "I know we're not married, Ray Anne, but you're the closest thing I have to family. And I want you to know something." I hadn't expected my throat to start throbbing, but it's not like I was going to cry in front of her. "I will *never* abandon my family, Ray. It's what some men do, but not me—you hear me? I'm not breaking up with you or going anywhere. You're not alone."

She embraced my neck, sniffling, resting her chin on the top of my head. I closed my eyes, refusing to look at the tail wrapped around her throat. We stayed that way awhile, until she asked me a question. A hard one I hadn't seen coming.

"How come we never say *I love you*?"

I stood and dusted grass off my jeans.

"You've never told me, Owen, even when you proposed. And I've never said it to you either. Don't you think that's weird?"

Of course I did.

I actually had said it once, back in high school, but it was right after she'd been shot, and she'd been unconscious and hadn't heard me. And I hadn't said it since then because . . .

"I don't know why we don't say it, Ray. I guess we both have issues. Serious ones."

She didn't deny it.

"There you are!" Mrs. Greiner came up to us, pushing Jackson's stroller and panting like she'd been afraid she'd never see her daughter again. Unlike Ray, her mom had been an uptight, fearful person as long as I'd known her.

We all went inside and filed into the third row from the stage, next to Ray Anne's dad, then sang along to the music. Ethan held a microphone in one hand, the other raised high in the air to show everyone how devoted and spiritual he was. Or maybe he just really loved God, and that's how he expressed it. Every time he worshiped, colorful light would swirl around him—all over him and others throughout the sanctuary. Those who really meant what they were singing. I knew that was the case because the shimmering rainbow, made of familiar colors as well as some not found in the earthly spectrum, would dance around me too whenever I blocked out distractions and made a point to sing the words to God instead of just mouthing them.

I noticed some people would suffer a certain unfortunate fate every Sunday. The instant the singing started, Creepers would cover their ears, no doubt filling their heads with soul-noise interference so they couldn't focus.

As for me, I liked the way worship made me feel, like God was bigger than all my problems and everything was going to be okay, even if I couldn't imagine how. Which was definitely the case right now.

Eventually Pastor Gordon took the stage and instructed us to greet the strangers around us as if we were friends—not that he said it like that. I happened to glance at the back of the sanctuary and spot Detective Benny, of all people, in the back row. It was weird enough he was at church and had Zella and Gentry with him, but the way he was staring at me—like he was about to run down the aisle and choke me—told me something was definitely up.

I'd recently had two forbidden conversations, one with Veronica and the other with Officer McFarland. Did he know?

Pastor Gordon motioned for all to take a seat, then stood silently behind the wooden pulpit, heavy-eyed—not just his shadowy, slumbering soul, but his physical face, like something was seriously wrong. "For those who have not heard the tragic news, I regret to inform you that Deputy Officer James McFarland died last night in an unfortunate boating accident . . ."

I didn't hear anything after that.

Slowly, my jaw gaping, I turned and peered over my shoulder. Detective Benny met my gaze with a single, narrow-eyed nod. I faced forward again, my mind reeling. My heart hammering.

That was no *unfortunate accident*.

I'd given Officer McFarland a tip about Benny, and he'd obviously gone poking around. Maybe even questioned the detective. And now the man was dead. A shackled man, suffering for eternity . . .

Because of *me*.

Another casualty of my naive mistakes. And yet another victim of Masonville's secret society.

Ray Anne cried on my shoulder, even more distraught now. I wove my fingers between hers, determined to be strong enough for the both of us, trying to block out the mental image of James McFarland being murdered, only to have his soul ripped away and cast into the pit. Banished to eternal hopelessness.

I looked back a second time, and Benny was leaving, ushering Gentry and Zella out the back doors of the sanctuary. I figured he'd brought them along to threaten me—to let me know they were under his control, just like the rest of this town, and I'd better back off or who knows what would become of them. His own daughter, for crying out loud.

As for the guilt and grief over McFarland's death, I had no choice but to stuff it for now—to let it fuel my determination, not stop me in my tracks. I'd deal with the emotional fallout later, when Molek and the Rulers were defeated. And Detective Benny was behind bars.

That afternoon, I paced the empty sanctuary during a phone conversation with Elle. I didn't want to be confined to my tainted room. Elle was equally convinced McFarland's death was no accident. "The occult targets the people around you," she explained, "working their way to those you care about most. It's how they intimidate and silence potential whistleblowers like us. It's why we have to be so careful."

I chose to interpret that as her way of not blaming me for McFarland's death.

"Trust me, Owen, I'm working on a plan to expose these people as soon as possible."

She and I agreed she'd continue the investigative side of things while I stayed focused on the spiritual battlefront. I told her what to do to drive the nighttime intruders from her home and sent her screenshots of my note cards.

"It's that simple?" she questioned.

"Was for me."

I dodged explaining the rest of my unsuccessful night, just like I had with Ray Anne. It was too much to focus on at once.

"Hmmm . . ." Elle made the hum that meant she was concentrating. "Concerning the witches, do you think maybe we're dealing with astral projection?"

"Astral *what*?"

She explained that people can tap into demonic powers that make it possible for their spirits to leave their bodies and go harass others.

"You're kidding, right?"

"Unfortunately, no."

"So . . ." I walked up and down the center aisle of the church, trying to understand. "You're saying the human forms I saw last night could have been real people, not Creepers, whose spirits had left their bodies and actually been there, in the storage room?"

"It's possible."

I stopped and pondered the dreadful scenario. "That would mean Ray Anne was right, and Veronica really has been leaving the jail and stalking Jackson's crib. And those weird letters from the jail Veronica denied mailing to me really were from her. She completely lied to you and me yesterday about having changed her ways." I huffed into the phone. "Seriously, Elle, how much crazier can this spirit-world stuff get?"

A call-waiting beep interrupted us—and answered my question.

SEVENTEEN

IT WAS A COLLECT CALL from the Hilltop Correctional Unit. I told Elle I'd call her back.

Veronica whispered into the phone. "Listen to me. I found out someone was assigned to get inside your apartment and put a curse under your bed."

"I don't live in my apartment anymore," I said, "and don't act like you don't know that."

She was silent a moment, then spoke again, her voice pleading. "Owen, I just assumed it was your apartment. If you've moved, I have no idea where you live. I swear. But I'm telling you, someone snuck cursed objects into your bedroom. You need to go under your bed and get rid of them immediately. Take them outside and destroy them."

I charged up the stairs and into my room, lecturing into the phone. "I know about that astral project stuff, Veronica."

"Projection?"

"Whatever. I know you've been going to Ray Anne's to spy on Jackson and coming to the church to mess with me too. And those letters—"

"What? I don't know about any church, and I already told you, I'm done with that life. I haven't gone anywhere near Ray Anne or Jackson." She sounded convincing, but what else was new? "Owen, I called to help you. I meant what I said—I'm on your side." Her voice broke with emotion. "And I could really use someone on mine." There was a pause, then, "I've got to go."

She hung up, and I scolded myself for being tempted to feel bad for her. Veronica was a wicked foe, not a friend—as slimy as the soaked strands of hair that were stuck to her astral-projecting cheeks last night. *That's* why the assailants didn't morph into Creepers when I gave the spirit-world orders: because they weren't Creepers. They were witches and warlocks performing a sinister stunt I never dreamed was possible.

I dropped to my hands and knees and searched the dim, dusty space under my bed. Nothing there but a toppled stack of books. But when I slid the pile aside, I knew something wasn't right.

I put my phone in flashlight mode and aimed it at an odd heap shoved against the wall. It looked like small bones bound together by a thread of bright-red yarn, placed on top of a nest of . . .

Is that human hair?

I used the corner of a book to snag the mound and slide it out from under the bed. Sure enough, there was a wad of long hairs in all kinds of shades—human hair colors. The bones looked like chickens' wings and legs. Or maybe bats'?

In the center of the mass was an ordinary gray rock with a white pentagram painted on the smooth surface. I might have dismissed the whole thing as some stupid scare tactic had the sound of hissing not filled the air as soon as I moved the bizarre pile.

I took the plastic bin my mother had given me and dumped the contents on the floor. Then I scooped the cursed objects into the bin and hurried outside, hoping I wouldn't run into anyone and owe an explanation.

I marched toward the pond, looking for a place where I could get rid of the objects.

I settled on drowning it.

I walked to the edge of the pond and dumped the nasty clump into the water, then used a stick to drive it down into the mud bottom.

Done.

Back in my room, there was no more trace of any snake bodies winding in the walls or the unnerving sound of hissing. Their witch-crafted nest was gone.

I glanced at my cell, wishing I had Gentry's number to call and check on him. On the burner phone, I saw that my father had texted me: **Please wait for me. I'll explain.**

Was he letting me know he was coming to Masonville?

I didn't want to see him. At least I didn't *want* to want to see him.

I didn't text back.

I drove by Gentry's that afternoon, and shocker, his mother said he wasn't home, and she didn't know where he'd gone or when he'd be back.

Finally, it was almost 7:00 p.m.—time for six local student pastors to meet up on the front steps of Masonville High with Ray Anne and me. Isolation came naturally to me, but if Ray and I were going to succeed at our mission, I had to get over that.

She and I stood side by side outside the school, waiting—hoping the pastors were already called to join us and we wouldn't have to do much persuading. I was prepared to do most of the talking. She kept dabbing her eyes with a tissue and apologizing. "I'm so sorry, I can't stop crying."

I assured her it was okay and kept that same upbeat tone while explaining that, as it had turned out, she'd been right about Veronica. "It really has been her making appearances," I said, "but there's still nothing to fear—she's no match for Scripture. Quote it, Ray, and she'll run."

She didn't ask any questions or even nod. It was like she was too afraid to even acknowledge what I'd just said. On top of that, she changed the subject—my go-to maneuver, not hers.

"Where are all the Creepers?" she asked me. Other than an occasional fleeting glimpse, they were nowhere to be found on or around the school building.

I peered into the sky at the same spot where we'd witnessed Watchmen come pouring into our realm. "Maybe Heaven's army is on its way, and they know it."

The black Suburban drove slowly in front of the school, drawing our attention until it passed.

Ethan was the first to arrive, five minutes early. He managed to make Ray Anne laugh with one of his corny jokes. I wondered if she'd have laughed if the joke had come from me, but I shrugged off the pointless question.

The last guy showed up twenty minutes late, but at least all six student pastors—four men and two women—were finally here, gathered on the steps. They looked young, all but one in their twenties.

Ethan was the only person among them who had a defender seal. I was sure Ray Anne would have noticed it on him by now had she not been so anxious and distracted.

There was an awkward silence, like it was sinful for people from different churches to mingle. But that wasn't as big of an issue as the fact that two of them were shackled. There was no way the metal-lugging lady and guy would believe what we had to say, and it's not like they were in a position to link arms and fight alongside us. How could any shackled person be called to join us?

I was curious about how these people were responding to the Rulers' intensified presence in Masonville and hoped I had enough compassion to detect it, along with any chain-links or cords—baggage of the soul—they might have been lugging around. At the moment, they all appeared fine.

We circled up, facing one another, and when Ethan offered to open the occasion in prayer, a refreshing breeze blew like some sort of divine thumbs-up. His prayer was a noble one, humble and sincere, asking God to please help us work together for the greater good.

Then I spoke up, and while I introduced Ray Anne and myself, she and I both spotted one of those massive stained-glass bowls high in the air, steadily lowering toward us—a reassuring sign that something good was about to go down.

I gave a less sensational explanation of Masonville's current spiritual condition than the one I'd recently given Pastor Gordon, making a case for why we needed to start praying together, avoiding eye contact with the two shackled people in case those disgusting black scales covered their eyes. "I imagine you've noticed how lots of people around here are struggling with things like despair, strife, addiction, slumber—kind of like they're asleep, spiritually speaking. And as you already know, pornography is a big issue too."

Of the four males there besides me, all except Ethan lowered their heads. And the shackled woman too. Sure enough, as each of them eventually looked my way again, I saw it. Streaming movement in their eyes.

"The thing is, you guys . . ." I kept talking despite the huge distraction, fixing my gaze on their foreheads. "If we're going to help people, we have to start with ourselves." I swallowed my pride. "I mean, I'm having struggles myself. But it's all intended to stop us from doing what we're called to do, especially the mission to work together to transform our town."

It took me off guard when the shackled lady came and stood beside me, announcing we were all invited to attend and bring students to a concert her church was hosting. Then she returned to her place—the open cuffs on the ends of her chains slamming the cement steps—and smiled at everyone, as if that one church event was the answer to everything.

Ethan spoke up, agreeing we should start praying together as a group—now but also weekly, suggesting Masonville High as the location since the students were our biggest concern. But another guy, Brandon, shot the location down, insisting his church would be more comfortable than an outdoor spot with no AC. Then that shackled concert girl, Shelly, said she could only commit to meeting once a month, at which point Brandon mumbled something under his breath that apparently offended Shelly; she crossed her arms and shook her head.

Out of nowhere, a guy asked the others how they go about doing Communion with their students, and the subject switched entirely to that. I tried to get us back on topic, but Brandon was dominating the conversation, breaking down the process he used to pass out wafers and juice in under five minutes.

I looked up. The stained-glass bowl was fading, disappearing into the sunny sky.

This was *not* going as planned. And somehow it hadn't dawned on me that our gathering might draw major spirit-world attention. It wasn't lower-level Creepers; they remained out of sight. The Ruler Strife rose up from beneath the parking lot, in broad daylight, and charged our way. He stared me down like he knew I'd been sipping on his toxic oppression.

Then he eyed Shelly. Her shadowy soul leaned forward, out of her face, and growled at Brandon, gums flared, before slipping back inside her skin.

I slapped my hand over my mouth. Had my soul, under Strife's influence, been doing that same lurch-growl thing at people?

I saw the dread on Ray Anne's face and wrapped my arm around her. She moved and hid behind me—a first for my normally daring girlfriend. But when the next being showed up, even Strife cowered like a cornered mouse.

EIGHTEEN

IT WAS ONE OF THE TWO Cosmic Rulers Ray and I hadn't seen before. A beast all her own.

The hood on her black cloak came to a point exactly like witchcraft Creepers', and her face was only a slightly lighter shade of green than that witch character in *The Wizard of Oz.* Black knotted hair draped down past her emaciated waist, and in her right hand, she toyed with what looked like a key chain of bones—the same shapes and sizes as the ones I'd dumped in the pond a few hours ago.

She didn't walk, but sailed along the earth toward us, mumbling to herself with insane amusement. Strife stepped back, deferring to her, giving her room to close in on our group, still gathered on the front steps of the school. No wonder there were no base-level Creepers crawling outside the building. Even they feared her arrival.

As the group continued their meaningless discussion, she eyed each one of us like tasty morsels for her next batch of brew.

I could feel Ray Anne trembling against my back, tugging on the bottom of my shirt.

The witch's eyes met mine—her irises so horrifyingly black, there was no distinguishing a pupil. She moved within arm's length from me, proving my suspicion right—she was nearly three times my height.

I tilted my head back, and she held my gaze. "I see you." Her voice was shrill and raspy, like grease sizzling in a frying pan. "And you see me, don't you?" Her chapped lips parted in a predatorial grin, as if she'd been looking forward to this for centuries.

I didn't nod, much less answer. I wasn't supposed to communicate with her—with any demon. Plus, my jaws felt like they were locked. I was sure I could have pried them open and blasted her with the Name above all names, but first, I hoped to uncover her assignment—her strategic weapon against the people of Masonville.

I'd stood in the presence of intense hatred many times; it seeps from every Creeper, no matter its rank or assignment. But *this* degree of loathing rivaled Molek's. I felt her hostility physically bearing down on me, like it might snap my spine.

I was no longer aware of the conversation around me. It was as if the evening air had become a kind of shrink-wrap, enclosing the assailant and Ray and me, isolating us from the land of the living.

The Cosmic witch extended her neck at the most unnatural, disturbing angle until her pointy noise nearly touched mine. I covered my face with both hands.

"Break all the rules, boy. Every last one of them." Her mouth reeked beyond description, and mounds of death dust flung off her tongue onto the back of my hands and wrists. It stung.

She backed away like she was leaving, turning her back to me, only . . .

There she was again. Another version of her, on the flip side.

This side was arrayed in solid white, plump, and dressed like a nun—not the sweet, charitable kind, but a ruthless old hag with a scowl. Her hair was completely tucked away in her head covering, her pale, wrinkly face bulging out from skin-tight fabric. She wore a long necklace with ornate charms—symbols of world religions, including an upside-down cross. And in her hand, she clutched a thick, menacing paddle with a word singed into the wood: *LAW*.

I blinked, and she was in my face again, her eyes a captivating blue but squinting into merciless slits. She smacked the paddle hard against her blistered hand, and a wave of asphyxiating guilt washed over me, literally taking my breath away. Just like the smoky shadow in my nightmare.

"Keep the rules, boy. Every last one of them." Cobwebs shot out of her mouth and stuck to my face, blanketing my nose and mouth. I clawed at my face, struggling to breathe, but my hands couldn't touch the spirit-world strands.

"It's you." I didn't mean to talk to her. I was only thinking out loud—marveling that I'd finally come face-to-face with the demonic creature responsible for the webs I'd seen for years, strewn all over things and people—the living and the dying. This was a black widow that veiled half herself in white, no doubt the dominant Ruler among the seven.

My hands were still stinging, and I gasped for air, but unlike my nightmare, there was no faucet to rinse my hands and no way to wake up and catch my breath.

Intuition kicked in. I turned and dropped down, shoving my face into the divine light around Ray's feet. The cobwebs incinerated. Don't ask me what the people around me were thinking as I pressed my cheeks against my girlfriend's ankles. I didn't care—all that mattered was that I could breathe again.

I plunged my burning hands into her aura, and instantly, the pain ceased. I was sure a prayerful plea to God would have accomplished the same thing—he is the Light—but I took advantage of the shortcut.

Apparently the two-faced Ruler didn't like that I'd found relief. She hissed at me, extending a flapping forked tongue the length of a yardstick.

As an act of defiance, I stood and squared my shoulders, forcing myself to make eye contact. Right away, she shoved her face in mine and gnashed her rotten teeth. "Poor orphaned Owen," she sneered.

I admit, the words sliced like razors, especially given what I now knew about my father's neglect—that I essentially had been orphaned. But I refused to internalize the label.

The law-obsessed Ruler began moving in tight circles around Ray Anne and me, spinning faster and faster—a disorienting kaleidoscope of night and day. And she kept shouting, "Keep the rules! Break the rules! Keep the rules! Break the rules!"

I had an epiphany. The sixth and seventh Rulers were two in one. Legalistic religion and lawless witchcraft, trampling the earth with the same crushing pair of feet. Holier-than-thou saints and hell-conjuring Satanists, all brainwashed slaves of the same demonic tyrant—both camps convinced they're far superior to the other.

She didn't take off on a broom or disappear in a puddle of holy water. She created a dust devil that I imagined the people there could see and soon vanished in the traveling swirl of dry Texas dirt.

Ray Anne's head pressed into the middle of my back, and she clung onto my triceps as we stood there panting, disconnected from our surroundings.

I finally came to grips enough to realize the student leaders were all staring at us.

"What were you *doing*?" Ethan asked.

All I could manage was a shrug.

They were content to look away at that point and resume their conversation, which had thankfully returned to the subject of prayer yet somehow escalated into a full-blown conflict. Brandon insisted he'd already developed prayer guides we could use while Shelly argued that if we were going to start meeting regularly and praying together, we should use the prayer program her church had followed for years.

Ethan tried to suggest a compromise but got nowhere. After all, Strife was still there, hunched over, growling and whispering in people's ears. Brown sludge dripped like sweat from his face as he pitted them against one another, inciting their pride as if they were puppets on strings in his huge hands.

All the student leaders except Ethan had spirit-world cobwebs clinging to them, left behind by the paddle-carrying warden of religion. And no doubt true to her assignment, they kept defending their own specific traditions, unwilling even to listen to others' point of view.

I watched like an outsider as the disagreement intensified, and death dust mixed with tiny black chunks began spewing from their mouths—only from the Lights', though. No matter how often the shackled two chimed in with remarks as inconsiderate as the others', no grossness came out through their lips. The stuff kept flinging off the Lights' tongues, sticking to all of our faces and chests and also hovering in the air, but they couldn't feel the sting like Ray and I could. They couldn't rinse off in our auras either, and I was sure, stopping to pray together was out of the question now.

Within minutes, the spiritual airspace around us turned dim and ashen gray.

Once again, my nightmare in living color.

"Please, guys." I was done downplaying the real issue. Even if they weren't predestined to join us, they deserved to know the truth. "There's a demonic Ruler of Strife here, and he's provoking us. I feel his effects too. We have to resist him."

Brandon laughed, even though he was a Light. "Good way to ease the tension, man."

I glared at him, then spoke the straight up truth to the group as frankly as I ever had with anyone, besides Ray Anne. "I'm dead serious, you guys. Our town—make that our whole nation—is counting on us to overthrow a reigning Spirit of Death named Molek and seven Cosmic Rulers that have descended on Masonville. They're out to destroy us, and there are thirteen people—students, I think—marked to die any day now unless we find a way to intervene." All they did was stare. "Look, I get that I sound crazy, but the Bible has plenty to say about ruling powers of darkness."

That's when Strife charged at me, crouching down on all fours and snarling in my face.

"Jesus!"

That got him to back away from me, but so did everyone else.

"Was that really necessary?" Shackled Shelly. On my last nerve.

Several Creepers rose up from the concrete steps and swarmed her and the shackled guy, covering their ears—that white-noise technique I absolutely loathed.

Ray Anne finally stepped forward and stood beside me, even though she was still shaking all over. Ethan looked at her and gasped, his lingering feelings for her on full display. "Ray Anne . . . are you okay?"

She was pale. "Do you believe what Owen just said, Ethan?"

All heads turned to Masonville's most eligible young bachelor. He eyed the group before answering. "I believe we're in a spiritual battle. So, in a sense, yes."

It's hard to explain the relief that came over me, hearing someone actually say they believed me, even somewhat—someone smart whose opinion carried weight. For the first time, I thought, *Maybe, just maybe, this guy and I could actually be friends.* I could have used one.

But no, there was way too much awkwardness between us.

Brandon tossed his hands in the air like he'd had enough, and the webs clinging to his sleeves swayed with his every move. "Sorry, guys, but this isn't what I expected." He hightailed it toward his car in the parking lot, calling back at us, "No hard feelings, but I can't be a part of this."

One by one, others followed. Strife abandoned the scene too, until it was just Ray Anne and Ethan and me in front of Masonville High, engulfed in a blanket of dark haze Ethan couldn't see.

So much for worshiping together like we'd seen the Watchmen do here.

Ray Anne clung tight to my hand when all six of Molek's brown bats descended on us, flying in circles above our heads. They swooped down, flapping their bony wings, stirring the haze. Then they opened their mouths and inhaled the paranormal pollution, sucking it out of the atmosphere. Every last bit was gone in seconds.

They flew away in a lopsided formation.

Ray Anne elbowed me in the ribs, pointing behind us, at the school building. Custos was on the roof, mounted on his breathtaking white horse, his armor shimmering. His gaze followed the bats. Then he looked at me. *Really* looked at me. I got the hint.

I turned to Ray Anne. "I'm sorry to run like this, but I have to go." I started sprinting to my motorcycle. "Go to your house and wait for me—I'll be there soon!"

I wouldn't normally leave Ethan and my girlfriend alone, but this couldn't wait.

I sped past the Masonville city limits sign, then parked and ran through the cornfields, using my GPS pin to show me the way. It took half an hour, and the sun had nearly set, but at last, I spotted the dim shape of the run-down little house.

I shined my phone light, and just like I thought, the bats were clustered where I'd seen them the first time. They took turns craning their necks down, making gagging sounds that made me want to gag too.

I charged toward them, and they took flight, allowing me to stare down at my opponent. Molek was still buried in dirt up to his chin, but his clawed fingertips had breached the soil, his disturbing eyes wide open now. Slowly, he was chewing and swallowing, ingesting the potion the bats had slurped out of the air and regurgitated into his mouth. His tongue and chin and thin lips were covered in the stuff.

In my nightmare, I'd had no clue what that substance was or why it coated Molek's mouth. But I did now. The Lord of the Dead was feasting on Lights' conflict, nourished and strengthened by the discord among God's people.

I shuddered.

Hadn't I feared this all along? That no matter how hard I tried, I'd never succeed at getting people to believe in the mission and cooperate? Not one person tonight had been on board. Well, except Ethan. He seemed to be holding up well under the Rulers' concentrated influence. Better than me, honestly.

I took a final gaze at Molek. "You're defeated in Christ's name." He groaned like I'd stepped on his face but kept chewing.

I'd seen enough. I walked away, ignoring the threats and insults the bats spoke over me, still soaring above their master's recuperating body. I passed through the rows of corn, looking in every direction for the wise old man. My circumstances were more complicated than ever—surely he knew it and cared enough to show up and give me the guidance I desperately needed.

But he never came.

I parked in Ray Anne's driveway and knocked on her garage apartment door. Why wasn't her car there?

"Coming," she called out.

Okay, so she *wasn't* out with Ethan. I felt the tension leave my shoulders. As far as I knew, she still hadn't seen his defender seal. I was grateful for that—and felt a tad guilty for keeping it from her. But it was one less thing she could admire about him.

Ray Anne opened the door with Jackson on her hip. Her eyes were bloodshot like she'd been bawling.

"Are you alright?" I imagined the sight of that two-faced Ruler had really freaked her out.

She nodded, but her frown gave her away.

I eyed the driveway. "Where's your car?"

"I didn't want to be alone on the drive home. So Ethan drove me."

This was no time to be jealous, and I should have appreciated that he'd been there to help her. But what I knew and what I felt didn't always line up.

"I'm glad you're here," she said. "My parents just left to go get my car."

It was like she was a little kid, afraid to be home alone.

I started to step inside, but just then something purred really loud, like a bobcat curled up inside a megaphone. I looked toward the sound, and on my left, a mega-sized cardboard diaper box was wedged behind the front yard shrubs. The open lid flaps jostled.

I pointed to it. "What's in there?" Her mouth moved, but nothing came out. "Tell me you didn't put that box out here for that pathetic Creeper."

She swallowed hard. "He was getting chewed up by ants."

My mouth fell open. "Ray Anne, you know earthly insects can't bite a spiritual being."

"But they did."

"You're kidding, right?"

She didn't say anything.

"He's a *Creeper*, Ray Anne, and he keeps coming back to pull at your heart strings. He's deceiving you, the same way Molek tricked me."

She switched Jackson to her other hip, and, off topic as it was, I noticed how good her figure looked in her leggings and T-shirt.

"It's not like he talks to me," she said. "He just hides there and sleeps."

I huffed. "You swore you wouldn't feel sorry for it."

She huffed harder. "Can we please just drop it?"

Drop it. Great idea.

I didn't ask her permission, just traipsed behind the bushes and hoisted the box off the ground. I hadn't expected it would weigh anything, but it felt like a bowling ball was in there. I stepped through the hedge of bushes into the Greiner's front yard, and Ray Anne came running outside, still holding Jackson. "What are you doing?"

I held the box straight out, then let it go, drop-kicking it. The box sailed all the way into the street, but the Creeper passed through the cardboard and hunkered in a tight ball in the grass a few feet from me. It covered its head with both scrawny arms and squealed. Immediately, a stampede of Creepers came advancing down the street.

"Look what you did!" Ray Anne said. "They're coming to hurt him."

"Good!"

She tucked her chin and winced. Jackson eyed her face with his miniature brow furrowed, like he knew his favorite person was sad. I hurried to her, careful not to squeeze her arm too hard while leading her inside.

She pulled away from me, then practically barked, "Shut the door." She set Jackson on a blanket on his belly. "I don't want to hear the torture."

I shook my head, marveling at how deceived she was—at how the kingdom of darkness was managing to use her merciful nature against her.

I asked her to come sit by me on her futon. She grabbed some tissues and eventually lowered beside me, leaning away.

I did my best to talk some sense into her, the same way she'd pled and tried to warn me a few months ago, when I'd fallen for evil in disguise. But she stared at her shaggy rug the whole time, rocking back and forth, like she was in a trance.

"Are you even listening to me?" I asked.

"Veronica's going to kill me."

"What?" I moved to the floor and faced her on my knees. "Why would you say that?"

"She was back today. Over there." She pointed at Jackson's crib. "She looked straight at me and told me."

A sense of hatred toward Veronica welled up in me, expanding like a poisonous vine taking over my chest, but I worked to tame it before it wrapped around my soul.

"There's no form of evil we have to fear," I told her. "Nothing can harm us."

Ray Anne slid to the edge of the futon and vented like a pot boiling over, like there was no truth to what I'd just said. "She swears I'm gonna die young, just like my uncle. My mom's brother was only twenty-three when he died. And my brother was only fifteen when he . . ." She swallowed instead of saying it. "Veronica said early deaths run in my family, and she promised I'm next. She vowed to end my life when I least expect it, then she'll get Jackson, and there'll be nothing I can do about it."

There are moments when divine revelation comes so swiftly, so obviously, it's as if the earth stops spinning. That's what happened as I knelt there, listening to my girlfriend pour out her petrified heart.

The kingdom of darkness had overplayed its hand.

I clutched her clammy fingers. "Ray Anne, what if that curse is fear? That snake in your neck was moving the whole time you talked about every scary thing you dread. Maybe your family does struggle with fear more than most, and maybe it even has something to do with the premature deaths, but you don't have to give in. All we have to do is figure out how to break the curse off you."

I couldn't exactly rip the snake out of her neck and dump it in the pond with the ones from my room, but I was sure there was a way she could be delivered. I knew evil masquerades as having the upper hand yet never truly does.

Ray Anne gripped the back of her neck, nearly hyperventilating.

"It'll be okay." I said it over and over, but it didn't help. "Should I go get your mom?" I couldn't just sit there, watching Ray Anne gasping in panic.

"No. She overreacts to everything."

True, but I didn't want to make the mistake of underreacting either. I'd never seen my girlfriend this distraught.

Ray begged me again not to involve her mom, so I hugged her and did my best to coach her through some calming breaths. Then I bolted off the floor, inspecting the place, looking under her bed and beneath the crib. "Have you seen any bones and yarn, like, in a nest of hair?"

She shook her head.

"Someone planted one in my room at the church. It was a witchcraft curse."

"Who would do that?"

"I have no idea." I kept searching. "If you happen to find something weird like that, get it out of here immediately. Throw it into a drainage ditch in the street or something."

I went back to my same pose on my knees in front of her, leaning in close. "I don't know how to break curses off people yet, but I'm absolutely positive God has a way. And I'm telling you, I *will* figure it out, Ray Anne. I won't rest until I do."

She released her head into my chest and cried on my T-shirt. "Where's all my faith gone?"

Honestly, I'd been wondering the same thing. I ran my finger over her defender seal, still as vibrant as ever. "It's still here. Your destiny hasn't changed. You've just let the voice of evil paralyze you."

"Thank God I have you." She pressed her soaked cheek against mine. "I . . ."

I thought this was it. She was going to say she loved me.

"I'm so sorry I can't get it together," she said.

I kept holding her, swaying with her. "You don't have to apologize for anything, Ray."

I stayed there until she finally relaxed enough to fall asleep in my arms.

Back at the church, I took Daisy outside. I gazed up at the moonlit balcony attached to my room, then eyed the pond a short distance from where my dog was sniffing around. All was still. No sign of Custos or his warriors and no waterlogged witches. No squalling babies either, thank God.

I'd promised Ray Anne I'd uncover how to break curses, and I intended to keep my word.

I couldn't think of a single person to call on for help. Betty didn't need all this stress, and my father was no longer an option. I actually considered Ethan but immediately shot the idea down. My situation had to be far beyond anything Mr. "Sheltered All My Life" had ever experienced. As noble and spiritual as he was, he wouldn't know how to fix this. They didn't exactly teach how to disarm curses at choir practice.

It was time to take the training wheels off my spiritual maturity and figure this curse-breaking thing out myself. With God's help, of course.

I didn't need more motivation, but some came anyway. I spied a brood of spirit-world snakes slithering in and out of the pond at the exact spot where I'd dumped the cursed objects. So, even though I'd removed the curse from my room and submerged it under water, it hadn't drowned out its power.

I popped my knuckles, sensing it was going to be another sleepless, intense night.

NINETEEN

I SAT ON MY BED WITH MY LAPTOP. "Lord, show me how to break curses—how to get rid of the snakes, starting with the one in my girlfriend's neck."

I knew if I did an online search for articles, I'd have to weed through all kinds of New Age, mystical websites—as if trendy witchcraft is an effective way to combat overt witchcraft. So, I pulled up the Bible online and searched the Scriptures.

It turned out nearly 170 Bible verses address curses, confirming what I already knew—they're a real thing, not some hokey superstition. I clicked through the list of Scriptures and nearly fell off my bed when I saw that the King James Version describes curses as a *hissing*.

Yes, people could attempt to curse others through spells, rituals, and cursed objects, but based on all I was reading, no snake—no curse—was allowed to penetrate a Light without cause. And get this: throughout the Old Testament, there were examples of people—and even God—declaring that whoever attempted to loose a curse on a person who served God evoked a curse in return. That would mean whoever put that hairy-yarn thing under my bed had invited those same snakes on herself. Or himself. And same for all the covens cursing Elle and Ray and me.

Was it wrong that I was happy about that?

Yes, I quickly learned. A verse in Luke said to bless and pray for those who curse us.

There went my biblical backing for revenge.

I also learned that curses could come on people without any use of witchcraft, when people live in stubborn defiance to God. Acts of rebellion could open a spirit-world snake hole of sorts for serpents to slither into people's circumstances and work against them, binding them to ongoing failure and misfortune—the exact opposite of blessings. And if I was interpreting the Scriptures correctly, curses could even be generational, meaning parents could pass down their serpents to their children, grandchildren, and so on.

I cringed. Given my family history, it was a wonder I didn't have snakes coiled around every inch of my body.

One verse stood out to me. Galatians 3:13. It basically said that on the cross, Christ took the curses on himself that we deserve so we can be free of them. It wasn't fair to him, but what else is new?

I pressed my palm over my mouth, sickened at the thought of having my own hands and feet nailed down, enduring the agony of crucifixion, while feeling snakes crawling all over my body.

I took some deep breaths, working to force the mental image to fade.

So, the way I now understood it, that hissing curse wrapped around Ray Anne's spine had no right to be there, sentencing her to nonstop discouragement, panicky dread, and—God forbid—a premature death. But as long as she caved to fear instead of clinging to faith, it was never going to leave. Ray Anne needed to stand up for herself. For her God-given rights.

Surely once I explained the simplicity of that to her, she'd have a change of heart and be brave enough to command the curse to go. I would have gone to her and told her right then had it not been two in the morning.

I'd just closed my laptop when Daisy sprang awake and growled at the window.

Here we go again.

I peeked out the sheers. Nothing on my balcony, but the way my dog was carrying on, something had to be out there. I grabbed my baseball bat and flashlight, ran downstairs, then charged out the door with my dog, ready to face whatever person or paranormal being had made the mistake of trespassing. Sure, I wanted to protect the church's property, but this went way beyond that. I took it personally that someone or something would try to get past me.

I made it all the way to the pond, where my flashlight illuminated a cluster of spirit-realm snakes slithering above the sunken thread, bones, and nasty clump of human hair.

"Christ took this curse for me."

The serpents dove down, away from me, hunkering under the water. But they were still alive.

Maybe Veronica had been telling the truth, and I needed to completely destroy the hexed objects.

After some thought, I decided God was bound to approve of me annihilating demonically charged objects off the face of his earth. I just had to decide how.

Incineration came to mind.

I ran back to my room and grabbed a box of matches, then dragged a metal trash can full of tree limbs from behind the building, all the way to the pond. I used two long sticks to fish the red-threaded blob out of the water, covered in the mass of snakes, and dumped the mess in the trash can.

I tossed in a few lit matches, but the fire only consumed the tree leaves and limbs. It startled me when, out of nowhere, a huge hand formed, made of flames. It gripped the snakes and nest, crushing all of it with a blazing balled fist. Instantly, the cursed objects and serpents turned to ash.

"So freaking cool."

If only I could have captured stuff like this on video.

I stayed and watched the ashes trickle toward the bottom of the can, acknowledging that Veronica had been right about needing to destroy the thing—even though her helpfulness majorly contradicted the acts of viciousness she was also unleashing on me.

Still standing at the pond, I had that undeniable sense someone was watching me. I shined my flashlight across the water. Sure enough, the wet witches—Veronica included—glared at me from the other side, their ankles submerged in pond water.

Somehow it was freakier now, knowing they were not Creepers but real people—rebellious spirits roaming outside catatonic bodies. They whispered at me, their lips moving as my flashlight remained fixed on their cluster. I'd run them off last night; surely they knew to keep their distance from me. But clearly, they hadn't given up their assignment against me.

I didn't have my note cards, but I recited verses as I recalled them, starting with the one I'd just used on the snakes. One by one, the spirits ran forward, charging into the water without causing any splashing. But instead of coming at me, they disappeared under the tide, resurfacing in the center of the pond. Like a scene from a horror movie, their heads bobbed, eyes hovering just above the waterline.

It didn't come naturally, but I turned my back on them, proving I wasn't afraid. I walked toward the church building, and when they didn't follow, I knew my act of faith had worked. And when they sank out of sight completely, it felt like the tables had turned in my favor for the second night in a row.

I was calling Daisy to me when an infant's cries echoed in the distance. *The* infant.

I looked around. "What *is* that, Lord?"

No internal answer.

Even in bed with my music playing in my ear pods, I could hear it. I quoted every Scripture I knew and even yelled the name of Jesus, but there was no silencing the child.

I'd found nothing in the Bible about wicked wailing babies. Believe me, I'd checked.

I thanked God when Custos appeared and knelt in the center of my room. His arrival shut the baby up, and once I finally quit analyzing whether or not my father was on his way to see me, I fell asleep.

On Monday afternoon, the Masonville High multi-purpose gym was a sea of tan chairs—occupied ones facing empty ones where students would soon sit.

So, this is how the mentoring program works.

I was the youngest mentor here by far. And the only one who could see Creepers scampering across the ceiling, weaving in and out of the walls and hovering as high as the basketball goals, spying down on us like starving vultures. They didn't move as quickly as when Molek was here, infusing his army with sinister strength, but they were still on the hunt.

While waiting on Gentry, I texted Elle: **Did you get rid of your night-time stalkers?**

She texted back immediately: **Your strategy worked, thank you!** Seconds later: **We should write a book about all of this someday.**

Maybe, I replied. **Let's see how things turn out first.**

I hit send, then typed: **And if we survive.** But I deleted that faithless remark.

I hadn't heard anything from my father since his last confusing text. My frustration toward him was growing, but apparently I hadn't become so bitter that I'd provoked Creepers to chain my neck.

I dragged my thoughts back to Gentry. Finally, a chance to talk to him. He was among a flood of incoming students, his head draped in a hoodie that hung so low, I was surprised he could see to find me. I didn't pick up on any facial mask of addiction or disgusting belly dagger today, but the black streak under his chin was in plain sight.

Numerous students escorted Creepers, tethered to them by their spirit-world chains and cords, but thankfully Gentry didn't have that going on. His four open chain cuffs dragged the gym floor—a lot of metal baggage for a fifteen-year-old. He sat across from me, and I smiled. His mouth stayed flat. The puffy bags under his eyes made me wonder if he'd slept at all the night before. And his bottom lip was cut in the center, crusted with dried blood.

A dark-skinned armored Watchman appeared out of thin air in a swirl of light and stood behind Gentry, watching us. I wanted to take in every detail of his armor, but I needed to stay focused. And try not to squint. It was awesome the way the Creepers raced to the other side of the gym, all hunkered down and nervous now that a Watchman was here.

I reached out to give Gentry a fist bump. He gave me one but rolled his eyes.

"So, they obviously told you I'm your mentor." He barely nodded. This was way more awkward than I'd expected. "Umm . . . how are things?"

He gave me a disinterested shrug like we were total strangers, like he had no memory of the good times we'd had when he was younger.

He grabbed something out of his backpack and began toying with it, clutching it tight enough to conceal it from me. It reminded me of Hector last school year, how he'd obsessively hold that vocatus crystal— an occult object Veronica had given him.

"So, you like wearing hoodies, huh?" I tried a lighthearted approach. And seriously, it was ninety degrees outside.

Another disinterested shrug.

I get that it was impulsive of me, but I hadn't come here just to be dismissed by him. And I mean, the guy's life was in jeopardy. I leaned in. "Gentry, I know this won't make sense to you, but you're in serious danger. Like, life-threatening. And I'm here to help, but I can't unless you open up to me."

I knew I probably sounded fatherly and weird, but this was my chance to talk to him without any Creepers closing in and covering his ears. That Watchman was protecting him, guarding our conversation.

Gentry didn't flinch or even ask why I suspected his life was on the line. Instead he crossed his arms, still clutching something. "My life completely sucks. What else do you want to know?"

"What sucks about it?"

He was pouty and shifty-eyed, the same way I'd been with the school counselor here when she'd tried sticking her nose in my business.

He mumbled, "My stepdad wants me out of the house."

"Why?"

He stared at his Converse, tapping the gym floor. "My brother Chase is a Marine, kicking butt overseas. And Lance is like a god around here, training at the police academy. Then there's me—the loser flunking ninth grade."

From the pictures of Chase I'd seen a while back, Lance and Gentry's oldest brother truly was a man's man. And after Lance had survived his nearly-fatal wounds from Dan's school shooting, he'd become a town hero. They'd even named a street after him. But that didn't make Gentry a loser. "Dude, it's only the second week of school; I'm sure you can pass ninth grade. And just because your older brothers have accomplished some things doesn't mean there's anything wrong with you."

He shook his head, and I caught an unnatural flicker in his brown eyes. The indwelling presence of evil, badgering him from within. This wasn't the time or place to try casting it out, but I felt bad for Gentry, having to live like that. *With* that.

How had he opened himself up to such a severe degree of evil influence? I was certain it had to do with Veronica—or Eva, as she'd told him to call her.

"How'd you bust your lip?" I asked.

"A guy accused me of being a traitor and socked me in the mouth."

"A traitor?"

"Hector thinks I reported him for selling at school, but I didn't."

I already knew there were no coincidences, but this was even more confirmation. I knew Hector from last school year. Another one of Veronica's blind followers. He'd wrestled Jackson out of my arms at the secret ritual.

"Hector's who you get your stuff from?" Drugs, we both knew.

The third shrug in less than a minute. In other words, *yes*.

"How'd you meet him?"

More looking down and fidgeting. "He used to hang around Eva. He was cool at first, but he hates me now."

I wasn't surprised Veronica was intertwined in the situation.

Gentry's fingers were really moving now, spinning something around and around.

"What's in your hand?" I couldn't keep ignoring it. But he kept his palm closed as tightly as his mouth. So, I straight up asked him, "Is it a vocatus?"

He finally looked me in the face. "You—you know about that?"

I nodded, then assured him he could tell me anything and everything—and he needed to.

Slowly, Gentry relaxed his hand, exposing the oblong crystal—the reward for having been selected to join Veronica's exclusive, seemingly-innocent meditation group.

"Eva gave it to me last school year," Gentry said.

"You were in her program?" I had no clue she'd been targeting middle school kids too.

He coughed like he was buying time to think. "I learn from her, if that's what you mean."

"You mean *learned*, right?"

He blinked fast. "Forget it. It doesn't matter."

"Yes, it does." I scooted my chair closer to him. "I know you won't understand this, but I've been called to protect you, and that's what I'm trying to do. Seriously. So please tell me, have you been visiting Veronica—Eva—in jail?"

He stuffed both hands into his jeans, I think because they started shaking, either from nerves or withdrawal. "She . . ."

"Yeah?" I put a reassuring hand on his bony shoulder, and the Watchman stepped forward, resting his hand over mine. Instant peace.

"Eva comes to me," Gentry finally admitted. "Don't ask me how, but she meets with me in the woods. When I go by myself."

I almost used my free hand to slap an open palm against my forehead. Gentry was entangled in even more of a spirit-world mess than I'd realized. And he didn't have a clue.

There was only so much I could explain, especially while seated within earshot of others. "Meeting with her like that, it's extremely dangerous."

"I know." Gentry's eyes became glossy, and he looked away, pulling his hood down lower, covering most of his face. I finally let go of his shoulder, but the Watchman's hand remained, a look of concern on his ageless face.

Gentry whispered, "She says I *have* to meet with her and tells me when and where." He tugged nervously at the cuffs of his long sleeves. "I'm scared not to."

Finally, some vulnerability.

"I need you to come see me after school." I told him where I was staying and the street the church was on. "There's a lot we have to talk about, but not here, in a crowd."

"I have detention after school, and my mom said I'm grounded tonight. But I can probably come tomorrow."

Give me a break. He snuck out whenever he wanted. But he shot down all my attempts at talking him into it. "Tomorrow, then," I finally conceded. "And *please*, Gentry, between now and then, stay out of the woods and away from Veronica—Eva—no matter how she's threatened you."

He gave a reluctant nod. "I can try, but she'll get mad."

I understood where he was coming from; I'd been there myself a few months ago. And to make matters worse, Gentry was shackled, not a Light like me, *and* he was housing evil inside—about as defenseless as it gets. "I'll be here for you through this," I vowed. "Every step of the way."

The Watchman left, vanishing as unexpectedly as he'd arrived. So of course the Creepers took over the gym again.

Principal Harding walked by, still mummified in webs—trapped in religious traditions and legalism, I now understood. She scanned the crowd with a satisfied smile. I scooted my chair back, trying to look as casual as everyone else.

I noticed a purple-haired girl seated nearby—not because of her hair, but because she had a black streak across her throat, identical to Gentry's. That, plus a Creeper looming behind her back, staring her down. Those signature eyes: blood-red misshapen pupils inside a yellowish ring. And that dreaded name scraped into its face: *Suicide*.

"Hey, do you know her?" I pointed.

Gentry nodded. "Presley. She's in my support group." He huffed. "It's so obvious they put all the suicidal people together."

"Wait . . . you're suicidal?"

He sank lower in his chair. "The counselor lady already told my parents, so don't bother tattling on me." He froze. "Wait—you're not gonna tell Lance, right?"

"Your brother and I don't talk anymore."

He spun the vocatus back and forth between his index finger and thumb, like he was flaunting it now, but his shoulders slumped.

"Have you ever attempted suicide?" I asked him.

It took him a while to confess. "Yeah. Everyone in the group has."

"Including Zella?"

He nodded. "All of us."

Not good. "How many are in your group?" I held my breath.

"Thirteen."

My stomach twisted . . .

We've marked all thirteen . . . The words came back to me—Molek's messenger bats, commissioning the Rulers. *Every one of them must die.*

I knew then that all thirteen members of Gentry's support group likely bore the demon world's mark to die as soon as possible. And all basically wanted to.

Gentry smirked like he was half-kidding. "So, are you out to protect just me or the whole group of us?"

I leaned back in my chair, tilting my elbow to steal a glance at my luminescent seal. "I believe it's my job to defend all of you."

He kept his chin down but cut his eyes up at me, his gaze no longer boyish or timid. It was a chilling stare that made the hairs on my neck stand at attention. Gentry's voice lowered and his face morphed into a sinister scowl. "What makes you think you can possibly defend *any* of us?"

My heart rate spiked. The devil inside him had just questioned me. My best guess: another Creeper named Suicide. For all I knew, the exact one that had squeezed itself inside Meagan our senior year and provoked her to end her life.

"Gentry, listen to me." It was my way of calling him forward, so to speak—communicating with Gentry instead of the assassin within. Immediately, his gaze softened. "You're in deep trouble," I told him, "but there's a way out. I can help you."

He nodded, actually seeming grateful, wiping his damp eyes on his sleeve before admitting, "I don't think I can live like this much longer."

Every Creeper in the gym turned and faced Gentry, including the one attached to purple-haired Presley. It was the worst time to have part ways, but the bell rang.

At least I had some answers now. And I knew I'd better get some solutions fast.

TWENTY

I LEFT MASONVILLE HIGH and headed to Ray Anne's, lost in thought. Why would the kingdom of darkness target thirteen suicidal kids? It's not like they were outspoken Lights on a mission to overthrow evil's plot. Then again, maybe it was the other way around. Maybe the thirteen students were suicidal *because* the kingdom of darkness was after them, targeting them specifically, for reasons I had yet to uncover.

I parked against the curb in front of Ray Anne's house at the same time her mom was backing out of the driveway. The windows of Mrs. Greiner's white Explorer were down, and Jackson was waving his little arms in his car seat strapped in the back.

Mrs. Greiner saw me and stopped. I approached her open window. Her aura illuminated the floorboard and pedals.

"Good morning, Mrs. Greiner."

"Hey, Owen. Ray Anne has a lot of schoolwork today, so I'm taking Jackson to the zoo." She peeked at Jackson in the rearview mirror and spoke in baby talk, naming the animals they'd see.

I'd never seen Mrs. Greiner's shoulder-length hair tied back in a ponytail before, which wouldn't be worth mentioning except that for the first time ever, it gave me a clear view of the back of her neck. I tried not to cringe. An eyeless serpent was coiled at the top of her spine, in the same spot as Ray Anne's.

Maybe I'd been right, and Ray's fear really was a generational curse?

"I trust you're not staying long?" Mrs. Greiner didn't like me being alone with Ray in her garage apartment, and ever since I'd proposed, I got the feeling she didn't like me coming around as much. She still liked *me*; I just think in her mind, I'd become the person who might one day take her daughter away. Her only child, since Lucas died.

"I'm here to cheer her up," I said.

Oops. I would have hit a rewind button if only life came with one.

"Is something wrong with Ray Anne?" Mrs. Greiner plunged her head out the window, her cheeks instantly red. "Please, Owen, if something has got my girl down, I need you to tell me right now. Is she upset because we've had a difficult time paying her college tuition?" She lowered her voice so Jackson couldn't hear. "Or because caring for a child is too much? She doesn't tell me anything anymore."

Because you're an overbearing worrywart, I thought. Not that I completely blamed her. Mrs. Greiner's fifteen-year-old son had committed suicide, despite her best efforts to rescue him out of his depression. But from day one, the way I'd witnessed her hover over Ray Anne seemed to me like more than devoted motherly concern. The wide-eyed, panicked look on Mrs. Greiner's face right now was full-on fear, like a child eyeing a closed closet door, convinced there's a flesh-eating monster behind it. And it was hardly the first time I'd seen her like that.

It was the identical expression Ray Anne had lately, especially while rehearsing the ways Jackson might come to harm. The exact same curse coiled around her neck.

"Ray Anne just has a lot on her mind," I told her mom. The truth minus specifics.

Unfortunately, Mrs. Greiner only kept interrogating me, probing for details.

"She'll be fine," I said repeatedly, watching in revulsion as the snake embedded in Mrs. Greiner's skin started twisting, roused to action by her fearful fretting.

I tried to assure her all was well, but nothing I said relaxed her. Or the serpent.

Mrs. Greiner put her SUV in park and took her foot off the brake. "Maybe I should stay home with Ray Anne today."

"No," I said. "I'll help her get her homework done, then I'll get her out of the house for some fresh air."

It wasn't easy, but I finally talked Ray's mom into backing out of the driveway and leaving.

I had my fist up, ready to knock on Ray Anne's door, when I saw that diaper box behind the shrubs again, farther from the door this time. I sidestepped over to it and folded the lid back.

"Sick!"

There were *two* pale-pink Creepers in there now, their arms and legs wrapped around each other and their faces crammed together—not like hatchling creatures snuggled in a nest, but more like a pair of villains with their hands all over each other.

To make matters worse, a bath towel lined the bottom of the box—the same shade of light blue as I'd seen folded in laundry baskets at Ray Anne's.

She put it in there.

To make the monsters comfortable.

They saw me and started squealing, clinging even tighter to one another's emaciated bodies.

I heard the door fly open, and Ray Anne hollered, "Hey, what's going—"

It was super awkward when she realized it was me messing with the box. We stared at each other, both aware she'd just set out to defend demons.

"Ray Anne, you'd seriously run out here and use your light to protect them from other Creepers?" I picked up the weighted box and turned it upside down, but all that fell out was her towel. "You're acting like they're your pets."

"What do you mean, *they*?"

Ah. She didn't know another one had joined the party. And by *party*, I mean the evil operation to gain access to her life through her misguided sympathy, no doubt to eventually harm her in some devastating way. Maybe even fatally—the very thing she feared. It was my worst fear too, though I tried to suppress it.

I dropped the box on its open lid, and the fakers whined like it actually hurt them to fall.

Ray Anne made her way over, inching behind the shrubs in denim shorts and sandals. She peeked beneath the overturned box. "Another one?"

"What'd you expect? When you play around with evil, it grows bigger and stronger, Ray Anne. It's only when you hate it and make it go away that it gets weaker and backs off."

"I'm not *playing around* with them."

I grabbed the towel and waved it in her face. "You made them a *bed*." I kicked the box, but not nearly hard enough. It wedged sideways in the bushes. The Creepers scrambled to get back inside like frightened toddlers. "What's next?" I asked her. "Bath time and bottles?"

She crossed her arms airtight. "I can't help that I have a heart."

That one made my blood boil, but I took a deep breath and forced myself to chill. "Babe, there's never any form of evil that deserves the slightest bit of mercy, no matter the situation."

I waited for her to realize and admit how unreasonable she was being, but she just stood there, eyes going glossy. "I can't deal with this right now." She turned her back on me and headed toward the door.

I could take the easy way out and blame what I said next on the effects of Strife's presence in Masonville, but the anger surged from within and came bursting out of my mouth. "What *can* you deal with anymore, huh, Ray Anne?"

She jerked to a stop, like I'd hurled a javelin into her back. And to my instant regret, I basically had. "Please," I begged her, "ignore what I just said. I didn't mean it."

She didn't move a muscle at first, then finally stormed past her door and stomped into her front yard. She dropped to the grass and wrapped her arms around her bent knees, dropping her head onto them. I lowered beside her beneath the beaming-blue sky, as close to her as I could get. I rubbed gentle circles between her shoulder blades, not willing to let the thought—or icy feel—of that snake inside her stop me from consoling her. It ran the full length of her spine.

"Please don't." She moved my hand away, then reached and cupped the back of her neck above her shirt collar, covering the reptile's head. "Is there anything else in me or on me I need to know about?"

"No, Ray Anne. I swear."

"You promise?"

I'd just sworn, but I promised too, then assured her once again, "It's okay, you don't have to cover anything up."

I rubbed her fingers, but she refused to loosen her grip on her neck. "You were right, Owen. I can't deal with anything anymore."

"That wasn't fair of me."

"It's true." She looked up at me, more angry than sad, I think. Furious at herself. "I've never felt so defeated. So helpless to stop being afraid and suck it up and get my act together."

"Fear's paralyzing," I reminded her, trying to understand and encourage, not lecture.

"And faith is liberating," she said. "But for the life of me, I can't seem to conquer this anxiety—this overwhelming fear that, any day now, the worst is going to happen. To me, yes, but to Jackson, too. He's who I'm really worried about. And if something ever happened to you, Owen—"

Even with her hand on the back of her neck, I could still see the snake's body begin to twist.

"You're panicking over Jackson," I said, "just like your mom panics over you."

"What?"

I wanted to explain things, but not here, in her front yard, where deceiving Creepers were jumbled in a box. We needed to distance ourselves. Get as far away from all things oppressive as we possibly could.

I stood and reached out to her. She grabbed my hand, and I led her to my motorcycle, then handed her a helmet.

"Where are we going?"

I gave a playful shrug and grinned, pretending not to know.

She cracked a smile for what seemed like the first time in forever, then hopped on.

She spotted the familiar lakeside gazebo before I did, nestled in its scenic spot two towns away from Masonville. It was the same lake we'd escaped to the night of our senior prom. I veered off the road and parked in the grass.

We walked hand in hand up the steps into the white wooden gazebo and stood in the center, looking out at the rippling water and surrounding trees. It felt like the shade was fanning my stressed soul. I hoped she was experiencing similar relief.

It had been quiet for all of sixty soothing seconds when Ray Anne dug her nails into my hand. "How are we supposed to work with other Lights and carry out Arthur's instructions when our meeting on Sunday was such a total disaster?"

Her question was timely and important—vital, even—yet it totally clashed with the calming bird chirps and rustling leaves around us. I had a lot to tell her, and yes, we had some serious things to discuss. But I was nineteen years old and full of energy, desperate to let loose a little. She needed that even more than I did.

I started untying and removing my shoes, then emptying the pockets of my basketball shorts.

"What are you doing?" She crinkled her nose.

I flashed her a flirtatious smile, then ran toward the lake, pulling my T-shirt off and tossing it to the grass. My feet sank into the mud as I charged into the water, trudging deeper until the tide had engulfed my shorts and water sloshed above my waist.

I turned to wave Ray Anne on, but she was already barefoot and running toward the water—smiling, even. Having fun for a change. Shorts and T-shirt and all, she ran to me, and I spun her around, then dunked her completely under water with me. We came up for air at the same time, both cracking up and basking in the cool water mixed with the toasty feel of the sun on our heads.

The water was all the way up to Ray Anne's shoulders. She brushed her soaked hair away from her beautiful face, then interlocked her fingers around the back of my neck. I've got to say, it took me by surprise when she wrapped her legs around my waist. I didn't recall ever being *that* physically close to her before. The feel of her body against mine, her soft skin touching me all over . . .

Was there even a word in the human language to describe the feeling?

Yes, I was insanely attracted to her, but coupled with all the emotion—the intense attachment I had toward her—it was like the perfect explosive combination.

No, more like the perfect storm surge. She was saving herself for marriage, so there was nowhere to go from here except to stuff all that desire into a musty storm cellar known as *restraint*. It wasn't gratifying or fun, but I'd come to understand by now: she wanted to be treasured, not targeted. And she wanted to honor and obey God.

How could I not admire that?

She rested her chin on my bare shoulder and stroked my hair above the back of my neck like she was filled with affection for me. She seemed determined to forget about spirit-world invaders for now. Minutes passed, and the water lapped against our skin, both of us content to be so close.

"I know why I've never told you I love you, Owen."

I waited for her to explain, feeling like I'd forgotten how to breathe.

"It's because I'm terrified of losing you—of having no control and suddenly being separated from someone I can't imagine living without. And I think somehow, if I guard my heart against saying those words, it helps silence the fear. At least most of the time."

"Maybe because of how you suddenly lost your brother?"

It took her a second to confess. "Probably so."

I waded through the water, still holding her, feeling a sense of pride, as if I were bravely leading us somewhere important, even though I was only treading through a small hill country lake.

"I want this thing out of me," she said, snapping me back into reality—a world where curses coil inside of people.

I told her all I'd learned about curses, reciting the verse out of Galatians and also describing how things had played out the night before with the snakes and cursed objects from the pond. "If you'd just stand up to the curse that's got you," I told her, "resist all the fear, and come at that snake with that verse, it would have no choice but to go."

"Seriously, Owen? I know that verse—you don't think I've tried?"

"You have to really believe it, Ray Anne."

"Stop it!" She was instantly irate. She let go of my neck and pointed in my face. "You have no idea what this is like. How overwhelming it feels. I'm trying not to fear, but I've never, in all my life, been hit *this* hard with something so terrifying."

"I'm sorry." I hugged her. "I'm sure it's much harder than I understand."

She hugged me back, and her voice softened. "I'm praying and trying, Owen. I really am. I don't know why my faith is gone or how to get it back. I'm sorry too."

It was the kind of deflated, defeated apology that made me want to keep pleading—keep encouraging her—until it finally clicked and she realized the fight was already won. But this was her battle, not mine. Her spiritual crossroads to navigate and hopefully find her way back soon to the Ray Anne I'd always known and fallen in love with, even if I had yet to say it.

She was still toying with my hair but had gotten really quiet. I sensed it was my turn to explain why I'd never told her I loved her, even though everything within me did. The problem was, I didn't exactly understand why. Not entirely.

"I guess for me . . ." I paused, soul-searching, hoping something authentic and mature would come to me. "I think I feel unworthy of being loved, so it's like I don't have the right to say it to you."

Whoa. Finally, some clarity. And unbearable humiliation.

I couldn't believe I'd just made a confession like that about myself, especially since I'd always considered myself a confident guy.

Ray Anne leaned back and looked up at me, her brow furrowed in sympathy. "Of course you're worthy of love."

I turned my head, loathing that I'd come off as needy. Eventually I asked her, "Why are there some things we can't seem to believe, even though we know we should? Good things? True things?"

She nestled her face into my neck, beneath my chin. "I wish I knew."

I kept holding her and walking, eventually circling back, content to be quiet awhile—my way of accepting there were some things I couldn't fix, no matter how much I wanted to. And maybe I wasn't supposed to try.

We made it to shore, and as we approached the gazebo, traipsing through the tall grass in our waterlogged clothes, I thought of more things I needed to get her caught up on. Like what was feeding Molek, refueling his strength, and how the thirteen targets were the suicidal students in Gentry's support group. I knew I should also tell her about the snake in her mom's neck. Surely Ray Anne hadn't seen it, or she would have told me. But when I opened my mouth to start talking, I got the feeling I shouldn't bring up any of that heavy stuff.

Not here.

Not now.

And thankfully I didn't, because I'm sure it would have ruined what happened next.

As we stood embracing one another in the center of the gazebo, soaking wet yet warm, Ray Anne stared out at the serene lake, then up at me. "If we get married someday, can we have the ceremony here?"

Wow.

I was so elated, so over-the-top ecstatic that she would even think of that, I told her yes, like, four times.

To this day, it was among our sweetest, most unforgettable moments.

And we really needed it before heading back to the war zone awaiting us back home.

TWENTY-ONE

On the drive back to Masonville, Ray Anne and I spotted a food truck and stopped to grab a bite. While seated side by side on a wobbly bench, I delivered the depressing news about her mom's infested spine, identical to hers. "It's a curse that runs in your family, I think."

Thankfully Ray Anne was almost done with her taco by then, because she completely lost her appetite. She changed the subject, too distraught to even discuss it, I think. Her new way of coping lately.

"Sunday's meeting was an epic fail," she said. "How are we ever going to gather people onto your land when, from what I can tell, Ethan's about the only one in Masonville who's on board?"

He was more than on board. He was an official spirit-world defender, like us. But I still couldn't bring myself to tell her that.

"Don't you think we should get with Ethan soon and discuss things?" she asked. "Maybe he'll have suggestions about what we should do next."

Of course we should. But as disgraceful as it is to admit, I was willing to compromise the fate of our town—and ultimately our nation and world—just to avoid having to endure seeing my girlfriend interact with him. Jealousy burns the soul *that* bad. "Let's give it a few days and see what happens," I said. "I have some ideas." Never mind that we had no time to waste, and I didn't have any strong suggestions about what to do. But I told myself I'd figure something out.

I had to.

This time, I changed the subject—to the suicidal students in Gentry's support group.

Ray Anne pointed out the obvious. "Warning them that Molek and Cosmic Rulers want them dead won't work."

She and I brainstormed one intervention strategy after another, but they all had gaping flaws.

Ray Anne lowered her head and sighed. "Who am I to try and help anyone right now, anyway? I can't even help myself."

I looked around, suspicious. Sure enough, I spied a Creeper next to a dumpster, its gaze fixed on Ray Anne. "That thought didn't come from you, babe." I pointed to the liar. "He hit you with that."

We threw away our trash and left.

The sun was beginning to set as I pulled up to Ray Anne's. She invited me inside, I think so we could pray, but I stayed outside when I spotted that infamous diaper box, tattered and jostling behind the bushes. The two predators had dared to move their "home" a few feet from Ray's door.

I pointed to it. "They keep coming back because you allow it. Let's command them to go once and for all and throw that box away."

She winced. "But they need shelter."

I sighed. *Here we go again.*

"Ramus was out here yesterday," she said, "and he didn't seem bothered by it. He just glanced at the box, then took his usual post on the roof."

"Because he expects *you* to deal with it. Watchmen leave certain things to us—the things we can stand up to ourselves. They step in and help when we need it." I'd witnessed it more than once.

"We've had such a good day. Can we please not argue about this?"

"But you're not using your head, Ray Anne."

She put her fists on her hips and told me I had no business telling her how to handle the situation, which of course, made me defensive. "'Cause you think I could never have more spiritual insight about something than you?"

It went downhill from there. We shouted back and forth—until that unholy mix of death dust and black grit came billowing out of our mouths. *Our* mouths—the last two people on earth who should be guilty of helping Molek regain his strength.

Before we had time to even discuss it, two of Molek's fat brown bats descended on us and sucked the stuff out of the air, then flew away.

"Ugh!" I punched the brick wall, skinning my knuckles. "We just made Molek stronger."

Ray Anne tossed her hands up. "See? I told you it wasn't worth fighting about."

"You're totally missing the point."

We were both panting and tense, ready to keep defending our stances, but we couldn't afford to spew out more nourishment for our opponent. We had no choice but to shut up.

Neither of us brought up praying. Or said we were sorry.

I walked away, battling heart-pounding intensity—my own flaring temper intensified by Strife's proximity. I lowered onto my bike, about to slide my helmet on, when a realization came to me. I called out to Ray Anne as she stood eyeing me from her doorway. "Hey, do you remember what Veronica told you the day you first met her? The prediction she gave you?"

She grimaced. "Something about me having kids, even though I'd *just* found out I never can."

I flinched, surprised by how bluntly she'd spoken of her infertility. I cleared my throat. "Veronica said you'd have twins someday." I nodded toward her two identical Creeper pets. "Think about it."

Slowly, and finally with some hesitancy, Ray Anne stared down at the box.

"Veronica was possessed," I said. "She was telling you evil's plans for your future."

If that didn't make Ray Anne reconsider the situation, nothing would.

I was walking my motorcycle out of the driveway when a spotless red Ferrari parked against the curb in front of Ray Anne's house—same model and color as the one I'd seen in the woods at the human auction.

When Dr. Bradford exited and stood next to his car, I dismounted my bike. He told me hello, then called out to Ray Anne, "How's Jackson?"

She managed to say, "He's fine. He's not here." Thankfully Mrs. Greiner hadn't made it home with him from the zoo yet.

Dr. Bradford approached Ray Anne, dragging half-a-dozen chains up the driveway, holding what looked like a small piece of paper. "Please, I want you to have this. It's the least I can do."

He handed Ray Anne the paper—a check. She unfolded it, then mumbled like she could hardly read. "Five thousand dollars . . ."

"My grandson should lack for nothing."

"He doesn't," I said, walking back to Ray Anne and crossing my arms.

Dr. Bradford eyed me with confident ease, sporting high-dollar gray slacks and a navy-blue sports jacket. "What do I have to do to convince you that I care and am trustworthy?"

Ray Anne clung to my arm.

"I can tell you," he said, "I have many regrets. I would do things much, much differently if only I could, starting with my misguided admiration for your grandparents, Owen." He angled toward me. "It took me far too long, but I finally came to see them for what they really were—manipulators who preyed on me during my most vulnerable, impressionable time in life. I was a young man starving for parental acceptance and guidance.

"And it's true, I got caught up in the supposed power and vitality offered to me, only to someday realize I'd bought into a terrible, pernicious lie." He teared up. "I admit I'm still searching for truth. For redemption, if such a thing exists. But I've turned my back entirely on that society and severed all alliances. Steadily, daily, I'm becoming a new person, forging new loyalties."

He made it sound so easy, like all he had to do was tell the occult, *I quit*. "They just let you walk away?" I asked.

He glanced over his shoulder, a common gesture in this town. "It's been extremely difficult and risky. I'm so grateful for your mother, Owen. Susan has been an invaluable source of advice and comfort."

Did he *really* just imply that my mom had been open with him about her childhood, about her involvement with and escape from the occult? "My mother never talks about anything related to her past."

"She does to me." Dr. Bradford touched his chest as if he was speaking from his heart. "I believe it's been as healing for her as it has for me."

Ray Anne was teary-eyed, like she was buying all this. I admit he looked sincere, but I wasn't willing to go off appearances. Or be a coward. "Are you willing to tell us everything you know, like what happened to the missing Masonville kids?"

He took a big step back and shook his head. "I got out before the abductions. I know nothing about that."

It occurred to me my next question could end up costing me my life, just like questioning had cost Officer McFarland his. Poor man. "Tell me, who is Veronica Snow's handler? You're bound to know."

He shifted his weight and wiped his forehead, now beading with sweat, then leaned and whispered in my ear. "I suggest you never speak of her handler again."

"Why?" I demanded. "If you have so much regret, how about you help expose the criminals around here?"

He whispered again. "If you value your life, you'll stop seeking him out. That man shows no mercy to anyone who poses a threat to his anonymity."

A quiver swam the length of my body. As strongly as I considered Dr. Bradford to be a liar, his words of advice rang true. I knew Detective Benny was dangerous, but maybe he was even more cutthroat than I suspected.

Ray Anne tried to give Dr. Bradford his check back, but he refused it. "I hope to see my grandson soon."

He drove away after that, but Ray Anne started heaving like she had asthma. "I told you he was going to try to get visitation with Jackson! And Owen, it's not our job to confront Veronica's handler. She can stand up to the detective herself. That's not our battle to fight."

"But it is, Ray Anne." I wiped a strand of hair away from her clammy face. "Veronica said her handler has been issuing orders, rallying covens across the US to work against you and me and Elle—anyone viewed as a threat. And he's vowed to kill Veronica if she doesn't go along with it all. He's the human force leading Molek's charge against us. The person enforcing the Rulers' agenda."

"And you believe Veronica?"

"Yes. I mean, I think so."

That was just it. I didn't know what to believe. Veronica Snow, Brody Bradford—two corrupted people claiming to be remorseful and caring all of a sudden.

It was one thing to question and scrutinize the motives of spirit-world beings that appeared to bear light, but trying to sort through mixed signals from humans was proving even harder. And Ray Anne, the one person I would normally lean on to help me make sense of things, was trapped in her own whirlpool of confusion.

She burst into tears, as fragile as a teacup. "This is too hard." She collapsed onto her driveway and dug her fingers into her scalp, sobbing as loud as I'd ever heard her.

I dropped down and tried to get her to look at me. "Sweetheart, please listen."

"I can't! I can't!"

"Shh." I rubbed up and down on her back, trying to stop what looked to me like the onset of a panic attack. And hoping I could ease her out of her fear-ridden state before . . .

Too late. I wasn't surprised the kingdom of darkness had dispatched forces in immediate response to the distress call Ray was broadcasting for countless miles through the spiritual atmosphere. But I was startled by who they sent.

TWENTY-TWO

BACKED BY A MOB OF CREEPERS, Veronica stood at the edge of Ray Anne's driveway, draped in a black hooded robe that reminded me of the Cosmic Ruler witch. I had no way of knowing if it was a Creeper disguised as her or her astral-projecting spirit. Either way, she wasn't welcome here.

Ray Anne was still on the ground, sobbing with her head down, and any second, she was bound to smell the Creepers, then see Veronica and freak out even more.

Veronica took steps toward us, and I jumped to my feet. "You can't come near us."

She kept advancing.

"In Christ's name."

She stopped like she'd rammed a brick wall.

Ray Anne lifted her head, and I tensed up, anticipating a full-blown meltdown. "Who are you talking to?" she asked me.

What? I looked between my girlfriend and the evil entourage. Veronica was standing directly in front of Ray Anne, within ten feet of her, with a row of Creepers towering behind her like linebackers. I pointed. "Look!"

"At what?" Ray said.

Veronica stared me down, her words dripping with contempt. "Your pathetic girlfriend crossed a line and has lost her senses."

"What's going on?" Ray Anne gasped between sobs.

"Tell her, Owen." Veronica formed a lethal grin. "Tell her Eva's been at Jackson's crib, and here I am again, but now she's such a weakling, she can't see me anymore. And warn her that Mother Punishment will be here soon to take Jackson. There's no protecting him—or the thirteen cowards you know full well you cannot save." She snickered.

Mother Punishment. That had to be the two-faced witch.

I took a big, bold step forward. "In the name of—"

I hadn't even finished when Ramus's armored feet slammed the driveway behind Ray Anne and me, his jaw tight with fury.

Veronica arched her back and hissed, then scurried back, escaping behind the wall of Creepers. That's when I noticed they all had the same assignment on their mangled faces: *Suicide.* They had the nerve to advance, tiptoeing forward while huddled shoulder to shoulder like they were terrified but had been ordered to do this. Their nightmarish eyes were missile-locked on Ray Anne, who sat with her face buried in her hands.

Ramus tilted his head down and looked straight at me, pleading, it seemed, for me to do my part. I quoted a go-to verse I'd seen beat back the enemy before: "I've been given authority to trample on snakes and scorpions and overcome all the power of the enemy. Nothing will harm me."

"Or Ray Anne," I added.

Trample on *snakes* . . . why hadn't I paid attention to that before? Now wasn't the time to analyze it.

Ramus leaped forward, up and over Ray Anne and me, and shoved the two Creepers in the center of the pack, yet the whole line of them slammed backward onto their crooked spines, screeching like hogs snagged in a trap. They scattered in every direction, fleeing so fast, they looked like black streaks.

Ramus paused to look over his shoulder at Ray Anne, gazing at her with sympathy. Then he flew straight up, racing into the early evening sky.

Ray Anne wiped her cheeks. "I know I'd better stop complaining before I draw the enemy here."

I lowered beside her, slowly this time, dreading the news I had to deliver. "They were here. Right in front of you. So was Ramus."

"No . . . that's not possible."

"I think your fear is sabotaging your senses, like my deception weakened mine a while back, only your senses are gone completely."

She trembled all over, still hunched over on her driveway, too distraught to cry now.

"We'll get through this," I assured her.

"No." Dread covered her face. "I don't think I can live like this much longer."

"Ray Anne . . ."

Did she mean that? And had she really just said the *exact* same words Gentry had today?

The unanimous assignment I'd just seen on all six Creepers was way more serious than I'd thought. Those Suicide devils weren't just here taunting Ray Anne. They were getting to her, maybe at times when I wasn't around to witness it. "You'd never hurt yourself, right?"

"I . . ." Her hesitation freaked me out. "I hope not," she said. "But promise me no matter what happens to me, you'll protect Jackson."

I was so stunned, all I could do was press my hand over her mouth and silence her. That kind of hopeless talk could lure a mass of Creepers from zip codes away—ten times as many as the horde that Ramus had just run off. Of all the people I needed to be concerned about, Ray Anne was at the very top of my list now.

We spotted Mrs. Greiner's SUV approaching, and Ray Anne hurried to stand, wiping her blotchy face and tightening her ponytail before her mom saw her and figured out something was terribly wrong.

I faced my girlfriend. "This is serious, Ray Anne. I'm extremely worried about you."

"Not now."

Mrs. Greiner pulled into the driveway and exited her vehicle. "How are you, honey?" She made a beeline for Ray Anne, and as usual, hugged her longer than hugs generally last.

"I'm good." Ray Anne avoided her mom's gaze. "How was the zoo?"

"We had fun. Are you sure you're—"

"Owen and I had an awesome day. I'm just tired, Mom."

I'd never seen Ray Anne lie outright before. She opened the door to the back seat of the SUV and started unstrapping Jackson, talking to him in a high-pitched, motherly tone. Her voice cracked, though, her distress seeping through.

Mrs. Greiner stood next to me. "Spending time with you today was obviously what she needed."

I nodded, knowing it was a dishonest gesture. I hadn't managed to encourage her one bit, not really.

Ray Anne pulled Jackson into her arms, then flashed a fake grin at her mother and me, bouncing Jackson like she didn't have a care in the world—as if she could still see perfectly well into the spirit realm and hadn't just confessed to me she was entertaining giving up on life.

"I'm gonna reheat some leftovers for dinner," Mrs. Greiner said. "Owen, you're welcome to stay."

Ray Anne's dad arrived and parked his truck behind the SUV. He told Ray and me hello before catching up to his wife at the front door.

I stood close to Ray Anne in the driveway, torn in two like a thin sheet of paper. I knew what I needed to do, but Ray Anne would be furious with me. Maybe enough to break up and never speak to me again. But from what I could tell, her life was on the line.

I had just seconds to decide whether or not to act—to drop a truth grenade or keep it to myself, undetonated.

I decided that, as deadly as grenades can be, they can also save lives.

I cleared my throat, but it didn't make the nervous lump go away. "Mr. and Mrs. Greiner?"

Ray Anne's mom stopped just short of going inside and faced me, her husband right behind her. Ray Anne flashed wide eyes at me, silently begging me to keep quiet.

"I think your daughter is suicidal."

TWENTY-THREE

ONE LOOK AT RAY ANNE'S PAINED FROWN and I knew that of all the things I'd ever done that had disappointed or hurt her, I'd never wounded her like this. She'd given me no choice, but I still felt like a traitor. Like I'd betrayed my best friend.

The next two hours were a stressful mess as the four of us sat facing one another in the Greiners' living room, Jackson rolling around on the carpet while Ray's tearful parents asked one pointed question after another. Ray Anne kept downplaying things, trying to ease her parents' concerns and keep them out of her business, which obligated me to recite things she'd said and done that pointed to a need for intervention—all while being careful not to slip up and mention any spirit-realm factors.

It felt like I was on the witness stand, testifying against my girlfriend. Ray Anne refused to look at me.

In the end, her parents insisted she move out of her garage apartment and back into her old bedroom in the house for now, where they could keep a closer eye on her. And Mrs. Greiner went online right then and made Ray Anne appointments with not one but two counselors. Tensions were high—so high that Creepers kept poking their hideous heads into the house and scoping out the scene, but none was willing to set foot in a den of Lights.

There was that tantalizing scent that always filled the air when the Greiners—a shackle-free family—were all together, but that wasn't enough to lift Ray Anne's mood, even a little.

Come to think of it, with her senses disabled, she couldn't even smell it.

She finally looked in my general direction, and there was no disguising her scowl of contempt. I could only hope she saw the compassion on my face.

Mrs. Greiner said she wanted to be alone with her daughter, and about that time, Jackson started throwing a fit. I did something I never thought I'd do. I offered to take the playpen thing to the church and watch Jackson for the night—you know, to give Ray and her parents a break. Ray Anne didn't like the idea of parting with him, but she might have felt differently had I told her that "Eva" threatened that Mother Punishment would be here soon, coming after him. And Ray wouldn't be able to see her.

I'd been around Jackson a lot, but never babysat him—or any kid—in my entire life. I didn't think Mrs. Greiner would trust me with the little guy overnight, but surprisingly, she welcomed it.

I followed Ray Anne into her apartment, and she gathered Jackson's things in cold silence. It felt like I'd lost her—her trust, for sure—but if I hadn't confided in her parents, I'd have run a greater risk of *really* losing her. Like, permanently.

"Don't worry," I told her. "Your parents love you. They're doing what's best for you."

She ignored me.

I knew her parents really would do anything to protect their daughter, but I also understood they seriously underestimated the role spiritual forces played in a situation like this—not because they didn't believe on some level, but they'd never witnessed it or seemed to ever take it in consideration in connection with their son's suicide. Kind of like, out of sight, out of mind.

Ray Anne headed toward the door with Jackson's belongings, but I stood in front of her, stopping her in the doorway. I wanted to tell her I loved her, once and for all, but the risk of rejection was at an all-time high. "I'm here for you. You know that, right?"

She stared back at me with heavy, hopeless blinks.

Seeing Ray Anne like this, so broken and crushed, was a bigger nightmare than the one I'd had where bats plunged down Molek's throat and I was nearly choked to death by a possessed shadow. Worse than every other fearful thing I'd lived through. And I couldn't fix it.

It was 11:00 p.m., way past Jackson's bedtime. I did my best to give him a decent sponge bath in my bathroom sink, then I put him in his pj's and set up his foldout crib in the corner of the room. It felt different being alone with him, like I was guarding Fort Knox all by myself.

At least the snake nest was gone from my room and nowhere near him. There was a strong chance the astral-projecting witches might show up outside again tonight, but they knew better than to barge into the building, much less my room. And if Mother Punishment came sailing through the walls, hunting for Jackson, I still trusted he was safe with me. The same all-powerful Name I'd seen restrain every force of evil that sought to harm me was sure to work on her, too. There was only one bizarre exception . . .

Nothing I'd said had driven away the invisible crying infant or the stalking presence from the sanctuary when they'd come to torment me. At least there was no sign of them at the moment.

Jackson started fussing, and I mixed formula in a bottle. I daydreamed again about what it would be like for Ray Anne and Jackson and me to pack up and flee Masonville. Turn our backs once and for all on this toxic, murderous town and do what was best for *us* for a change.

I gave Jackson his bottle, then walked around the room with him, patting his back, trying to get him to fall asleep the way I'd seen Ray and her mom do. Within minutes, his eyes drifted shut, but a slamming sound overhead woke him, followed by quick footsteps. Jackson had heard it, so I knew it was a material world intrusion. Finally an actual break-in?

I felt completely vulnerable with Jackson in my arms—like a squirrel forced to defend its young against a pit viper. And the only Masonville cop I trusted had been murdered.

In the seconds it took me to set Jackson in his playpen and grab my baseball bat, the prowler began stomping down the creaky third-floor steps, then the hallway, stopping outside my room.

I dropped to the floor and spotted two semicircular shadows looming in the gap beneath my door. I grabbed my cell, resigned to dialing 911, praying an emergency operator would answer right away.

I held my breath and kept silent, but Jackson started crying. There was no hiding now.

"I have a gun." I announced my lie loud and clear.

Then came a knock. Not an aggressive pound, but a polite tap. *Seriously?* "Uh . . . who is it?"

"It's me. Gentry."

I sighed long and loud, grateful it was only him, yet still taken aback. I opened the door. Gentry's eyes were bloodshot, like he'd either been crying or getting high. He wore one of his signature hoodies, of course, and clutched a duffel bag. "My stepdad kicked me out. I didn't know where else to go."

"Sorry to hear that."

I was willing to invite him in, but first I wanted to know, "Did you break in upstairs?"

"I knocked and knocked on the front doors of the church but figured you couldn't hear me. I walked around the back of the building and saw the open third-story window, and I mean, a tall ladder was right there."

I didn't recall an open window when I'd been in the storage room the night before, but it was possible, I guessed. "And you knew this was my room?"

"No." He shrugged. "I thought maybe it led to another hallway or something and I'd find you eventually."

I welcomed him inside, and he furrowed his brow when he saw Jackson fussing in his playpen.

"He's not my kid." I was super self-conscious that I was caring for a baby. "I'm just watching him for the night."

A sense of self-loathing washed over me. Had I really just referred to Jackson like he was some random child I happened to be stuck with, just to save myself a little awkwardness?

I walked over and picked him up. Gentry closed the door to my room, then leaned against it. "Whose kid is he?"

"Dan and Jess's son."

"So . . ."

"Yeah, he's the one Veronica kidnapped." I went back to patting Jackson's back and shushing him, feeling awkward again.

Gentry finally set his bag down, and the cuffs on the ends of all four of his chains clanked against the floor. He took a narrow-eyed, scrutinizing glance around my ugly room.

"I used to have a really cool apartment," I said. "I'm just staying here to help out for a while." Wow. My pride was relentless. "So what happened with your dad tonight?"

"Stepdad." Gentry sat but stayed by the door, still feeling unwelcome, I think. "He accused me of stealing and pawning some of his tools, and no matter how many times I swore I hadn't done it, he wouldn't believe me. He called me a liar and told me to get my stuff and get out."

Gentry had been accused of being a traitor and punched in the mouth, then called a liar and kicked out of his home, all in one day. "Dude, sounds like it's been rough."

He nodded. "You think I could crash on your floor tonight? I promise I'll figure something else out tomorrow."

I already had one houseguest, but that wasn't why I was reluctant. Gentry was housing evil; I'd seen it in him this morning. I didn't want him near Jackson while I slept.

"Ah, if it's not cool with you, I mean, I can leave."

I couldn't exactly explain my hesitation, and it wasn't like I could try casting the Creeper out of him. Gentry would have freaked, I'm sure. At the same time, he was safe here with me from the spiritual powers that were out to eliminate him. So, the only solution I could come up with was to commit to myself that I'd stay up all night and keep an eye on both Gentry and Jackson.

I gave Gentry a pillow and the only extra blanket I had. Meanwhile, Jackson was asleep again, so I laid him in his playpen. The smell of detergent on his pj's was the same as Ray Anne's clothes, and it made me really miss her. Surely she'd understand soon why I'd done what I did today. And she'd start winning the battle against her soul and be strong again. And still want to be with me and marry me someday in the gazebo by the lake.

Gentry spread the blanket out on the floor and sat on it. "My brother Lance said you'd changed and gone all psycho and stuff, but, I mean, you seem alright to me."

I sat on the foot of my bed. "Unfortunately Lance and I didn't see eye to eye on some things."

"He said you claimed you could see messed-up stuff on people and scary creatures everywhere."

It was basically an accurate description.

"Is it true?" Gentry probed. Unlike this morning, he was looking me in the eye. That repulsive mask of addiction faded in and out as my thoughts jumped all over the place, my compassion coming and going. "Can you really see stuff?" he asked me.

I'd never had a shackled person believe my paranormal accounts, but if he was at all open to the truth, it was worth the long shot . . .

"There's a world that exists on top of our world, Gentry. And yes, I see it."

I expected him to laugh and grow scales over his eyes. Instead he asked, "Something happened in the woods, and that's when it started, right?"

Another detail Lance had obviously blabbed to him. But I didn't want to make this about how I'd gained my powers, and I definitely didn't want him knowing about the well on my property. God forbid curiosity get the best of him and he'd go serve himself a drink like Walt and Marshall had.

Okay, I'd served it to them. But I'd miraculously managed to forgive myself for the lethal outcome and vowed I'd never tell another soul about the well, much less where it was.

"Gentry, what matters is that there really is a fight between good and evil—a literal war—and you're right in the middle of it. You and the others in your support group."

Sure enough, those vile black scales I'd once seen on Jess and my mom began sliding up his eyeballs—a sickening manifestation of spiritual blindness.

I figured I'd shut up before his eye sockets became solid black, overtaken completely—a truly terrifying sight. But something else happened. About the most incredible thing I'd witnessed in a while, which was saying a lot.

TWENTY-FOUR

THE LIGHT AROUND MY FEET went from a soothing gold to a flash of glaring brilliance. I had to shield my eyes, but when I moved my hand seconds later, it had gone back to normal—and a pair of masculine hands made of the same golden illumination was reaching out from my aura. They were at least three times the size of mine—even bigger than a Watchman's. Same hands that had crushed the curse in the trash can.

The supernatural palms moved away from me, leaving a glistening streak behind like a jet trail, traveling like liquid gold across the room, reaching . . .

For Gentry.

The hands gently rested on him, covering his chest and neck and head, similar to how Jackson's tiny body fit in my hands. Both thumbs reached and extended up and—I couldn't believe it—pulled the blinding scales down, uncovering Gentry's eyes.

"What do you mean, we're in a war?" he asked me.

I stood, in awe of the situation. I knew this was it—my chance to testify without the shroud of darkness filtering out the truth before it had a chance to reach his soul. "Gentry, God loves you. He loves you more than you can imagine. You have no idea how he feels about you."

As much as I intended to make a solid case for the existence of spirit-world beings and explain the conflict he was in, the only thing that would come out of my mouth in that moment was an outpouring of God's affirmation and affection toward Gentry.

I could literally *feel* it. Like, tangibly sense God's over-the-top attachment toward Gentry. It was like a dam had burst, exploding from my gut and rushing toward Gentry's parched soul.

He tucked his head. "I don't believe in God."

I hurried over and lowered in front of him. "Yes, you do. You're just afraid he'll let you down and hurt you like people have. And you don't want to give up control—being your own god."

The words coming out of me seemed to be just passing through my brain, not originating there.

Gentry tucked his chin lower into his chest. "Look, I don't need to be preached at."

And just like that, the miraculous hands eased away from him, slowly letting go, then vanishing into the aura around my feet.

"Gentry—"

"I'm tired." His eyeballs were blanketed in black now. To make it worse, a different set of eyes stared me down through the slimy veils. The Creeper inside of him.

Gentry lay down and turned his back to me. Conversation over.

Yeah, it was rude of him, but I knew better than to take it personally. This was spiritual warfare—the way it goes when God reaches out to someone who doesn't want his touch. When a guy harboring a devil believes his life is better off without God interfering in it.

The same messed-up mindset I'd had for eighteen years.

I didn't say goodnight or anything—just turned off the lamp, then lay in my bed, restless on top of my covers. Awareness rolled in like crashing waves . . .

The aura around my feet wasn't just heavenly illumination, as if I was merely reflecting spirit-world light the same way the sun's rays reflected off my motorcycle's rearview mirrors onto my face. The aura on me was *alive*—a living, loving spirit in and of itself.

The Holy Spirit.

Had to be.

And another epiphany: God wasn't just watching over me from the distant cosmos or even occupying the same room as me. He was taking each and every one of life's steps with me, from *within* me. And the inexplicable love he'd expressed to Gentry through me . . .

It was soul-soothing beyond words, and believe me, I wanted to receive it for myself too—but I couldn't. It was like I was sure, without a doubt, that God cared immensely for Gentry—even while being rejected by him—but there was no way God could possibly feel that way about me. Of course it was irrational, but it felt like my unshakable reality.

I had another revelation. In the woods recently, and countless other times, I'd wondered how a loving God could make a place like hell. But now I realized that God didn't want Gentry to go to hell—the only place in the entire cosmos where not *one* of God's attributes is found. No, people banish themselves there by refusing his outstretched hands.

It was a game-changing realization I'd desperately needed for a long time, one that finally debunked my false, conflicting assumption that God could be merciful one minute and cruel the next.

And yet I was still all torn up inside. *If only people understood.*

I was full of hyped-up energy, which helped keep me awake so I could sit up and check on Jackson every so often. At some point though, I relaxed enough to accidentally fall asleep. I woke to an ear-piercing sound, as loud as a foghorn, only high-pitched.

I bolted out of bed, groggy and disoriented, my head pounding. Gentry's pillow and crumpled blanket lay on the floor. It didn't take long to scan the four corners of my room and realize he wasn't here. Where had he gone?

Jackson started screaming his head off, and I picked him up, aware now of the unmistakable smell of smoke.

Fire alarm.

I grabbed an open duffel bag with my free hand and started chucking stuff in it—my keys and wallet, my best Nikes, a few of my childhood photos off the floor. And thank God, I remembered to grab Arthur's prophecy out of the nightstand.

I tossed Jackson's baby bag over my shoulder before rushing to the door and throwing it open. A heated blast of air and the distinct smell of burnt wood rushed past me, barging into my room like a smoldering tidal wave. I didn't see any flames, but the hallway—my only passageway to the stairs, then out of the building—was filled with billowing smoke.

Daisy darted into the hall, disappearing into the darkness. I called for her, but she didn't come back. I pulled the collar of my T-shirt down over Jackson's face and tried making a run for it. But the singed air was too polluted to get through. By the time I ran back to my room, it was gray with smoke, and Jackson was coughing.

"God, help me."

I opened the double doors and charged onto the balcony suspended some twenty feet above ground. I figured if I had to, I could jump and endure the bone-breaking pain of hitting the ground, but how was I supposed to do that while holding Jackson?

He started squalling, and I held him up in front of my face, trying to calm him. But he wasn't crying.

Of all the times to hear that invisible child.

I yelled for help, but there was no one around. I searched my bag for my phone, but I hadn't grabbed it. I had no choice but to sit Jackson on the balcony floor and run back inside for it. I searched frantically through my bedsheets and on the floor, choking on the scorched air. And then I remembered . . .

My nightmare.

The smoke, suffocating me.

Had it been God's way of preparing me to die tonight?

I couldn't allow myself to think like that, especially with Jackson here, counting on me. He started crying, and I had two children bawling in my ears now. I couldn't find my cell or the burner phone. I grabbed a pillow and charged back outside, thinking maybe I could wrap it around Jackson and lower him somehow. But there was nothing to lower him with.

I tossed the pillow aside and scooped Jackson up, holding him against my chest. He was shaking like he knew his life was in danger.

A short distance from us, menacing flames lined the sanctuary's outside wall, devouring the building from the ground up like scalding tongues. Creepers converged on the scene, drawn to disaster like wolves to an injured lamb.

Behind me, my room was so dense with smoke, all I could see were flashes of bright-orange and yellow. I knew any minute, the fire would spread onto the balcony, igniting the wood like a match.

"Custos!"

Where was he? And the Watchman with the shield on his back that I'd seen protect Jackson before?

Smoke was pouring out of my room onto the balcony, a swirling mix of dark gray and jet black, sparks spinning like flying dragons.

In a matter of seconds, my entire room was engulfed. It was so blazing hot, I leaned over the balcony railing, straining to keep a tight grip on Jackson's squirming body, both of us sweating.

There was the distant sound of sirens—too far away to bring relief. Sure enough, flames reached out from my room and grabbed hold of the balcony. Everything in me wanted to back away from the flesh-eating heat, but there was nowhere to go.

"Please, God! Don't abandon me!"

As the words left my mouth, I thought someone had plunged a sword through my lower back, and it had come bursting out beneath my rib cage. It was *that* painful. But I looked down and there was no weapon in me. Just such indescribable agony, I might have raised my hands and surrendered to the fire had it not meant sealing Jackson's fate too.

I realized the pain had registered in my soul, but it wasn't like I could stop and make sense of it right then.

There were all kinds of explosions and popping sounds, like my aerosol cans were detonating in the bathroom and the balcony was breaking away from the building. I gazed over the railing at the grass, contemplating whether Jackson would survive if I stepped onto the handrail, keeping him tucked into my chest with the pillow, then fell backward, slamming the earth on my back. I'd crack my skull and break my spine. Probably end up dead or paralyzed. But it was the right thing to do—the only hope of saving him—and now was the time to do it.

But I just stood there.

Unwilling to sacrifice myself for him.

Jackson and the invisible baby both continued wailing. Then I got a mental image so vivid, it was like it was really happening—me leaving Jackson on the burning balcony to free up my arms so I could hang from the floor of the balcony, then let go. I saw my feet slamming the earth, my arms and elbows bearing the weight of the fall, but me surviving. My future intact.

Without Jackson.

I'd battled a lot of temptation, but this . . .

I didn't understand it. I'd been willing to risk everything to protect him before—why was I such a coward now?

"Owen!"

For the first time in my life, I was relieved to hear Ethan's voice. He was running toward the balcony, dragging the massive ladder. "Hold on, I'm coming!"

He positioned the ladder and started climbing. That's when I spotted the sopping-wet witches huddled by the pond. They were staring straight at me, no doubt willing my destruction.

I refused to look at them a moment longer and instead watched Ethan race up the rungs, knowing any second the building and balcony could collapse and incinerate him along with Jackson and me. Maybe it was a weird thing to think about in a life-and-death moment, but I couldn't escape it any more than I could outrun the flames: Ethan hadn't hesitated to risk being burned alive in order to save Jackson and me.

He's a real man. I'm not.

I recognized it as the kind of crippling thought a Creeper would launch at my mind, but I couldn't see any near me.

Finally, Ethan got to the top of the ladder and reached out. It was only when I handed Jackson to him that I realized how severely my hands were shaking. Ethan started down the ladder, holding tightly to Jackson, and I followed with my bag and Jackson's strapped around my shoulders. I so despised myself for my lack of bravery, I figured a Creeper would have a chain fitted around my neck before my feet touched the ground—the automatic bondage of an unforgiving grudge, whether aimed at someone else or in this case, myself. Instead I was met with a flurry of firefighters and church staff charging onto the scene, all looking me over and asking if I was okay. I told them I was fine—my go-to response.

Even after watching Ethan deliver Jackson to an EMT and knowing full well he'd be fine, my body was riddled with adrenaline like I was still about to burn to death with a child in my arms. I attempted to get to him but was told to back away from the ambulance.

I kept bending and shaking out my hands and legs, trying to chill out. Unfortunately that haunting infant's cries kept brushing past me—from down low, like it was being dragged past me on the ground.

Horrible.

I called for my dog, praying she'd escaped the building. I made my way around to the front of the church. While walking across the parking lot, watching firefighters work to tame the raging blaze, I finally crossed paths with Gentry.

"What happened, Owen?"

I shook my head.

"I went outside to get some air," he said, "and all of a sudden the building was burning up."

His slurred speech told me he'd gone out to get high, but all I cared about was that he was alive.

"I'm glad you're okay," I told him. "Have you seen my dog?"

He pointed. "She took off that way."

She made it out. I sighed in relief.

Someone tugged on my shoulder. I turned, and Mrs. Greiner was fanning herself with both hands, her eye makeup smeared. "Oh my gosh, are you okay? Where's Jackson?"

I pointed to the ambulance where they were treating him, and she ran over there. I looked for Ray Anne but didn't see her. I decided her parents probably hadn't even told her there'd been a fire. She'd have gone ballistic, especially knowing Jackson was here.

Ethan approached me, and before I could thank him for what he'd done, he offered me the key to his apartment. "I have a guest room," he said. "You can stay as long as you need. And I can let you borrow some clothes."

Oh yeah. Other than the shirt and shorts I had on and the shoes I'd shoved in my bag, everything I'd had in my room was ash, including both cell phones.

I reached for a handshake. "Thanks, man, I really appreciate it, but I've got a place to stay." Never mind that it was my mom's and I dreaded the thought of being there, even for a few days. But the idea of staying with Ethan was worse. Being in his presence was awkward. Like I was nothing.

He shook my hand, our identical defender seals momentarily in line with one another.

"About what you did . . ." How do you thank a person for saving you and a child from a horrendous death?

He smiled—with the same warmth as his father. "Hey, you'd have done the same for me."

I averted my eyes. *Would I?*

Jackson was released to Mrs. Greiner, and I kissed his forehead before she took him home. I had no way to warn her that a Cosmic Ruler was after him. And I still didn't understand why the underworld was so determined to get him.

There was no sign of Gentry now—or Daisy—but that black Suburban was parked across the street, watching my insane life unfold. Surprisingly, not one Watchman had shown up all evening. I figured maybe it was because Custos knew Ethan would save the day and had entrusted Jackson's life and mine to him. No need to dispatch Heaven's troops when Ethan's around.

Detective Benny pulled up, and I took that as my cue to leave, even though it meant leaving Daisy behind. I vowed I'd find her tomorrow.

I showed up on my mom's doorstep at sunrise—without being followed—and let myself in. It was technically my house, willed to me by her parents. I was glad to see it was still clean. Thankfully I'd left a few shirts and a pair of jeans here when I'd moved out. My mom was asleep, and I showered and sank into my old bed without her knowing I was there. A familiar feeling.

I dropped my head onto the dusty pillow with no pillowcase, totally exhausted. But it's impossible to close your eyes, much less sleep, when an invisible baby is crying and an unseen tormentor refuses to leave you alone.

TWENTY-FIVE

THIS TIME IT SOUNDED like the distraught infant was in the closet, sobbing behind the closed door. And I could feel that other presence standing beside the bed. Gazing down at me.

I jerked my head off the pillow, and no surprise, saw nothing. But it was there. No question.

I sat up and unleashed the ultimate, undefeatable weapon. "In the name of Jesus Christ, according to Luke 10:19, whoever you are, I command you to go now—away from me and out of this house!"

The unholy presence remained, and the infant cried harder.

I was so infuriated, I sprung out of bed, and while standing in the center of my old bedroom, I quoted more verses. But instead of fleeing, I felt the stalker move in circles around me.

More livid than scared, I stormed to the closet and threw the door open, shouting more spiritual truths at the unseen child, not caring if I woke my mother.

And how weird is this? The baby went from sobbing to sniffling, like it was somehow comforted I'd found it. Meanwhile, I sensed the predator closing in, hovering behind my back.

I knew better than to commune with spirits, no matter their form, but the exhaustion and frustration and total desperation got to me. Without thinking, I turned around and belted out, "Who are you?"

There was a knock on the bedroom door, and I grabbed the knob and rushed to open it.

"Owen?" My mom gasped, then grinned. "What are you doing here?" She hugged me. I couldn't squeeze back tightly with all her icy chains and didn't bother trying. I didn't feel like being affectionate, and I still wasn't used to this from her.

"The church burned down last night," I told her.

"Oh no." She looked genuinely concerned, like a normal mom, even though she had nothing but contempt for churches.

When she offered to make breakfast, it really seemed like this whole experience was a dream. Breakfast had been my chore my entire childhood. She set the meal on the kitchen table, and even though it was only a bowl of Cheerios, from all appearances, she was still sober.

"Are you dating Dr. Bradford?" I was too grouchy to mince words.

"We're just friends. Good friends."

Yeah, right. She didn't know how to be "just friends" with a man. "You know he's in the occult?"

"*Was.*" She poured more cereal in my bowl, her hand trembling now. "There's a big difference."

I kept my gaze on my food, using my spoon to dunk dry Cheerios in milk. "How come you're willing to talk to him about your past but not me?"

Her eyes pooled. "I would never burden you with the atrocities I've witnessed." She put the milk back, then slammed the fridge and stormed out of the kitchen. I found it oddly comforting, my mom acting a little like her old self.

I was so tired, the second I ate my last spoonful, I went back upstairs. This time, for whatever reason, my old bedroom was quiet. I slept hard until nearly five o'clock in the evening, when Pastor Gordon showed up at the door. Another first: I actually felt comfortable welcoming someone inside my mom's house.

We sat across from one another in the living room, and my mother was quick to retreat to her bedroom, as uneasy around pastors as I was Creepers. Gordon said he was relieved that Jackson and I had made it out safely last night. Then he asked me questions, including if I had any thoughts about what might have started the fire.

"I have no idea," I said.

"Please don't think I'm accusing you, Owen." He stared intently at me, even though his soul kept nodding off. "That said, if this turns out to be intentional—a case of arson—the insurance company may try to accuse us of having set the fire to collect the insurance money, and therefore, refuse to pay for the damages. They know we're embarking on a remodel."

"Arson?" I slid to the edge of the sofa. "Why would someone want to burn the church down?"

Duh. I immediately knew the answer, but it wasn't something I could share. I had enemies in this town that wanted me dead—Detective Benny being the primary culprit. Or maybe Dr. Bradford was as entrenched in the occult as ever and out to eliminate me and his grandson with the simple strike of a match.

"It's my understanding you had a friend staying the night?" Pastor Gordon asked.

"More like a little brother. A freshman, Gentry Wilson. I'm his mentor. He had nowhere else to go."

"I see." He nodded. "And how well do you know him?"

"He's got some issues, but I mean, he's no arsonist." I couldn't name the real suspects—they were among the most highly esteemed men in Masonville. But the last thing Gentry needed was to get blamed for the church fire. He'd been falsely accused enough.

"Detective Benny is looking into the matter," Pastor Gordon said. "He assures us he'll get to the bottom of it."

I rolled my eyes. There was no telling how Benny would manipulate and sabotage the investigation, even if it meant pinning the crime on a vulnerable high school kid.

I walked Pastor Gordon to the door and asked him to please keep an eye out for my dog. Before he left, he reached into the back pocket of his slacks. "I almost forgot. This came to the church for you."

Another letter from the Hilltop Correctional Unit, only the handwriting was different. A nice cursive.

I went back upstairs and sat at the antique desk in my old bedroom and opened the envelope.

Owen, I hope this letter arrives in time. Be aware of your surroundings, especially on these hot summer nights.

Veronica was intentionally vague, but I got the message. The fire was no accident. And she'd known it was coming.

Here are the cities I hope to visit someday, the ones we talked about . . .

More code speak. She was referring to the cities that had already fallen to Cosmic Rulers, leaving Masonville as the final targeted town to collapse. I read through her list of twenty-three US cities—some densely populated and some as backwoods as Masonville.

This time, the letter was signed from Veronica, not Eva.

My mom knocked, and I shoved the paper into my lap. "You want to come with me to Kohls?"

I know most women shop, but this was the first time I'd seen my mother get fixed up and excited about it.

"That's okay, Mom. You go ahead."

She turned to go, but I called to her. I had no way of knowing her true motive for her recent life change or how long it would last, but I still felt I owed it to her to say something nice about it. "You look beautiful, Mom. I'm really proud of you."

Her eyes welled up. "Thank you, Owen. That means a lot."

She'd been gone about an hour when I heard a heavy vehicle door close outside. I looked out my window, and that black Suburban was parked in the driveway. An unfamiliar man in a suit sat behind the wheel, but I recognized the man who'd just gotten out of the passenger seat, even with his dark sunglasses on. He started toward the house.

I could hardly catch my breath.

My father. Approaching the door.

TWENTY-SIX

HE KNOCKED. I stood there with my hand on the doorknob, trying to reel in my emotions so there'd be no hint of them—no weakness—when I opened the door.

Finally, I turned the knob.

"Owen." He removed his sunglasses. "I can't tell you what a relief it is to see you."

I didn't say anything back. It was awkward, but I was mad at him. Supposed to be, anyway. The resentment would come and go.

"May I come in?" He stepped inside and shut the door fast, as if it was dangerous to be outside. Then he took a slow glance around the living room, studying every detail.

Back when I'd lived here, I never would have imagined in a million years that my father would someday show up and set foot inside my house. It was surreal, seeing him here.

I kept my emotions in check, playing it cool. But on the inside . . .

My father's home. Even as a diehard atheist, I'd prayed for that. I'd just had zero faith I'd ever see it.

He walked to the sofa and motioned for me to sit next to him. I lowered beside him, our auras nearly touching.

"That Suburban you were in has been following me," I said.

He nodded. "I've had my men keeping an eye on you."

"Your *men*?"

He angled more toward me and searched my face. "The only way I know to do this, Owen, is to start at the beginning and tell you everything I'm able to disclose."

"The truth is all I've ever wanted. The whole story."

He cleared his throat. "You have no idea how incredibly head over heels in love I was with your mother."

Were my eyes seriously starting to pool? I clenched my fists, digging my fingernails into my palms, displacing the internal ache.

"My parents had someone else in mind for me, an Ivy-League girl, but my mind was made up. I couldn't wait to spend the rest of my life with Susan. We eloped at the age of twenty and started our lives together in New Haven, Connecticut. Honestly, my best memories in life are from those days.

"But it didn't take long to realize something was deeply troubling Susan. She would look over her shoulder everywhere we went and wake up most nights screaming from some terrorizing nightmare. She finally came clean with me about why she'd run away from home—her escape from her parents and the occult. Unfortunately, that vindictive society soon tracked us down in New Haven and started threatening her constantly, in all kinds of terrifying, demented ways."

"So, what'd you do?"

He clasped his hands the exact way I did sometimes. "She begged me not to go to the police, swearing it would only make things worse. So I did the only thing I knew to do. I trailed a vehicle as it followed her to work one afternoon, and when she went inside, I confronted the driver in the parking lot, demanding that he call off the operation. He told me I'd have to talk to the man in charge, and I was so young and naive, I actually got in his car with him, then boarded a private plane for Texas.

"He and I landed in Masonville that night, and he drove me to some forested land. I followed him on foot until we arrived at a secluded, candle-lit pavilion. I'll never forget the thick wood beams overhead with ropes dangling down. I was afraid they were going to hang me."

I gulped. The occult had met for generations on the land I'd inherited. Was the pavilion still there, somewhere on my property, or had my father been taken to a different patch of woods entirely? My stomach was twisting in knots. "Please, keep going."

"A man in a ram's mask emerged from the forest, followed by some twenty people, draped in black hooded robes. They encircled me in the pavilion. The masked man ordered me to drop to my knees. When I refused, I was struck on the back of my legs. I hit the ground."

My father gripped the sofa cushion beneath him, nervous, I think. "I'd been so sheltered all my life from harsh realities," he said, "I actually thought if I explained how much I loved Susan and begged those people to leave her alone, they'd have pity and relent. But they showed no mercy. They admitted they were determined to kill Susan for having defected from their society. And that's when . . ." He lowered his head and sighed. "They dealt me the terms."

"Okay?" I waited.

"I'm so sorry, Owen. I didn't know."

I tensed my abs, as if that would help soften the blow of whatever information he was about to deliver. "Go on. Please."

"They said they'd give up on their vengeance against Susan if I'd—" He paused. "If I vowed that we'd give our firstborn to them someday." He stared at the hardwood floors now—anywhere but my face. "We didn't plan on having children anytime soon, and I thought it was a ridiculous demand anyway. I told myself we'd never have to actually follow through on it. I just needed to say whatever was necessary to make it out alive so I could go to the FBI and put an end to this sadistic group once and for all. Unfortunately I was so unknowledgeable about the occult and their rituals—about the binding power of spiritual oaths and the global underground influence these people had—I repeated their words after them and made what I thought was a meaningless vow, sealing it with a drop of my blood.

"They roughed me up so badly after that, I was surprised I regained consciousness. I managed to make it back to New Haven, but I didn't want to scare Susan by telling her the truth about where I'd been and why I was so battered. So I told her a contrived story. Meanwhile, I went immediately to a family friend of mine, an FBI agent, and reported everything. I didn't understand at first why he refused to help me, as did the second agent I spoke with. But I soon discovered they'd both been threatened and blackmailed by the occult and weren't willing to risk being whistleblowers."

He slumped and held his forehead in his hand. "Days later, while Susan was at work, I saw a positive pregnancy test in the trash can. She'd obviously tried to conceal it from me, afraid I'd resent her for the timing of it, I think. But I wasn't upset at all. I was happy, but also . . . terrified.

"I started making plans that instant to move out of state with Susan—flee the country if that's what it was going to take to protect my family. I marched into the closet and grabbed a suitcase . . ." He needed another pause. A long breath. "But the phone rang, and a man warned me that the secret society was already aware of the pregnancy— there was nothing they didn't know about us. And there was nowhere we could run where they wouldn't track us down and take the newborn I owed them."

I sat still as stone, my heart racing. "So, what'd you do?"

He stood and paced the living room. "I returned to Masonville to find Susan's parents. She'd told me they held prominent positions in the occult, particularly her mother."

He took another glance round the room, and it felt like my chest caved in. "You came *here*, to this house?"

He swallowed hard, then pointed in the direction of my mom's lounge chair. "Your grandparents sat over there while I got down on both knees and literally begged them to help me—to have compassion on their daughter and soon-coming grandchild and use their influence to call off the mission against us. To help pardon me from the satanic vow I'd made in ignorance."

"And?"

He faced away from me. "Once again, I was given only one option— a cruel, devastating form of penance in exchange for breaking a vow to the kingdom of darkness." He stuffed his hands in his pockets, I think because they started trembling. "Susan's parents would see to it that her life and yours would be spared, along with mine, providing I never made contact with either of you ever again, from that moment on. *Ever*."

I stood, even though my legs felt numb. "But I thought it was *your* parents who manipulated my mom into abandoning *you* when she was pregnant with me."

"My parents did talk Susan into leaving me, but it was only because I went to them and managed to convince them I wanted out of the marriage. I never could have rejected Susan and my unborn child, but my mother was all too willing to send her away."

He faced my direction but kept his head down. "My parents aren't the same hard-hearted people they used to be. And Owen, it was the only way at the time I knew how to protect your mom and you. I didn't want either of you to ever think I'd forsaken you."

"But that's exactly what you did."

He finally looked me in the face. It was only then that I noticed Creepers had flocked to the scene, spying, pressing their huge bodies and mangled faces against every window in the room. But I couldn't have cared less about them at that moment.

"Owen." My father approached me. "I'm not here to make excuses— only to own up to the choices I made as a young man, when I was terrified and in over my head. Susan's parents warned that the instant I spoke to their daughter or our child—to you—their society would know, and they'd close in swiftly on you both, no matter your age or how much time had passed."

"But why?" I shouted. "Why would my own grandparents want to separate you from us?"

He stayed calm. "Darkened people do cruel things. And there's nothing crueler than forcing a father to abandon his wife and child." He reached toward me. "Son—"

"Don't touch me!" I dodged his hand. "You could have found another way. You could have fought for us!" The anger in me was hotter than the fire that had nearly killed me.

"I was so young, Owen. And they had supernatural means to carry out their directives. Evil powers."

"That's your excuse for turning your back on us?"

He took calming breaths, clearly working to keep his peace. "I couldn't see Susan again without risking that she'd be killed—that both of you would be brutally murdered—so I did what I thought I had to in order to protect you at the time."

I squared my shoulders and addressed him like a prosecutor, not like a son. "All this time, you let my mom believe *she's* the one who left *you*, and she's despised herself for it. Nearly drank herself to death over it."

His whole body crumpled, and he shrank to the sofa. "You have no idea how much I agonize over that." He bent so far forward, I thought he might fall to the floor. "It was me who sent financial support all those years, not my parents. I wanted to provide for Susan and you."

"Am I supposed to say thank you?" I wiped my cheek against my shoulder, absorbing a runaway tear into my shirt.

"I know it's inexcusable, Owen. I messed up everything and failed your mother and you in the worst of ways. And yes, I kept up with where you lived and even risked everything for the chance to catch brief, distant glimpses of you several times. But I know that doesn't begin to heal the wrong—the void of my absence."

He stood and stepped toward me, but I turned my back on him. I could feel his breath on my neck. "I've put us all at great risk by coming here today, but I had to see you. And Son, it's because of you, my love for you, that I devoted my life to learning all I could about spiritual laws—how to break demonic-world oaths and satanic vows. And I run a covert, global operation to rescue children around the world who are trapped and abused in the occult. Believe me, Owen, I'd always planned to meet you and tell you everything someday, at the right time."

I whipped around and faced him. "Oh, really? And when was that going to be?"

"When Susan's parents passed away."

I threw my hands in the air. "They've been dead for over two years."

The front door opened, intruding on us.

"Owen, whose vehicle—"

My mother's shopping bag hit the floor. Her mouth moved, but nothing came out. Finally . . .

"Stephen?"

I think my father stopped breathing. "Hello, Susan."

TWENTY-SEVEN

NEITHER OF MY PARENTS BLINKED.

My mother's voice shook. "What—what are you doing here?"

"I came to see my . . . our son. I apologize for barging in on you unannounced." My father gulped. "I was just leaving."

"You are?" I said. "Already?"

He leaned toward me and whispered. "I have to. If you only knew the danger I've put us in today—I don't have a choice."

I let him hug me, then squared my shoulders. "You do have a choice. Don't run off like this, Dad—not again." I looked toward my mother, her bottom lip quivering. "She deserves a better goodbye. An honest one this time."

Mom furrowed her brow in pained confusion. My father squinted the same way I always did when battling an emotional lump in my throat.

He gave me a single nod.

And with that, I walked away, past my mother and out the front door, so my parents could finally be alone. Together, after having been torn apart for a lifetime.

TWENTY-EIGHT

I SAT ON MY MOTORCYCLE in my mom's gravel driveway, engine off, staring up at the early evening sky. I was relieved my parents were talking.
Still, I wished I could go back in time and fix everything somehow. Redo
our family history, starting with both sets of my grandparents. Had any
of them ever stopped to consider the domino effect of their decisions?
How their kids and grandkids would pay?

How *I'd* be impacted?

The thought came boomeranging back at me: Was I thinking about
how my choices would someday affect my kids and grandkids?

Then again, if I married Ray Anne, would I ever even have any?

Suddenly I was desperate to hear her voice. I reached into my pocket
for my cell but pulled out my wallet instead—a frustrating reminder
that my phone had been burned up. Elle's bookmark was wedged in my
billfold. I read it.

"Even if my father and mother abandon me, the LORD will hold me
close, Psalm 27:10."

Pretty relevant to my life. And so like Elle to somehow know it would
be. But the longer I considered the verse, the more resentment ground
within me like a bag of rocks in my chest . . . Where was the Lord when I
was seven years old and my mom left me home alone all weekend while she

stayed across town with her boyfriend? I'd curled up in her bedsheets and cried the entire time. And where was God when I was trudging through snow at four years old, our pantry so empty I was willing to eat grass if I found any, and I fell into a sewer pipe and nearly died? Apparently some man had finally pulled me out, but was I supposed to believe God had been "holding me close" as I was trapped and freezing for hours?

I shoved the bookmark back in my wallet and did the usual—stopped thinking and suppressed emotion. I needed God to help me save lives in Masonville; I couldn't afford to anger him with bitter accusations.

Still seated on my bike, I turned over my shoulder and commanded the Creepers still spying into my mom's house to go at once. Watchmen reached up out of the earth and snatched the Creepers by their feeble ankles, yanking them underground, demolishing their stakeout. Heaven's army usually invaded from the air—this stealth attack from below was extremely cool.

An hour passed, and I remained amazed that my parents were actually in the same room together. I wasn't willing to interrupt them.

I drove to the church—what remained of it—and searched for my dog, but sadly, couldn't find her. I determined I'd keep trying. I headed to Ray Anne's house, anxious to tell her my father had come to town, but even more eager just to see her. If she refused to speak to me, I'd settle for just being near her. I pulled down harder on the gas.

"I love you."

It was weird how easily I could envision her sweet face and say it into the wind, as long as she wasn't there to hear it.

As I turned into her neighborhood, it occurred to me that I'd never once heard my mom tell any man she loved him, and she hadn't said it all that often to me over the years.

I'd told her even fewer times.

I knocked on the Greiners' door and also at the garage apartment, but there was no answer. No one home. I had no choice but to move on to my next important stop.

I raced to the edge of town, parked among the cornstalks, then began the trek to the abandoned house, as hollow as the principality buried beside it. At least I hoped Molek was still there, stuck in the dirt.

Thankfully there was some daylight left. I had no cellular GPS—no phone—but I was confident I could find the spot by memory now. I had to. It was my duty to make sure Molek stayed down and the Rulers didn't prevail. It was Ray Anne's calling too, but she was buried alive herself right now in paranoid fear.

I'd only begun to traipse past rows of cornstalks, mulling over my father's shocking admissions, when the distraught infant came at me again—screaming its head off this time, like it was being tortured.

It's indescribably distressing to cover your ears, only to have a noise get louder.

I charged ahead, determined to stay on mission, even with that foreboding presence surrounding me like it was somehow in front of me, behind me, and hovering on both sides.

My will to keep going took a huge hit when my body began physically reacting to the affliction. It was like something was moving inside me, clamping down on my heart like an iron claw, then twisting in my gut, then lower still, pressing against my bladder until it felt it might burst. I had no choice but to stop and hunch over, cradling my midsection with both arms. The experience reminded me of when I'd first drunk the well water and it had wrecked my insides, only this was much, much more painful.

"God, help me."

It only got worse. The aggressive sensation traveled back up, assaulting my gut and heart all over again. And with it came crippling emotions I couldn't begin to process.

I didn't recall this form of anguish while spying on any of the Cosmic Rulers, but I still wondered if this internal torture was their doing. "No evil has any authority over me," I uttered. But up and down the sensation went, moving through me like a hostile hand tearing apart my organs—like those insects from hell that, months ago, had infested my apartment were now squirming inside me. I moaned. How long could my beating heart take this degree of torment?

I hit my knees in the dirt. "God, please."

There was no spirit of Suicide around. The pain alone was enough to make me want to die. It was *that* bad.

I collapsed onto my side and crunched into a ball. Just when I thought things couldn't get any worse, I felt a baby nestled against my chest, writhing like Jackson would do when he didn't feel well.

"Get away from me!"

A tiny hand hit my sweaty neck and clung to my skin. And then came the crushing. It was like the child's invisible accomplice had lain on top of me, pressing its massive weight against my right shoulder and hip and legs. It felt like more than one tormentor—like a dogpile of them was smothering me.

"God, where are you?"

The full-scale assault continued: the excruciating movement inside me. The mountain of oppression bearing down on me. The ghostly infant haunting me.

"Jesus!"

I don't know how long I lay there, disoriented and groaning. I only know that at some point, that gentle yet commanding voice I'd come to know spoke from within.

STAND UP.

I couldn't stop clawing the sides of my head, much less stand. "I can't."

I waited for another instruction—something more doable. But it never came.

Still lying on my side, feeling as if a mound of steel had me pinned down, I realized I had a choice. I could lie there in defeat or try to stand like I'd been told. *Try,* at least.

I pushed against the ground, but my upper-body strength was practically nonexistent. "Lord, help me stand."

I was in no less pain when I finally sat up. I could still feel the baby on the ground next to me. It paused for brief moments to catch its breath before wailing again, like real babies do.

"Lord, help me stand," I pled again, feeling an intense, incompatible mix of faith toward God and contempt, to be honest.

I rose to my knees, then dragged my foot across the dirt until the sole of my shoe was flat on the ground, my aura shining around it.

"Lord, help me stand."

I bent forward and breathed—in through my nose, out through my mouth—as the inner affliction bore down on my bladder again. What kind of evil was this?

"Lord, help me stand."

I held out hope Custos would come lift me up. At the very least, the old man. He'd rescued me twice before, when I was too weak to help myself. But minutes ticked on like hours, and no one came. I had to use both hands and press against the earth with all my depleted might. Soon, I was bent over, but on my feet. The weight of the invisible monster pressed down hard on my back.

"Lord, help me stand. All the way."

I wanted to hit my knees again, not straighten my spine and lengthen my tortured gut. But inch by inch, I lifted my upper body until at last, I stood upright. The oppressive weight bore down on my shoulders now, the baby still protesting at my feet.

WALK WITH ME.

Another divine instruction that seemed out of reach. I didn't feel like I could take a step, much less walk, but I moved my foot forward a few inches. "Help me walk with you, Lord."

I managed one step. Then another. Then another. The pain the same. My resolve renewing.

I finally managed to walk, struggling the same way Ray Anne had after back-to-back surgeries. I begged God with every ounce of humility in me to please, please, *please* take away the agony—even slightly. And silence the infant, which was still following right behind me.

But he didn't.

Over an hour after I'd started the trek, I finally arrived at the little abandoned house, no less miserable. But I had to force my focus off my pain and onto what mattered most right now.

I moved to the front left corner of the house, then leaned forward to sneak a peek.

Molek was only buried up to his waist, and he used his long spirit-world fingers to claw away physical-world matter, scooping dirt and tossing it aside, freeing himself from his soil prison. Next to him, his boxy throne poked out of the dirt, and he worked to unearth it as well.

I continued spying as one of those hateful bats descended, landing on top of Molek's thorn-crowned head. The Lord of the Dead tilted his head back and opened his mouth so wide, he could have swallowed the fat winged creature. Instead he let the bat spit that black-grit death dust concoction onto his outstretched tongue. There was no telling what conflict had created this latest batch—which Lights were feuding instead of loving.

The bat flew away, and Molek resumed digging, faster now, still chewing his nasty potion.

Out of nowhere, he turned his head my direction and froze.

"I'm breaking free." His voice was the sound of a thousand high-pitched whispers, aimed at me. Mocking me. Scorning my heavenly assignment to defend and liberate people. "I am free," he asserted, "but you'll never be."

That horrible agony traveled up through my midsection again, and I knew . . .

The war raging over my town was about to come to an inescapable standoff. And so was the turmoil inside of me.

TWENTY-NINE

IT WAS ALREADY DUSK, so I had to speed to my property to make it to the Caldwell Cemetery in time. With Molek strong enough to have nearly dug his way out, the Rulers were bound to execute their deadly assignment against the thirteen marked students, including Gentry, any minute now, while also ramping up for their full-on takeover of Masonville. I hoped to spy on the Rulers and get some idea of their next move, then interrupt their plan somehow—with wisdom, not fear.

I was no stranger to these woods, even at night—the eerie squeals and rustlings that could just as easily be a demonic tyrant as a forest animal. But I'd never had to journey out here with an invisible baby crying its lungs out and a hidden stalker pressing in on my still-throbbing insides.

"What kind of punishment is this, God?" I kept asking.

Despite the pain, I managed to jog part of the way in the sparse moonlight. I finally arrived at the Caldwell Cemetery. Well, at least where the fenced-in graves and Mary statue normally sat. Now a blistering portal lay open in the earth like a sweltering, gaping mouth. All seven Rulers—including two-faced Mother Punishment—hovered at the edge of the pit, gazing at those big cone-shaped bone platforms spinning over the crater.

I assumed they'd mount their demonic pulpits, but I was wrong.

Molek's messenger bats flew up and out of the pit, circling overhead. "The time has come," they demanded in unison. "You must combine your powers."

The Rulers growled and hissed at one another as if they loathed the thought. But the bats threatened, "If you refuse to do as our Master says and this territory is lost to the Light, you'll be cast into outer darkness with him!"

It didn't matter that the Rulers outranked Molek—he'd used the currency of hell to order them around. *Fear.* And I found the strength to inflate my chest at the bats' words: *lost to the Light.* They were afraid of the power in us. The presence we Lights house within.

It was also a sobering reminder of the responsibility we had to engage in the spiritual battle.

The Rulers seemed oblivious to me as I looked on from behind a tree—except Mother Punishment. She stood stiff, her white-robed side facing me, her narrow eyes scanning the exact spot in the woods where I was hiding. She whipped her paddle against her palm and smiled.

I sensed she was welcoming me to watch and listen to their plans, as if I could never dare stop them.

A four-fingered scorched hand the size of a battleship—I'm not exaggerating—reached up from the pit, grabbing all six massive platforms and crushing them with such force, I wondered if it could be Satan himself.

The bones and rubble snapped and cracked, rolling like pebbles inside the huge palm, and the fragments cried out like they were alive and could feel the pain. Then the hand opened, and amid the crushed platforms, numerous winged beasts the size of my Labrador retriever flew out. They had heads like wild boars and insect-like bodies. The gruesome creatures quickly assembled the bony wreckage into a single structure using their double set of arms and hands that looked as human as mine.

They constructed a giant, lumpy chair of crushed bones—a single asymmetrical throne, suspended above the blistering abyss. All at once, five of the Rulers charged toward it, colliding midair like debris in a tornado, punching and clawing and tearing at each other, striving to be the first to the throne. But not Mother Punishment. She stayed planted on the ground, eyeing the dogfight. She lowered her white-cloaked head, as if pretending their savagery actually grieved her. Then she began floating up into the air like cigar smoke.

She reached the airborne brawl, reared back with her paddle, and struck Lust in the back so hard, he went careening down into the pit, howling the whole way. One by one, she pounded the other Rulers, beating them until she was the only one left. With her green witch's chin lifted, she sank onto the hovering throne, sitting tall with that threatening grin of hers. Immediately, the bones cried out again.

It was dizzying watching her morph from the self-righteous saint in white to the pointed-hat witch in black, like a disorienting kaleidoscope of spinning colors.

Lust sailed sheepishly up through the air and out of the pit, his head down, facing away from Mother Punishment. He lowered onto the throne, disappearing inside of her. One by one, Despair, Strife, Addiction, and Slumber did the same, succumbing to her dominance.

"You disabled the radiant one?" the encircling bats called out.

The Rulers answered in unison, but the Mother's voice overpowered them all. "She's under lock and key."

Who? I wondered.

"You know what must be done to the thirteen," the bats sneered.

Mother Punishment nodded. "Under the cloak of darkness tomorrow."

An inevitable deadline. But at least now I knew part of their plan.

Instantly, the spirit-world spun like I'd seen it do before, and all earthly matter returned as the Cosmic Rulers vanished. It was only then I realized the infant had stopped crying while I watched them. But now it was back. I squeezed my head, off balance and despairing. I squatted on the forest floor, desperate for relief. "God, you have to help me!"

Instant, inexplicable silence and peace. And the feel of a warm hand on my shoulder.

I clamped down on the old man's fingers with my own. "You have no idea how glad I am you're here." I jumped up. "How'd you do that—stop the torment so fast?"

"It's what mercy does."

Even in the dark, with only our auras for illumination, I could tell he was grinning at me.

"Why are some baby and horrific presence after me?" I pled.

"That's a question for God, not me."

"I've asked and asked. He won't answer."

"That's a lie, and you'd be wise to never utter those words again." He hadn't ever put me in my place like that. "God always answers, in his timing and way."

"Okay, I'm sorry." I rubbed my stomach, relieved my insides were no longer being ravaged. "I have a million questions for you, like how to stop the Rulers and save the thirteen students tomorrow. But first . . ." I had to know. "Are you a heavenly being? Some kind of messenger from God?"

"Knowing who I am is far less important than knowing who *you* are."

I barely resisted sighing. "Please don't get philosophical with me— there's no time. Just tell me who you are."

He stepped so close, the brim of his cowboy hat nearly grazed my hairline. "I will. As soon as you tell me who you are."

My hands balled into fists—now more than ever, I needed straight-forward answers, not some rabbit-trail essay prompt. "All about me" was a weird conversation to have standing next to a cemetery in Creeper-ridden woods at night, knowing thirteen students were scheduled to die in twenty-four hours.

But fine.

"Uh, I'm Owen James Edmonds." I couldn't contain this sigh. "I turn twenty next month. Besides teaching myself to play a guitar that burned up in a fire with the rest of my stuff, I hardly know what I do and don't like to do anymore, because my life has been turned completely upside down and consumed by some calling I've been given to save the people of Masonville from demonic dominance—plus thirteen people targeted to die tomorrow. And I have a red glowing seal in me that says I'm a defender, even though I've never been good at defending people." I waved my arm in front of his face. "See?" I crossed my arms and huffed. "Okay, your turn."

"That was only a description." He pressed his index finger into my chest. "You haven't told me who you *are*—your identity, as you see it."

Maybe it was Strife's influence, or having narrowly escaped dying in a fire—or my nonstop concern for Ray Anne, or having just seen Molek nearly back in action—but I couldn't handle this. I exploded. "That's enough! I've dealt with secrecy all my life, and I don't need it from you." As bad as it sounds, I did want to punch the old man now. Or tackle him to the ground and physically force him to tell me what I needed to know, even though he was as muscular as me.

"I'm trying to help you," he said. "That's all I've ever done."

"Well, it doesn't *help* when you keep stuff from me." I was so loud, a flock of birds took flight. "And how am I supposed to make sense of who *I* am when no one wants to tell me who *they* are? Or every time I finally think I know someone, it turns out they're not who I thought they were?"

I didn't realize I was spitting in his face until he gripped my shoulders and gently pushed me back. "You'll never have peace, much less win the war on Masonville and fulfill your destiny, until you're certain of who you are. And just as importantly, who you're not."

My heart was pounding, but what else was new? "Look, I'm trying to figure it out, okay? But it's kind of hard when your own parents have lied to you over and over and let you down more times than you can count."

He flipped on a flashlight I hadn't noticed he had with him, and—I couldn't believe it—turned his back on me and started walking off.

"So that's it? You're leaving?" I huffed. "Guess I should be used to people doing that by now. You especially."

He stopped but stayed facing away. "You gonna stand there and keep whining about how bad you have it or walk with me?"

The second time tonight he'd put me in my place. "Fine." I caught up with his aura.

He shined the flashlight ahead. "Neglect and abandonment cut deep, Owen, and there's no shame in mourning a painful past. It's a crucial step. But it's not the final destination, Son. Never let the rejection suffered at the hands of others define who you are—how you view yourself." He quickened his pace. "Now, there's something you need to see."

We strode further, through a section of woods I'd never traveled before. I didn't smell or spy any Creepers, but then again, they always gave the old man lots of space. I stayed close to him, relieved that with him near, my tormenting symptoms were staying away.

As we neared the road that ran along the backside of my property, the old man finally stopped. He aimed his flashlight in the distance, illuminating a large pavilion constructed of thick wood beams that formed a roof over a dilapidated wood-plank floor. It was like a log cabin, only without walls. It took my breath away.

"This is the place my father *just* told me about, where the occult people took him twenty years ago and nearly beat him to death. Where he made an oath to give his firstborn child to them. *Me.*"

The old man handed me his flashlight, and I stepped into the pavilion, aiming the light overhead. "My father said there were ropes hanging from these massive beams." A single frayed one swayed in the breeze now.

The old man removed his cowboy hat. "Back when T. J. Caldwell ran his plantation out here, this was where he held public lynchings. Generations that followed kept up the sick practice."

I wanted to vomit. "Shouldn't it be covered in vines and greenery by now?" The question had no sooner left my mouth than the realization came to me: people were *still* using this place. Masonville's occult society.

I vowed right then and there, "I'm going to bulldoze all of this to the ground!"

The old man motioned for me to give back his flashlight. "Or you could use it for good. That's how you really turn the tables on the kingdom of darkness."

His comment was a sobering reminder. "Molek is about to dig himself free," I said, "and the Cosmic Rulers have converged into one on a giant throne. They're plotting to strike down thirteen students tomorrow night, but I have no idea how. Time is running out."

The old man nodded. "That's why I must show you this now."

He turned his flashlight off, immersing us in the dark, and instructed me to get down at the center of the pavilion floor. I hesitated, but he assured me he'd be right next to me.

We knelt down, and he rested his palm between my shoulder blades. "Use your hands to dig."

"What?" I pressed against the wood planks. "I can't dig through this."

He said nothing else. So I cupped my fingers and, idiotic as it seemed, began to scoop. I gasped when the wood supernaturally shifted and piled like particles of dirt. Soon, I was digging deeper, past a cement foundation, into actual soil.

"What do I do now?" I asked.

"Keep digging."

Needless to say, I had no idea what I'd find, and I was slightly creeped out. But I trusted him enough to keep plowing with my hands, eventually stretching out onto my stomach to reach further down.

"I don't see anything."

"You will," he asserted. "And you'll never forget it."

THIRTY

A FULL ARM'S LENGTH BELOW THE EARTH'S SURFACE, the ground gave way, and my hand slipped into chilled air. I pulled my arm back and peered into a dim underground hole. The cold air reeked of death and decay.

From my vantage point, prostrate on the pavilion floor, I stared down into a small underground cavern, the edges dim with green-tinted light. The space was as long and narrow as a grave, walled in by soil. I spied the back of a Creeper's battered head and shoulders protruding from the dirt, occupying most of the space. The demon shouted in English.

"You're supposed to be dead!"

"Do your family a favor and end your misery!"

"Death is your only way out!"

"You can't live like this much longer!"

On and on the instigator spewed suicidal insults, and having no need for breath, didn't even pause between sentences. The Creeper's foul mouth faced away from me, yet its hatred rose up like lethal fumes, its murderous words provoking me to give up.

The Creeper jerked backward, disappearing underground. That's when I saw the shadowy form of a stiff body wrapped in what looked like thin layers of gauze, encircled in chains and cords from the shackled neck down. The only skin visible in the mummified shroud was the pale face of a young man, his eyes shut.

I shuddered. "It *is* a grave."

The old man patted my back, but it didn't take away the dread.

"Why was that Creeper bullying him to kill himself when he's already dead?" I asked.

"Keep watching."

Now a different kind of light filled the grave, pure and soothing. The young man's eyes opened, blinking, as he began to breathe, slow and steady.

"He's alive!" But as the color returned to the boy's face, I slapped a hand over my gaping mouth. *It's Gentry.*

A robed Watchman pressed his glorious head through the side of the underground chamber, resting his left cheek against Gentry's chest, his gaze fixed on Gentry's face. The Watchman was so enormous, the distance from his dark hair to his perfectly defined chin stretched the entire width of the grave. He spoke, his voice youthful, yet deep and assertive.

"You're meant to live, Gentry."

"God willed that you be born."

"He has a meaningful future planned for you."

"God loves you and longs to heal your pain. All of it."

I inhaled an incredible aroma, like fragrant incense, overpowering all stench of death.

Gentry's face was dormant and expressionless, yet a tear trickled from his eye. I watched in stunned wonder as the Watchman's hand breached the soil wall, clutching a glass bottle the size of a salt shaker, as ornate as Mrs. Greiner's crystal vases. There was shimmering liquid inside. The heavenly giant touched it to Gentry's cheek, guiding his tear into the bottle.

The Watchman backed out of the claustrophobic space, and instantly, the harsh green light returned, along with the rancid smell of death. Even worse, Gentry stopped breathing. It was a helpless feeling, looking down on him as all color left his face and his eyes collapsed shut. That Creeper shoved itself back into the grave, assaulting Gentry with the same cruel remarks as before.

I scrambled to sit upright. "What's happening to him?"

The old man exhaled a heavy sigh. "This is the state of the human soul when a person attempts suicide, yet survives."

"I don't understand."

The man stood, then gripped my arm, helping me to my feet. "The moment Gentry set out to kill himself, the demonic world dug a spirit-realm grave and trapped his soul inside. Night and day, they call to him, accosting his mind and emotions, seducing him to murder himself again—to finish the job this time. But the voice of hope calls to him as well."

I stepped back, afraid that my foot might slip into the grave.

"So, Gentry's soul is stuck out here, on my land?"

"No." The old man used his work boot to slide dirt into the hole, covering the nightmarish spectacle. "Gentry's soul is inside his body, but wherever he goes, his soul remains trapped in a spiritual grave, battling conflicting voices. Despair versus destiny."

The duality of realms was an abstract concept to grasp, but all that really mattered was Gentry's survival. "How can we get him out of there?"

"Only he can." The old man stomped the pile of dirt, now level with the earth's surface, and the pavilion's wood floor returned—a spiritual phenomenon as seemingly natural as the rustling of the leaves on the trees surrounding us. "It's Gentry's choice."

For once, I didn't need the mysterious man to elaborate. I understood: if Gentry chose to believe and side with God's voice of truth—take the loving hand God was reaching out to him and refuse to listen to the enemy's lies any longer—his soul would escape that grave. And given my experience breaking free of chains and cords that, just months ago, had me bound, I was sure it would go a long way for Gentry to ask God's forgiveness for having tried to murder himself, as the old man had phrased it. I knew better than anyone that forgiveness causes major chain reactions in the spirit-realm. The good kind.

Most importantly, Gentry needed to be liberated from his shackle, and I knew the solution for that too. But I couldn't share it with Gentry if he wasn't willing to listen.

"Owen." The old man called to me, but I was lost in thought, staring at the lone rope dangling from the rafters. "Don't try to intervene alone tomorrow. You need another's help. Don't be too proud to ask for it."

Naturally, I thought of Ray Anne, but she was out of commission.

I turned to face the old man, eager to ask more, but he was gone.

Abandoned again. It was such an intense thought, I scanned the dark pavilion and surrounding woods, questioning if it came from me or . . .

An unmistakable sewage smell wafted my way. I knew who was there, stalking me and launching that depressing statement at my mind. An old nuisance, back again. "Demise, you have no permission to speak to me."

The sewage smell faded into the night air.

I lingered under the pavilion, sickened by the thought of the horrific, unjust acts performed here, under this very roof. The pleas for mercy that had gone unanswered. The innocent lives lost at the hands of humanity, received by Molek as a reverent offering.

Like the final pieces of a puzzle snapping into place, as I stood there pondering the pavilion's gruesome history, the Rulers' deadly plan for tomorrow night suddenly became clear to me—as obvious as the stench of death that engulfed Gentry's spirit-world grave. It was an unthinkable maneuver, a tragedy the people of Masonville had yet to suffer. So atrocious, the whole nation would be stunned.

I took off running as fast as I could in the dark woods back toward the Caldwell Cemetery so I could find my way from there to my motorcycle, praying the whole time. "Please, *please*, God, help me find Gentry."

It was 10:55 p.m. when I arrived at his house. Eleven o'clock by the time the door finally opened to my knocking. I was prepared to face his stepdad and insist I speak with Gentry. If Gentry wasn't home, I'd plead for his stepdad to tell me where I might find him. But it wasn't the stepdad at the door.

"Lance." I gulped. "You're back."

THIRTY-ONE

"WHAT ARE YOU DOING HERE, OWEN?"

It didn't matter how close of friends Lance and I had been when I first moved to Masonville, or that I'd run to his side when he'd been shot in the school hallway and was bleeding out on the floor. He apparently had nothing but contempt for me.

He flipped on the porch light and stepped outside, dragging his chains over the door's threshold. I resisted raising my brows at his sculpted biceps, even bigger now that he'd been through the police academy. And he'd grown nearly as tall as me since I'd last seen him—technically, the night he and the other masked guards at the human auction gagged and hogtied me, though I hadn't realized Lance had been among them until after the fact.

"I have to talk to Gentry," I told him.

"He ran away two days ago."

"Your stepdad kicked him out," I clarified.

"No, he didn't. How would you know, anyway?"

"I've been looking out for your brother lately. Trying to, at least. He's on drugs—and dealing, I think. And Lance . . ."

Gentry had asked me not to tell his secret, but I was sure if Gentry knew how much his big brother really cared about him, he'd have told

Lance himself. Still, this was the ultimate déjà vu, having to tell Lance yet again that someone close to him was suicidal. Last time it hadn't gone well, to say the least. "Gentry's attempted suicide before, and he's going to do it again. Tomorrow night."

Lance crossed his hulking arms. "I can't *believe* you're pulling this again."

"There are twelve more students who are going to do it too, including his girlfriend, Zella. A group suicide, on my property." A sacrifice of young lives hand chosen by Molek, the Lord of the Dead—so sadistic, it would grant him the spirit-world rights he needed to return to my land and join the Cosmic Rulers. Together, they'd wreak untold devastation on Masonville and beyond. But I couldn't explain that part to Lance.

He narrowed his eyes. "My brother told you this?"

I hesitated. "Not exactly."

He rocked back and forth on his heels, smirking. "Let me guess. You saw some invisible monster at the school, chasing his friends and him with an axe?"

"It's not like that."

He thrust his face in mine, smirk gone. "It's your morbid, psychotic stories that push people over the edge, Owen. If you hadn't scared Meagan so bad and put thoughts of suicide in her head, she'd still be alive. Walt and Marshall too."

"That's not true!" My temper spiked as hot as his. "I've only ever tried to help people and warn them. But you were too stubborn to listen to me before, and you still are."

I guess I should have seen it coming—he shoved me. "You stay away from my brother, you hear me?"

I stumbled backwards but managed to stay on my feet. "Please, Lance, for once, hear me out. I could use your help!"

Creepers rushed to the scene, lured by our conflict, but I kept my eyes on Lance, ready to cover my head if he started swinging. He kept his fists at his sides, but his shadowy soul lurched forward, leaning out from his torso and growling at me like a Rottweiler.

He'd always been one to rage; maybe that was what made him susceptible to Strife's influence.

Truth be told, for as long as I could remember, I'd been raging too.

No, I didn't go around taking it out on people, throwing punches; I kept my fury bottled up, battering my own frustrated soul.

Who was I kidding? Of course Strife had been able to sink his meat hooks in me.

I squared my shoulders, determined to try to get through to Lance one last time. "You and I both know there are some horrible, dark things going on in this town, led by some seriously corrupt people. Even you got caught up in it, Lance. But I'm begging you—there are powers at work here more deadly than you can imagine, and they're after your brother. I'm serious. I need you to trust me and help me stop this. Fight on the right team. With me."

His breathing quickened and his eyes became glossy—a major show of emotion for him. But he didn't break. "Get off my property, or I'll drag you off."

What could I do except turn around and leave?

As I drove out of Lance's neighborhood, it occurred to me to find Zella's house and try reasoning with her, but it's not like Detective Benny would let me anywhere near his daughter.

I pulled up at my mom's, and the black Suburban was idling out front in the street. At least I knew now the men in that SUV weren't out to harm me.

My mother and father stood by the passenger door, facing one another—two silhouettes on a dark night. I turned my engine off, but stayed seated on my motorcycle in the driveway, giving them space.

My mom looked up at him. "Stephen, I . . ."

I think she was trying to say the three most important words but wasn't any better at it than me. Like mother, like son.

He embraced her. "My heart never left you, Susan."

My mother's body went limp in his arms, like she'd waited a lifetime to hear that.

"We can't be seen together." He held her, swaying side to side. "But I'll be in touch. You have my word."

He looked my direction and motioned for me to approach. I did, and he wrapped an arm around my shoulders, still holding my mother in the other.

None of us said anything.

There was no need.

Minutes later, my mom sobbed like a homesick child as she stood next to me, watching the Suburban's red taillights move down the street. We wandered into the house, both of us keeping to ourselves, enduring the void of my father's absence.

I still felt the sting of his decision to distance himself from me nearly my entire life, but somehow the resentment was no match for the attachment I still had toward him.

Mom started up the stairs, and I asked to borrow her cell phone. She handed it to me, then locked herself in her bedroom. I could only hope she wouldn't start drinking again.

I texted Ray Anne and called her multiple times, but there was no answer. Was she ignoring my calls, or had her parents taken away her phone? Hearing Ray's voice on her voicemail greeting made my insides ache.

Minutes later, just after midnight, there was a knock at the door—so soft, I barely heard it.

I glanced out the peephole.

Zella. A black line above her shackle, across her throat. And a hulking Creeper behind her, attached at the wrist to one of her chains, with one of the cords hanging from the back of her head burrowed into its palm. I opened the door, and the Creeper's stench of festering mold accosted my nose. Tears streamed down Zella's cheeks, and she wrapped both arms around her waist like she was trying to console herself. For a moment I feared my theory about tomorrow's group suicide was wrong and her boyfriend was already gone.

"Did something happen to Gentry?" I asked.

"No." She wiped her nose on the long sleeve of her maroon hoodie. "Not yet."

Had she not been escorting that towering Creeper, I'd have invited her inside. I went out to her instead, closing the door behind me, ignoring the ice-cold intruder.

"I snuck out and walked here," she said. "Gentry made me swear not to tell, but I have to. I don't know who else to go to."

I didn't waste time asking how she'd known which house was my mom's or that she could find me here.

"Me and Gentry are in a support group with people who've tried to kill themselves before. Now Gentry's telling us we need to do it again, for real this time. Together. Tomorrow night. No backing out."

"I know, Zella."

She looked up at me, her teary eyes wide. "How?"

She was shackled, so not likely to believe me, but I was still willing to tell her the facts—how she and Gentry and the others were targeted to die. But I had to navigate the conversation carefully. The Creeper behind her already had its hands out, poised to cover her ears. "I know you think the group suicide is Gentry's idea, but it's not. An evil influence put the plan in his head."

"I know who."

"You do?" Now *I* was surprised. Did she actually believe in the existence of demonic beings?

I waited impatiently for her to get a tearful sob under control. "It was Eva. Gentry said she came to him last week and told him we have to do it—including where, what time, and how."

"Eva," evil's puppet. I should have known.

I popped my knuckles, struggling to make sense of Veronica's motives and methods. And the stupid two-name thing.

"And Gentry wants to go through with it?"

"Yes." Zella cleared her throat. "Eva said lots of innocent people have been murdered in those woods behind the school, and their spirits still roam the land, angry and unable to rest. They haunt Masonville High and make people do bad things, like when Dan Bradford shot up the school.

"And they're going to keep forcing people to do bad things unless a group of us sacrifice our own lives—you know, to show the spirits that we care and we're sorry for what happened to them. Then they'll move on and leave that land and our school alone forever. No more violence.

"And since we're the suicidal ones—the ones willing and brave enough—it should be us."

My jaw could not have dropped any lower. Yes, countless people had been murdered on that land—my land—but the rest was outright lies.

There were demons all over my property and the school, not vengeful ghosts, and demons don't *force* people to do violent stuff. They manipulate people by taunting them with cruel lies—the very thing "Eva" was doing to Gentry. And the remedy was citywide prayer on the land, not more senseless deaths.

I was practically choking on the putrid smell of mold wafting from the Creeper behind Zella, but it was too dark outside to see the word etched into its forehead. I clutched her thin shoulders. "What's the plan? The location and time?"

"Tomorrow at midnight. We're supposed to meet up at that Mary statue in the old graveyard and take some pills Gentry is bringing. He swears it'll be painless."

I thought for sure the moldy Creeper would react as Zella revealed evil's top-secret plot. Gnash its jagged teeth or something. But it just stood there, threatened by my aura, I supposed.

"You're not planning to be a part of this, right, Zella? You know it's all a deception?"

That did it. The Creeper snarled at me like a prehistoric beast.

She started to sob again, silently at first. Then through gasps, she confessed. "Part of me doesn't want to die, but . . . part of me does."

Oh yeah. Zella's soul was trapped in one of those spirit-world graves where evil advice and hope-filled assurances were yanking back and forth on her mind and emotions in a ceaseless tug-of-war. And with her father being entrenched in the occult, and her mother likely active too, who knew what her life was like?

"Zella—"

Before I could attempt to sway her, she threw her arms around me, squeezing my ribs, burying her damp face in my T-shirt. "I'm not gonna do it, Owen—I'm not! I want to live and move out and get away from this town. From my parents. But someone has to go to the cemetery tomorrow night and stop Gentry and talk the others out of it too. They won't listen to me. I know they won't!"

"Shh." I rubbed circles on her back, trying to calm her the way I'd seen Ray Anne ease Jackson during his crying spells. "Don't worry, Zella. I won't let this happen."

She finally released me, and I asked if she knew where Gentry was.

"He won't tell me. And, Owen, if you go to Principal Harding, or word gets out at all that someone's trying to stop the plan—if our group doesn't follow through—Eva told Gentry someone else would die in our place. She mentioned something about a special child worth more than all of us."

It felt like I'd been hit by a torpedo.

Hadn't Veronica told me Mother Punishment was coming for Jackson? He was evil's fallback plan.

For the life of me, I couldn't understand why they were so obsessed with that little boy. What made him such a coveted prize to enemy forces?

Zella started fanning her face like she was burning up, not surprising given that she was wearing a hoodie in August. I knew there had to be something to it. "How come Gentry and you always dress like that?"

She sniffled while pushing her sleeve up past her elbow, then held her forearm in my face. Even in the moonlight, I could see the scabby streaks.

"You guys cut yourselves?"

She nodded, then started to pull her sleeve down, but I reached and stopped her. "Wait!"

"What are you doing?" She tried to tug her arm away, but I held on.

"Zella . . ." I couldn't make sense of it. "You have a defender seal."

"A what?"

"You—you're shackled, yet marked for the mission. How's that possible?"

The Creeper tugged on her chain, and she stepped back.

I knew the moldy monster was going to freak, but I had to say it. "You've been set apart, Zella. By God."

Sure enough, her tormentor roared, then pressed its rotten mouth against her ear. "Go," it hissed.

Zella pulled her sleeve down. "I've got to go."

"Hold on." I pulled my mom's phone out of my pocket and aimed the screen light at the Creeper's face. A scarred assignment ran the length of its forehead and wrapped around the side of its bald head.

I'd commanded Creepers to go from places before, but never from a person tethered to one. There's a first time for everything, right?

"In the name of Jesus, Deception, let go of Zella."

The thing instantly foamed at the mouth and started convulsing.

"What's going on?" Zella asked.

I stayed focused, repeating the command.

The Creeper ripped Zella's cord out of its hand as if it was suddenly scalding hot, then scrambled to pull its wrist out of the chain cuff.

"I was gonna ask you for a ride home," she said, "but seriously, never mind." She started down the driveway.

Unlinked to Zella, Deception rushed into the street, where two more Creepers came climbing out from a covered sewer hole. The three of them eyed her like snakes tracking a mouse.

"Zella, please." I caught up to her. "Let me give you a ride."

She threw her hands in the air. "You just went psycho on me."

"I'm sorry. There are things you don't understand. Things you don't see."

Like a dimmer light switch steadily rising to max power, the gruesome mask of addiction came into view, covering her entire face. The sharp barbed wire dangling at her chin. The dagger in her gut.

"Zella, I know you're really stressed out and scared, but don't go use. It's not what you need."

"I don't do drugs."

I didn't call her on the lie.

She grabbed the sides of my arms. "Just promise me you'll stay sane and make sure no one dies tomorrow."

"I'm willing to die trying," I vowed. The three onlooking Creepers cackled, apparently pleased with the mere mention of my death.

Zella finally agreed to let me fetch her an Uber, but she insisted on waiting for her ride at the corner by herself. I looked on from a distance as those Creepers in the street—Deception included—pounced on her, attaching themselves to her chain and cords.

The old man's lesson clicked. *An empty house can be occupied again by worse tenants than before.* A shackled person freed of a Creeper can end up with more attached than before.

Zella's car arrived, and as I turned to go inside the house, I noticed the lid on my mom's mailbox was wide open. I peeked in and retrieved two envelopes—neither marked with an address or stamp. My first name was written in pencil on both envelopes—one in nice cursive, and the other, sloppy kid font.

Once inside and seated on the sofa, I opened the cursive one and read the blue-lined paper.

> *The people who need us the most can turn out to be our biggest*
> *backstabbers, the worst kind of traitors. Be careful, Owen.*
> *– Veronica.*

Gentry came to mind. He'd been labeled a traitor. Then again, the accusation had come from Hector—a major fraud himself.

I tore open the other envelope, unfolding the second letter, scanning the scribbled words.

> *Expect to cry some bloody tears tomorrow. This one's going to hurt.*
> *– Eva*

Clearly a reference to the Bloody Mary statue, the location for tomorrow night's group suicide.

I dropped the stationery and cradled my head, my mind reeling. A helpful warning and a vicious threat, sent from the same woman.

Was this the kind of maddening mind game occult people play?

I was crumpling both letters when it hit me: *There's someone who'd know.*

I raced upstairs and knocked on my mom's bedroom door.

THIRTY-TWO

My MOTHER'S MAKEUP was smeared down her face, and she was lying in bed on a mound of crumpled Kleenex, but thankfully, not sipping alcohol. I lowered onto the corner of her mattress.

"Mom, I know you hate talking about anything related to your past, but please, I need you to help me make sense of something. Lives are on the line."

She raised her eyebrows but nodded.

I summarized the bizarre situation, asking if she understood how someone associated with the occult could be helpful and hurtful at the same time, using two different names.

"It's simple."

"It is?" I scooted closer to her. "Tell me."

She closed her eyes and spoke robotically, like emotions weren't allowed. "The abuse children suffer in the occult is so unbearable, so totally overwhelming, they often dissociate—invent an imaginary personality that can survive the pain that would otherwise crush them. They may create numerous personalities, each designed to protect them from specific threats. It's a desperate form of denial and escape. And it's not uncommon to give the personalities names."

"That's insane."

She opened her eyes. "Owen, I don't know what you've gotten yourself into, but if someone in the occult has befriended you, end the relationship immediately. And don't believe a single word they tell you. Not *one* thing."

It was surreal having such a candid talk with my mother on a topic that had been forbidden all my life. I saw it as my one chance to ask her, "You know your 'friend' Dr. Bradford was in the occult—do you honestly believe he got out?"

I expected her to launch into a lengthy defense of him. Instead, her eyes pooled. "Of course I question it at times. But for once in my life, I'm trying to trust that people can change." She clutched a wad of tissues. "I have to believe that."

In order to believe *she* could change.

I wasn't suddenly infused with any new confidence in Brody Bradford, but for my mom's sake, I found myself hoping I was wrong and he truly was a transformed man. She had suffered more than enough betrayal.

She closed her weary eyes, and I politely left the room. I shut myself in my old bedroom and sank to the floor, needing to sort through the traffic jam now gridlocked in my mind.

I'd heard of dissociative identity disorder but never understood it, much less thought I'd come face-to-face with someone who actually had the condition. The way I now understood it, "Veronica" was truly done with the occult and genuinely trying to help me, but "Eva" was as committed as ever—intentionally plotting against me, taking orders from her handler.

One person with two opposing personalities that had never met. Maybe more than two.

Then there was Zella, also being raised in the occult. Could I trust the details of her story tonight? Her motives? Her sanity?

And how in the world was she marked as a defender?

I gnashed my teeth, loathing the mounting uncertainty, enduring the physical symptoms of fight or flight. I was tempted all over again to take off—run away with Ray Anne and Jackson and never look back. Instead, I rose to my knees.

"God, I want to intervene and save these students' lives—you know

I do. And I want to stop the evil in this town and see your will come to pass here. But as usual, I don't understand who's for me or against me—who's lying or telling the truth. But I do know tomorrow night will make or break everything, so please, Lord, show me what to do."

I collapsed onto the bed, seriously missing my dog but grateful that the wailing baby and unseen stalker had left me—at least for now. "Whatever you say, Lord, I'll do it."

There was the rapid sound of tapping on the window. At first I was sure it was the witches, but when my eyelids sprang open, I saw raindrops pelting the farmhouse glass. The scarce morning light had turned the white walls a bleak gray. The seriousness of the day's objective weighed so heavily on me, it hurt my chest to inhale. But I wasn't willing to lie there cowering.

I sat up, and Ray Anne's face consumed my thoughts. I felt like I'd lose my mind if I didn't get to see her this morning. And hopefully hold her.

I wanted—really needed—her with me for tonight's mission, but I knew the odds of her being strong enough weren't good. Plus, her mom probably wouldn't allow her out of the house for long, if at all. As of now, my only plan was to show up at the Mary statue and beg the students not to kill themselves. I held out hope I'd piece together a better strategy.

The old man had warned me not to go alone, but what choice did I have?

A knock on the front door jarred me out of bed.

Elle. Dressed to impress. High heels and all.

I welcomed her into the living room, and she held a gold iPhone out to me. "I figured you might could use my old cell after the fire."

Of course she did.

"Thanks."

"Is your mom home?" she whispered.

I nodded toward the stairs, and Elle spoke softer. "I located the boarding school Veronica Snow attended. It's in New Mexico. It took a lot of digging, but I found a certain signature on the visitation log."

Finally, physical evidence that Detective Benny was Veronica's handler—a child abuser and leader in Masonville's underground crime ring. McFarland's killer. Also the one inciting witches and warlocks from coast-to-coast to war against those of us committed to peace.

"Is it enough proof to expose the detective?" I asked.

She crinkled her nose. "The detective?" She leaned and spoke in my ear. "The name was 'B. Bradford.' I compared it with the doctor's signature—it's a match."

I sank to the sofa, reacclimating to reality.

My instincts had been right about Dr. Bradford's unredeemed motives, yet it hadn't dawned on me he could be evil's point man. Even worse than a dirty cop.

"And no, I need more evidence before coming forward," Elle said. "In the meantime, don't say anything to anyone, and don't get near him." She searched my face. "What are you thinking?"

I was sitting there contemplating whether or not my mom could handle the news that her faith in Bradford was a huge mistake after all. I was also weighing the rewards versus risks of telling Elle about tonight's group suicide. On the one hand, if anyone had my back and was willing to help, it was Elle. But as a reporter, she might feel a sense of responsibility to go public with the story, even knowing it could provoke evil forces and the human masterminds to retaliate.

"I just have some decisions to make." I left it at that.

"I understand, but don't wallow in uncertainty." Elle had never been much of a nurturer. She hurried toward the door, looking down at her phone, then glanced back. "How's Ray Anne?"

"Not so great. I'm about to go check on her. Why?"

Elle shrugged. "Just a feeling."

I didn't like the sound of that, especially coming from Elle.

She left, and I drove my motorcycle in the drizzle to Ray Anne's. There was nothing but a soggy, empty diaper box in the bushes outside her apartment now.

Her dad answered the door.

"How's Ray Anne? May I please see her?"

Mr. Greiner looked at me differently today, his eyes not narrowed for once, like he'd finally grown fond of me. "Now's not a good time."

"Why? Because she's still mad at me for telling?"

"Because she's not here."

"Where is she?"

He smiled, but I could tell it was 100 percent forced. "She's getting the treatment she needs."

Ray's mom came to the door, her pink-tinted eyes and nose bearing the signs of a tear fest. "Owen, difficult as it was, we committed Ray Anne to the hospital last night."

I couldn't catch my breath. "Like . . . a psych ward?"

Ray's mom started sobbing and stepped away. Eventually, Mr. Greiner nodded.

"Are you serious?"

"Owen, we—"

"Where is she—what hospital?"

"She can't have any visitors."

"For how long?"

"Five days. Maybe longer depending on her progress."

"Are you kidding me?"

Mr. Greiner stepped outside, his chest inflated like a bodyguard. "We weren't willing to sit back and lose another child to suicide, Owen. I'm sorry if you don't understand, but my wife and I stand by our decision."

I understood his decision; I just hated that I couldn't get to her. And nothing about her treatment plan would take the spiritual battle into consideration—how frustrating would that be for Ray Anne?

I dug my fingers into my scalp, resisting punching the brick house. "Where's Jackson?"

Mrs. Greiner stepped outside and stood beside her husband, still weeping. "Jackson's grandfather asked to see him. We thought now would be a good time, while Ray Anne is away. Dr. Bradford picked him up this morning."

The earth might as well have quit spinning. My world came to a standstill.

I wanted to say something. To tear into both of them, even though they had no idea they'd done anything wrong. *Terribly* wrong. But my jaw was clenched too tight to mouth the words.

Mrs. Greiner hugged me. My arms hung heavy at my sides. "We

can't lose heart, Owen. We're hopeful Ray Anne will recover quickly from this and be back home soon. She's a remarkable young lady. A radiant person."

And just like that, it came back to me . . .

The chilling question Molek's bats had posed to Mother Punishment and the indwelling Rulers last night: "You disabled the radiant one?"

"Under lock and key," they had replied.

Ray Anne . . .

THIRTY-THREE

I SPED TO BRODY BRADFORD'S HOUSE, the biggest mansion in Masonville. The childhood home of Dan Bradford, the most notorious school shooter in America. I pounded on the double doors with both fists, calling Jackson's name.

No answer.

Five more minutes of pounding and shouting. Nothing.

I pressed my forehead against the door, still trying to come to grips with how the secret society had managed to confiscate Jackson *again*. And how spiritual forces had successfully masterminded sidelining Ray Anne at the height of our mission. They'd known what a threat she was to their agenda.

I had no way to go get her out. As for Jackson, even if I had trusted Masonville's police force, I couldn't report him as a missing child this time. His own grandfather had him—a plot concocted by Mother Punishment, I was sure.

While rushing to my motorcycle, I called Elle, careful to avoid saying names. There was no telling who might be listening to our calls. "You know the handler?"

"Yes?"

"He's got the child. You have to track him down, Elle. *Please*."

I'd never heard her breathe frantically before. "I have an idea." She hung up.

I paced in the street beside my motorcycle, already outplayed and outmatched fifteen hours before the group suicide was even set to go down.

Hard as I'd tried to beat my opponent, I'd walked right into a lose-lose trap.

If I managed to talk the students out of taking their lives tonight, I'd be guaranteeing that Jackson paid the price—his life in place of theirs. But I couldn't just sit back and let the students die. Either outcome would grant Molek the spirit-world right to set up his throne alongside the Rulers.

"How could you let this happen?" I raged at myself. And, I admit it, at God.

I grabbed my helmet and held it in the air, ready to hurl it at the concrete as hard as I could.

I can't take this anymore, God! You picked the wrong guy. This is too hard.

A crippling sense of despair came over me like a weighted blanket of rage and sadness.

Wait a minute . . .

Instead of throwing my helmet, I slowly lowered it onto my bike, then turned to look over my shoulder. There were the two big-eyed, pale-pink Creepers, soaked and shivering in a mud puddle in the grassy empty lot across the street from Bradford's house, clinging to one another's bruised bodies. They whimpered, stealing timid glances at me.

I'm exhausted. I've done all I can—this is too much pressure.

I stepped toward them.

I'm gonna lose. I always lose. It's what I do. No—it's who I am.

I stopped at the puddle, and they leaned away, tucking and covering their heads like helpless victims.

I have to leave town. Escape. I can't save anyone, and I can't survive here.

Their mouths weren't moving, but that didn't fool me.

"It was you." They covered their ears, but I kept talking. "You two were on assignment at Ray Anne's, pumping her head full of discouragement and defeat, acting like victims to deceive her into believing that's what she was, like you're trying to do to me now."

There's no hope for me. There never was.

"She felt sorry for you while all along, you worked to make her feel sorry for herself."

I'm not enough. I don't have what it takes.

I bent down, hovering over the malicious pretenders. "Is that the best you can do?"

No one loves me. Everyone rejects me. I'm always abandoned.

I huffed.

I don't deserve to be loved. Not me.

Then finally, a silent moment in my mind. But all of a sudden . . .

I'm nothing but an orphan.

"No!" Anger took over. I reached out and tried to choke their feeble necks, but of course, my hands passed through them. So I stepped into the puddle, and sure enough, my God-given aura penetrated the water like a sizzling electric current, pumping them full of pain.

They howled and leaped out of the water—out of my aura—then stood upright for once, only as tall as children yet eyeing me with aggressive scowls. Villains now, not victims.

"In Christ's name, stop your deception and go!"

Their skin started melting like wax, and out from their dripping, dissolving frames stretched two fully-grown Creepers—sure enough, the word *victim* was carved into both of their faces. Their playbook officially disclosed.

They charged past me, hissing until they disappeared into the Bradfords' house.

Home sweet home, no doubt.

It was a victory, but it's not like I could celebrate. A much bigger battle was still looming. I sat on my bike and lowered my head. "Lord, it looks like evil has already won and there's nothing I can do. But the kingdom of darkness relies on distortion—false impressions, as if it can't be beat. So tell me, God, where do I go from here?"

Nothing hit me but the drizzling rain.

I gripped my handlebars and closed my eyes, inhaling deep, exhaling long. "Tell me, God. I'm listening."

More controlled breathing. Then the sudden mental picture of a person's face. The last guy I wanted to see.

"Really?" I gnawed my bottom lip. "Fine."

I drove to Central Hospital and tracked Ethan down in a hallway in the radiology wing. The floors were covered in death dust, like every hospital I'd been in.

"Owen, what are you doing here?"

Petty as it was, I couldn't stand seeing Ethan in scrubs and that white MD-monogrammed coat of his. I knew it didn't make sense, but it felt like he'd stolen my dream career out from under me. Still, I managed to say it. "Ethan, I need your help tonight."

"Absolutely. What can I do for you?"

I fought back my annoyance at his too-nice persona.

"I need you to please meet me at Masonville High at ten o'clock. Something really bad is going down in the woods at midnight, and we have to go out there and stop it." I was relying on Elle to find Jackson, trusting we'd have rescued him by then.

Ethan wanted the details, but I couldn't risk word getting out—not until Jackson was safe. "Please, just meet me tonight, and I'll lead the way."

He looked at me for a couple of moments, then nodded. "Okay, man. You can count on me."

I knew I could. That was just it—his character was so squeaky clean, so solid and dependable, I couldn't relate to him.

He gave me his phone number, then started to walk away.

"Ethan?"

He faced me. It was too late now to turn back.

"How come you're such a good person? Like, how do you do it?" I immediately regretted asking. It felt like I was a tail-tucked dog that had just acknowledged him as the alpha.

He gave me a kind smile. "Well, I definitely have my struggles. That said, it's been a huge blessing to have parents that are people of faith. And growing up in a church community has been invaluable."

"It has?" I didn't mean to sound so surprised.

"I mean, there were times I didn't want to go, and my parents made me. But looking back—all the Bible stories I learned at Sunday School, the songs I memorized and sang, plus my mom and dad praying with me at dinner and bedtime, the unconditional love and acceptance they always showed me . . ." He shrugged. "It's caused me to want to know God myself. And he's never let me down."

It felt like a raw egg was oozing down my face—shame I couldn't hide. One, for having only seen the faults in the church, hardly ever any potential upside. Two, for despising Ethan all this time when his only real offense was liking the same amazing girl as me. And three, my bitter envy. I couldn't imagine dinnertime at the table with adoring parents, much less having been tucked in bed—and with a thoughtful prayer.

Ethan's parents had loved and wanted him. But mine . . .

"So, I'll see you at ten o'clock?" He hurried toward a nurse's station.

"Yeah."

I wandered out of the hospital, tempted to feel sorry for myself, even without any Creepers shooting pathetic thoughts at my head. But there was no time for that.

I raced to the cornfields and jogged to the abandoned house, anxious to know whether Molek was still restrained or roaming free. When I saw that he was gone—his throne missing too—my gut throbbed with adrenaline.

I tried jogging the whole way back but had to settle for a fast-paced walk a few times, sucking in air while mentally sifting through every detail Zella had reported to me. Was I overlooking something?

My motorcycle came into view as I recalled that Creeper she'd had with her. *Deception was linked to Zella*, I thought, *yet she had clarity of mind—enough to choose life over suicide and realize the other students needed rescuing.*

The demon hadn't done its job at all.

I slid my helmet on, then froze.

Then again, maybe it *had* executed its assignment—using Zella to deceive *me*.

But not for long.

THIRTY-FOUR

I WAS A SWEATY MESS and still out of breath as I entered the atten-
dance office at Masonville High. "I'm Owen Edmonds, Gentry Wilson's
mentor—is he in class today?"

I was surprised I cared enough to see it, but the forty-something-
year-old lady behind the desk had a mask of addiction fitted on her face.
"There's no mentoring today."

"I know. Can you please just tell me if he's here? There's been an
emergency." It was true enough.

After using my ID to verify I was, in fact, in the mentorship program, she clicked on her mouse. "He's marked absent today."

I knew it. "What about Zella Benny, his girlfriend?"

More clicking. "Absent as well. Do you mind me asking—"

"There's a purple-haired girl . . ."

"Presley Baker?"

"Presley—that's it. Is she here?"

Three more clicks. "Hmm. She appears to be absent too."

Of course she was. I couldn't name the rest of the thirteen students,
but I didn't need to. I was sure they'd all skipped today.

I stormed out of there, still convinced a group suicide was set to go
down, but also suspecting Zella had lied to me about what time and

maybe where—even though she was somehow marked as a defender. By midnight, the horrific ordeal would be long over, already making national news. For all I knew, the students were in the woods now, gulping down pills—if that was truly how they planned to do it.

I clung to the hope that they weren't dead already.

I hurried toward the main exit doors but paused to take a sweeping glance around the foyer. Not a single Creeper visible anywhere. Unheard of in this school. They were bound to be in the woods, frenzied spectators to their Creeper King as he attempted to raise his throne.

I charged through the parking lot in the rain and called Ethan. I got his voicemail. "Hey, I need your help now, not tonight. There's no time to meet up at the school. If you have any way to find the Caldwell Cemetery in the woods behind Masonville High, go there—I can't really explain how to get there. If you don't see anyone there, or can't find it . . ." Where else was I supposed to tell him to go? "Just search the woods for people, okay?"

I started my bike and called Elle. She sounded fairly confident she'd locate Jackson soon, but she admitted getting him away from Dr. Bradford would be tricky. "Do whatever it takes," I told her. "And Elle, please don't go public with this until you have Jackson, but any minute now, there's going to be a group suicide somewhere on my property—if it hasn't happened already." I didn't waste a minute explaining. I hung up and sped off the parking lot.

The skies were gray and pouring, but that didn't explain why the spiritual atmosphere was dormant. I'd expected to see battalions of Watchmen and hordes of Creepers, as intense a battle as the last time Molek had attempted to reclaim Masonville.

I raced down the one-lane, unpaved street that ran along the back of my acreage, dodging waterlogged potholes. I finally made it to the make-shift road that, months ago, had served as the secret passageway through my property to the human auction. I drove down the path, aiming to get as close to the Caldwell Cemetery as I could before venturing there on foot. I knew the students weren't likely to be there, but I had to check.

I parked under a soaked cedar, then charged toward my ancestors' graveyard, where the Mary statue stood. Lightning cracked like a leather whip, lighting up the overcast woods brighter than the sun for seconds at a time.

There was still no sign of paranormal life in the trees or air. It made no sense.

I tripped over tree limbs and stumbled a few times but kept running. Then suddenly, with every stride, my feet began to sink into the earth up to my ankles. I don't mean I was traipsing through mud. I was slipping through the ground supernaturally. My Nikes—aura included—sank like I was standing in quicksand, only they didn't create holes in the ground.

I got stuck in one spot and kept sinking until the ground was at the middle of my shins. Then came a distressing sensation, like there was nothing but air underneath the soles of my shoes—as if I was somehow floating underground.

I pulled one knee up, removing my foot with ease, and stepped to the side, where it turned out the earth was solid—as in, not swallowing my shoe. I pulled my other leg out, and, once standing securely on un-sinking turf, lay flat on my stomach, thinking maybe I could plunge my head down and spy underground.

I assumed I'd peer into another spirit-world grave, which I dreaded, but I couldn't ignore what might be happening. I grabbed a small but firmly rooted shrub with my right hand, closed my eyes, and held my breath, then pressed my face down in the same spot where my feet had fallen. And down I went, until my upper body was suspended above an underground void so immense, I gasped, horrified of falling in. I clung to the shrub with all my strength.

It was endless miles wide and unfathomably deep—not hell's fiery chambers but a spirit-realm space of some kind. There was a shifting mix of darkness and radiance, but the lighting was eclipsed by the action and noise.

It was the most intense, loudest battle I'd ever seen. Hundreds of armored Watchmen wielded giant swords and shields, taking on gangs of Creepers as the demons whipped long chains around, attempting to maim and bind the Watchmen. Heaven's army was too strong to be restrained, but the Watchmen would grit their teeth and groan when metal links struck their necks or slammed their helmets, crashing against their shiny armor.

Extra-tall robed Watchmen dumped a few of those stained-glass bowls on the fray, but they were half full—with only enough shimmering liquid to disable handfuls of Creepers. And I could hear people—humans—talking. Some praying. Others casting spells. All at once.

"Custos!" I spotted him diving down—headfirst, shield extended. He blasted through a clustered wall of Creepers, and it sounded like freight trains colliding.

No wonder the skies had been empty. The war raged underground.

Everything in me wanted to stay there, watching the action unfold, but who was I to be lying down during the heat of battle, spectating while God's army fought with all their might? I jumped to my feet and resumed sprinting in the wet woods, praying I didn't fall through the ground and plummet into the gargantuan war zone.

Finally, the Caldwell Cemetery's black iron fence was within sight. Not surprisingly, I didn't see any students at the Mary statue.

As I stood there contemplating my next move, my own battle caught up with me. More like overtook me.

The crying infant wasn't close by or pressing against me now; it was screaming between my ears, as if it was lodged in my brain. And that haunting, stalking presence . . .

I felt it inside me, like it had made itself at home in my bones.

I slowed to a jog and clawed at my head and chest, moaning and praying without words for God to send the old man to my rescue again. But like the torrential downpour, the assault continued to batter my soul, overwhelming me completely.

"Who are you?"

How could I fight an enemy I couldn't see or comprehend? One that had withstood every spiritual weapon I'd aimed at it, even the name of Christ? And the crying inside my head . . . the sheer decibel level was maddening to the point of insanity.

I hit the soggy ground on my knees. "Tell me what you are!"

It's me. It was my own voice, answering me.

"Get out of my head!" I was on all fours now, crawling like an animal.

I can't.

"Why not?" I gave in to the lunacy of conversing with myself. But there was no reply this time.

I collapsed facedown, scooping fistfuls of mud and dumping it on the back of my head—a useless attempt to bury the noise echoing through my mind, ringing louder than the church fire alarm had.

"Please, God, help! Have mercy on me!"

My nose and mouth became covered in mud, smothering me. I lifted my chin and spotted a puddle catching drips falling from tree limbs. It was just beyond my reach. I dug my fingers into the ground and pulled myself forward, then rinsed my face in the water, inhaling lifesaving breaths.

I hovered on my forearms and elbows, coming unglued inside, staring down at the puddle in the storm-shrouded daylight.

At my reflection.

But instead of my face, it was the single most terrifying image I'd ever seen.

THIRTY-FIVE

I COULDN'T TELL if the face reflecting up at me was male or female or if it had skin or scales, but its eyes were completely gone—just two dark, empty sockets. It had a sunken nose and razor-thin lips pressed tightly together and sewn shut with thick thread in a messy crisscross pattern.

I tilted my neck to the left, and the bald head moved in sync with me, like a mirror image. Like it *was* me.

The ears were grossly malformed—clumps of flesh with no openings.

I extended my arm, the hysterical child still screaming in my brain. I reached out until my fingertips grazed the water's surface. The reflection moved too, only its arm was broken off—nothing from the bicep down.

I reached with my other arm. Same thing. No elbow or forearm or hand. Just a shredded bicep.

I stayed fixated on the monstrosity but spoke to the infant, desperate for some silence. "Shh. Don't cry." Just like Ray would soothe Jackson.

Had the wailing actually eased a bit?

"It's okay, I'm here. You're alright."

It was absurd and insane, but the more I coddled the infant, speaking words of comfort, the more settled it became. But nothing I said silenced it completely.

The hideous image in the water—the villain inside me—couldn't move its lips, yet it managed to utter a single word. In my voice. In my head.

Orphan.

I rose to my hands and knees and shoved my face so close to the reflection, my nose touched the water. "I am *not* an orphan! My mother raised me. And my father walked out, but he's in my life now." I waited for a response, then shouted, "Do you hear me?"

The creature in the water shook its head, and I realized I was shaking my head too.

I lost it.

I punched the puddle. Drove my fist into the mud. Pulled my own hair. "Stop torturing me!"

"Easy, Son." The old man's soothing voice. He placed his warm, dry hand on the back of my neck.

"Help me!"

"Calm down." He let me catch my breath, then pressed down gently until I was face-to-face with the horrid reflection again. The baby was no longer sobbing, but sniffling.

"What do you see?" the old man asked me.

"Pure evil. With no eyes."

"No eyes to see you. To look you in the face. To behold your expression. And the ears?"

"There aren't any."

"No ears to hear you. To listen to you. To understand." He lowered to one knee behind me. "The mouth?"

"It's sewn shut."

"That's right. No affirmation. No words of affection. No guidance or wisdom or prayers."

I cupped my face, enduring an avalanche of emotions. The monster couldn't mimic my gesture. "It has no arms."

"No holding you," the old man said. "No hugging. No pats on the back."

I'd never felt such hatred. Or sadness. "Make this demon go!"

"Look at me, Owen."

I turned my head and stared into his golden-brown eyes, my own pooling.

"It's not a demon, Son."

I searched his face. "Then what is it?"

He wrapped his strong arm around my shoulders, pulling me into a fatherly embrace. "It's the wound you carry. In your soul."

Slowly, reluctantly, I looked down at the monster again.

And for once, I let myself think it.

And feel it.

And finally say it: "I wasn't raised in an orphanage. But all my life, I've felt like an orphan."

"I know." The old man rose and stood behind me. "God knows."

My stomach dropped when the earth beneath my knees gave way, and I started sinking. I reached for the old man's hand but couldn't find it. I looked for him but didn't see him. Within seconds, I was buried up to my waist.

"I'm falling!"

I grasped at every twig and rock within reach but kept sinking. The baby in my brain sobbed again.

I was up to my chest in mud when my worst enemy approached. Molek circled me, stalking me on his hands and knees like a prowling lioness. "You're too late," he raved in shrill whispers. "They're as good as dead. All thirteen—and the little boy."

"No." I kept working to pull myself out but only became more entrenched. "You're a liar!"

My shoulders sank, restraining my arms.

How had it come to this? My enemy, unearthed and free, while the ground swallowed me alive?

Molek hovered over my head, watching me fall with his hollow-white pupils in a sea of black. "My son . . ." It was the cruelest thing he could have called me, especially given our history. "You're rejected." That thick black concoction shot off his tongue and stuck to my face, stinging my skin.

"Abandoned."

More pain.

As my head sank into the soggy soil, a final insult sliced my skin and soul: "Orphaned."

Everything went black. I was freezing. My face was burning. I was no longer falling but stuck, unable to move—not a muscle. And I could barely breathe.

I knew then that this was how I would die. Trapped and alone. The infant wailing within was my own nagging pain, I understood now. A lifetime of neglect. The tormenting fear of abandonment.

God . . .

I couldn't speak. My thoughts were all I had. Honest thoughts, finally. *It's so unfair. My shattered family. Loss after loss my whole life.* Ethan's face surfaced in my mind. His self-confidence and success—my fears and failures.

For once, I let myself feel the full brunt of suffering. The ache of injustice. The crushing grief of unspoken disappointments. It felt like my pounding heart was fracturing into a thousand agonizing pieces. It was becoming impossible to breathe.

Finally, the infant inside me was silent.

Any minute now, I'd face my Creator—the one who had given me this life and was taking it now. All that was left for me was to choose.

Do I blame him . . . or trust him?

I was shivering uncontrollably. I could hear Molek pacing above me, no doubt counting down the seconds until I died. He couldn't capture my eternal soul, but he was sure to revel in my failed earthly mission.

I inhaled, but there was no oxygen. No time left. Nothing but a last thought. The choice of a lifetime. My final decision . . .

Lord, even when my father and mother abandoned me, I trust you were there, holding me close.

A warm hand plunged down and gripped my arm, then tugged with massive force, pulling me up and out of the ground until I was lying in the dirt on my back.

I wiped mud from my eyes, working to pry them open . . . "It was you."

The old man was on his knees, hovering over me.

I pushed up onto my elbows. "When I was four years old and trapped in that sewer pipe, *you* were the man who pulled me out. I remember now."

He grinned and nodded, then his lips flattened with urgency. "Hurry." He stood and pointed. "That way." He turned to go.

"Wait!" I scrambled to my feet, feeling strangely lighter now.

He charged deeper through the woods in the direction he'd pointed.

I tried to follow him but couldn't begin to keep up. Still, I kept running, even as the rain poured harder. Eventually, I recognized the path. Sure enough, minutes later, I spotted the old wooden pavilion. I stopped and gulped for air, looking up at the roof. It was covered entirely by witches, those astral-projecting people, draped in their sloppy white dresses. They were on their knees, as if praying to their god.

But that was nothing compared to the ground around the pavilion. It was gone—as in, completely open to the underworld.

I stepped as close to the edge as I could stomach and stared down.

Same as before, the powers of heaven and hell collided in heated conflict in that cavernous space, so wide and deep it appeared endless. In the center, directly under the pavilion, a huge mass of bones—the Rulers' throne—rose slowly from the turmoil. Mother Punishment was still perched on top, the other Rulers tussling inside her so that I got brief glimpses of their deranged faces.

The throne rocked and teetered, unstable and unbalanced like all things evil. With every tilt, I caught peeks of Molek's empty throne dangling below, attached to the Rulers' throne by a chain that whipped his empty chair around like it was made of flimsy black plastic.

The sound of countless people's pleading voices filled the atmosphere, as loud as a crowded stadium—a clashing mix of prayers and hexes. I'd come to cherish a certain voice so much, it stood out to me above the masses.

"Protect Owen and show him what to do. Don't let the students die, Lord."

"Ray Anne!"

She was nowhere near, yet by my side, fighting for me and with me in a dimension that transcends time and space.

My phone rang, and it was like an alarm clock waking me from a wild dream, only this was really happening. "Hello?" I said. "Ethan?" The signal in the woods was too weak, and our voices kept cutting out. I finally hung up, pinned my GPS location, and sent it to him, but there was no time to stand there staring at the screen to see if it went through. I had to get inside that pavilion.

I was standing some twenty feet back from it, and the rain pouring off the roof formed walls on every side, blocking me from seeing in. Normally, I'd sprint over there. But normally there wasn't an open war zone where the ground should have been.

How was I supposed to get there?

I looked around, searching for a solution, and spotted a teenaged girl emerging from the woods, headed toward the pavilion. Her short purple hair was soaked and plastered to her head, her tight jeans so waterlogged she struggled to walk.

As she approached the ledge—the underworld drop-off—I cried out, "Presley!"

She didn't hear me. And she didn't fall. She made it all the way to the wall of water, ducked her head, and slipped inside.

Of course. Just because the spirit world was open didn't mean the material ground had caved in. The two realms were overlapping. But that didn't make my next step any easier.

I held my foot out, hovering it over the bottomless gulf, debating which would be more terrifying: to look down or close my eyes. I settled on looking straight ahead. The witches on the roof had spotted me and were pointing and cursing, but I tuned them out.

It took longer than I wanted, but I managed to put my foot down far enough to feel the ground beneath my shoe. When it was time to step out with both feet and stand entirely on the invisible, I couldn't help but look down. Sure enough, I remained secure at ground level, but I still felt like I was falling. Totally disorienting.

I took short, quick steps, wondering if this was what Jesus felt like walking on water, trying to get to the pavilion as fast as I could. I was almost there when a fanged Creeper came racing up from the depths beneath me, its arm outstretched like it was reaching for my ankles. But the instant its clawed hand touched my aura, the beast howled and recoiled, thank God.

Finally, I made it to the rain wall. A deep breath, then I passed through, into the pavilion.

THIRTY-SIX

To MY EYES, the pavilion floor was as transparent as the surrounding land, but it was what I beheld in the physical realm that freaked me out. Like in decades past, thick ropes hung from the antique beams in a makeshift circle, each dangling in front of a student as they balanced on tree stumps, facing one another with their eyes closed.

Unbelievable. It wasn't the first time I'd marveled at history repeating itself on my land, deliberately provoked by age-old evil.

No one moved or uttered a word. Behind each guy and girl, a spirit-world grave was positioned like an open mouth.

The chains attached to their shackled necks stretched down with no slack in them as Creepers yanked on the links from the under-earth cavern. It looked like they were working to pull the students' souls out, into eternal suffering, even though the people were still alive.

Everyone had on a rain-soaked T-shirt marked with words they'd apparently handwritten themselves in black permanent marker. It reminded me of Creeper graffiti.

Goodbye.
Don't cry for me.
No more pain.
I'm sorry.
I'm free.

In all caps across a young man's chest: *NEVER FORGET ME MOM. I LOVE YOU.*

As the lightning-fast chaos raged beneath my feet, I spotted Gentry. His rope hung in the center of the circle, his back to me. I wasn't surprised to see Zella among the ring of students—an active participant, not some whistleblower.

Gentry tilted his head back, gazing into the rafters. "Eva" peered down at him, crouched among the wooden beams, barefoot and draped in the same flimsy dress as the rest of the witches. She gave a single nod.

"It's time." Gentry grabbed his rope with both hands. "Here's how to tie it."

The other twelve opened their eyes. That's when his girlfriend spotted me. "Owen!"

Gentry whipped his head around at me. "What's he doing here, Zella?"

"I told him midnight, I swear! And I never mentioned this place!"

Eva rushed toward me in the rafters, crawling on her belly like a spider.

"Please Lord, keep him safe." Ray Anne's voice, still fighting for me.

An armored Watchman's hand reached up from beneath the pavilion and launched blinding orbs of radiance at Eva. She covered her eyes, and when the shimmering dots slammed her, she fell from the rafters. The Watchman caught her—her rebellious roaming spirit—cradling her just below ground level in his sculpted arm. "You don't belong here."

"I'll go back!" she pled, her hands up. He gently released her, and she ran up and out of the pavilion—back to her incarcerated body, I presumed.

"Where are you going?" Gentry watched Eva flee. He and I had to be the only two who could see her—me because of my supernatural senses, and Gentry because he'd ignorantly dabbled in the paranormal.

He rushed at me, his possessed eyes browner than normal. "You can't stop us, so unless you want to stand there and watch, you'd better leave."

The Rulers' throne continued to rise beneath us. If only he could see *that.*

"I did come here to stop you, Gentry." I looked past him. "All of you. You can't go through with this."

"Why not?" Zella asked, her voice emotionless.

"Because . . ."

How could I make them understand?

Gentry got in my face, same as his brother once had in these woods. "You gonna tell us our souls are in danger of hell's flames?" He had Lance's sarcastic smile, too.

"Yes, they are. But it's not just that."

Molek's bats flew up from below, flapping around the ring of students. I knew their presence was enough to incite evil thoughts.

"We can't back out now," Presley said.

"There's nothing to go home to," Zella piled on.

Gentry left me and returned to the center of the circle, resuming instructing the others on how to tie and knot a noose.

Then, suddenly, I saw it, plain as day. My next move.

"You guys!" I ran to them. "Please, give me a minute—just one minute to explain."

Gentry mumbled something about hell again—I think telling me to go there—and all six bats swarmed me, morphing into a multitude of smaller bats that looked like an actual earthly species but still reeked of spoiled meat. Within seconds, there were untold thousands of them—a blur of so many wings, I couldn't see my hand in front of my face. They hissed at me.

I covered my head and stumbled backward, losing all sense of direction, including up versus down. Pounding rain hit my head, and I realized I'd staggered out of the pavilion.

I commanded the bats to back off, keeping my head covered and falling to my knees, at the mercy of God's intervention.

"Owen!"

It sounded like Ethan, but I couldn't see past the dizzying blur of brown.

"Jesus!" Ethan's voice again—not cursing Christ, calling to him.

Instantly, the flying pestilence flew down, disappearing into the spirit world like water swirling out of a toilet bowl. There stood Ethan, soaking wet in his blue scrubs, wide-eyed, no doubt trying to make sense of what I was doing on my knees.

He reached out to help me up, and I defied my pride and took his hand.

The Rulers' huge throne had risen within a few feet of ground level, Molek's throne still dangling below. He was seated on it now, pulling on the chain, working with all his might to hoist his smaller seat of dominion as high as the Rulers'.

"You're just in time, Ethan."

"What's going on?"

"Follow me."

Ethan trailed me through the deluge of water into the pavilion, then gasped. All thirteen students were tightening nooses around their necks. "Stop!" he yelled.

They flinched but remained determined.

Ethan snatched his cell from his pocket and started dialing 911.

"It won't work," I said.

He searched my face. "We have to call the authorities!"

"Put the phone down," I told him. "We're the authorities here."

"Owen, are you—"

"Trust me. I know what we have to do."

He hesitated a second longer, then put his phone away. "Tell me."

"I have something I *have* to communicate to them, but dark forces will keep interfering. Unless you fight them off—meaning, stand here and pray."

"That's it?" He caught himself. "I mean, yeah, I can do that."

He didn't waste time. He spoke softly, pacing the edge of the pavilion, striding on top of a cosmic clash he had no idea was there. He left behind glistening footprints I'd only seen one other prayerful person make—Betty. It was another mystery I couldn't stop and try to figure out right now.

Instantly, the Creepers pulling at the students' chains began to thrash, covering their own ears for a change.

Once more, I approached the group. Gentry scowled at me, his eyes even darker. "Leave us alone!"

"That's just it." I stepped into the center of their circle and eyed each one of them. "You're not alone."

I braced myself for those horrid black scales to overtake their eyes. Instead, a burden-easing warmth filled the pavilion as Custos and a platoon of armored Watchmen rose up into the space, positioning themselves above us, underneath us, and around the circle, encasing us inside a protective sphere. The graves vanished in their golden light.

Without any cue that I detected, the Watchmen all extended their jaw-dropping wings, creating an impenetrable fortress of feathers—luminescent layers of interlocked metal, not wispy quills. There was so much heavenly light swirling on the students' bodies and faces—so much peace in the air—several of them started tearing up, responding emotionally without explanation.

"It's not death you guys want." I was loud and bold. "It's *life*. A sense of hope and happiness and assurance that you matter and have a good purpose that's worth existing for. And you've tried to find life in all kinds of ways, but nothing's worked—I know, I've done it too. So, you think by 'bravely' escaping this world, you'll finally find the life you're looking for somewhere else. Or maybe just sleep forever.

"But I'm here to tell you the God-honest truth." I eyed their shackled necks. "You won't."

Gentry tried to interrupt me, but I didn't let him. "Life is something that comes to us *here*, while we're alive on this earth. It pursues us, because, you guys, life is a presence and person who loves us—a Creator who really does care. It's taken me a while to get that through my head, but I'm starting to.

"It's no coincidence that each of you is here, with a rope around your neck." I kept turning, working to face all of them. "Evil has a plan to kill you today because God has a plan for your life—a vital plan that seriously threatens the kingdom of darkness. And I so wish I could explain this to you guys, but just please, *please* believe me when I say . . ." I eyed their arms as they clung to their nooses. "I can see that all of you are marked by God to defend others from the exact hopelessness that's got a hold on you now. Every one of you. Whether you believe in God or not, you're already sealed, just like me." I turned and eyed Ethan's red-glowing symbol. "And so are you."

Gentry huffed. I faced him. "All of us are destined to work together and change this town, this planet, for good. And the next generation needs us too." I got down on my hands and knees, desperate to convince them. "I'm begging you, don't leave me to do this alone. Don't leave each other. Don't leave this world before your time."

I admit, I tensed with aggravation when their attention was drawn away from me because Ethan started singing some old hymn, hands raised and all. But man, when the Watchmen started harmonizing with him, I unclenched my fists. Absolutely incredible.

I wished everyone there could hear it, but even without it, one by one, the students began removing the rope from their necks and stepping down from the tree stumps. They began to hug one another and cry—a change of heart that was no less supernatural than the war raging underground.

"I'm here for you," a young man told Presley.

"Same," she said.

Zella removed Gentry's noose and hugged him. "I love you so much."

Along the outer edges of the pavilion, the old wood floor began appearing, the spirit-world portal closing. *Finally, the ordeal's over.* I held out hope Elle had rescued Jackson.

What went down next happened shockingly fast.

The Watchmen retreated, plunging down, giving me a full-on view of the action directly under us. The Rulers' throne was nearly to our feet now—the chair back inches from the soles of our shoes. Mother Punishment still sat on it, but she was leaning side to side, frantically looking down. Molek's throne was still attached, dangling at the bottom of the chain, having failed to ascend. He'd abandoned his throne and was racing to climb the chain links as if his immortal life depended on it.

I let out a moan when that humongous black hand I'd seen before reached up from the deep and clutched both thrones. A booming voice spoke in a language I couldn't understand, but the furious outrage was clear. This was it. The seven Rulers and Molek were about to be cast into outer darkness. The portal was closing, the pavilion floor steadily returning, but I still had a front row seat to their demise.

"Get away from me!" Gentry said.

My attention shifted above ground when Gentry pushed away from Zella's embrace, his eyes completely unrecognizable now.

"In Christ's name," I commanded, "come out of him!"

Sure enough, a Creeper marred with *Rejection* came barreling out of Gentry's chest—my first successful exorcism. The tormentor expanded to full size, only to be sucked down into the portal below like a clump of dust in a vacuum.

Gentry's eyes were his own again, thank God.

"It's over now," I told him, reaching to pat him on the back.

He lowered his head, his bottom lip quivering.

"I was ready to die today," he uttered. "And you'd have gladly let me if you knew all the ways I've betrayed you." A tear fell from his face. "I planted that curse under your bed the day you moved into the church. And I stole both your phones the night of the fire and dumped them in the pond so you wouldn't be able to call for help. And I set the fire that was supposed to kill you. And the baby."

I felt the inner ache and shock of having been stabbed deep in the back. But I was willing to forgive and start over, to allow him to begin earning my trust all over again. Unfortunately, I wasn't given the chance to say it. The underworld portal had been reduced to a round opening the size of a sewer manhole cover, and up came Molek, leaping from the clutches of that punishing black hand. He rushed like a bullet out of the pavilion into the woods.

"I don't deserve to live!" Gentry shoved his way through the group and ran out into the rain. Zella started to follow, but I grabbed her arm. "Don't! Stay here—I'll go find him."

"Let me go!" She broke free and chased after him.

Ethan and I fled the pavilion, but Gentry and Zella had already sprinted away. We searched the nearby woods for them, calling their names. A half-hour later, there was still no sign of them—no evil spirits either, or witches. The remaining students were weepy and exhausted, their weary expressions pleading to leave the pavilion and dangling nooses behind. I led the way to the nearby road, desperate to get a strong enough cell signal to call Elle for an update.

Sure enough, as we exited the woods, I spotted her—a microphone in one hand, an umbrella in the other—concluding an on-camera broadcast next to her news network van. She handed the mic to the cameraman, nodding to dismiss him.

I ran to her. "Where's Jackson?"

"He's safe. Back in the care of Ray Anne's parents."

I let out a huge sigh. "How'd you pull that off?"

She looked past me, like she hadn't heard me.

"What are you doing here?" I asked her. "How'd you find us?"

"I tracked the cell I gave you. And I came to do my job. I reported the truth to the people of Masonville. They have a right to know and see what's going on."

As if on cue, cars began turning onto the street and parking along the sides of the road. Hysterical parents came flying out of vehicles, running and searching students' faces as all eleven huddled together in the rain. It was obvious when a distraught father found his son among the group. He hugged the boy and wouldn't let go.

"You did it, Owen." Elle gave me a rare smile. "Are you up for a TV interview?"

I winced, and she got the picture. "Well," she said, "I'm still going to report that you intervened."

"Ethan too," I told her. "I couldn't have done it without him."

She nodded. "How do things look from your point of view?"

I knew what she meant. "The darkness took a huge hit today. Unfortunately there are two students still out there we have to find." I saw people flooding the woods, already searching. "How'd you get Jackson back?" I wanted an answer this time.

She diverted her eyes and fidgeted with the ends of her hair, a look of hesitancy I'd never seen on her before. "Elle, tell me."

She grabbed me by the hand and led me to the other side of the news van, away from the growing crowd. "The black Suburban," she said. "Your father's men. I had them locate the child and retrieve him."

"What? I don't understand."

She scanned our surroundings. Coast clear, she whispered up at me. "Owen, I'm about to trust you more than I have anyone else in this town. Under the circumstances, I believe Stephen would approve."

"My father?"

She cleared her throat. "I work for the news station. But Owen, I'm here in Masonville because I'm also employed by your father. This is where he assigned me."

Seriously? "So . . . you're like, one of his operatives?"

She nodded, pressing her index finger to her lips, cautioning me to say nothing more.

It was another unforeseen spin of reality that would take some time to process. And even though it wasn't necessarily a bad secret, it was still a secret, and I'd had my fill of them.

"Elle, why—"

She answered a call on her phone and, no surprise, hurried off.

I turned and nearly slammed into Lance. "Owen!" He gripped my arms—more like a friend than an adversary. "Where's my brother? Is he alive?"

"Yes. But he took off in the woods with his girlfriend, and we can't find them. People are looking."

"He's okay, though, right?" Lance squinted, as if he could hide his pooling eyes.

"No, Lance, he's not okay. I tried to help him, but . . ."

Lance stepped back and stared at the wet grass, squinting harder now. "Thank you, Owen." Then he ran off, sprinting into the woods, shouting for Gentry.

I stood in the street, in the midst of what felt like a toppled anthill of frantic people. More press vans pulled up, and there were parents and students darting every direction, searching in the mayhem for their loved ones and friends.

Not one person had come looking for me, wondering if I was okay.

A familiar feeling began rising in me—the crushing sense I was all alone in the world. But I knew better now . . .

It's all right, I thought to myself.

You're always with me, I thought to God.

THIRTY-SEVEN

FOUR DAYS LATER, on Sunday morning, Gentry and Zella still hadn't been found. The search continued, but the rumor around town was that they'd run away together. I feared Gentry had taken his life somewhere on my land and talked Zella into doing it too, but I prayed I was wrong.

I thought maybe the Rulers' defeat had been enough to rid my land of its Creeper infestation, but a quick drive past Masonville High and my acreage made it easy to see that wasn't the case. Even though it appeared the Rulers had been punished and cast away from Masonville—banished to outer darkness, along with their detestable throne—Molek's army still roamed the land.

It made sense. The spirit realm's terms of justice had yet to be met the way Arthur had outlined in his prediction—God's way—and nothing else would do.

There was no denying it: my mission would definitely continue.

Still, this recent victory had served to get seven high-ranking Rulers away from earth's inhabitants. Even if there were more just like them, that had been a battle worth fighting. And the triumph not only bought us more time to follow through on Arthur's instructions but had saved human lives. *Defenders'* lives.

There was no telling where Molek was, a demonic fugitive who'd managed to escape hell's punishment for the time being. Maybe he was hiding somewhere? I thought perhaps it was possible; his master wasn't all-knowing. And until the people of Masonville did their part to evict him, his army would remain, and the Lord of the Dead would always find a way to try to reclaim our town.

I wasn't discouraged, though. We had a glowing-red-seal army of our own now—even if the students were shackled and vulnerable at the moment.

Ethan had texted me and said Pastor Gordon was looking for people to help clear the charred rubble at the church that morning, before what remained of the building was bulldozed to the ground. It was the least I could do. And maybe some of my stuff would be salvageable.

I pulled up in the lot early, missing Ray Anne so much, I could hardly eat lately. I'd never gone this long without seeing her, much less talking to her. But other than that nagging dilemma—and the fact that I still hadn't found my dog—I had more peace of mind than ever before. No more crying baby or invisible spy. No more giving in to the oppressive sense I was destined to be rejected and alone.

No more orphan identity, even when Creepers shot the cruel accusation at my mind.

Ethan handed me gloves and a mask, and we got to work—two friends, serving side by side. But minutes later, we stopped and stared out at the parking lot, both of our jaws gaping. It was like all of Masonville had come out to help, shackled and Lights alike.

"I put the word out that we needed help," Ethan said, "but this . . ."

As if that wasn't surprising enough, the people started applauding, taking turns shaking my hand and Ethan's, hugging our necks and thanking us for saving the students' lives. One by one, all eleven of them showed up, flocking to me like ducklings to a feathered mother.

"What are we supposed to do now?" Presley asked me. I gathered she wasn't talking about the church cleanup.

I eyed her shackled neck. "I need to explain some things to you guys and teach you."

Another one of them reached out and shook my hand. "I'm Austin. And I'm ready to learn."

"Me, too," the others chimed in.

"How about we meet this Wednesday night?" I threw it out there.

They nodded enthusiastically. "Where at?" Austin asked.

"You're all welcome at my apartment," Ethan offered.

And just like that, a plan was in place.

"Thanks, Pastor Owen," Austin said.

"No." I laughed awkwardly, my face feeling frozen. "I'm not a pastor. Like, *at all.*"

Ethan gripped my shoulder and spoke in my ear. "To them, you are."

Yet another one of life's ironic twists I never saw coming.

Pastor Gordon descended carefully out of what used to be his office, visibly shocked by the number of people there. He balanced on top of a stack of wood pallets, and people gathered around him.

Gordon started by thanking everyone for coming out, then frowned. "The insurance is refusing to pay our claim on the building, and we can't possibly afford to build from scratch. And we can't afford to buy this property either. So for now, I'm not sure how we'll continue gathering as a church."

I wasn't trying to be a hero. It just came to me, as natural as breathing. I raised my hand. When Gordon acknowledged me, the offer rolled off my tongue. "If you can raise the building funds, you're welcome to build on my land. For free, I mean." That was one way to get people on my property.

I thought Gordon was going to fall off the wood pile. "Owen, I . . . I don't know what to say."

"That's amazing," his assistant said, "but where are we supposed to meet in the meantime?"

I raised my hand again. "I know of a temporary solution, at least for the next week or two. It's in the woods, but it's close to a road. There's a large pavilion on my land." The students were still gathered around me; they lowered their heads. "It needs to be used for something good."

Gordon eyed his son.

"It's unconventional," Ethan told his father, "but I think it's doable. Neat, even."

More applause. I stood there in awe. Had I really just witnessed

Masonville's townspeople agree that my land would be the new location for worship? It was like I'd pulled off Arthur's prophetic mandate without even trying. Like God had it all worked out way before I did.

"Pastor Gordon?" We all looked back at the speaker, the man in a tan suit. Dr. Brody Bradford, of all people. "I'd like to personally donate the remaining finances needed for the church rebuild . . ." He looked straight at me. "On Owen's beautiful land."

I narrowed my eyes. *Of course you would.*

Even more applause. And more confirmation that the kingdom of darkness and its secret players were never going to stop working against us in the fight over this town—right up to the point of ultimate victory or defeat, I was sure.

As Ethan began giving instructions about the day's cleanup, my pulse quickened at the sight of Mrs. Greiner's SUV turning into the lot. I hurried to where she parked, eager to hold Jackson—and keep him away from Dr. Bradford. I spotted him in the backseat . . . then cupped my mouth and gasped. "Ray Anne!" She was in the backseat too. She threw her seat belt off and ran to me, and I spun her in circles in my arms.

"I was released this morning," she said.

I set her down and stared at her face. There was a glow—the natural kind, like old times.

"How are you?" I asked.

She wrapped her arms around my neck. "I figured it out, Owen. How to get free from petrifying fear." She smiled and teared up. "I had to stop running and face it. Head-on."

I pulled her into a tight embrace. "I know what you mean."

I wasn't trying to check; I just happened to notice as I ran my hand along her back and neck—there was nothing there. No more coiled curse.

"Ray, your senses . . ."

"I can see again. It all came back to me."

I hugged her again, exhaling in relief.

I looked into her gorgeous blue eyes, ready to finally say it—the three words I'd kept on lockdown for way too long, for all the wrong reasons. "Ray Anne?"

She smiled bigger, like she knew what was coming. But the sound of a dog barking stole my attention.

"Daisy!" She was in the field across the street.

She didn't budge. Just kept her head low, barking, seemingly at me. Ray and I ran that way, hand in hand, but Daisy turned away from us, disappearing into the tall grass. We searched for her, following a path of trampled grass. Turned out, my dog led us right to them . . .

Gentry and Zella were hunkered on the ground, their hair and skin filthy, wearing the same T-shirts they'd had on when I'd last seen them. Gentry rocked back and forth, head down, knees drawn into his chest. Zella was curled in a ball on her side, pounding her forehead with her fist.

Ray and I knelt beside them. "What are you guys on?" I asked.

"We didn't mean to," Zella cried.

"Didn't mean to what?" Ray Anne tried to touch her shoulder, but Zella wailed and recoiled in fear.

Gentry mumbled to himself, an angry rant. None of his words made sense.

"We were lost in the woods and dying of thirst." Zella's voice shook as violently as her body.

I felt my pulse begin to hammer at the base of my neck. "Did you guys drink from a—"

"Shhh!" She covered her head. "The monsters will find us!"

Ray and I looked at each other, knowing what they'd done.

"How long ago was it?" I asked.

"Three days," Zella said.

They'd survived past twenty-four hours, which probably meant the well water wasn't going to kill them. It also meant nothing was ever going to be the same for them, or Ray and me, or this town.

She and I were no longer the only ones with spiritual eyesight.

"Listen to me, Zella." Ray Anne was careful not to touch her. "You're going to be okay."

Zella pointed to Gentry. "He's not. He's not okay!"

I said his name, trying to get him to look at me. Instead he lurched forward and threw his arms around my neck, squeezing me in an overly tight embrace. "Help me, Owen!"

"I'm here for you," I assured him.

He clung to me like a traumatized child, trembling like an earth-quake. Uncomfortable as it was for me, I let him stay that way. Then out of nowhere, he pushed me away like he couldn't stand me. He started mumbling again, and his voice turned to a shrill whisper. An unsettling quiver ran up my spine, but I stayed focused on trying to comfort him.

I put my hand beneath his slobbery chin, slowly tilting his head up. "Gentry? What's going on? Tell me what you see."

He narrowed his eyes at me. "A weakling who'll be dead within a year."

Before I could even react, Detective Benny came charging through the grass, shouting into his cell phone, "I got 'em!"

Another officer assisted him in dragging Zella and Gentry into the back of a squad car. The commotion caused everyone in the church parking lot to gasp and gawk.

Ray Anne ran up to the car and pressed her palms against the back-seat window, calling to Zella, "Don't cry! I promise, I'll find you!"

That was all she could say before Detective Benny drove off.

It was dusk when Ray Anne and I stepped into the pavilion.

We'd agreed there was no reason to heed the death threat launched at me through Gentry's lips. He was clearly possessed, and Ray and I were both done listening to the enemy.

I'd spent the remainder of the afternoon recounting the whole story of this place to her—the century-old lynchings, my father's tragic vow made beneath the rafters, the miraculous rescuing of thirteen students, just in time.

Thankfully someone had taken the ropes down.

Ray Anne walked to the center of the pavilion and lowered her head. I hugged her from behind. "Are you okay?"

"My heart breaks for you." She clutched my hands at her waist. "The impact this place has had on your father and your mother, and you. On so many families."

I turned her around to face me. "It is sad, Ray Anne." A soothing breeze grazed past us. "But just think, we're closer than ever to fulfilling

Arthur's prophecy and cleansing this land. And look at what's happening here now." My cheeks curved into a grin. "You and I, standing here unharmed, still together despite everything we've faced."

She smiled up at me. "I know our mission isn't over and yet I can honestly say, I'm not afraid."

"Neither am I." I pulled her to me, my heart pounding close to hers. "And I can also honestly say . . ." My eyes started pooling, but for once, I didn't hide it from her. "I love you, Ray Anne. I love you more than words can ever explain."

"Oh, Owen . . ." She clasped her hands behind my neck. "I love you too. And yes, I will."

I hadn't realized until then that we'd been swaying, but I stopped. "You will what?"

Her eyes welled with tears, even as her smile widened. "If your proposal still stands, I want to marry you."

I didn't move—not a breath or a blink, in case I'd somehow heard wrong. Finally, I asked her, "Are you serious?"

"Yes!"

I scooped her in my arms and spun her around, both of us laughing. And crying. And saying over and over without restraint how much we loved each other and couldn't wait to be together—for life.

"Congratulations." The deep voice shocked us both. We turned, and there, in the corner of the pavilion, stood the man in overalls—the one who'd saved my life, basically all my life. "The two of you make an exceptional couple," he said. "Now, I need you to follow me—both of you, right now."

"Who's he?" Ray Anne whispered.

I started to explain but stopped. "Actually, I don't really know." I fixed my gaze on the man's golden-brown eyes and stepped toward him. "Please, I'm begging you—who are you?"

He peered at me the way only he could, like he was seeing clear through to my soul. Then he pressed his palm over his heart and bowed his head. "I'm a humble servant of the Most High."

And with that, he turned and started walking away, gesturing for Ray Anne and me to follow.

We stepped out from under the pavilion, and, before our eyes, his work boots, overalls, and cowboy hat gave way to blinding brilliance and spectacular armor. He quickened his pace as his stature stretched twice as tall—taller than some of the trees. Ray and I hurried to keep up, both of us speechless as a gigantic shield appeared in his right hand, and to his left, an enormous, majestic white horse.

Custos's horse, rushing to his master's side.

ACKNOWLEDGMENTS

I first acknowledge Jesus Christ, whose presence and goodness graced me to walk through the most difficult valley of my life during the writing of this book.

I acknowledge my husband, Patrick, and our children—Madison, Avery, and Levi. You never cease to inspire and motivate me. I love you beyond words.

I acknowledge the "Delusion Dream Team" ladies, who've proven to be the most caring of friends and most courageous sisters in Christ. Your prayers are quite literally transforming the world.

I readily admit that I began this publishing journey as a novice fiction writer, and if it were not for the editing genius of Sarah Rubio, this book and series would be seriously lacking.

I am grateful for the support of the Tyndale staff. Your belief in this project is a gift.

Finally, I thank God for the readers who have reached out and expressed their enthusiasm for the Delusion series. I celebrate each and every story of how the Lord has used this project to reveal himself as the Way, the Truth, and the Life.